...and for honor.
But a secret of the
past could destroy
them both.

Praise for
PATRICIA POTTER
and her bestselling novels:

"Patricia Potter looks deeply into the human soul and finds the best and brightest in each character. This is what romance is all about." —Kathe Robin, *Romantic Times*

"Pat Potter proves herself a gifted writer as artisan, creating a rich fabric of strong characters whose wit and intellect will enthrall even as their adventures entertain."
—*BookPage*

"When a historical romance [gets] the Potter treatment, the story line is pure action and excitement, and the characters are wonderful." —Harriet Klausner

The Perfect Family

"The reader loses all sense of time as they become entangled in a web of mystery Ms. Potter spins in *The Perfect Family* . . . flawless characterizations. . . . You are holding a work of art when you pick up a book by Patricia Potter."
—*Rendezvous*

"This is a novel that will long be remembered by those who read it." —Harriet Klausner

continued . . .

The Black Knave

"Patricia Potter has taken a classic plotline and added something fresh, making her story ring with authenticity, color, exciting action, her special humor, and deep emotions. *The Black Knave* is *The Scarlet Pimpernel* with twists and turns that make an old story new."

—*Romantic Times* (Top Pick)

"I couldn't put it down! This one's a keeper! Pat Potter writes romantic adventure like nobody else."

—Joan Johnston

Starcatcher

"Patricia Potter has created a lively Scottish tale that has just the right amount of intrigue, romance, and conflict."

—*Literary Journal*

"Once again, Pat Potter demonstrates why she is considered one of the best writers of historical novels on the market today. . . . Ms. Potter scores big time with this fabulously fine fiction that will be devoured by fans of this genre."

—Harriet Klausner

Broken Honor

Patricia Potter

JOVE BOOKS, NEW YORK

BROKEN HONOR

A Jove Book / published by arrangement with
the author

PRINTING HISTORY
Jove edition / January 2002

All rights reserved.
Copyright © 2002 by Patricia Potter.
Cover art by Donald Case.
Cover design by George Long.
This book, or parts thereof, may not be reproduced in any
form without permission.
For information address: The Berkley Publishing Group,
a division of Penguin Putnam Inc.,
375 Hudson Street, New York, New York 10014.

Visit our website at
www.penguinputnam.com

ISBN: 0-515-13227-6

A JOVE BOOK®
Jove Books are published by The Berkley Publishing Group,
a division of Penguin Putnam Inc.,
375 Hudson Street, New York, New York 10014.
JOVE and the "J" design
are trademarks belonging to Penguin Putnam Inc.

PRINTED IN THE UNITED STATES OF AMERICA

10 9 8 7 6 5 4 3 2 1

author's note

Although the seed of *Broken Honor* was suggested by an actual event during World War II—the capture of two Nazi treasure trains—the characters and events in the book are completely fictional, the result of the author's "What if?" mechanism.

prologue

Sam Flaherty sickened as he finished his walk through the first boxcar and entered the second.

He barely heard the sound of crackling gunfire outside as he looked around at the contents of the car. Silver gleamed despite the dim light: silver candlesticks, silver serving dishes, silver tableware.

"Look here, General," a sergeant said.

Sam stopped just inside the entrance of the next car. Trunks lined its interior. Sergeant Major Hawkins Jordan had opened one. Thousands of rings with myriad stones sparkled up at him. Wedding rings, engagement rings, dinner rings. Silent testimonies to love and hope and life.

He leaned against the edge of the door for a moment, the sickness in his stomach worsening. God knew he'd seen enough death these last four years, but there was something especially obscene about the trunk.

"I want an accounting of every item," he said. "And I want it quick. I don't want us delayed here longer than necessary."

"Yes, sir."

"Send someone for General Mallory. He'll be responsible for finding a place to store these things and try to get them back to their owners."

Jordan looked skeptical. "They're probably all dead, sir."

Sam's eyes roamed the contents of the boxcar again. Other cars held paintings, ornate silver pieces, clocks, jewelry, furs, carpets, and even trunks full of gold dust. All probably looted from Jewish families in Hungary and bound for Nazi officials in Berlin. Sam's regiment had received word of the train from headquarters, and it had been tracked by U.S. planes. His men had blocked the tracks with tanks.

The SS put up little fight. Many were being held prisoner down the tracks. The few who did fight, were dead.

The train contained a treasure but, to him, it was a nuisance. Sam's regiment had been pulled back from the front lines for a short rest. He wanted to be back in the midst of the fighting as the British and U.S. forces headed toward the heart of Germany but then they had been ordered to take the train. His superiors had witnessed the devastation of the occupied countries and wanted to deprive the German hierarchy of as much of their ill-gotten treasures as possible. Thus his regiment had been diverted into a relatively quiet sector of Austria while others were racing across Germany.

He would secure these . . . goods, then get back in the fight.

He finished his walk through the train. His chief of staff, Colonel Edward Eachan, would work with Mallory to inventory the goods and safeguard them. Then perhaps he could get on with the real work of war.

Still, he paused at the back of the last car. One particular painting caught his eye. A portrait of a young girl with a wistful expression. It was a stunning painting, the colors so vibrant and real she could almost step out of the frame. But what really captured his attention was her likeness to the daughter he and his wife had lost years ago.

He hesitated. It would do no harm to borrow the painting for his quarters. He would be here no longer than a week or two, and then he would return it.

"Sergeant," he said to the man still trailing him. "Send that painting to my quarters, but make sure it is included in the inventory."

"Yes, *sir.* Anything else, sir?"

Sam swallowed. It was the damned trunks. The wedding rings. How could anyone look at them and not despair for humanity? "No," he said after a too-long pause.

Sam's gaze took one last journey around the boxcar. *So many hopes*, he thought again. *So many broken dreams.*

one

Irish Flaherty nearly knocked his coffee cup over as he scanned the morning headlines.

His hands stilled, and his heart beat louder. He read the article swiftly, then closed his eyes against the words.

COMMISSION INVESTIGATES POSSIBLE U.S. THEFT OF NAZI WAR LOOT.

The headline had captured his attention, but it was the body of the story that made his blood run cold. His grandfather's name. *General Sam Flaherty.* The general had been more than his grandfather. He had been Irish's salvation. His mentor.

Honor. Duty. Country. Those three words had been drilled into him since he'd been a tyke. They'd meant everything to his grandfather, to his father, and to Irish. They had dominated all three men's lives. His father, in fact, had given his life for them.

He himself had spent the last twenty-two years in the army, including four years at West Point, and had just made lieutenant colonel. He'd completed a long and ugly tour in Bosnia and then Kosovo, where he supervised the collection and destruction of illegal weapons, and his promotion put him in line for battalion commander, something he didn't particularly want. He preferred field command of intricate investigations rather than desk duties.

Still, he was glad to be out of Kosovo. He was sick of the hatred and violence that continued to sweep that tragic, torn country, and upon returning to the States, he'd taken accumulated leave. He'd headed for the Colorado ranch left to him by the General.

He came here this time to think. He had his twenty years. He could retire, and rebuild the ranch, which was now merely maintained by a friend. But the army had been his life for so long, he knew he'd be lost without it.

And now his grandfather's name was being besmirched, his reputation destroyed.

Irish tried to control his anger. His fingers thrummed on the table. Why now? It was fifty-seven years since the end of World War II, fifty since his grandfather went into retirement and started Flaherty's Folly, a ranch that reflected his wry humor.

Irish saw his grandfather in his mind's eye. A man bigger than life, Sam Flaherty's bulk had been much like John Wayne's. And his weathered face had reflected that same kind of rough integrity.

Irish read a paragraph again. *A Presidential Advisory Commission looking into Holocaust assets in the United States had determined that items from a Nazi gold train captured by U.S. forces toward the end of World War II had vanished. Members of the American armed forces at the highest levels had been implicated in their disappearance. Among them were three generals, including Samuel Flaherty.*

For the first time, Irish was glad his grandfather was dead. Otherwise, the story—and its implications—might well have killed him.

The one thing Irish did know was that the General had nothing to do with a theft, particularly of items looted by the Nazis.

And if it were the last thing he did, Irish would prove it.

MEMPHIS, 2000

Amy Mallory barely caught the story on page three of the newspaper. She probably would have left it until later if she didn't teach advanced American history at Braemore, a prestigious private liberal arts college. Her students were bright and eager, and she knew some of them would have read the story and might well have questions.

The one thing she did not want was to appear unaware. Her tenure hearing was imminent, and she wanted no complaints from students. Once she had tenure, she could relax. Her future would be assured.

Three more weeks.

"Damn," she muttered to herself as she went back to the newspaper to read the entire story.

G.I.S CALLED LOOTERS OF JEWISH RICHES. . . .

Bojangles, her mongrel dog, whom everyone else called the ugliest dog in the world, huddled next to her legs, knowing her departure was looming. He was a ridiculously needy dog who made her feel guilty every time she left the house.

She leaned down and petted him while her eyes scanned the article. They stopped at the name of General David Mallory. Her hand left the dog and she clutched the paper. David Mallory. Her grandfather.

He and two other generals were named in the article as possibly being involved, at the very least negligent, in the loss of treasures from a captured train. Missing were two trunks of gold dust, paintings, and other goods.

"Not Grandfather," she whispered, remembering the battle of wills they'd engaged in. Her mother had died when she was entering her teens, and she'd been sent to her grandfather. They'd detested each other on sight. *She* was the bastard daughter of a flower child who had run away from home. *He* was a martinet who tried to run his family as he'd run a regiment.

It had taken them years to come to an accommodation.

She'd ended up loving him—perhaps more for his flaws than for his virtues. He'd died at eighty-three of a bullet he'd put in his own head, and it had broken her heart.

He had flaws. Many of them. But dishonesty was not among them.

"No," she said, hearing her own outraged whisper. "No, I don't believe it."

Bo whined, feeling tension in the room. He didn't like tension. He didn't like a break in the routine. He didn't like strangers. He was afraid of everything, including a leaf blowing in the wind. After finding the sad-sack dog in the animal shelter, she had named him Bojangles for the dog in her favorite song, hoping it would give him a bit of self-esteem. It hadn't.

But she loved him for that, for all the insecurities that resided inside him.

"It's okay," she whispered to him, and he collapsed in relief at her feet. When she left, he would, no doubt, go and wrap himself around the toilet, his place of safety when he was alone. Like the ostrich who hid his head, he thought himself invisible there. He'd be deeply distressed to know that both his tail and his nose were visible.

She tore out the article. She would research it later. If nothing else, she owed it to the man who had half-raised her.

She made sure that Bo had his sock, which, like Linus's blanket, was his security, locked the back door, then grabbed the papers she'd graded the night before. She paused at the front door. Bo had already left for the bathroom, the sock hanging forlornly from his mouth, his tail drooping.

"Ah, Bo," she said. He turned, a hopeful look on his face.

"I'll play ball with you tonight," she promised, absolutely positive that he understood her. He did like to chase balls. It was the one thing in which he excelled, and he knew it.

His tail lifted and wagged. Amy felt better.

Now if only she could solve her other problems that easily. She turned the lock on the front door, the tone of the article nagging at her. She had never liked the military. In truth, she despised it. Its rigidity, she'd always believed, had driven her mother away from home and had made her grandfather a humorless, stiff man who thought he must always be obeyed.

But he would never betray his trust. She knew that as well as she knew how to breathe. "I won't let them do this to you," she promised, only barely aware that she uttered the words out loud.

WASHINGTON, D.C.

Assistant to the Deputy Secretary of State Dustin Eachan had known the story was coming.

He'd been warned days earlier by a friend who had attended Harvard with him. He had hoped against hope that it would be lost, ignored. After all, the incident had taken place more than fifty years ago.

But the recent flurry of news about Swiss banks and sales of art masterpieces known to be stolen by the Nazis had made this a good story. The fact that American servicemen, including high-ranking officers, might have looted Jewish possessions would be just too juicy for the newspapers to ignore.

He'd been waiting for the ax to fall. It fell today.

He knew that some, if not all, of his fast-track success in the State Department came from his family connections. His grandfather had been a two-star general and then a Washington lobbyist for defense contractors. He'd known everyone worth knowing, and the fact that the talented Dustin Eachan was Edward Eachan's grandson had sped his progress.

He'd worked damn hard for it, too. He wanted to be the first career State Department official to become Secretary of State. He had the political, family, and professional credentials to do it. He was close now to selecting the perfect wife.

He was perfectly positioned. If nothing went wrong.

And now the goddamn story implied his late grandfather might have committed grand theft.

And Sally. God, Sally would be devastated. He remembered the painting that she treasured as she cared for no other possession. Could it have been one of the stolen items?

He picked up the phone. He would cancel an engagement and take her to dinner tonight. She would need him. Hell, she always needed him.

He hesitated for a moment. He had tried to keep a distance. He cared far too much for her, and he had to be careful. She was his cousin; they had the same grandfather. He had been madly in love with her as a young man until it had been made plain that he could not marry a cousin.

His feelings for her had been one reason he hadn't married yet. He hadn't found anyone else he wanted to marry. But now a wife was essential to his career, and he liked, if not loved, Patsy Sandiford, the daughter of an administration official. For the past few weeks, he had been thinking about asking her to marry him.

He looked at the receiver in his hand, then dialed Sally's number.

two

COLORADO

Irish rode his favorite horse up into the hills, relishing the exercise and the time to think. He also needed to dissipate the frustration that knotted his stomach. He'd spent the last two days in a fruitless search for clues. He'd crawled through the attic of the ranch house and peered like a peeping Tom through decades of old papers.

He couldn't help but feel guilty. He was an investigator, used to digging into the dark recesses of people's lives. He hadn't wanted to do it to the person he'd loved and respected above all others. It made him feel dirty. Even treacherous.

It didn't matter that he was doing it to save his grandfather's reputation, not to destroy it. The simple fact was, he might be intruding into places best left alone. But if he didn't, others might. And those others might not have his care in doing so.

He'd hoped to find a diary, papers, journal. Anything.

But there had been nothing, and that was far more suspicious than documents would be.

Could there be any place other than the ranch house where the General might have left papers? Or had someone been there before him?

He wished now he had taken the time after his grandfa-

ther's death to go through his files. It hadn't seemed necessary at the time. A meticulous man in all things, his
grandfather had put all his important papers—the deed to
the ranch, a few minor investments, and insurance poli-
cies—in a safe deposit box and had left exact instructions
with his attorney as to their disposition.

At the time of the General's death, Irish had been in
Special Services, on an overseas assignment. He had flown
in for the funeral but then had to leave immediately. His
subsequent visits to the ranch had usually been working
vacations, trying to keep the ranch viable. He hadn't had
time to go through piles of paper. Or maybe he'd avoided
it to avoid the reality of his grandfather's death. Sam Flaherty had been the only person who'd ever accepted him
for who he was.

There had always been dozens of details to go over with
Joe Mendoza, the ranch foreman. Irish had planned to retire here, once he got his twenty years. Now he was a few
years past that mark. A steady string of promotions had
kept him in the army, along with a hesitancy to give up the
only life he'd ever known. He'd wondered whether he
could ever relinquish the adrenaline that coursed through
him when he neared the end of a hunt.

After reading the article about the commission report
and making several phone calls, to little avail, Irish was determined to prove his grandfather innocent. There had to
be something. His grandfather was known for his attention
to detail. He'd even dictated every part of his memorial
service. Irish had found journals written through most of
World War II. They had stopped, however, in June 1944,
the date of the European invasion.

Nothing after that. Not so much as a letter. It was as if
every piece of paper relating to the final campaign had
been eliminated. Had his grandfather expunged everything
from those years? He couldn't quite believe that. But there
had been no evidence of a break-in over the years.

Oh, he'd realized his grandfather had never wanted to

talk about World War II. He'd wondered about it, then credited it to modesty, although modesty was not usually a virtue of general officers. Perhaps the events had been too painful. Irish did know something about that. He'd lost his best friend in an investigation. He couldn't imagine losing hundreds, even thousands of men. In truth, he'd never wanted that kind of responsibility. He'd liked the lone wolf role he'd perfected over the last few years.

His grandfather had certainly been loquacious enough about other topics, particularly about his earlier years in the army and western novels. But he'd always been reticent about what everyone called the "Greatest War."

Had there been an ominous reason behind that silence? The feeling of uncertainty had clawed at Irish all day. Could there possibly be something?

He watched the sun disappear behind a snow-covered mountain. He gloried in a sky that was clear and so blue it hurt. The first few stars were just barely visible, and a silver disk of a moon appeared translucent. Another thirty minutes and it would be dark.

He started back toward the ranch house. The ride had served the purpose of clearing his mind. He'd made his decision, one he knew he'd really made days ago. He would ask for an extended leave. He sure as hell deserved one.

Irish knew he had to get to the bottom of the charges. The investigator inside him was raging. The absence of any records or memoirs had raised the hackles of every instinct he had. It was uncharacteristic of the General. Someone must have taken them.

He had to do something about the commission report and its implications. He had to do it for the General. And for himself.

He'd read the public part of the report. He'd thought about picking up the phone and contacting the commissioners, accusing them of character assassination. He'd even dialed the first three numbers after locating the office. But then he wouldn't get *any* cooperation.

No, he had to get his facts straight first, compile evidence. That meant securing top-secret information, and that might be difficult, even for him.

Perhaps he would start with the other officers named in the report. The names were imprinted in his mind. Brigadier General David Mallory and Colonel—later General—Edward Eachan.

MEMPHIS

Amy Mallory grabbed a quick lunch with her teaching assistant, Sherry Machovitz, who had become both friend and valued ally. She had also been her house sitter when Amy did an occasional visiting lecture, a necessity to gain her tenure.

The last few days had been so busy she hadn't had time to think of her grandfather, or of the article that had been shoved back on her desk. Once the tenure hearing was over, she would think about it.

Like Scarlett O'Hara, she thought, then grinned at the idea. She was as unlike Scarlett O'Hara as poor Bojangles was unlike the fearless Lassie.

But she was a devotee of old movies, and *Gone with the Wind* was her all-time favorite despite its skewed history. She knew she *shouldn't* like it. She had a doctorate in history, and her colleagues scorned such mindless entertainment. But she harbored a deep rebellious streak, something she suspected she inherited from her mother.

Her mother had been a hopelessly idealistic and extremely impractical romantic. Amy thought of herself as a practical idealist with a touch of romanticism. As long as it was from a distance. She wasn't sure she believed, as her mother had, that she was destined for any great romantic love. She was, in fact, quite convinced otherwise.

She liked to believe in the abstract that there were knights on white horses, but for herself . . . there were only mules.

And while she might like mules, she did not want to marry one.

"I found two of your people," Sherry said with a wide grin. "They are husband and wife. I even have their phone number. Now getting them to talk to you . . . well, I leave that in your experienced hands."

Amy gave her a rueful smile. "They didn't want to talk?"

"Nope," Sherry said. "They are now fine, upstanding Republicans."

Amy chuckled. She had done her dissertation on the protest movements of the twentieth century, arguing that the protests of the sixties and early seventies against the Vietnam War and segregation—they became linked in the minds of many people—comprised the first national American protest completely free of economic interest. The abolition movement also was moral in nature, but she'd contended it was far smaller and less national in scope.

Perhaps because her mother had been a part of protests, she was interested in their leaders and what had happened to them in the years since the protests ended. Although her dissertation had centered on the protests themselves, she'd continued to study the effects of those years on the people who led the movement, and planned a book on the subject. There was, she'd found, no common denominator. Some had wasted their lives, unable to survive productively without a cause; others had continued their activism in both governmental and private roles; and still others had turned into what they had once despised the most: their parents.

This, she often thought, was *her* romanticism: the mysteries and contradictions of history, even modern history.

And it was safe.

Emotional and physical safety meant a lot to her. Her childhood had been chaotic—she'd moved from one city to another, often as a member of an extended family where drugs flowed freely. She was the one who insisted on going to school, on trying to bring some order to their lives. She had been the parent.

Her attention turned back to Sherry. "Good work," she said. "I'll call them tomorrow and try to make an appointment."

"They're in Chicago," Sherry warned.

"Are you up to house-sitting with Bojangles again?"

"Are you kidding?" Sherry said. "It's a refuge."

Sherry lived with two other graduate students in a small house with only one bathroom. Though her assistant liked her housemates, she relished the privacy she had at Amy's. And Sherry was the only person who had any kind of rapport with emotionally challenged Bojangles.

In all, Sherry was the best thing that had happened to Amy in years. She was sharp, efficient, fascinated with the same obscurities as Amy, and loved dogs, cats, and anything else with four legs and a tail. It was complete compatibility. Too bad she would probably leave at the end of the year for an instructor's post at a college in the Midwest.

They talked about one student who showed particular promise, then Amy looked at her watch. "I'm going to run home before my afternoon class. I left a paper there."

"Right," Sherry said with a lifted eyebrow.

"All right," Amy said. "I have office hours this afternoon, and Bojangles. . . ."

"You don't have to convince me. He has my heart, too."

Amy paid the bill, which she often did. Sherry had stopped protesting after Amy had pointed out that Sherry had refused to take pay for house-sitting, and it would have cost her a fortune to board Bojangles. It had become a good arrangement.

Amy got in her twenty-year-old yellow Volkswagen, which she loved just as she loved Bojangles. It was another stray that needed constant and tender care. It had, in fact, been her very first car. Her only car. She wondered what that said about her.

Her house was ten minutes away. It had consumed nearly every penny she had, but it was hers. And that had been very important to her. She impatiently waded through heavy traffic. She had just enough time to get there, take Bojangles out for a short walk, and make it back in time for her class.

While waiting at a long light, her mind flipped over her schedule for the next week. Examinations. Grades. Most important, the tenure hearing in three weeks. And then she had the summer to work on her book. That damned article about her grandfather crept into her mind. She vowed to look into that, too. She owed it to her grandfather.

She had lent three boxes of her grandfather's papers to one of her colleagues who specialized in World War II. Perhaps she could find something there. She would go through them again before she started her book.

Satisfied that she was doing what she could for his memory, she pressed her foot on the gas, turned left into her neighborhood, then another left. As she reached the house, she saw flames dart out the window, then spread up the side of the house.

Bojangles!

She grabbed her keys, ran to the front door, and un- locked it. Fire was already filling the house with smoke. She grabbed a sweater resting over a chair and held it to her face. The bathroom. If something had scared Bojangles, he'd be hiding behind the toilet. Amy felt heat as she ran through the hallway toward the bedroom and its bathroom.

"Bojangles," she called.

She heard a bark and then she saw him streaking toward her. For once, his belief in her overcame his fear. She picked him up and ran for the door, aware that the fire was following her. The smoke was acrid, the heat unbearable. Bojangles huddled against her, his faith in her giving speed to her feet.

She didn't think she'd make it. Her throat burned and

flames were everywhere. She couldn't see anything; only familiarity with the house kept her going in what she hoped was the right direction.

Fear was suffocating her as much as the smoke. Then she saw light where she'd left the door ajar. Flames ate away at the bottom of the door. Praying, she pushed open the screen and burst through it. She stumbled down the steps, trying to take them in one single leap. Bojangles flew out of her arms but other hands—neighbors' hands—reached for her and the dog, dragging them away from the fire.

Sirens. She looked back. *Her home.* Her first home was a roaring inferno. She suddenly realized that cinders had burned through her pantsuit, and Bojangles was frantically licking himself and whining plaintively.

She stooped down and took him in her arms, burying her head in his wiry fur as fire engines pulled up in front of the house and men jumped down and started unrolling hoses. One pulled her away.

But she couldn't help looking up and watching everything she owned going up in flames. Everything but Bojangles.

If she'd been a few moments later. . . .

Even through her shock, her practical mind ran over this morning's routine. She knew she hadn't left anything on. Not a stove or an iron or another appliance. She was meticulous about that. She'd always had a fear of fire, especially after her mother had left hot oil on the stove and it had caught fire. Amy had been burned when she'd tried to put it out with water. The next-door neighbor had heard her scream and came in, smothering the flames with baking soda.

Bojangles licked her face, and she realized she was shaking.

A fireman came up to her. "Ma'am? Were you inside?"

She nodded. "I'd just driven up when I saw the flames. I went in for my dog." She clutched Bojangles tighter as he tried to snuggle even closer. His fear of the stranger was palpable.

"You should go to the hospital and get checked out."

"Just a few surface burns," she said. "I'll put salve on them."

He studied her for a moment. "A fire investigator will want to talk to you."

She stared at his frown. "Why?"

"My men smelled accelerant," he said. "The fire spread too quickly to be an accident."

She knew what that meant. Her legs suddenly felt rubbery, and she trembled all over. Bojangles whined in distress.

A fire was bad enough, but to think. . . .

Who could possibly want to set her house on fire?

three

Dustin Eachan stared at the painting hanging in his cousin's living room and felt a prickling along his back.

"We should report it," he said. He couldn't look at his cousin. He knew he would see a feeling of betrayal on her face. He wouldn't have suggested it if he hadn't known she would refuse. He certainly didn't want the public to know that his family had stolen art treasures. God help his career then. Still, he felt he had to say it.

"No," she said. "I won't do it."

"Then you need to put it away," he said. He knew how much the painting meant to her. It was the last present her father had given her. The fact that it hadn't meant anything to her father didn't destroy her pleasure in it..

"They're dead now," she said quietly. "It can't mean anything to anyone but me. It's not as if it was really worth any money."

"It's on a partial inventory list. I saw it. *Sea Scape* by Ramon Castelli. Someone might remember it," Dustin said.

"Why? You told me the painting isn't worth much."

That was when she was desperate for money. He had bailed her out financially—not for the first time—and she had offered the painting in exchange. He'd refused to take it because he knew how much it meant to her. And in truth it wasn't worth a fortune, though it would have sold for about fifty thousand.

To Sally, though, it was her only inheritance from a father she'd adored.

"Will you do that?" he asked.

"Store it away?"

"Yes." He turned and looked at her. She was the most beautiful woman he'd ever seen.

If only he had lived in the sixteenth or seventeenth or eighteenth century, when marrying cousins was acceptable. But he didn't, and it wasn't—especially for someone who planned to go into public service. Some states even prohibited marriage between first cousins. He remembered his mother's horror when she'd first realized that he felt more than cousinly affection for Sally. She had been merely sixteen then, and he'd been twenty-two.

So he had taken over the role of protector instead, pushing his wayward feelings aside. He'd told himself that there were other women in the world. He was, in fact, almost engaged to Patsy Sandiford. Patsy was beautiful and bright and committed. She was involved in a dozen causes and held a master's degree in international relations. Her pedigree was impeccable. Just like his. At least, just like his before the goddamned commission report.

And she would marry him in a New York second. He had known that for months.

He liked her. He had just about decided love didn't matter. They would have affection and similar interests and great sex. Did he really need more?

Then he would see Sally, and know that he did.

He stuffed those feelings back in the mental box where they belonged.

"Will you put it away?" he repeated.

Sally looked at him for a long moment. She was unlike all the other members of the Eachan family. Where most of them were dark-haired with blue eyes, she had golden hair and green eyes. They weren't vividly green, not like emeralds, but a soft, vulnerable gray green with flecks of gold. "Where?"

"A safe deposit box," he said.

"And if someone asks me if I have anything. . . ."

"They won't," he said with more assurance than he felt. "They looked into events that happened fifty years ago. They won't be crawling through all our possessions. . . ."

"Then why . . . ?"

"Someone might see it and say something," he said.

She looked at him with those damned eyes that made him feel like God. "All right, if you think that's best."

"I do, Squirt," he said, using his old pet name for her. They had virtually grown up together. He had soothed her when her father disappeared for months at a time, leaving his wife and daughter in the not always gentle hands of their grandparents.

Dustin's father was with the State Department and often left his children home when stationed in what he said were dangerous countries. Dustin had been shipped off to the grandparents, where he'd been the golden child. He'd been fawned over by grandparents who adored him but disliked Sally's mother and, therefore, her child.

His cousin had been a lonely child, and now she was a lonely adult who'd never learned to trust anyone but him, and there wasn't a damn thing he could do about it.

The ironic thing was that he wasn't very trusting himself. He had always felt deserted by his own parents, and had turned away from them when his sister had drowned when she was seventeen and he was fifteen. It seemed all his parents cared about was covering up the fact that she had been high on drugs.

He'd learned then that all their talk about duty and honor meant little. Everyone took shortcuts to get what they wanted. You didn't get where his father had without leaving a few bodies in your wake, even your own children's.

The only person he'd allowed himself to care about after that was Sally. She always made him feel better about himself. Better and worse.

She nodded. "I'll do it tomorrow."

He went over to the cabinet where she kept the scotch and took out the bottle that was always there. For him, he knew. She drank wine.

He poured a sizable measure in a glass and added some ice, then gulped it. "How's your job?"

Sally shrugged. "It's fine," she said without enthusiasm. She was a public relations officer, or more accurately, an escort for foreign dignitaries visiting the State Department. It was, in fact, a good job for her. She was uncommonly good-natured and competent in her own way, as well as a very decorative part of any office, but she never stayed anywhere long. At thirty-five, she still didn't know what she wanted to do when she grew up.

Or maybe she did. She'd always liked to draw and paint, but she'd never persevered with any studies in that area. "I'm not good enough," she'd always claimed.

He thought she was, but she'd never been able to commit to art—perhaps because she was opposed to everything her mother liked. Nor could she seem to commit to a job any more than she could commit to a man. She'd had more boyfriends than he could count, but never one that lasted more than six months. He'd never known how he felt about that.

"Do you believe Grandfather was involved?"

"Well, he took one painting at least," Dustin said. "We know that," he added as he looked back at the art hanging on the wall. It was the one really nice thing in the apartment. The other furnishings were either cheap imitations or hand-me-downs. Possessions, other than the painting, had never meant much to her. Another attempt at avoiding commitments.

He, on the other hand, believed in nice things, and had accumulated them carefully. Every piece of furniture he owned was of the best quality. Every painting on his walls had a pedigree. They had been part of the package, the weapons he'd gathered to take him where he wanted to go.

He'd always wondered why his soft spot—his only one—had to be his cousin.

"Daddy would have been pleased," Sally said. "He always thought Grandfather was such a paragon of virtue. He would have loved the fact that he had feet of clay." Her voice was cold. She'd always blamed their grandparents for her father's problems.

Dustin did not reply. His view of their grandparents was different from hers. They had been aloof, but he also had that quality and he understood it. It had always been difficult for him to show affection, even when he felt it. Men didn't do that. He didn't know whether that belief had been bred or drilled into him. He just knew that emotional detachment had become a part of him.

He also knew why his grandparents had disinherited Sally's father and basically thrown him out to die of alcoholism. He had been a thief and a liar. But Sally had never seen that part of him and the family was not one to bare unpleasant secrets. God knew, though, those secrets had ultimately hurt Sally, for she had only seen her father's charm.

Now they had only each other. His parents and grandparents were dead, and Sally was estranged from her mother, her only other relative. Only Dustin remained to console her after yet another relationship went bad, or a job didn't lead to what she'd hoped it would.

An alcoholic's child. She always tried to please, and did it in all the wrong ways.

But was he much better? He was ready to marry someone he didn't love to advance his career. He also knew most of his colleagues didn't like him, that they felt he would sell his best friend for a promotion. *And they could be right.*

Now his family *would* respect that, he thought bitterly.

It was a family tradition. Ambition meant everything. More than loyalty or honor.

"Will you take the painting tomorrow?" he said, returning to the subject. The last thing he needed now was evidence that his family had stolen art treasures.

"For you," she said. "Not for Grandfather."

He bent down and kissed her forehead. He touched her cheek for a moment, and she bent her head so it rested on his hand. The gesture was so filled with trust that he felt an ache in his heart.

His colleagues would laugh at that. None thought he had one.

He sighed, sure now that she would do as he asked.

Dustin lowered his hand and went to the door, knowing he shouldn't stay one moment longer, or he might do something he would regret.

"Let me know if you need anything," he said.

She looked at him with those soft eyes. "I always do," she said with a wry, even sad, smile. "Don't you ever get tired of me?"

He shook his head. "Never," he said.

MEMPHIS

Amy spent the better part of two days at the police station going over every part of her life.

Who would want to do her harm?

The very thought that someone hated her that much sent icy tremors through her. She knew of no enemies. Not even anyone with the slightest grudge.

During the past two nights, she'd often found herself shaking as she recalled those few horrible moments in the house. She would smell the smoke, feel the heat, experience the terror. In her nightmares she didn't always make it out of the building. She would wake up drenched with sweat and hug Bojangles until he yelped.

She had found a temporary haven at a suites hotel that

permitted dogs. When she wasn't at the police station, she was talking to the insurance company and trying to decide whether to rebuild. She wondered whether she would ever feel safe there again.

"You still haven't thought of anyone who might want to do you harm?" the police detective asked for the tenth time. "A boyfriend? Anyone?"

She shook her head. It had been a long time since she'd had a serious relationship, and that one ended by mutual consent. He'd received a job offer in another city, and neither was committed enough to the other to marry and give up a career.

"Keep thinking about it. No matter how far-fetched," Jim Evans, the frustrated detective, insisted.

She nodded. How could she help not thinking about it? She doubted, though, if she would come up with any kind of answer. She liked almost everyone and everyone seemed to like her, although she had few really close friends.

"You haven't found any clues at all?" she asked. "You're absolutely sure it was intentionally set? I had a gas grill," she added hopefully. "Maybe a leak. . . ."

He shook his head. "The fire investigators found traces of accelerant at the side of the house. It looked professional." He hesitated. "Is there anything you might be working on that someone might not like?"

"People don't set fires because they don't like a historian's take on the past," she said. "There's nothing that should upset anyone, certainly not enough for arson."

"But someone *did* set a fire," he said.

She bit her lip. She still couldn't imagine what anyone might want, what motive anyone might have for hurting her.

"Was there anything on your home computer that wasn't on the office computer?" he asked.

"Just some notes on a book I plan to write. Almost everything was backed up on my office computer."

"You haven't received any suspicious E-mail? Threats?"

"No. None of the above. I really live an uneventful life, Detective."

His eyes narrowed. "Can our people look through those computer files?"

She knew they couldn't do so without a search warrant, and she was the victim, not the perpetrator. "After I back them up."

"And you didn't have any other papers in your house?"

"Not that would interest anyone," she said. For a moment she thought of the boxes of World War II documents she'd saved from her grandfather's attic years ago. Another professor had had them for months. But she didn't want to bring Jon Foster's research into this. Her fifty-year-old papers couldn't have had anything to do with the fire. With the exception of Jon and Sherry, no one even knew she had them. He certainly had no reason to harm her.

The detective stood. "We're questioning people we know like to set fires," he said. "It could just be a firebug who struck at random."

That was the first comforting thought he'd offered, even if it was disconcerting to think someone would cause such destruction for a thrill. It was better than the alternative, however. She nodded. "That must be it," she said.

His expression expressed some doubt. "Could be, Miss Mallory, but I think you should be careful. And if you think of anything, anything at all, call me."

"I will," she assured him.

She hugged herself against the cold that had settled deep inside her and started for her temporary lodgings. She'd borrowed a friend's laptop to use at the hotel. She didn't want to work in the darkened halls of the university—not now—and she felt reasonably safe in the hotel. And Bojangles was there.

She found herself doing something she had never done

before. She looked at everyone with suspicion: the driver of every car, even pedestrians walking near the hotel. She wondered whether she would ever stop looking now, and that question filled her with anger. No one had the right to do that to her, to change the way she looked at the world.

Bojangles barked when she arrived at her room. She unlocked the door and leaned down to pet him. His furry face looked worried, his long eyelashes trembling nervously. He'd been even more timid than usual since losing the one safe place he knew.

"Ah," she said, "it's all right, Bo. No one is going to hurt you or me."

But she found herself looking out the window and wondering whether she really believed it. Or ever would again.

She felt so alone. So damnably alone.

Who?

And, more important, why?

four

Irish stared at the burned ruins of what once had been a
home.

So that was the reason he hadn't been able to reach Amy
Mallory, the explanation behind the "this number is no
longer in service" message.

He'd researched the two generals other than his grandfather: Mallory and Eachan. They, like his own grandfather, had surprisingly few progeny. From the three, no
child still lived. There were four surviving grandchildren,
including himself. Two others had died: his brother and an
Eachan child. If he had been a superstitious person, he
might have thought the families cursed.

Irish had discovered a great deal about the others in the
past three days. He knew their jobs, their school records,
their credit reports.

He'd pondered which to visit first. He hadn't particularly been encouraged by what he'd learned about Dustin
Eachan. Irish had friends who interacted with the State
Department. None of them thought highly of the man they
all considered too ambitious for the department's good. He
was a man, they said, who always chose the expedient
way, who let nothing stand in the way of promotions.

He probably would not be overly pleased about opening

the investigation wider. Hell, he was probably hiding in a closet now.

Eachan's cousin didn't sound too encouraging either. She was in substantial debt, had changed jobs seven times in ten years, and was currently working for the State Department.

Amy Mallory, on the other hand, seemed the epitome of stability. Not even a parking ticket. History professor. She would keep papers, memoirs, journals—if indeed any existed. He'd decided to start with her and had tried for two days to reach her by phone. Then he'd jumped on a plane.

He had three more days of his scheduled leave remaining. He'd already talked to his commanding officer about taking an extended leave. But he'd learned long ago not to waste time on hopeless causes. If he didn't find anything in Memphis or in Washington, his next stop, he would forget it.

Or try to.

Damn, General! What in the hell had happened? He could see his grandfather in his mind's eye. He'd been integrity itself, drilling into his grandson the concept of honor every day of his life. He'd called the man "Grandfather" but he'd always thought of him as "the General."

Honor. How in God's name could he allow his grandfather's honor to be stripped from him?

Which was why he was standing in front of a burned-out shell of a house.

He looked around. No cars. He would head for his hotel and call the university. He probably couldn't get her private number, but he should learn where she might be the next day. Or at least locate her office.

He would wear his uniform, since it often impressed. Or intimidated. Those were the only reasons he wore it these days; CID agents—even military members—usually wore civilian clothes.

Irish took one last look at the house. An accident? Or another coincidence? He only knew he didn't like the feeling in his gut. He knew it too well, and it always meant trouble.

Amy clutched the telephone to her ear and listened to Sherry's excited voice.

"When I told him you wouldn't be in today, he wanted your address and phone number," Sherry said.

Amy sat down on the bed. She'd been arguing with insurance adjusters all day about the value of her electronic equipment. For some idiotic reason, they didn't understand that all her receipts went up in the fire. They also expressed concern that the cause was arson. There would be, they said, an investigation before they could pay out.

As if she would have burned her own house with her livelihood, dog, and herself inside.

Thank God, she didn't have a class today. Fortunate for the students anyway. She'd had Sherry cancel her appointments.

"Amy?" The voice on the other end of the telephone sounded concerned.

"He didn't say what he wanted?" She didn't want to talk to another insurance agent, fire investigator, or police officer for the next ten years. Especially not today.

"No but he's one hell of a good-looking guy. He's in uniform and looks very cool in it."

"What kind of uniform?"

"Army. I think. He had enough decorations to fill a Christmas tree."

Army. She got an all-too-familiar bitter taste in her mouth. She tried to wash it out with the glass of wine she'd poured on her return from the insurance company. For a moment her throat tightened, constricted. She had to force out a breath of air.

This had to have something to do with her grandfather. Possibly the article she'd seen a week earlier . . . a lifetime ago. She'd forgotten all about it after the fire.

She knew one thing. She couldn't cope with it today. Maybe not tomorrow.

"What should I tell him?" Sherry prompted.

"Nothing," Amy said. "Tell him you couldn't reach me."

There was a silence, then in a small voice, "He's standing here."

Amy groaned. Sherry was usually more protective of her than this. The soldier must be *very* good-looking.

"Tell him I'm going to Alaska." That seemed as reasonable as any place to her. She wondered if there were firebugs in Alaska.

"I think he'd follow you there. He has a determined glint in his eyes."

If she knew Sherry, her assistant had already assessed every physical characteristic of her unwanted visitor, down to his shirt size. "What color are they?"

"Paul Newman," Sherry said.

Now she knew how the man had gotten as far as he had. Sherry was a sucker for Paul Newman. Amy sighed. She might as well get it over with. "Tomorrow," she said. "At the office."

She heard Sherry talking to someone, then a question. "He wants to know if he can take you out to dinner tonight."

"No," Amy said abruptly.

Whispers again on the other end of the line, then Sherry's questioning voice. "You won't reconsider?"

"No," Amy replied.

Sherry sighed again. "You have a class at nine and meetings at ten and eleven."

"Two o'clock," Amy said. "At the office." A week ago she wouldn't have thought twice about meeting someone outside of the office. She didn't like the fear that had become a part of her.

She hung up and leaned against the headboard of the bed. Bo crawled up beside her, and she rubbed his head.

Amy had never been a coward. She had taken care of her mother in down-and-out neighborhoods since she was in grade school. She'd learned to be tough. Lenis Mallory had been into drugs, and though she tried to quit, she'd always fallen back on them. She was one of those flower children who had never grown out of it.

Amy had loved her with all her heart. She had been gentle and sweet, and had a voice that would make angels weep. But she'd had no strength. People had used her. Strength was important to Amy. She hated the feeling of being out of control.

She rose, went to the small kitchenette, and made a cup of coffee. She could only guess at what her insistent caller wanted. Something to do with her grandfather, probably with the recent investigation. Well, she wasn't going to give him anything that might hurt her grandfather's reputation. But first she had to know if she had anything that might. That meant going through the boxes of her grandfather's papers that were now in the hands of Dr. Jonathan Foster.

Amy was everything her mother wasn't: practical, ambitious, independent. But she shared her mother's distrust of authority. She'd seen—and heard—too many things as a kid. She was not going to let anyone take advantage of a Mallory. She certainly wasn't going to salute at the sight of a uniform.

Her hand was still on the phone. She picked it up and dialed the history department's number.

An answering machine answered. Jon Foster wasn't in. She knew, though, that he kept her grandfather's papers in his office. He often worked late there, preferring the messy comfort of his office to the tidiness of his home. It was an escape from a marriage well on its way to going bad. His wife was demanding and perennially unhappy, Jon had confided to her over lunch one day when she'd teasingly accused him of being a workaholic.

She looked at the clock. Five o'clock. He was either at

a deli picking up a sandwich or he'd given in to his wife's complaints. She looked up his number, wishing for her address book that was now only wisps of smoke, and called. He wasn't home, his wife said curtly, adding that he was probably working late "as usual."

That meant he was out to supper.

Amy had keys to the building and to her office but not to his; he kept it locked, as did they all. Student thefts of examination papers were always rumored if not proven.

He should be back by seven at the latest.

She would be there.

"Come on, Bo," she said. "Let's get some supper."

She missed her kitchen. She missed being able to make a salad or cook a steak or a grilled cheese sandwich. She missed her home office with its eccentric computer. Most of all she missed her books: six rooms of books that would take decades to replace.

Don't think about it. There's nothing you can do now. But, dear God, she hoped they found the individual responsible.

They would get some hamburgers and bring them back, then she would run over to the university. She opened the door and Bo hung back for a moment, then reluctantly followed. Obviously uncertain about his new environment, he'd moped ever since they arrived, even whimpering occasionally. He knew something was wrong.

She tried to call Jon's office when they returned, Bo's mood decidedly better after a hamburger. Again no answer. It was probably a waste of time to go by his office, and yet she did have some work to do. She had to complete backing up all the computer files at her office; she was insistent on always having a second copy of everything, and her second set had been destroyed in the fire. She'd already backed up her chapters of the new book, but not the raw notes for her dissertation. There were names in them she needed.

The depth of her loss kept slapping her.

Amy almost decided to take Bo with her, then decided he would be happier here. She grabbed her purse, then left and drove to the campus just a mile away. It was still daylight, though it would be dark soon.

An hour, she promised herself. Only an hour. It shouldn't take longer than that to back up what she needed. If Jon didn't appear by then, she'd try to call him again. She really wanted to go through those boxes before she met with an army investigator or whatever he was.

The doors were still unlocked, and she took the stairs to her second-floor office. Jon's office was about ten doors down and on the corner. He was a tenured full professor and thus had more space than her small cubbyhole. She went past her own office and down to Jon's. She tried the door. It was locked.

Amy turned to leave, then thought she heard someone inside. She stopped, listened for a second. Then she knocked, first tentatively, then louder. Nothing. She started back toward her office, then decided she would find the security guard, something she wouldn't have considered two weeks earlier.

Her skin crawling with the kind of fear she hadn't known two days before, Amy took the steps two at a time, hoping she could find Claude, who was often on duty. He was a large, black man who exuded both goodwill and competence. She finally found him checking offices on the first floor.

"Dr. Mallory," he said with a grin that quickly disappeared when he saw her face.

"Can you check Dr. Foster's office? I knocked and no one answered, but I thought I heard someone inside."

He nodded. He used his cell phone to call the campus police office, asking for backup, then started up the stairs. "Stay here, Dr. Mallory," he said.

But Amy couldn't do that. She followed him closely, her breath catching in her throat as they reached the last step. A feeling of dread smothered her. "Let's wait until someone comes."

"It's probably nothing. We've been having trouble with mice, and that's most likely what you heard. Nothing ever happens around here."

Just then, Jon's door opened and a man stepped out. A ski mask covered his face, and he was carrying a box. He saw them and stopped, the box falling from his hands. Then a gun was in his hand. The movement was fast. Incredibly fast, even graceful.

Amy's gaze went to Claude. His hand reached for his holstered pistol. The sound of gunfire came just a second after the crash of the box. It echoed through the empty hall.

It was like nothing she'd ever heard before, so loud that her ears rang. She saw Claude stop, his hand dropping the pistol, blood blossoming over his uniform shirt. Paralyzed, she felt rooted to the spot as the man aimed at her and shot again.

She felt as if a train had hit her. Shock clouded pain, and she felt herself fall. Then nothing.

five

Dustin's fingers tightened around the phone as he listened
to the voice on the other end. "I just thought you'd like to
know someone else is looking for the same records you
asked about."

He swore under his breath. He hadn't expected that.
He'd hoped the whole bloody thing would just fade away.

"Do you know who?"

"An army investigator. Name of Flaherty. Ring a bell?"

Dustin didn't like the amusement in the voice on the
other side of the line. Of course, he knew the name. One of
the other generals implicated—or at least named—in the
report.

"What did they tell him?"

"Same thing they told you. And gave you. No more. But
my contact in the commission's office said this Flaherty
wasn't going to back off. I just thought I should warn you."

"Thanks," Dustin said. He hung up, leaned back in his
chair, and stared outside at the view that was his, due to his
position.

He thought about the caller. Cecil Ford was a subordinate who'd hitched his star to Dustin's. He was, in fact,
Dustin's gofer, a man who, like Dustin, would do nearly
anything to get ahead. And had. Dustin trusted him only

because it was in Cecil's best interest to be loyal. If that ever changed. . . .

Dustin weighed his options. He'd asked for a copy of the commission report and supporting documentation. He received the first. The latter had so much blacked out that it was of little use. Even the list of stolen items was incomplete; several pages from the original forty-five page inventory were missing.

But the major theft—two trunks of gold—had been documented elsewhere. *Two trunks of gold.* They would have been worth millions at the end of the war.

Dustin had never questioned the source of his family's wealth, although his great-grandfather had emigrated from Scotland with very little. He had fought in World War I and won the Congressional Medal of Honor, which meant his son—Dustin's grandfather—had a automatic appointment to West Point. In the ensuing years, the Eachan family became very wealthy. Dustin didn't know the particulars. He'd just enjoyed it.

But he'd never lied to himself, either. He knew much of his success came from his lineage. A heroic great-grandfather. A grandfather who was a three-star general. A father who was a career diplomat who had become an ambassador and finally president of a major university before his death in a plane crash.

Dustin was easily admitted to Harvard despite less than exemplary grades. He had any number of sponsors, including the Vice President of the United States. He had immediately been scooped up by the State Department at graduation, and his family had a sufficient number of friends to speed him up the career ladder. He had every intention of eventually being appointed Secretary of State. That had, after all, been driven into him all his life. It was expected of him.

Therefore he was very careful politically, and even more careful in his personal life.

He wondered how quickly support would erode if it

were suspected that his family had built its wealth on stolen gold—Nazi wealth.

And if he discovered his grandfather was guilty, then what? Hide the evidence?

Dustin felt no obligation to those people who once owned the objects. They were dead, and he knew it would be next to impossible to find any of their rightful heirs. He didn't want the expanding scope of national recriminations over something that happened before he was born to destroy everything he had worked for. Damn the interfering fools who stirred up something that should have been forgotten.

He also knew he couldn't press any harder to see the top-secret files without having questions asked about *him*.

Dustin wished he had more real friends. He'd always been somewhat of a loner. Oh, he could be loquacious enough in a crowd. And charming. But other than Sally, he'd never really had any close friends. He'd often regretted that, and wondered at it. What in him kept people at a distance?

He ran down the list of his acquaintances in the government, someone who might ask the questions that he didn't feel he should, not without drawing attention to himself. Cecil was out. He was already linked to Dustin. There was only one name that came to mind. Alf Adams had been his roommate his third year at Harvard. Alf—short for Alfred, which he hated—was now with the CIA. They continued an active, if not particularly chummy, tennis relationship. They tried to play at least once a week and, equally matched, they often traded wins.

Dustin seldom asked favors, and he hated to do so now. Asking a favor meant having to return it. He hated that kind of debt.

But first, he decided, he would go to his vacation home on the Maryland Eastern Shore. It was time for a long weekend anyway. Time to get back to the sea again.

*"I must down to the seas again, to the lonely sea and
    the sky,
And all I ask is a tall ship and a star to steer her by,
And the wheel's kick and the wind's song and the white
    sail's shaking,
And a grey mist on the sea's face and a grey dawn
    breaking."*

He'd often wondered why Masefield's poem so res-
onated in him. Now he knew. He wanted to feel free.

Dustin rubbed the knots forming in the back of his neck
before turning to the stack of papers on his desk.

MEMPHIS

Amy woke to waves of pain. She remembered being told
that she would be all right. A nurse? A doctor? Then she'd
been moved again. But everything was hazy, so hazy. Everything but the pain. When she moved, she felt as if a red-
hot poker had been applied to her side. Her head pounded
as she slowly opened her eyes. It took her a long moment
to focus. She bit down to keep a sound from escaping her
lips. Then she was aware of someone else in the room. No,
two people.

Sherry was sitting next to her. A man in uniform stood
at the window, looking out. She tried to place him but she
couldn't.

She moved, and he whirled around. In her foggy state, he
did it with such grace and speed that it made her dizzy.
Dizzier and more confused than she already was. What . . . ?

Then she remembered. The halls of the history building.
A man in a ski mask. A gun. Grace. She'd had the impression of grace then, too. Then the sound of a bullet exploding
from the gun. The stunning impact.

The pounding in her head worsened. She felt as if it
were going to explode.

"Sherry. . . ."

Sherry had been staring at the stranger. Now her gaze dropped back to her. "Amy. Thank God. We were all worried about you."

Amy's mind frantically tried to recapture those moments before the shot. Something important. A man in a ski mask. A box. The security guard.

"Claude . . . the security guard?"

"He's in critical condition," Sherry said. "The doctors think he'll make it."

Stunned, Amy could only look at her. Why had she asked him to go with her? Why couldn't they have waited for someone to accompany them? He was married with two young children. She'd seen the photos.

She closed her eyes for a moment. Grief was like a parasite, chewing her up inside.

But then she heard movement next to her, and she opened her eyes again. The man in uniform was beside her, and despite the pain and grief, she was momentarily distracted. She knew now why Sherry had been so insistent on her meeting with him. He *did* have striking ice-cool blue eyes, and small lines—laugh or worry lines—crinkled around them. The color was a more intense blue than any she had ever seen before. His face in totality was not handsome. It was too angular for that, but an indentation in his chin broke its austerity. His lips had an odd little quirk that made him look permanently quizzical.

He was, she guessed, in his early forties, but his face looked older, as if weathered by sun and weighty matters. *Or command*, she thought, as she saw the ribbons on his uniform and the oak leaf clusters. Ordinarily, she wasn't impressed by the military. The exact opposite, in fact. But Sherry was right. He did look "cool." And that was not a word she ever used.

"I'm Colonel Flaherty," he said, the twist of his lip turning into a half-smile that acknowledged her. As she'd suspected from Sherry's smitten reaction, charm radiated from him.

Amy did not smile in return. He was an intruder here, not a friend. And she certainly didn't want to talk to a stranger. Not now, not until she got her thoughts together. She forced her gaze away from him and back to Sherry. "How . . . long have I been here?"

"About sixteen hours," she said. "They had to take a bullet out of you, but the doctor said you'll be just fine." She hesitated. "The police were here. They waited most of the night and today. They finally gave up, but they want to talk to you as soon as possible."

Amy weighed that. Something nagged at her. Then she remembered what she'd been trying to remember. Boxes. She started to mention them, then stopped. What was the stranger doing in her room?

"Jon?" she asked. "I want to speak to. . . ."

There was a stricken look on Sherry's face. She touched Amy's hand. "He's dead," she said reluctantly. "An automobile accident last evening. Hit and run."

The room started to blur. New pain ripped through Amy. A kind of pain far different from the physical pounding in her body. And anger. Deep, bitter anger.

"No" she whispered. "It can't be."

The colonel looked at Sherry. "Jon?"

"A history professor at the college. He and Amy were friends."

And the burglar was coming out of his office. Amy's heart beat faster, almost frantically. Sherry wouldn't have known she had gone to see Jon last night, that she had wanted to retrieve her boxes. And now Jon was dead. A coincidence? She did not believe it for a moment, but she was not going to mention it in front of this man.

"I'm sorry, Miss Mallory," he said in a soft voice. "I wanted to reach you this morning, and called the college. Miss Machovitz had just arrived at the office and learned of your . . . injury. I don't think anyone knew about your friend then."

His voice was deep, soft, and soothing. Too soothing.

She didn't trust it. She wondered whether he had connected the two . . . incidents. "Why are you here?" she asked.

"The police were here all night, waiting to see you," he said soothingly. "When they left to get some lunch, I told them I would stay with you." He looked at his watch. "They should be here any minute."

Then it struck her. *Flaherty*. Sherry had not mentioned his name yesterday, and she'd been so busy with details with the insurance company she hadn't asked. Flaherty. It was the same name as one of the generals in the newspaper story. Her eyes narrowed. Everything bad had started to happen after she'd read that article.

"What do you want?" Amy asked.

He looked uncomfortable, but determined. "Information. I don't know if you're aware of a recent commission report. On war thefts. Second World War." He said it all in clipped sentences, his magnetic blue eyes studying her with an intensity that burned like a laser.

"I'm aware," she said simply.

"I thought you might have some papers that would shed light on it." It was both a statement and a question. It was a particularly effective form of interrogation. She had used it herself in interviews.

She was silent. In truth, she didn't know what she had. But after the last few days she was not going to share anything with anyone. "Why . . . would you believe I do?"

"You're a historian," he said. "A very good one, I understand. And you're the only descendant of General Mallory. It stands to reason. . . ."

How would he know whether she was a good one or not unless he'd checked into her background? The thought chilled her. And that chill laced her reply. "It is not my field, Colonel."

"I know," he said with some amusement in his voice.

"Your field is war protestors. I probably shouldn't have worn the uniform."

"Then why did you?"

"It often helps me get into places I otherwise might not," he said with a disarming charm that she knew had been lurking there, just waiting to be sprung on her. She was, however, in no mood to be charmed. Particularly by someone named Flaherty who got himself into her room through false pretenses, who had apparently snooped into her life.

"Well, I can't help you," she said, tamping down on the waves of pain assaulting her. "I just want to rest. And," she added pointedly, "to talk to the police."

He studied her for a moment. "Why were you in Sammons Hall last night?"

"It's none of your business," she said, her anger overcoming curiosity. Too much had happened in the past week. Things she didn't understand, and now this . . . stranger apparently wanted her to trust him. She didn't. She wondered whether she would ever trust anyone again.

She turned to Sherry. "Bo?"

"As soon as I knew you'd be okay, I went to your hotel and explained everything. They let me in and I got Bo for you. He's at my house."

"Who's Bo?" the uniform said.

"Amy's dog," Sherry said helpfully.

Amy closed her eyes. She was tired, so very tired. Her head hurt, and her side felt as if it were on fire. She was also confused. Angry. She thought of Jon, and grief flooded her again and lodged in her heart. He had been a good friend, and she would miss their conversations and his humor. And somehow, for some reason she didn't understand, she suspected she was in some way the cause of his death.

She opened her eyes again. The colonel was still standing there. Stiff and straight. Tall. Several inches taller than her own nearly six feet, which usually made her self-conscious.

He was lean in build and she sensed, rather than saw, raw physical power. He also gave an impression of restlessness even where he stood still. She would bet her last paycheck that he ran three miles before breakfast and worked out daily in a gym. The thought did not endear him to her.

His eyes, though, were difficult to read. He wore the investigator's mask. She had seen it too much in the past several days. Resentment replaced some of her confusion. They wanted information. They seldom gave it. *Well, not this time, buddy.*

"What do you do in the Army?"

"I'm in criminal investigation."

She should have guessed from his insistence. "CID?"

He looked startled. "Yes, ma'am."

"I didn't think colonels conducted investigations."

"You know about us, then?"

"Oh, yes. I know about most law investigation agencies," she said dryly. "Certainly enough to know that colonels supervise. Warrant officers and civilians do most of the . . . work."

He looked uncomfortable, and that gave her momentary satisfaction. She didn't think he looked that way very often.

"The police know I'm here unofficially," he said after a short pause.

She moved then, and the pain that had been under control—barely—became white-hot agony. She clenched her teeth to keep from moaning.

But Sherry saw it. "Squeeze the button beside you," she said. "There's a drip to control the pain."

Amy didn't want a drug. Not until she saw the police. Maybe not even then. She'd seen too much of what drugs did. She didn't even take aspirin. Instead, she waited until the pain receded.

"Go away," she told the colonel.

He hesitated a moment. "I told the police I would stay with you. They've checked my credentials."

Ah, the fellowhood of cops. Not once, apparently, did they question whether the colonel had a personal motive. She bit down on the pain again. "I still want you to go."

"Will you talk to me later?" he persisted.

"Why should I?"

He raised an eyebrow.

"Your name is Flaherty. So is one of the generals involved with the treasure trains."

"I'm his grandson," the colonel said.

The pain was tolerable again. "Why didn't you tell me that in the beginning?"

"Does it make a difference?"

"Of course it does," she said, steeling herself once more against a new wave of pain. "You have a personal interest." It was almost an accusation. He'd appeared the day after someone tried to kill her, several days after her house was burned.

"I do. I don't deny it. And you do, too."

"It was fifty years ago. It has nothing to do with my life now."

"Then why was your home destroyed? Why did someone hurt you last night?"

"You tell me," she said, anger and pain coming together in an explosion. "You certainly appeared at a curious time."

He shrugged carelessly, but she saw the tension in the set of his shoulders. He wasn't nearly as relaxed as he wanted her to believe. Why? What did he think she might know that would help him in any way? Or did he think it might hurt him?

"I saw the article in the paper," he said after a moment's silence. "I knew my grandfather well. I couldn't believe he would have anything to do with a theft."

"And you think my grandfather might have?" she asked indignantly.

"It might well have been none of them," he said soothingly, "but now they're all tainted by insinuations. I tried to locate witnesses. Many of the supporting papers are classified or names are blacked out. I hoped your grandfather might have left some documents."

The documents. *The boxes.* Was that why Jon had died? But why? Terror ripped through her, but she didn't want him to see it. Men like him—investigators—used fear as a weapon. She had seen it used with her mother. But where were the boxes now? In her mind's eyes, she saw the masked thief dropping one. Had he picked it up before fleeing?

"Why," she asked, "didn't the commission investigators talk to me?"

He shrugged. "They were concerned with the events as they happened more than half a century ago. We weren't alive then. There was no reason to come to us."

"Then why are you involved?" she asked testily.

"I want to know the truth. Our grandfathers were indicted by innuendo. I owe it to mine to clear him."

"At the expense of others?" she accused him. "As you said, it was fifty years ago. Let it go."

"You're a historian. Can you really do that?" It was a challenge.

No, she couldn't. Which was why she wanted to go through the boxes again. But she wasn't going to admit that. She didn't know whom to trust now. *Jon. Dead.* Her house burned. She had been shot. She knew enough about anatomy to realize that if the bullet had been inches to the left. . . .

"Do you remember anything about the man who shot you?" he asked, as if reading her mind.

She wasn't going to tell him anything. Not until she talked to the police. She shook her head and turned to Sherry. "The police don't have any idea who did it?"

Sherry shook her head. "A second security guard saw him flee, but he was masked. They want to talk to you, of course, and they're dusting for fingerprints."

Amy saw the intruder in her mind's eye. Masked. Gloved. Dressed all in black. And graceful. Like her visitor. *An athlete's grace.*

She fought a wave of fear. Did someone know she was going to Jon's office? If so, how? And if not, how did he know to look in Jon's office? If, she reminded herself, he had been after *her* boxes. Maybe, just maybe, he had been after something else.

She only knew she was not going to mention them until she knew what happened to those boxes. There had been three of them. The thief had one box in his hands before he dropped it. Had he taken others before she arrived?

You're being paranoid. It wasn't your box. Jon's office was lined with them. Notes. Reference books. Manuscripts. It could have been anything.

She had to make sure.

And she couldn't do it with the Army investigator in the room. The one with his own agenda.

"I want you to go," she said again. "I'm hurting and I'm tired and I want you to go."

He studied her for a moment, his eyes making requests she wasn't ready to grant. "I'll be back," he said. "And," he added, "I'll wait outside until the police arrive."

His words struck her as ominous. "You don't believe. . . ."

"No," he said. "The police think it was just a burglary gone wrong. But I told them I would wait."

Amy just nodded. She wasn't surprised at his persistence. But at the moment she wanted him gone. He was a disturbing presence in more ways than one.

She watched unwillingly as he put on his hat, and drat it if he didn't look even better.

Amy turned away. She waited until the door closed,

then looked at Sherry, who had a dazed expression on her face.

"Sherry?"

Sherry stirred herself back to reality. "I'm sorry, Amy," she said. "I thought he had a right to be here."

"He wanted you to think that," she said flatly. "He lied."

"He never actually said. . . ."

"Same thing as," Amy said. "Do me a favor. Don't tell him anything. Anything at all."

Looking abashed, Sherry nodded. "I swear."

Amy remembered what the colonel said, that the police would be back soon. But he'd made sure he asked *his* questions first.

A simple burglary gone wrong. If that was what the police thought, then they probably hadn't collected her boxes. She tried to move toward the phone, but her body objected and she fell back. "Sherry," she said, "call the campus security office. See if they retrieved the box the man dropped. Ask them to check to see if there are any other boxes with my name on them. If so, ask them to lock them up."

Sherry looked started. "Do you think that's what the . . . burglar was after?"

"I don't know, but I want to go through them, and I won't be able to do that if the police take them."

Sherry stood.

Amy reached out her hand. "Thank you, Sherry."

Sherry's hand squeezed hers. "I'll make the calls outside. You need some rest."

Amy was grateful. Her head was swimming with emotions. She needed time to think, to cope with all the questions and fear and grief. *Claude. Jon. Why?*

Was someone also after her?

Or did she just have a dark cloud floating over her head? Coincidence. A burglary she interrupted. A burglary that had nothing to do with her? She wished that with all her heart.

But her analytical mind told her that was foolish. Too many coincidences meant none at all. Everything that had happened was tied together in some evil way.

And what did Colonel Flaherty have to do with it all?

six

Professional courtesy. One investigator to another. It usually opened a lot of doors.

But not at Braemore, not on this campus. And not with its small security force. Irish thought about trying a little intimidation, then discarded the idea. One of theirs was down. One of their charges was wounded. Another was dead, but that was still deemed a hit and run.

The security officers had said they had been instructed by the Memphis police not to say anything and, still stunned by what happened, they obeyed. He'd also called on the Memphis detectives working the case. They were friendly enough—he was a colleague—but they had little information. About all he learned was that it was being worked as a burglary of a professor's office, one that went awry. Miss Mallory was just unfortunate to be in the wrong place at the wrong time. No, they couldn't share any more information. No, he couldn't go into Jon Foster's office.

Another door slammed in his face.

Flashing his military credentials, he had talked to others in the Sammons Building at the college and discovered a great deal about Amy Mallory. She apparently was one of those people who was interested in everyone, and showed it. From the janitorial staff on up, everyone seemed to like her, though few claimed a really close relationship. They raised disbelieving eyebrows when he asked whether they knew of any enemies she might have.

And his own impressions agreed with that assessment. She'd been undaunted this morning, despite being nearly killed, and appeared more concerned about the security guard, her friend Jon Foster, and her dog, than herself. He'd also been intrigued by the mild hostility when she'd seen his uniform. Not rabid, merely wary.

Because of her grandfather? Her mother? He already knew from his research that the woman had been unorthodox, a flower child who had never quite conformed to society.

Amy Mallory had used what must have been a chaotic childhood to succeed in a particularly demanding career, one that required discipline. He admired that.

He'd also liked the smoky gray eyes and the short, dark hair that wrapped appealingly around her face. But she was no real beauty. The description that applied was "pleasantly attractive." He suspected, though, that when she smiled, she would be very pretty indeed.

He thought about Amy Mallory again, and wondered whether another visit would produce anything. He'd not missed the suspicion in her eyes, the growing awareness of danger as he'd talked.

To his surprise, she had not expressed the outrage that many would after a random act of violence. Nor had she expressed surprise at what would have been a really astounding run of bad luck. She must suspect a connection.

What?

He went over everything he knew about her. There was nothing that should suddenly plunge her into danger. Could it be mere coincidence that the report on the thefts had just recently been published?

It was a far stretch. . . .

And yet deep in his bones, he knew there was a connection.

If there was, why had anyone gone after her alone? Why not him?

He wondered about the other descendants, Dustin and Sally Eachan. Had they had sudden accidents?

He had to find out.

Irish went down to the desk of his hotel and told them he would be staying at least two more nights, maybe longer.

There was never really a decision to make. He didn't like the fear in Amy Mallory's eyes. He didn't like people who hurt women.

But to accomplish anything, he needed her trust. And he didn't blame her for not giving it readily. God only knew she'd had a horrendous few days. Why should she trust anyone, particularly him? He'd appeared on the scene just as everything had happened.

After arranging for the longer stay, he returned to his room. He plugged in his electronic notebook, and in minutes had the home and office numbers of Dustin Eachan and the home number of his cousin. He started dialing his cell phone.

An hour later, he was completely frustrated. He couldn't get through to either one of them. He left several messages, using his name and expressing the urgency of the matter.

He looked at his watch. He could try the Memphis police again, but he didn't want to press them. He didn't want them to contact his commanding officer. Doug Fuller was a friend, but he was also a stickler for protocol. He wouldn't approve of Irish using his badge for personal reasons.

Fishing. He was supposed to be fishing. He'd just been looking for a different kind of catch. Information. And now. . . .

Now he was beginning to think he was looking for some bad guys.

After fifty years. It didn't make sense.

And it particularly didn't make sense that someone was going after one of the descendants of the officers involved in a theft so many years ago. She had to know something. Even if she didn't know what it was.

Or was he just taking two and two and making five?

He looked outside. It was late, and yet he was restless. Frustrated. Unable to relax. Something was going on that he didn't understand, and he didn't like that one damn bit. He thought about Amy Mallory in the hospital room. Why her? Of all of the descendants, why had there been attempts on her life? According to the police, there didn't seem to be anything else in her life that might inspire such sudden violence. No stalkers. No boyfriends. No enemies.

Unable to rest, he decided to make one more effort to talk to her. He would wear civilian clothes. The uniform, he'd sensed earlier in the room, had had the opposite effect than what he'd hoped for. Instead of assuring her, it had turned her off. But he should have guessed. She'd done her research on protest movements, perhaps because of her mother. It stood to reason that she didn't like the military.

He changed to a sports shirt and jeans. He would find some flowers and try to reassure her that he was one of the good guys. It was obvious that his poor attempt at charm hadn't worked.

It took him an hour to find flowers, finally resorting to a grocery store after he found all the local florists closed. It was after ten before he reached the hospital. Probably too late, but at least he could leave them at the desk and return in the morning. He would leave a note of apology for pushing himself on her today. Damn, how long had it been since he apologized?

The halls were quiet. Only one person was at the nurses' station, and she was on the phone. He walked down to the room. If the light was on. . . .

It wasn't. He turned and started back toward the station when he saw another man, one in a florist's uniform, stop at the desk. His hands were full of a huge bouquet that partially covered his face. The bill of a cap shaded his eyes. Did florists really deliver this late? He sure hadn't been able to find one open.

His own small offering from the grocery store looked rather pitiful. He was thinking about throwing it out and starting over in the morning when he heard the man ask for Amy Mallory's room.

The nurse looked up from the phone call with a hassled look on her face. "You can leave them here," she said.

The deliveryman hesitated. "You look busy. I don't mind."

A buzzing sound distracted her, then another. "Three ninety-six," she said in a distracted voice. "The hall to your left."

The deliveryman nodded, cast a quick look at Irish and gave him a careless shrug, but kept his face partially covered by the huge bouquet. Irish felt a quickening of his pulse. His eyes scanned the man, including his hands. Despite the hot weather, they were gloved. Irish's instincts tingled.

He nodded amiably and leaned on the nurses' station counter as if he were waiting to speak to the nurse. He wondered where the other nurses were. He knew there had been a cutback in personnel in most hospitals, but this reminded him of the movies he'd often sat through with total disbelief. People running through empty halls.

He waited until the deliveryman had turned the corner, then followed. He ducked back when he saw the man look around. The glance, he thought, was meant to look innocent but instead looked furtive. But then Irish's entire career involved furtiveness, and maybe he saw it when it wasn't there.

Irish waited just a second, saw the door close behind the deliveryman, then walked softly to the door. He pushed the door open slightly. The flowers had been dumped on a chair. The man was leaning over a sleeping Amy Mallory, a pillow in his hand.

The man whirled around.

"Not today, you don't," Irish said softly as he imprinted the lean and hungry face in his mind.

He knew instantly that the man recognized him. Not specifically. Not as Irish Flaherty, but as an opponent. As a cop.

The man spun around, dropped the pillow, and his hand went behind his back. Irish knew what he was after. He dived for the man, tackling him. A pistol skidded across the floor as a plastic pitcher and books fell from the stand next to the bed.

Both he and the intruder went down as they wrestled for the gun. The assailant was strong, powerful, skilled . . . and desperate. Irish barely avoided a kick to his groin and landed a blow on the man's cheek. He used his body to block the assailant's desperate attempt to reach the gun—just inches from their hands.

He heard Amy's exclamation, then her frantic screaming for the nurse. The intruder must have heard it, too, because he pushed with almost superhuman strength and rolled over on Irish before kneeing him and reaching for the gun.

Pain ripped through Irish, but he managed in one desperate movement to stick out his foot, tripping his opponent.

The man landed on his back and hit the side of the bed as Irish kicked the gun under the bed. His opponent groaned at the impact, then managed to get to his feet and avoid Irish's grasp. He ran toward the door, hitting a nurse as he did so. He shoved her against the wall and disappeared.

Irish reached for the gun. The nurse screamed. He started for the door, but a crowd now blocked it. The intruder was gone. He groaned as he straightened. Damn, but he must be out of shape. And practice. It had been years since he'd had a physical encounter with a bad guy.

The room filled. Nurses, attendants. Voices babbled.

Amy Mallory sat up in the bed and stared at him. The pitcher, plastic glass, and telephone were scattered across the floor, along with pools of water. Wilted and crushed flowers added flashes of color in the shambles.

Everyone stared at him—and the gun—with horror.

He lowered it to his side. "It's over," he said. "Someone intended to hurt Miss Mallory. Someone posing as a delivery-man. He might still be in the hospital. Alert security." Useless. The intruder—no, hit man—would be long gone. He thought about going after the intruder himself, but he knew he was too late.

No one moved. Faces were full of indecision, even fear, as eyes moved from the pistol in his hand to Amy's stunned face. One nurse finally took a step toward Amy. "What happened?"

"I . . . don't know," she said, obviously bewildered. "I woke up, and two men were fighting. I know . . . the colonel."

"Colonel?" The nurse's eyes were suspicious as she eyed Irish. He knew how he must appear. His face hurt like hades; it must look battered. His clothes were torn and wet. The pistol was damning.

"Lieutenant Colonel Lucien Flaherty," he said, clipping his words. "Army Criminal Investigation Division. I came to see Miss Mallory. An intruder had a pillow in his hands and was leaning over her. I think he meant to kill Miss Mallory." He looked for a place to put the gun, but there was none. He finally walked over to a windowsill, and placed it there, knowing that the longer he held it, the less likely anyone would listen. "It was the intruder's gun," he explained.

He heard the gasp from the bed. Of course she hadn't known what was going on. He couldn't even begin to think what she thought when she woke—probably from a drugged sleep—to two men fighting in her room.

The nurse gaped at him.

"Call the police, too," he said.

She turned to the crowd accumulating in and outside the room, and he wondered where everyone had been a few moments earlier. They were dressed in a variety of clothing: scrubs, white uniforms, cheerful lab coats with cartoon figures. Then yet another person came into the room, spreading the others like Moses parting the Red Sea. Even if the newcomer hadn't been wearing a white coat, he had the professional assurance that screamed "doctor."

"What's going on here?" he asked as he surveyed the mess on the floor, Irish's disheveled appearance, and then, warily, the gun that was very visible on the windowsill.

"One of your patients was attacked," Irish said.

"Attacked? In this hospital?" Disbelief dripped from his voice. "I think you had better move away from that gun."

Irish moved away. Then two men in security uniforms pushed into the room. Irish motioned to the gun. One of the security officers reached in a pocket, took out a handkerchief, and gingerly took the pistol.

"Is it all right if I get my wallet?" Irish said.

The security guards exchanged looks, then nodded. Irish very slowly and carefully reached inside his pocket with one hand, holding the other in plain sight. When he extracted his wallet, he pushed it open and showed his badge to the guards. The one not holding the gun took it and studied it.

"I want the room cleared of everyone not directly involved," one of the security officers said.

The room emptied except for the doctor, a nurse, and Irish.

The doctor leaned over Amy, giving her a cursory examination. Her I.V. had dropped from her arm, evidently pulled when she'd moved during the scuffle. A nurse started to reattach the needle.

"I think you should get a fresh one," Irish said.

The nurse looked startled, then turned to the doctor, who straightened and eyed the I.V. uncertainly. "You don't think . . . ?"

Irish shrugged. "I don't think he had time to touch it, but this is the second attack on Miss Mallory."

The doctor nodded at the nurse, and she started to unhook the bag.

"I think you should preserve it," Irish said, looking at the security officers. The older one nodded. "I'll take it," he said, putting on a pair of gloves and taking the half-full bag.

Irish looked down at Amy Mallory. Her gray eyes were wide, filled with confusion and pain and fear.

"I don't understand," she said.

"I saw a deliveryman bring flowers in the room. He wore gloves. It seemed a little strange, since it's so hot outside, so I followed him. I'd just arrived with some flowers of my own—an apology for bothering you earlier." He looked at the crushed flowers strewn around the floor, mixed with the more expensive blooms of the intruder.

He hesitated, then said, "I saw him lean over you with a pillow in his hands. It's the best way to. . . ." He wasn't sure how to put the rest of the sentence. Her eyes had already widened with realization.

Then they locked with his. Weighing him. Judging him. Believing him?

He wasn't sure. He wasn't sure of anything.

"I should thank you, then," she said softly, but with no conviction.

His explanation did sound lame. Arriving late at night with flowers? Following someone because he wore gloves?

The doctor finished his examination. "She appears to be all right." He hesitated. "Perhaps we should have security post a guard tonight."

"I'll stay," Irish said.

"No." It was a flat rejection from the woman in the bed. "Security would be fine, thank you."

"I'll see to it, then," the doctor said, and left just as the nurse returned with a new I.V. bag. She attached it to the

stand, then stood aside as someone knocked on the door
and two uniformed Memphis police officers appeared at
the door.

One of the security officers went out in the hall for a
moment, then all three came back into the room.

The nurse hesitated. "Hon, do you want me to stay?"

Amy Mallory shook her head. "It's all right. I'll be
fine."

"I'll send someone to clean up. If you need anything
hon, you just press that button."

Irish watched as the patient tried to smile. It was a brave
if wobbly attempt. "Thank you."

"Miss," one of the uniformed officers started as he took
out a notebook. "We need some information. Why. . . ."

She shook her head. "Some detectives were here earlier
in the day. Someone shot me last night, and a few days ago
my house was destroyed by fire. The fire department said
it was arson." She was talking in reasoned tones, but Irish
saw the shock in her eyes.

"Their names?" the officer asked.

"They left cards. . . ."

She looked helplessly where the stand had been. Irish
leaned down and straightened the stand, the pitcher, the
glass, and two sodden cards. He handed them to one of the
officers, who hadn't taken his eyes from him. The two security men stood behind them.

"He says he's some kind of army cop," one of them told
the officers. He held out the pistol. "He also says the gun
isn't his."

Irish patiently held out his wallet again. It was scruti-
nized far more carefully by the police officers than it had
been by the security guard. "Do you have any other
weapons with you?" the older one asked.

He shook his head. "The gun isn't mine. It belongs to
the intruder."

"Stand away from the bed, and stay there until we get
some word from the detectives."

Irish glanced at the woman in the bed. Her face was white, her fingers clenched on the blanket. Her gray eyes were huge. It was obvious she was trying to stifle the terror she must feel.

"It'll be all right," he said to her even as he wondered whether anything would be all right for her again. He knew what it was like to have your life hang in the balance. A movement to the right rather than the left could mean death. But it came with his chosen profession, not hers. That kind of fear should never have invaded her life.

And his gut told him it wasn't over. He also knew no police department would provide the kind of protection she might need, not even on the basis of events during the past few days.

He listened as the police asked all the expected questions. Who might want to hurt her? Then they turned to him. Doubt and suspicion laced their questions as they listened to his recital of the facts. Had he actually seen the man place the pillow over her face? How did he know that the man was, in fact, trying to kill her? Couldn't he simply have been picking up something that had fallen on the floor?

"He pulled a gun when I appeared," Irish said dryly. "I don't think he was a Good Samaritan."

One officer looked at him suspiciously. "You sure the weapon didn't belong to you?"

He knew, suddenly, that his were the only prints on the gun. The only other witness was the distracted nurse at the station, who probably wouldn't remember anything about the intruder except that he looked like any other deliveryman.

It was his word, and his word only; and no one, including Amy Mallory, seemed inclined to accept everything he said.

Thirty minutes later, the detectives Irish had talked to earlier came into the room, and the two policemen gave a brief account of what had happened.

Then they turned to Irish. All friendliness was gone. He surmised that they had checked on him and discovered he was here unofficially. "Colonel," one said, "your commanding officer would like to talk to you."

"But first we do," said the other. "Can you give us a description of the . . . assailant?"

"An inch shorter than I am. A little thinner. Light brown hair, cropped short. Brown eyes. I could give a description to a police artist."

"We'll take you down to the department when we finish here. But first I want to know your interest in this. And your interest in Miss Mallory, especially since it's not official." *As they had been led to believe.* The detective didn't have to say the words. They hung unsaid in the air but were evident in their suspicious eyes.

Irish *had* led them to believe he was on a case. Now they knew he'd lied. He wished now he had been more forthcoming, but he'd always known how he'd felt when outsiders wanted information.

It was too late now.

"Miss Mallory and I have a connection," he said. "Our grandfathers served together during World War II."

"And they were both accused—by implication, anyway—of stealing Nazi loot," Amy Mallory said, her gaze confronting his directly.

He nodded. "I came to talk to Miss Mallory about it, to ask whether she had any papers of her grandfather's."

The detective's eyes sharpened. He turned back to Amy. "Papers?"

Amy Mallory's gaze moved from Irish to the detective and back again. He could feel her indecision.

"Miss Mallory?" the detective said.

Her eyes met Irish's, then turned back to the detectives. They were defensive. "I told you earlier that Jon Foster had three boxes of my grandfather's papers in his office. That's why I went up there last night. I wanted to look through them. The . . . burglar had a box in his hands when

I encountered him. I don't know if it was one of my boxes or not. There's no reason to think it was. . . ."

"After we talked to you, we checked with campus security. We'll pick up the boxes from the security office," the detective said. His gaze went to Irish, then back to her.

"I don't even know whether the . . . burglar had one of *my* boxes. They're just old documents. Bits and pieces of things."

"We'll look through them later," one of the detectives said.

Amy tensed. "I want to go through them myself."

"We'll look through them first." He turned to Irish. "And what did you hope to find, Colonel?"

"Yes, Colonel," Amy said, "what did you hope to find?"

Irish shrugged. He'd learned years ago to protect himself, to reveal as little as necessary. It had been vital to his survival when he'd been pulled first one way, then another, by parents who detested one another. He'd never known a sense of belonging until he'd gone to live with his grandfather; now he was not about to betray that grand old man.

"A commission virtually accused my grandfather of theft," he said. "I didn't believe it. I hoped that Miss Mallory's grandfather had some journals or accounts of the incident, some clues as to what happened during those months. I planned to contact the families of each of the men mentioned in the report. Miss Mallory was first on my list."

"You could have told us that earlier," one of the detectives said.

"I didn't want any more publicity than there's already been," Irish said, "especially if there's no connection with what's been happening to Miss Mallory."

"There's nothing in those boxes," Amy insisted again. "I've been through them."

"What was the professor doing with them?"

"He specialized in World War II. I thought he might find something useful, even if I hadn't."

"What was there, exactly?" Irish asked.

"Maps, battle plans, notes. As I said, I didn't find anything really useful, but decided to keep them because Grandfather apparently put value on them. I mentioned them to Jon several months ago, and he asked to see them."

"He never mentioned finding anything?"

"Whenever I asked about them, he said he'd just taken a quick glance and was waiting until this summer, when he had some time to study them thoroughly."

"Anything from April 1945?"

"I don't know," she said, then added hopefully, "The burglar might well have thought he had something else," she said. Hope and defiance, and a certain resigned knowledge were in her eyes. She flushed when her gaze met his, and Irish knew immediately that Amy Mallory was not a devious soul. Not like he'd learned to be. Her emotions were written all over her face.

One of the detectives interrupted. "This is *our* investigation," he said curtly, frowning at Irish. "I would rather you wait outside. Then you can come to the station for that artist's sketch."

Irish hesitated. Then he looked back at Amy. "I'm sorry to be persistent, but those papers must have something to do with the attacks. If they didn't, I don't think someone would have attacked you again tonight."

She swallowed. Sympathy coursed through him. Sympathy and something else. A feeling of protectiveness. Their eyes met, locked for a moment, and he felt his heart beat faster.

"Why?" she said. "Why would this have started now?"

He hesitated. He had started checking into the commission report two weeks ago. Her house was destroyed ten days ago. Had his questions sparked a train of events? Was he responsible for all that had happened to her?

But before he could consider that possibility further, one of the detectives turned to the security guards still in the room. "Take the colonel outside and wait with him," he said.

One of the policemen put a hand on Irish's arm.

Irish shrugged it off, then turned to Amy. "I want to help."

Her eyes met his again, and for a split second he saw the fear she'd been so valiantly trying to hide. Fear and suspicion. Then she turned back to the detective, effectively dismissing him.

Irish turned and followed the security guards out. He'd lost this round.

Dammit! How was he going to get her to trust him? And if not, how in the devil was he going to get those boxes? They had to be the key to something. Just what, he didn't know.

But someone must. He realized that now.

For a moment he wondered whether he really wanted to pry into fifty-year-old secrets. What if his grandfather . . . ?

Also, his career might be on the line. His commanding officer would not approve of what he was doing.

But now he had no choice. Someone else was in the game, and he, or she, had deadly intentions. If Irish had unintentionally opened Pandora's box, then he was responsible for closing it again. Even if it meant ending his career. Or worse.

seven

Dustin Eachan looked down at the pile of messages. It had been an endless day, and he knew he'd been uncommonly distracted by personal worries. Usually, he could direct his attention to the immediate problem and wipe everything else from his mind.

Not today.

He'd asked his secretary to hold his calls as he'd tried to put together a list of options and recommendations concerning a coup in an African country. There were pleas for American help from the ousted government and a request for recognition by the new regime. He'd requested the latest intelligence on both parties and asked his staff to prepare alternative plans.

Dammit, the process of putting together options and making recommendations just didn't appeal to him today, and not only because there weren't any good ones.

He continued to flip through messages, stopping at two. One from a Colonel Flaherty, another from Sally with "Urgent" on it.

Dustin looked at his watch. After seven. Sally should be home. He hesitated over Flaherty's number. He knew a great deal about Flaherty. He had made the man his business since the Army officer first sought information from the commission, and none of what he'd learned made him feel good.

Flaherty was a bulldog. A maverick who got results. He'd been promoted despite some less than glowing reports, perhaps thanks to important champions.

That's what worried Dustin.

He'd done what he could to keep the commission report as low-key as possible. Then some damned reporter got hold of it, and now Flaherty was making waves that threatened to become a tidal wave.

He didn't need this now. His next career step would require congressional approval, and that meant extensive background checks, even more intense than those he'd already experienced. The opposition party would do whatever they could to block him. He'd made his share of enemies on the way up.

His grandfather's flawless reputation had helped him get where he was. So had his father's.

Now they could all be tainted by something that happened fifty years ago. There had to be a way of stopping Flaherty.

He called Sally first.

She picked up on the first ring. Dustin heard the panic in her voice.

"Dustin, thank God you called. A man named Flaherty called me. He said he was the grandson of . . . one of the other people named in the article. He said we may be in danger."

"Did he say why?"

"The granddaughter of General Mallory has been attacked, and it might have something to do . . . with the report about the train."

"That's nonsense," Dustin said.

"Will you talk to him?"

"Yes," he said.

"I did what you asked me to do. I. . . ."

"Don't say any more," he said. "Can you meet me at Art's for a drink?"

"Now?"

"In thirty minutes."

"I'll be there," she said.

He hung up the phone.

The call was made on a private line.

"You made a hell of a mess in Memphis. A simple, undetectable burglary, and you turned it into World War III. Killing a cop, for God's sake."

"A security guard," the voice on the other end corrected with a sneer. "Would you rather that I sat in jail?"

An implied threat radiated across the miles.

"Sloppy work. I expected better from you."

There was silence. Then, "Someone may have seen me."

"Explain."

"I . . . had a run-in at the hospital with Flaherty. He . . . could have seen my face."

"You know it's Flaherty?"

"I've seen his pictures."

A curse came across the lines. "Come back. I'll send someone else to tidy things. Did you find anything?"

"Nothing in Foster's files. There were some boxes with Mallory's name on them. I had one when the bitch showed up with the security guard. One of them might contain what you want."

"Where are they now?"

"The police probably have them."

A pause. "I'll have someone else try to get them."

"What about a tap on her phone?"

"They might be looking for it. Leave it alone for now. Don't go near her."

"I don't like that Flaherty saw me. Maybe I should. . . ."

"Get the boxes and get back here. We'll take care of Flaherty. And Amy Mallory, too."

MEMPHIS

The morning wore on endlessly. The detectives had asked question after question, then remained until a uniformed policeman arrived and took his post outside her door.

Amy wanted to go home. She didn't want to be guarded. She didn't want to be reminded of the last few days. *The last week.*

Then remembered there was no home to go to. She didn't feel safe anywhere, particularly not at a hotel swarming with people she didn't know.

Sherry couldn't help. She had two roommates. And Amy didn't want to put her friend in danger. She wouldn't feel safe in her office again, either, and that had always been her refuge.

Her blood froze every time she saw the uniform of her police guard when someone opened the door to come in the room. Even Sherry, who visited early this morning, had been disconcerted. Amy had already been told she would be released tomorrow morning if everything went well. She still had a headache and her side still hurt badly, but the burning agony had lessened. She wanted Bojangles. Amy wanted to bury her face in his thick fur and feel the comforting sympathy.

But where?

She spent the morning calling two academic friends, one of whom was a wizard on the computer and one who had gone to the Department of Defense as a researcher. She asked both to check on Lieutenant Colonel Lucien Flaherty and to get back to her as soon as possible. Then she called the security office at the university and asked about the box that had been stolen and any others in Foster's office.

Larry Green, the chief of security, came to the phone. She had met him several times, once when one of her students had been attacked on the campus. She liked him.

"Miss Mallory, I've wanted to come see you, but things have been hectic here."

"I'm so sorry about Claude. I want to see him, but he's still not allowed visitors." *She also had Jon's funeral to attend.* Her voice caught at that.

There was a silence on the other end. Then, "Claude died last night."

She didn't think she could feel worse than she already did. She was wrong. "Please tell his wife I am so sorry. He was just . . . trying to protect me."

"I hope you don't blame yourself," he said.

She was silent for a moment. She *did* blame herself. She didn't know why a black cloud was following her like Joe Blfsph in an old *Dick Tracy* comic strip. But that black cloud was a person, and by damn she was going to find out who.

"Miss Mallory?"

"I'm here."

"Can I do anything for you?"

"I . . . was just calling about the box that the thief dropped. The police asked about it, and I told them I wanted to be present when it was opened."

"That's odd," Larry said. "Someone came by a few minutes ago from the police department to pick it up, but I didn't remember seeing him here that night, or the next day, and I was surprised it wasn't one of the detectives working the case. I told him I couldn't release it without the proper paperwork." He hesitated, then added in a strained voice, "He protested until I started to call police headquarters. Then he left. Fastlike." A pause. Then anger laced his voice as he asked, "Do you think he had anything to do with . . . Claude's death?"

"What did he look like?"

"Tall. Six feet. About a hundred and ninety pounds. Dark hair."

It couldn't be her burglar. He'd been thinner than that. And Colonel Flaherty had said the assailant in her room had light brown hair. Still a chill ran up her spine. "Was there anyone with you?"

"The office was filled. We were raising money for Claude's family. In fact, we were just leaving for his house when you called. I'll put the stuff in our safe," he said, "and call the detectives who worked the case."

She heard voices in the background, and she remembered the faces. Pain twisted inside her as she saw Claude in her mind. Tall and proud in his uniform, his large hands fumbling with his wallet as he thumbed through photos of his family.

The silence on the other end stretched for a moment, then Larry Green spoke over other voices in the background. "I should have stopped him." Anger laced his words. And self-accusation.

"You didn't know," Amy said simply. She hesitated, then added, "But someone attacked me late last night. In my hospital room. I think he was trying to kill me. Someone—an Army officer—stopped him, but he got away."

"Flaherty?" the security chief asked. "The CID guy? He was here asking questions about you yesterday."

"About me?"

"About you and Dr. Foster."

Amy tensed. The colonel hadn't said anything about that.

"I didn't tell him anything," he said, as if he sensed her uncertainty.

"Thank you," Amy said.

"Do you have any idea of what's going on?" Larry's voice was rough with frustration and, she thought, exhaustion and grief. Security was a tight-knit group.

"I wish I did," she replied, knowing that her voice trembled. She hated that. She wanted to be strong and independent. She *was* strong. But how do you fight shadows?

Larry muttered something that was probably a curse. "I can't believe someone would actually pretend to be a cop."

"Maybe he *was* one," she tried to soothe him. But even

as she did, she knew—and knew he did, too—that it was unlikely. Why else would he have left as soon as Larry called police headquarters?

"You will be careful about the box?" she said. "Can you get the others from Jon Foster's office?"

"I'll do it now. The office has been secured. The lab people have been there to fingerprint, but they told me there are so many prints that it's almost hopeless."

"The burglar wore gloves," she said. "And a ski mask. I told the police that." Amy heard voices in the background. "And I want to contribute to Claude's fund. I'll send you a check."

"I'll stay here and call the detectives," he said. "Your boxes go into our safe, and I'll instruct my people that no one, absolutely no one, is to let them go out."

"Thank you," Amy said, then added in a low voice, "I'm sorry. I am so very sorry about Claude."

Irish spent the day at police headquarters. The two detectives—Rick Ames and Bill Davies—had been fairly helpful yesterday, but today they were tight-lipped. They watched him as he gave a description to a police artist who worked on a computer. It took an hour, but he felt he had a fairly good likeness despite the fact that he'd had only a quick glimpse of the man's face.

"How long are you going to stay in Memphis, Colonel?"

"I'm not sure. I want to be certain Miss Mallory is safe."

"Your interest again?" An eyebrow raised. These cops were not like the campus security. They were cynical and suspicious.

"Our grandfathers served together in Germany," he said patiently. "I hoped Miss Mallory might have some records relating to that. I met her yesterday."

"And why were you in her room last night?"

He told himself it was standard investigating procedure. Keep asking the same questions, but in different ways. Try to trip a suspect.

"I wanted to apologize for barging in on her."

Bill Davies frowned. "You indicated yesterday that you were on a case. Your commanding officer seemed unaware of that."

"I said I had an interest," Irish said. "I did not say it was an official case."

The detective named Ames glared at him. "Your commanding officer, Colonel Fuller, would like a word with you."

"I appreciate your passing along the message," Irish said.

"If you're holding anything back, I won't hesitate to file obstruction of justice charges," Ames said.

Irish understood. He would have felt the same way. "I wish I did know what in the hell was going on," he said. "I came here to seek information. I'm as puzzled as you by all these attacks on this particular young woman." He paused. "Are you taking steps to protect her?"

Now it was their turn to look uncomfortable. "We don't have the resources to guard people indefinitely."

"You mean unless they're of value to you?" Irish asked.

Ames leaned forward, steepling his fingers and resting his chin on them. "Believe me, Colonel, if it was up to me, she would have round-the-clock protection. I agree that she is probably in danger. But we don't have the funds to do it. We can keep a guard at the hospital, maybe a few days afterward, but that's it. And that, Colonel, is why we need to wrap this thing up." He unsteepled his hands. "You had the best go at him."

Irish already felt a hefty dose of guilt at his performance. What if he had been quicker? More prepared? He'd thought he was in good condition, but he'd been no match for the assailant. Not this time, anyway.

He nodded, silently assuming blame.

David broke the silence. "At least we have your composite."

"He was a professional," Irish said. "Everything about

this screams professional. The fire. The ski mask in the burglary. The way he handled himself. The descriptions vary, but not the height. I think it was the same person. He just made minor changes. Hair color, bulky clothes. When I was on the floor with him, I felt padding."

Ames looked at the composite, then back at Irish. "You're not going away, are you?"

Irish shook his head.

"Even if I ask your superiors to call you off?"

"No."

Ames sighed. "I don't suppose I can keep you away, but I want to know everything you learn. *When* you learn it."

Irish would have demanded the same thing. But he had told them everything he knew, which was damned little. He just hadn't told them his suspicions that this all had something to do with events that had happened before they were born. At best, the detectives would think he was reaching. At worst, it would be in all the newspapers. And that would alert whoever was behind what was happening.

Amy apparently was the key to everything. She was the unwilling catalyst. Or had he been that, and she the unwitting victim?

If so, she was his responsibility. And possibly the answer to the puzzle.

But how was he going to convince her of both?

eight

No protection after she left the hospital. Or very little.

A detective explained that sad truth to Amy as she waited to be checked out of the hospital.

She could move now without the stunning pain. Her headaches were gone. She'd stayed this long only to make sure there was no infection.

But what now? Even though she felt awkward about the policeman outside her room, he did represent safety. Now, according to the detective, they would patrol the area around the hotel frequently, but they just didn't have the manpower to do more. Did she have another place to go? Somewhere out of the city? Friends?

Not friends she wished to endanger.

She'd missed the funerals of her two friends. Jon's was yesterday, and Claude's an hour ago. She sent flowers to Jon's funeral and a check to Claude's family. Silently and alone, she cried for both men.

Visitors had dropped by. Sherry brought her books and clothes, and told her about Jon's funeral. The colonel stopped by several times, but he'd had nothing new to offer. Neither had the police. They'd shown her the composite sketch the police artist had produced from Colonel Flaherty's description, and wanted to know whether she could add anything. But she'd been in a drug-induced fog, the room had been dark, and she had barely caught a glimpse of the assailant.

She stared at the composite for a long time. This was the man who had tried to kill her. She hoped it was a close likeness. Flaherty said it was, but she'd too often seen composites that looked nothing like the real person. Still, she'd stared at it, memorizing every feature.

The detectives reported they had picked up her boxes from the security office and gone through them. Nothing interesting turned up. Could she review the contents? Perhaps she would find something they hadn't.

She intended to do exactly that. Until now, her concentration had been weakened by drugs. But on her release, the police said they would deliver the boxes to her hotel room. They had dusted for fingerprints, and now their only value as evidence seemed to be whether she could find something in them. She used her wound as an excuse not to go to police headquarters to pore over their contents.

And the colonel? She wished she could trust him, but after the last few days she couldn't trust anyone. Not even those eyes that made her *want* to trust him.

He'd shown up yesterday with flowers.

"To make up for the ones I squashed," he'd said with that odd little quirk of his lips that was too darn appealing. He'd dominated the room with his restless presence, and his attempts to tame it were very unsuccessful.

He had eyed the copy of the composite sitting on the table next to her. "No one you've met?"

The police had asked the same question. "No." She hesitated, then asked, "Is it very accurate?"

"I'm good at faces, Miss Mallory. And we were very close to each other. It's as good as one of those things can be."

"It's odd," she said, "looking at a picture of someone

you don't know but who tried to kill you." Her voice sounded calmer than she felt.

He nodded, hesitated a moment, then said, "The police said they didn't find anything in that . . . box that was taken from your friend's office. Would you mind if I looked?"

Her gaze met his. "I thank you for saving my life that night," she said. "And I appreciate the flowers. But I want to go through my grandfather's possessions before anyone else does."

He nodded as if he expected the answer. "And then?"

"Then I will decide."

He smiled at that. It was a very attractive smile, especially since it touched his eyes, making the skin around them crinkle. "I don't think I would ever want you as an adversary," he said lightly.

She fought an answering smile. He wanted something from her. It was nothing more. "Is this happening to anyone else?" she asked. "To the other families?"

"Not that I've discovered. I've warned them, though."

Thank God, he didn't add that he was not even sure that it was her relationship to General Mallory that had caused this . . . curse. Nothing else made sense. "You will let me know?"

"Yes." He paused. "Whoever is behind this must know that I'm here, probably even that I've contacted the Eachans. That might deter them."

"Or it might not," she said.

His silence gave her the answer.

"I have sources you don't," he said. "And neither do the police. I can help you."

She was considering that, and whether she could—or should—trust him when a nurse entered the room.

He stood for a moment, obviously uncertain, then gave her a slight smile. "I better go. I'll be back in the morning."

She nodded, feeling the oddest sense of loss, and unhappy at herself for regretting the interruption. She couldn't trust him. She couldn't trust anyone at this point. . . .

That had been yesterday, and she hadn't really expected him to return today. She'd tried to distract herself by making plans for the next few weeks. Her tenure meeting was in three weeks, and she still had some preparation to do. The bulk of the paperwork was done and had been submitted. But there were several additional letters she had requested that had not yet arrived, one last grant application she had almost completed, and the matter of ensuring that all her publications had been included. One had disappeared, and she was trying to find a copy. If only she didn't need to stay in Memphis.

Or did she?

Her classes were over now. She had one day's work on final grades and paperwork. She'd wanted to consult with Jon about one student. But Jon was dead. Jon, her mentor, who had written one of the letters of recommendation for her tenure.

A deep sense of loss flooded her again. Not because Jon couldn't help her, but because of their friendship. She also knew she had to be realistic, no matter how much it hurt. She'd lost her strongest supporter in a department that was none too friendly to women.

She would go through everything again, see if there was something she'd overlooked, perhaps even try to get more letters from her lectures at other universities. But how could she do that when fear haunted her? It was a living thing within her now. Boring in like a parasite.

If nothing else, her innocence was gone forever. So was the illusion of safety in her own home.

Maybe a week at the beach was what she needed. She would take the boxes that belonged to her grandfather—and the materials she'd put together for the tenure meeting, and Bojangles—and go somewhere no one could find her. And she *would* be careful. She would use another name at a motel; she could do that if she paid in cash.

Once she took off in the car, she would make sure no one followed.

She felt like a fugitive from a spy novel. There had to be an explanation. A logical, sensible, nonparanoid explanation. People just didn't try to kill people like her.

Oh, a random street mugging, maybe. Even a burglar. But someone desperate enough to go into a hospital room with flowers in her name? That was serious stalking.

She still couldn't believe what had happened. Despite an unusual childhood, she'd never really felt physically unsafe. She'd survived the constant moves, her mother's boyfriends, the lack of stability, but part of her had hungered for normalcy, or what she considered normalcy. Though a few of her mother's views took root in her, most had not. Like her mother, she hated injustice. Unlike her mother, she'd never believed that copping out—or breaking the law—solved the problem.

Her grandfather had had more of an impact on her than he had ever known. His sense of honor had invaded her psyche, despite her mother's disdain for the military.Which was why, she knew, she wanted to get to the bottom of this affair. Her grandfather would have wanted it. She knew that as sure as she knew that someone on the hospital staff would wake her at midnight.

"Ah, Grandfather," she whispered. "What is going on? What might you have left me that someone would kill for?"

Now she wished with all her heart that she had gone through his papers at the time of his death. But she'd been heartbroken. They'd had a long and rocky relationship, but in the end he was the only family she'd had. She hadn't realized how much she'd come to love him during his last courageous months. She was in college then, in an accelerated program that took all her time. It only made sense to sell his house. She had glanced through his belongings and sold most of them, but kept his papers, always intending to go back and examine them thoroughly. Instead, they had remained in a storage facility. She hadn't looked at them again until Jon had asked her whether he'd left papers. Or had *she* mentioned them to *him*?

Now she realized she'd been trying to escape the reality of her grandfather's death by putting his possessions in storage. She hadn't wanted reminders. When she was stronger, she'd told herself. And then she let month after month go by, then years.

The phone rang, and she picked it up. One of the friends she'd asked to check on Colonel Flaherty was on the line.

"I think he's who he says he is," Eric said. "I have a photo I'll bring over later. He's with CID, as he said, and apparently is one of their best people. Commanded a unit in Kosovo and is in line for battalion command. His grandfather *was* your grandfather's commanding officer during the last months in World War II."

"Is there any other family?"

"Doesn't look like it," Eric said.

"Does the man in the photo have dark hair, a lean face? A small indentation in his chin?"

"You described him."

So Lieutenant Colonel Lucien Flaherty was who he said he was. Why did she not feel safer? "Thank you, Eric," she said. "I don't think I have to see the photo."

"Righto. Anytime I can help."

"I might take you up on that."

"I'm surprised at you, Professor. Hacking into the Defense Department."

"All in a good cause, Eric."

"And that is . . . ?"

"My life."

There was a long silence, then he said somberly, "Take care."

"I will," she said.

She slowly put the receiver into the cradle. What now? She'd already been told she was being discharged today. An hour. Or two. And then the doctor would be here, telling her she could leave.

Amy sat on the side of the bed and tried to analyze her situation. Physically, she was much better. Her side was stiff, but the world no longer spun in crazy arcs. Emotionally, though, she felt overwhelmed. She hadn't felt that way for years, not since she was thirteen and her mother died, and there was no one to turn to, no one but a name that belonged to a man in an old photograph, a portrait of a man with a stern expression.

She'd been bewildered, then, when the social workers had come to get her. They wanted to know whether she had family. She had a photograph. Nothing else. It had been several weeks before they had located him because her mother used another name. Amy hadn't wanted to go with him then; she hadn't wanted to go with someone who'd disapproved of her mother. She'd been scared, but tried hard not to show it.

Amy was scared now, and she was still trying damned hard not to show it.

She dressed in a pair of slacks and blouse that Sherry had brought earlier, the few pitiful pieces of clothing she'd bought since her home went up in flames. She looked at them again and fought back tears.

There was a knock at the door, and then it opened. It was the police officer who guarded her room. And the colonel.

"Is everything all right, Miss?" the police officer asked. She nodded.

"The colonel asked to see you. Is that all right?"

Not exactly, but at the moment any company would be a diversion from her very dark thoughts. She nodded.

"I'll be outside if you need me," the officer said, casting a doubtful eye at Lieutenant Colonel Flaherty, dressed casually in blue jeans and a dark blue shirt. Unfortunately, he looked as striking as he had before.

"The doctor said you could leave this afternoon. Can I offer you a ride home?"

She hesitated, suddenly wanting to take him up on the offer. She didn't want to go to the hotel alone, and Sherry had a meeting with her adviser this afternoon. She'd had no idea how long it would take.

Her visitor held out a card. "You can call this number," he said. "My commanding officer will vouch for me."

"I don't have to," she said. "A friend of mine already checked you out."

He looked surprised, then impressed. "Good girl," he said.

"I'm not a girl, Colonel," she said a little waspily. She hated to be called a girl. She'd worked too hard to get her doctorate and now a full professorship.

"Irish," he said.

Her puzzlement must have shown in her eyes.

"Nearly everyone calls me Irish."

"Why?"

"If you had a first name like Lucien, you wouldn't ask that question," he said with that damnably attractive smile.

He was being charming, and she didn't want to be charmed. Still, she couldn't resist. "Where did Lucien come from?"

"Damned if I know. My mother had probably just seen a movie and liked it, and my older brother had been named after my father. At his insistence. I think Lucien was my mother's revenge."

"I like it," she said.

"*You* weren't called Lucy when you were a boy."

She couldn't help a smile. It was probably a weak one, but it was a smile. She couldn't imagine someone calling the man in front of her Lucy. But kids could be cruel. She'd been taunted as a child because she didn't have a father, then because she was so tall. She'd struck back once and bloodied a boy's nose. Her mother had been appalled. Violence, she'd said, never solved anything. But it *had* solved her immediate problem. From then on, the teasing was behind her back.

"You smiled," he observed.

"I did," she admitted. "You have to admit I haven't had much to smile about since we met." She paused. "And again, thank you. If you hadn't come in. . . ."

He shook his head. "I'm afraid I may have stirred things up. When I read about the investigation, I made some calls. Maybe if I hadn't. . . ."

"Has *your* home been invaded?"

He hesitated, then said, "I'm not sure. My grandfather had a ranch in Colorado. I inherited it, but I haven't spent much time there. When I read about the commission report, I did go through his papers. There was nothing there that touched on the months when he served in Austria. But someone could have gotten to them before I did. I've been gone for months at a time. There's a ranch foreman, but he has his own place and is often out on the range. A maid cleans my house every month, but she's completely trustworthy."

"And you've had no accidents?"

"No."

"Nothing suspicious?"

He hesitated, then shook his head. "Nothing but my encounter here in your room."

"You hesitated," she said.

"You're observant," he replied.

"Obviously not observant enough," Amy retorted. "Why did you hesitate?"

He shrugged. "I just returned from Kosovo after eighteen months there. My tour was supposed to be a year, and was unexpectedly extended even after I'd already received orders to return to the States. I didn't think much about it then, because unlike others, I didn't have a family. But now I wonder whether someone wanted to keep me out of the country."

"Why didn't anyone contact us?" she asked. "Anyone official, I mean."

"Third generation? No reason to. I don't think anyone really thought that the three senior officers actually stole anything. It was more about carelessness, and that was easily explained by the circumstances of the time. War was still raging across Europe. Who really cared about a train of wedding rings and second-rate paintings?"

"But the gold?"

"After more than fifty years?" he asked. "I don't think anyone thought it could be recovered, but now with the United States putting pressure on other countries to make reparations, it couldn't avoid looking into this. Unfortunately, our grandfathers aren't here to defend themselves."

"You think they're being made scapegoats?"

He shrugged. "A commanding officer is always responsible for the actions of his men. But I imagine their minds were on the drive across Germany, not inventories of trains."

Amy digested that, then, uncomfortable with more questions about her grandfather, asked, "What did you do in Kosovo?"

"Tried fruitlessly to keep the number of arms down," he said wryly. "Stockpiled arms and destroyed them. But there are so many of the damn things that they can go on killing each other for the next century."

The light had left his eyes, and she realized that he felt things far deeper than he wanted her to know. That made her want to trust him. Want to. But could she?

He walked over to the window. She wondered whether it was an attempt to remove himself from recent memories.

"You said you had an older brother? Where is he?"

"He died when he was twelve," he said flatly.

His voice was noncommittal, but she sensed pain in him. She wondered how old he'd been, but she'd already been too invasive. While inquisitiveness was in her nature, she didn't want to revive sad memories.

He turned around and looked at her. "And you? Any siblings?"

"I thought you knew everything about me," she said.

He had the grace to redden slightly. "I didn't check that closely."

"Didn't you?"

"I didn't find one," he said, obviously a bit abashed. "That doesn't mean there weren't any."

"Well, there weren't," she said without going into details she knew too well. She'd heard them too many times as a child.

A short knock came at the door then, and the doctor entered. "Ready to go?" he asked.

"Yes," she said.

He looked at the chart, then at her. "You'll probably feel some discomfort for a while. The bullet didn't hit anything vital, but you're going to be sore. The dressing needs to be changed frequently, but everything looks good."

"I can change the dressing," she said.

"I'll have a nurse and patient's representative come in. They'll give you instructions and a prescription for pain. I want you to take it easy." He hesitated. "You do have someone to look after you?"

"Yes." *Herself.*

"I don't want you driving for a few days," he said. "You've lost some blood. You need a lot of rest."

How could she do that when someone was apparently trying to kill her? But she didn't ask that question. Instead, her gaze went over to the colonel's, and his met hers. His face was impassive, and yet she thought she saw a flash of sympathy. That and a dime might buy her a cup of coffee, but wouldn't assure her that there wasn't poison in it.

At this point, she could depend only on herself. And so she paid lip service to the doctor, and later to the nurse with her prescription, knowing she wasn't going to pay any attention to either. Wise or not, she planned to retrieve her grandfather's boxes from the police and drive to someplace safe. She did agree to return to the doctor's office in ten days and make sure the stitches had dissolved as they should.

Then she was left with the colonel and his offer. Could she really trust him—and if not him, then who? A ride home would be safe, particularly if others knew about it. She would leave a message on Sherry's answering machine and also make it clear to the officer outside that Flaherty was taking her home.

And when she returned to the hotel?

A shudder ran through her. A gun. Should she get a gun? She, who had always been on the front lines for gun control?

She did know she was not going to follow the doctor's suggestion and not drive for several days. As soon as she could, she was going to get in a car and leave the city.

"The offer of a ride remains, Dr. Mallory," Flaherty said.

Her eyes turned to his. "Thank you," she finally said. "I would appreciate a ride. I'll call Sherry and let her know she's off the hook."

A gleam appeared in his eyes, and she knew that he knew exactly what she was doing. Protecting herself. Was it approval she saw there? Or chagrin? She wasn't sure.

She only knew that her trust was limited. Very, very limited.

WASHINGTON, D.C.

Art's was a small and noisy bar. It was a place Dustin wouldn't usually frequent, and a place his cousin would.

It was situated in a working-class neighborhood, squeezed between a laundry and a loan company.

Sally loved it. She was a princess there. The bartender

loved her. So did most of the customers. It was her second home.

It wasn't that she drank that much. She was cautious about that. Two drinks, maybe three. Nursing them. She seemed to feel more at home here than in her own home. He suspected he knew why. No one expected anything more from her than her quick smile.

Just thinking about it made him smile. Sally's smile was infectious. It always had been. He knew, though, that it curtained a well of insecurity. That insecurity had been her worst enemy.

He had tried to give her what she needed, but his own feelings were too dangerous, and he'd found himself backing away.

He parked his car, hoping it would still be there when he returned.

The bar was dingy and filled with smoke. He had quit smoking years ago, and nearly choked on it now. Sally was at the bar, leaning over it in discussion with the bartender. He sidled in next to her, but he didn't sit.

Sally looked at him and her eyes lit up, even in the dim light of the bar. The bartender frowned.

"Let's find a table," Dustin said.

She leaned over the bar. "Take tomorrow off," she told the bartender. "Your daughter's birthday is more important than a day's pay." She started to leave, then added, "Hey, I used to be a bartender. Ask your boss if I can fill in."

The bartender's face brightened. "I'll call him."

"He knows me," Sally said. "He'll agree. I'll phone in sick tomorrow at work." She looked around the bar, located an empty table. "I'll be over there with Dudley Doright."

Dustin felt the familiar ache. She'd called him that on and off for years, sometimes with affectionate teasing, sometimes with resentment. He couldn't quite catch tonight's nuance. It had started when she'd once tried to kiss him, and he had given her a stilted, uncomfortable lecture on why he couldn't do it. He'd been stiffer than usual because he'd wanted her so badly, even while not wanting her to know it.

"That is ridiculous," she'd scoffed at him. "It's only a friendly kiss, and even if it wasn't, cousins have married throughout the centuries."

But not in a straitlaced Episcopalian family, they didn't. And he knew that one kiss often led to another, and another. . . .

"Oh, pooh," she'd said. "You're such a Dudley Doright."

It had hurt then. But over the years, it had become an endearment of sorts. She was the outlaw, and he was the careful one.

He tried to ignore the yearning in him as they sat in a little booth, protected on both sides by tall wooden dividers. He waited until she had settled down, then leaned over, keeping his voice low. The feeling of privacy created by the dividers was, he knew, an illusion.

"Tell me what happened," he demanded. "You said it was urgent."

"A Colonel Flaherty called me. He said there had been attacks on General Mallory's granddaughter. He's one of the. . . ."

"I know who he is," Dustin said. "I had a message from him, too, but it just asked me to get in touch with him. What, exactly, did he say?"

"He asked whether anything strange had happened to me. A burglary or mugging. I told him no."

"That's true, isn't it?"

Sally hesitated just long enough to make his stomach twist.

"I'm not sure," she said finally.

"What do you mean you're not sure?"

Her gaze met his directly, and there was worry in it. "I had an odd feeling a week ago. It was several days after I took the painting to a safe deposit box, as you suggested.

I went in the apartment and I just felt . . . weird. As if something was wrong. Nothing was missing, though, and I'm not sure. . . ."

The knot of apprehension grew tighter inside him. "Nothing was out of place?"

She shrugged. "You know I'm not the neatest person. I never pay attention to where I put things. I don't even know why I felt uncomfortable. An unusual scent, maybe. I just don't know."

"Can you take some vacation time?"

"Right now?"

"Yes."

She shook her head.

"Then you will be sick. I'll take care of it. You go to my place in Maryland . . . until I can talk to this Flaherty and see what's going on."

He stopped, then realized that if someone was stalking all of them, they would know about his Maryland cottage. *They.* He didn't like the idea of unknown, unnamed, faceless stalkers. "There's another possibility," he said. "But it will take me tomorrow to arrange. We'll leave tomorrow after work."

"The day after tomorrow," she said. "I just offered to fill in for Robert."

He knew she wouldn't change her mind. Not when she got that stubborn look on her face.

"Then take your clothes with you tomorrow night, and I'll pick you up when you finish. I have a meeting the next day. I can't miss it."

Her gaze didn't leave his face. "That means you won't get any sleep."

He shrugged. "I've gone days without sleeping. I won't leave you alone."

She didn't ask questions. He saw both fear and trust in her eyes, and the latter made him straighten. He'd never been anyone's knight. And though he probably did seem like a Dudley Doright, it had always been for the wrong reason. Ambition. Pure, raw ambition. But now something ugly might be reaching out to touch the one person he cared about.

Your career, he reminded himself. *You can't let this affect your career.*

Whatever *this* was.

The first thing, after making sure Sally was safe, was to talk to this Flaherty and see what he knew. And Dr. Mallory.

He knew a little about her, at least her academic career. And a lot about Flaherty. He was someone who wouldn't let go once he sank his teeth into an objective. Dustin had decidedly mixed feelings about that. He didn't want Flaherty going back in his family's history. He couldn't afford it.

How in the hell could he find out what Flaherty knew and still keep him from probing any further into the Eachan family?

Well, dammit, he was a diplomat, wasn't he? This should be a piece of cake after the other negotiations he had conducted. He could deal in subterfuge as well as any man alive.

But first he had to make sure Sally was safe.

A waiter came over and they ordered drinks—a scotch for him and wine for her—and dinner. Hamburgers and fries. He ate them only with Sally, who loved both. He didn't trust anything else at Art's.

Her large blue eyes settled on him. The fear faded, and he felt ten feet tall. She reached over, and her fingers went around his. "I've missed you," she said.

Dustin felt his own hand tightening. Hell, he felt his entire body tensing. His eyes met hers, and awareness flashed between them.

He withdrew his hand as if burned. "From now on, I don't want you to open the door to anyone if I'm not there. I don't want you to meet anyone. I don't even want you to go out to lunch alone."

She tried to smile. "I can take care of myself."

"The hell you can," he retorted, but even he heard the softness that took away any sting. "I would stay tonight, but I have a meeting in an hour."

"What's going on?" she asked.

"I wish I knew. But once you're safe I'll find this Flaherty and try to find out."

"I still can't believe that Grandfather stole anything. He was so . . . righteous. He destroyed my father because he didn't live up to *his* standards."

"Your father destroyed your father," Dustin corrected softly.

"He had help," she said, her defense of her father as strong as always.

Their food came, and he ate fast, checking his watch as he did so. Forty minutes until the meeting. He had to have recommendations on the deputy secretary's desk by eight in the morning, and he'd called in several of his brightest and best assistants for one last evaluation. For the first time in his career, he wished he could brush his job aside.

Her gaze seldom left him. He knew she was weighing how much he had told her, how much he knew.

Too much. Far too much.

He left a couple of bills on the table, more than enough to cover the check and a generous tip. "I'll walk you home."

For a moment she looked rebellious, then nodded.

"I'll be over later," he said as they walked to the door and out into the hot, humid Washington night. He meant it as reassurance, but she stopped and looked up at him. He brushed a soft curl from her face and tucked it behind her ear. "It's probably nothing," he said. "Anything could have happened in Memphis. This Mallory woman could have enemies, a jilted lover. Chances are it has nothing to do with us."

"And my apartment?"

"I've seen it," he said wryly. "The aftermath of a hurricane."

She grinned at that. "Says the world-class neatnik."

At least a grin. And tomorrow he would make sure she was safe.

nine

The hotel room looked bare and lonely. Although it was called a suite, it had the same bland lack of character that every moderately priced hotel or motel had. The upholstery was slightly worn and stained, the carpet gray and thin. An aroma of cleaning fluid clung to it.

No Bojangles. No welcoming bark or nose nudging her legs. Only institutional indifference. Amy thought of her own house with its vivid warmth, and was sick to her stomach. She'd tried hard not to think about it these past days.

She'd learned to accept what couldn't be changed, but now she leaned against the interior wall of the room. She took a deep breath, then another.

"Dr. Mallory?" The colonel's voice was warm, full of concern.

She tried to smile. "Just dizzy for a moment," she lied. "And no one uses 'doctor' to refer to the holder of a doctorate. Call me Amy."

"Someone should stay here with you."

She shook her head. She hadn't told him she planned to take Bo and leave tomorrow. She didn't want to give anyone warning or an opportunity to stop her. In fact, she was becoming more and more determined to do it. Once

Colonel Flaherty left, she planned to go to the bank, which was just only blocks away; if she hurried, she could get everything accomplished. She'd already called the police. She was told her boxes would be delivered this afternoon. She had to be back before then, and before Sherry returned Bo.

All that movement was going to hurt like blazes, and she would still hurt tomorrow. But she wouldn't feel safe until she was out of Memphis.

She tried to hurry her benefactor away. "Thank you for the ride, but I think I need some rest now."

He looked at her with skeptical eyes, as if he doubted that she intended to rest. But she didn't care. It was none of his business.

After a moment's hesitation, he took a business card from a pocket and scribbled something on it. "My cell number," he said. "Call me if you need anything."

She took it. It would be rude not to. But she had no intention of getting any more involved with Colonel Flaherty. He made her wary in more ways than one.

She merely nodded, which was neither agreement or refusal, then opened the door for him to leave.

The wry look on his face told her that he knew she had no such intentions, and she felt a small twinge. He had saved her life. Still, she was not sure of his motives. All she knew was that he appeared when everything had turned bad. She wasn't at all sure their interests were compatible.

Part of her regretted the resignation on his face. But *she* was what was important now, she and Bo, and living beyond the next few days. She closed the door firmly behind him.

She waited just long enough to see his car disappear through her room window.

Amy looked enviously at the bed. No time now. Bank first. Then she could rest. Maybe. She wondered if she could ever close her eyes again without seeing blood, without fearing that someone was trying to get to her. Her body ached. It was telling her to rest even if her mind shied away from the idea.

Her mind turned to the boxes. The police had looked through them and found nothing. They believed that the burglar just grabbed the nearest thing when he heard someone coming. They were looking into Jon's background, not hers. The fact that he was killed by a hit-and-run driver around the same time as the burglary seemed too coincidental. As for the attack on her, that was attributed to the burglar's fear that she might have seen more than she had.

Any connection of these recent events to a fifty-year-old theft in another country seemed far-fetched to the detectives. And to her. But she couldn't dismiss it as easily as they had. It wasn't their life on the line.

Once the boxes arrived, she would go through them. Perhaps *she* would find something. But she knew she didn't want to ask the colonel for help.

She was afraid he would sacrifice her grandfather's name to clear his own grandfather's. She had little faith in authority figures, particularly the military. They had lied in Vietnam to protect their war and their reputation, overestimating enemy casualties to a criminal extent. Would they lie to protect another image? Would *he* lie to protect his family?

MEMPHIS

Irish made some calls to friends, one an intelligence officer in Memphis. They had worked together years ago and had remained in contact. He asked a few questions, got a name of a private detective who could be trusted. He then called the detective and asked where he could obtain a GPU device.

"Who you wanna track?"

"A young lady who might be in danger."

There was a pause, then, "Well, if Lieutenant Brannigan sent you, it must be okay."

Within hours, he had what he needed. He'd also picked up his .48 from his hotel room. He grabbed a hamburger and fries, then returned to Amy Mallory's hotel at dusk.

He already knew which car was hers. After looking around, he bent next to her car and put the homing device on the undercarriage, then returned to his own car. He didn't have the luxury of scanning the entire car for any other such devices. He could only hope there was none.

He drove to a secluded corner of the lot and selected a parking place that would be out of her sight if she looked out, but in a position where he could watch who came in and out of the door. Someone could, of course, approach her room from another door, but this was the most convenient—and private—one. This would be the entrance of choice.

Amy Mallory might not want him around, but he sure as hell wasn't going to leave her alone. Not with a killer around. He had another reason. If this had anything to do with her grandfather's papers, then he was a part of it, too.

And his antenna was up. He had great faith in his own personal antenna. His instincts had always been good. He'd been careful today, checking frequently to see whether he was being followed. He thought he might have seen the same car more than once on the way from the hospital to the hotel, and had made some quick turns, then hadn't seen it again. He would guess, though, that Amy's attacker probably already knew where she was staying. For a moment, he thought about checking on her, then squelched that idea.

The light was on in her room. The curtains were closed; he couldn't see whether anyone was inside. But the lights reassured him. The attackers had been professional. They wouldn't have left a light on.

He saw her friend leave through the door, and he slouched down in the car until he heard an engine start and the car leave the lot. Only then was he able to breathe easily and relax. He readjusted his long body in the confines of the rented car and kept his eyes on the door closest to her room.

The moon was half-full, casting shadows over the building, but the lights around the hotel were bright. A police car entered the parking lot, cruising slowly, and he ducked again. He really didn't want to explain why he was skulking around at this time of night.

The car stopped. A uniformed officer stepped out and took three boxes from the backseat. He locked his car, then took them inside.

The police officer came out almost immediately, stepped back into his cruiser, then drove out of the parking lot.

Several moments later, he saw Amy. She was carrying a suitcase and was headed for her car. A dog trotted at her heel, obviously unwilling to leave her side for any reason. She glanced around, and he didn't duck fast enough. In an instant, she was over to the side of his car.

He sighed, opened the door, and stepped outside.

Conflicting emotions crossed her face. Apprehension, then anger. "What are you doing here?"

He gave her a rueful look. "Looking out for you."

"I don't remember asking you to do that." Her voice was edgy. Well, his would be, too, if he had gone through what she had.

"You didn't," he admitted wryly, giving her the reassuring smile that usually worked. It didn't. She glared at him.

"Look, Colonel Flaherty, I appreciate your help earlier, but I don't need it now."

He didn't respond. Instead, he looked at the suitcase. "Leaving?"

"Yes. In the morning."

He wanted to ask where she was going, but she had told him several times before that her business was none of his, and he suspected she would only remind him of that.

"Perhaps that's the wisest thing to do," he said.

"How nice you agree," she said testily. She knew she was being unreasonable, but she just wanted to get away from everything and everyone that reminded her of the last few days. "I plan to go *alone*."

"I'm not sure *that* is the wisest thing to do."

"I don't care what you think," she said.

She looked tired and vulnerable. The T-shirt she was wearing showed the bulkiness of bandages on her side, and her face was pale. He had the damndest urge to take her in his arms and protect her. Even . . . kiss some of those fears away. He didn't think she would take that well. So he tried words instead. "Perhaps you should wait a few days. I could ask the police. . . ."

"They've already told me they can't do anything." Some of the control left her face, and her lips trembled for a moment. "And I don't intend to wait for someone to try again."

"Where . . . ?"

"Where no one can find me," she said. "Not even you."

"Your injury may need attention."

"It's much better," she said.

"You shouldn't be driving." He knew he should stop. With every admonition, her chin went higher and higher.

He understood why she didn't trust him. He wouldn't trust easily, either, if a stranger showed up on his doorstep after all that had happened recently.

He was impressed. She had the kind of gritty courage he admired. But it was also the kind of courage that could get someone killed.

He knew, though, he would get no further with her now.

Instead, he looked down at the dog. It was medium size, obviously part wirehaired terrier and God knew what else. It had a snaggle tooth and looked at him through scraggly whiskers. One ear was only half there. The other stood up as if it were saluting.

"Bojangles," he acknowledged.

She looked surprised that he remembered. He leaned down to pet the dog, and it scooted behind her. "He doesn't like men," she explained. "I got him at the pound, and I think he'd been mistreated, probably by a male."

He didn't press it. He knew enough about dogs to know it would take time for any stranger to win trust. Still, the dog said something about her character. She certainly did not pursue the beautiful and celebrated. Bojangles was, quite simply, a dog poorly endowed by his creator.

He was not going to say that, however. He'd already given her a card with his phone number, but he had the thought that she might well have thrown it away. He took another from his pocket. "In case you . . . misplaced the other one," he said.

To his surprise, she took it.

"I would appreciate it if you would leave now," she said.

He gave her a crooked grin that was meant to be reassuring. "All right," he agreed. "Try to remember, I'm on your side."

Her dubious look pierced through the shield he thought he had built around himself. Reluctantly he returned to his car. He noticed in the rearview mirror that she did not move until he drove out and down the road. He waited until he was well out of sight of the motel, then pulled into a parking lot.

She said she was leaving in the morning, but her eyes had said something else. She was not a practiced liar.

And he did not intend for her to get very far from him.

In addition to the unexpected protective feelings he had for her, he knew she was the key to a mystery he had to solve.

It had been all she could do not to cry as she stood next to the colonel. The tears behind her eyes were held back by sheer force of will. Dear God, how she wanted to accept his offer to look after her.

But no one could really take care of her. She had to do it herself.

Amy had been doing exactly that for years. And doing it well. She had never been a wilting flower. She'd received a doctorate and succeeded in one of the best private colleges in the country. She was close to catching the brass ring of tenure, and she'd done it all on her own. She'd sacrificed a personal life for that stability. And safety.

And now someone was tearing it away from her, or trying to, and she wasn't going to let that happen.

She hadn't really lied to Flaherty. She had planned to leave in morning. She'd just wanted to get everything ready. But now she knew it was important to leave tonight. She wouldn't travel long, just far enough where no one could find her.

She had never been so alone in her life. She wanted to trust Flaherty, but his appearance had just been too convenient. She couldn't get beyond that fact.

She hated feeling so vulnerable. She had to do something to regain control of her life. Going through her grandfather's papers might do that, and she had to do it alone and in safety. She was not going to risk those papers by giving anyone access to them.

She took Bo inside and stared at the boxes. They were more like snakes now, their contents possibly venomous. She was surprised the police had released them, but it made sense. They did the police no good at the moment. Only she might be able to find something important.

The cover on the top one had been taped down, but carelessly. It took her only a moment to undo it. She pulled it open and looked at the file folders inside. They were messy, with wrinkled papers stuffed indifferently in bent folders. She looked at the first folder. April 1945. The month before the train was captured. She opened the second box. The date on the folder she extracted was three months earlier.

She didn't have to time to go through them all. She wanted to get away from here before she did that.

Amy went into the kitchen. She'd already packed the dog food and Bo's dishes. She added a package of crackers and several sodas, then carried those out to the car. No one there. No Army colonel. No police. No lurking villains.

At least none she saw.

In another five minutes, she'd transferred the boxes, the files she'd copied from her office computer, and finally her new laptop to the car. It took all the energy she had. When she finished, she had to lean against the car for a moment. She was breathing hard, and her side hurt.

You can do it.

She went back to the room and took one last look. It was paid through the end of the month, but she would not miss its bland contents. Then she left the room, Bo beside her.

A feeling of excitement started to fill her, shoving aside the loneliness. She was still sore. Still hurting. Still afraid. But she was taking her life back. For the next ten days, she intended to be a wild goose, going where instinct called. And, in that time, she hoped she would become less important to whoever was haunting her. Or perhaps she would find a clue as to who or what was behind it.

Once in the car, she drove out of the parking lot, keeping both eyes open and roving. It was nearly ten. She planned to drive to Jackson, about ninety miles east. She could find a hotel there after taking several out of the way roads; she knew the area well.

Amy knew she couldn't go any farther than Jackson. She didn't have the physical strength. Not tonight. Any place, though, would be better than this hotel, this city.

After Colonel Flaherty had left her at the hotel the first time, she'd gone to the bank around the corner and withdrawn half her savings—ten thousand dollars—so she wouldn't have to use a credit card. She also bought a certified check, and mailed it to a post office in Savannah, Georgia, under the name of Susan Weir. It was an identity her mother had used, and she still had a Social Security card with that name on it. She had taken every conceivable precaution outside of selling her beloved VW. She wasn't ready for that. It and Bo were the only familiar possessions she had left.

She was confident she could disappear. She'd learned any number of how-to-get lost techniques from her mother and other miscreants during her childhood years. Although, as far as she knew, her mother had never tried to bomb anything, she had, on occasion, harbored fugitives, friends from the "glory days." Anyone who showed up on the doorstep received sanctuary—along with what little money her mother had. Sometimes it was given. Sometimes stolen.

Amy wished she could stop the thoughts flashing through her mind as she pulled onto the main highway. *Concentrate,* she ordered herself. *Concentrate.*

She looked in the rearview mirror. No one behind her. She drove toward the interstate, detouring once down a side street, then taking several more turns. Still no one behind her.

She hoped no one—not even the colonel—had believed she would leave the day she was discharged from the hospital. That hope brought back his face to her mind. She wished it wasn't such an attractive one.

A few more turns and she was on the interstate, heading east.

For the first time in a week, she felt free. Mistress of her own fate.

She only hoped it wasn't an illusion.

MARYLAND

Sally was unusually quiet on the drive up to Maryland's eastern shore.

Dustin would have to be back at work in the morning, but the next day was Saturday and he hoped he could find a better place for her. At the moment, though, he'd decided on a condominium rental unit. He had engaged the apartment in Cecil Ford's name, using the man's credit card. He'd repaid Cecil with cash and sworn him to secrecy.

"I don't have to stay inside, do I?" Sally asked.

"If I said yes, would you do it?"

"Probably not," she said with what sounded like forced cheerfulness. Still, his own urgency seemed to have seeped into her. At least a little. He was grateful, and saddened. Some of her joie de vivre—her essence—had faded.

He didn't want her to go out, but he knew he couldn't keep her locked up. It would be best to suggest what she *might* agree to. "I think you can go out if you don't use your name," he said. "But I don't want you to make any calls to me. *I'll* call *you.*"

She was silent for several moments, and he knew she understood the implications of his words. They did sound ominous, but he hadn't known how else to frame them. "I don't like this," she said. "Why don't we just go to the police? They can have the darned painting."

"We have no proof someone was in your apartment," he explained. "And probably no one was. I just don't want to take chances."

"The woman in Memphis. . . ."

"It could be just what the police there think it is: a simple burglary. It may not have anything to do with us. I'm just being cautious." He forced a smile. "You know that side of my nature." He hesitated, then added, "If we go to the police, we'll be telling the world our grandfather was a thief. God knows what else might surface."

"I don't care about Grandfather's reputation."

"I do," he said quietly. "It can destroy us."

Destroy you. The idea was in her mind. He knew it. Sally cared less about what other people thought. In fact, she had made a career of not caring. One of her first stabs at independence had been bartending, mainly because she knew it would upset her mother.

And she was right. He *was* concerned about his family's reputation. He'd worked too hard to throw it away now. He couldn't rid himself of the expectations drilled into him since he was a toddler. *Strive. Produce. Make your life count.* Counting meaning achieving. *Power. Prestige.* He had both now, and he could have a great deal more in a few years.

But only if he quieted the damned investigation. Only if he could keep this Flaherty from inquiring further. Perhaps if the interfering fool ended his queries, the story would just fade away.

There had to be a way to stop him. Dustin turned on the compact disc player. The music of Beethoven filled the car, and the silence between them. Several minutes later, Sally was asleep.

He glanced toward her. Even in the dim light of the interior, he could see the blond hair that framed her lovely face. His heart jerked. He wanted so many things. Some he could have only at the loss of others. Expediency over honor. Power over friendship. And he could never have Sally. Perhaps if he could . . . then other things wouldn't be so important.

But "ifs" had no value. "Ifs" represented failure.

He turned his attention to the road ahead.

ten

With every mile that passed, Amy felt safer.

She was stiff. Every time she made a rest stop, she knew there would be one agonizing moment when she stepped outside the car. But Bo needed his walks, and she would be unable to walk herself if she didn't take occasional breaks from one position.

She never stopped, though, unless she saw other people about.

She'd spent the night in Jackson, just ninety miles east of Memphis. Atlanta was approximately seven hours farther, and the Georgia coast another seven, depending on her speed. She kept under the limit and left the interstate several times to take country roads. She was convinced she wasn't being followed, and she didn't want to risk a ticket and questions.

She'd been to Jekyll Island years ago, so long ago that no one would know about it. She suspected it would be a good place to get lost. There were many motels, and she'd called from a pay phone to check on availability at the one she remembered. Rooms there had two doors, one to the parking lot and the other to the beach. They also had kitchenettes so she wouldn't have to go out. Best, of all, they didn't object to dogs. And because it was one of the few hotels that did not, there was always a large assortment. She'd be just another woman with her dog. She wouldn't stand out.

She shook her head to stay awake. She'd stayed in a motel just past Atlanta on the second night, but she came fully awake at every sound and didn't get much sleep. She'd also been too tired and sore to take more than a cursory look at the boxes, though she had lugged them in. At this point, she wasn't letting them out of her sight.

But her brief scan revealed little. There were no diaries, no written memoirs. She saw some scribbled notes, but the writing was barely legible. It would take time and concentration to decipher them.

Had Jon been through them? He'd certainly never indicated he'd found anything of interest, but then they had both been extremely busy the last weeks of the semester.

She thought about exactly when he'd asked about her grandfather. Not so long ago? They had worked together for five years, then three months ago. . . .

Three months ago.

The commission would have been working then. Had Jon heard of it? His field was World War II, and he'd been particularly interested in the efforts to trace the money trail between Nazi Germany and Switzerland. Had he chanced upon the commission report? Had he investigated further?

If so, wouldn't he have told her? Wouldn't he have warned her?

Wouldn't he have shared any suspicions he might have had about her family? Bring her into whatever project he planned?

Dread filled her. Had he used her? Had he been after something more than simply perusing the papers of a general to get more insight on him?

Is that why he'd died?

She couldn't bear to think that. Jon had been one of the two close friends she'd had.

Paranoia. It was smothering her.

She rolled down the windows. She relaxed as she passed over grassy marshlands, and the aroma of sea was like a drug. She'd always loved the sea. The constancy of it. The sense of renewal she always felt. One day, she hoped, she could live next to the sea.

An hour, and she would be in her room. She would take a hot bath, order a pizza, then start looking at her grandfather's papers. Maybe a walk on the beach to clear her head, especially since no one could have followed her. "We're almost there, Bo," she said. He wagged his tail and put his head in her lap. How nice, she thought, to be so oblivious.

She took another look in the rearview mirror. No familiar cars. She left I-16 to take a meandering route through south Georgia. Sometimes she went twenty miles or so without seeing another car.

Anticipation started to build as the smell of the sea grew stronger. A warm breeze blew through the car.

Safety. Just a few more miles, and she would feel safe again.

Where in the hell was she going?

Irish tried to stretch in his rental car, but this model was too cramped for comfort—or maybe he had been in it too long.

He'd spent the last two nights sleeping in his car outside a motel where he could keep an eye on her room. He hadn't really slept, merely dozed. His instincts were such that the slightest noise would wake him. But though he was used to sleeping anyplace under any circumstances, he now longed for a bed.

She had protected herself well, though. He'd been impressed at the precautions she had taken, the way she had doubled back several times. He would not have been able to follow her without being seen had he not had the electronic transmitter. He still didn't know if anyone else had put one on her car. He couldn't make a thorough check without being obvious. Neither did he know whether she had told anyone where she was going.

He would not stay with her much longer. If there was no attempt on her in the next few days, he would consider her reasonably safe. He would probably knock on her door, and let her know that there were still ways for people to find her—as he had—and leave his cell phone number again. She wouldn't be happy, but he would know he had done everything he could.

He couldn't help feeling a responsibility toward her. Guilt still gnawed at him. His questions could have caused her problems. And if they had, then someone had profited from the captured trains years ago. It hadn't just been carelessness or sloppiness or expediency that sometimes happened in the midst of war.

Or even minor theft by more than one individual during massive and rapid movement of troops. He'd seen it in Bosnia and Kosovo. Confusion in moving supplies. Someone takes one thing, and then another. Just a souvenir. Word gets around that it's easy picking. The command staff is more concerned with the next objective than securing enemy—or even friendly—possessions.

He supposed that's what he hoped to find. Some indication of carelessness rather than venality. The only way he could discover that was to find the names of those in charge of inventorying and guarding the contents of the train. Who had day-to-day access? That was something he'd been unable to find in the commission report. It placed blame in the command structure, which, of course, did have ultimate responsibility. But Irish wanted to know more. How much direct knowledge did the command have? When did the thefts actually occur? He wanted to know how the goods were inventoried and warehoused. Was the shipment intact when his grandfather left the area? None of these questions had been answered by the commission report, at least not what he'd been able to see.

The recent attacks on Amy fostered the idea that something far more sinister than piecemeal theft had occurred, and that someone was afraid a continuing investigation might lead to them. He wondered then whether the commission had been hampered in any way. He planned to ask them. He certainly had had problems when he'd requested supporting documentation. He would have to go through the Freedom of Information Act, despite the fact that he was an Army investigator.

It hadn't made sense then. It was beginning to make sense now.

If someone was trying to limit the investigation, then it had to be someone very powerful. Someone powerful enough to influence a government commission. Someone with enough money to hire a professional killer. Someone ruthless enough to burn down a woman's home.

Powerful and wealthy. Dustin Eachan fit that description.

He passed over a marsh, then a bridge, and finally another bridge, where he paid a toll. The sign read Jekyll Island. He'd never been to the Georgia coast and he was pleasantly surprised. The island was heavily wooded with windswept oaks trimmed with gray moss. He followed the tracking signal to a two-story motel that seemed to stretch a half-mile between the road and beach.

He pulled into a restaurant parking lot next to the motel lobby. He was probably about ten minutes behind her. He didn't see a car in the lobby area, so she must have registered. Then he saw her V.W. halfway down the row of buildings. He took note of the room number, then went into the motel office.

"Do you have a room?" he asked. "I have a friend staying in 226, and would like something near him." Room 226 wasn't hers, but the one next to it.

The clerk looked at his computer. "I have one four doors down," he said.

"I'll take it."

He wanted to lean over and look at the computer. Had

Amy Mallory used her name? She hadn't at the motel near
Atlanta. He had placed a call to an Amy Mallory and found
no one with that name was registered. Unless he'd missed
another tracking device on her car or she'd told someone
where she was going, or used a credit card, she would be
difficult to find.

She was damned smart.

He gave her another fifteen minutes for unpacking her
car, then went to his own room. He noted warily that his
unit, and thus hers, had two doors. It wouldn't be easy to
keep track of her.

He'd brought along a cooler of soft drinks and extra
coffee, along with bread and some sandwich meats. After
splashing water on his face, he set a chair next to the window where he could watch.

He wondered whether he was crazy. Whether this was a
wild goose chase. Still, he had time. And all his instincts
told him that Amy Mallory was the key to what he
wanted—no, needed—to know.

He had his laptop with him. Time to find out a little
more about the Eachan descendants while keeping an eye
on the parking lot.

It was going to be a long evening.

WASHINGTON, D.C.

The meeting seemed to last forever. Dustin fidgeted, something he never did. One of the reasons he was successful
was his policy of always, always paying attention to
whomever he was with. Or, at the very least, appearing to
do so.

But Brian Jordan, chief executive of one of the country's largest defense contractors, had asked to meet with
him. He had a major contract with the new leader of the
African country now dominating most of Dustin's time.

"He is a friend of this country," Jordan said.

"He's a friend to whoever fattens his Swiss bank account," Dustin replied dryly.

Jordan shrugged. "They all are. But in this case he is the lesser of two evils, and he needs a loan to arm his military."

And you are going to provide it. At a hefty profit. Dustin didn't put his thoughts into words. Jordan was a friend and supporter of the current president. He was also a major campaign contributor.

But damned if he was going to recommend sending more money to another dictator.

He stood and extended his hand. "Thank you for your time and your recommendations. I'll be sure to follow up on them."

It was standard Washington speak, but Jordan very nearly crushed his hand with his handshake. "By the way," he said as he finally relinquished it, "I've been reading about that commission report."

Dustin knew exactly what commission report he meant. There was a smug knowledge in the man's eyes. He knew why he had never liked the man despite his surface charm. There was a shark underneath it, and Dustin had always recognized it. He'd tried to stay away from him, but this time the blasted man had insisted on talking to him, and he'd used the vice president's name to get the appointment.

Dustin shrugged. "What commission report? God knows there are millions of them."

"The one about your . . . is it your grandfather?"

Jordan was not just being obnoxious. Dustin didn't know why, but he knew a fishing expedition when he saw one. Did Jordan think he could find some advantage here? A hint of a threat to force a favorable recommendation?

"I haven't paid any attention to it," he said lightly. "You must know how much theft—and how many mistakes— happen when an army's on the move."

"Of course," Jordan said. "I just thought you might have more information."

"Sorry to disappoint you," Dustin said. "If you've read the newspapers, you probably know as much as I do." He guided his visitor to the door.

"When can I expect to hear from you?" Jordan asked.

Dustin examined the man. He was perhaps twenty years older than himself. Fifty-five or so. He had a rough charm, a kind of man's man certainly. Gray hair he didn't try to hide. In fact, it softened his chiseled features.

But Dustin knew him well, and his reputation better. Both he and his father were ruthless in their business practices, and there were plenty of rumors about the elder Jordan's flirtation with unsavory governments.

He would use anything in Dustin's past for leverage. He was now putting Dustin on notice.

But Dustin put his best smile in place as he opened the door. "I have very little to do with it. I only make recommendations."

"I know it will be the right one," Jordan said, and it was all Dustin could do to keep from slamming the door behind him.

Did Jordan know something he didn't?

He made a phone call.

"Is anyone else snooping around the records?" he asked.

"Just the CID colonel. He's put in a request. I don't think he's going to stop."

"Doesn't he have anything better to do?"

The voice on the other end was silent.

"Give him something better to do," Dustin said, and slammed down the receiver.

Who had been searching Sally's apartment? And why? What did they think they would find? Something they could use to blackmail him?

He didn't think Jordan's comments were just friendly conversation. They were a message. Even a threat. Dustin

wondered how much Jordan would make on the potential
sale to the African despot. He sold armored vehicles,
among other things, and the sale would mount into many
millions of dollars.

Dread filled him. Something was happening. Flaherty.
The Mallory woman. The search of Sally's apartment.
Now Jordan's comment. Dustin hadn't questioned his re-
quest for the meeting when it was made two days ago.

But now. . . .

A subtle kind of blackmail? But what could Jordan
know that would give him any leverage? The newspaper
story had made the incident public. He'd thought it would
die a quick death.

Maybe if Flaherty stopped interfering.

Maybe . . .

eleven

Amy felt safe enough to take Bo for a walk on the lawn between the beach and the hotel. She double-locked the front
door from the inside. No one could get in there, and she
planned to keep the sliding glass door in direct range of vision at all times.

The tangy salt air filled her with a sense of security. She
almost felt as if she had come home. She often felt that
way around the ocean. She had once read that many people had that same feeling of familiarity with the sea because life evolved from there. She had no idea whether that
was true. She only knew it gave *her* a peace she didn't experience anyplace else.

Amy wanted to go down to the beach itself, but she
wasn't going to let her door go unwatched. After everything that had happened, she wasn't taking anything for
granted.

How long would she have to live like this? Why was
she not allowed to enjoy several days like everyone else?

At least she felt better now that they were settled. A hot
bath and an ordered-in pizza shared with Bo had made all
the difference. After this brief walk, she would start a serious review of the boxes.

She returned to her room and piled the boxes on the

sofa. She curled her feet under her and sat. Bo jumped up, stretching his body alongside hers.

She started reading.

Irish wearied of watching the front parking lot. He'd checked the locks of his own room, and with the door guard, he figured she would be pretty safe if she used them all.

He'd taken up a position then in front of the sliding door leading to the beach. An hour went by, and then he saw her. Framed by an outdoor light, she walked the dog, never going far from her own door. She didn't use the leash, but the dog stayed right at her feet. He saw her look toward the water, and could see the wistfulness in her stance if not her eyes.

He wanted to go out to her. Instead, he waited until she went back inside. He didn't like the sliding glass doors, but he thought he would hear any disturbance. He damn well hoped the dog barked.

He went out the front door, checked the parking lot again. Nothing suspicious here. It looked as if most of the occupants were attending some kind of conference. Little groups of people were returning with name tags. Most were wearing shorts and T-shirts. *A law enforcement seminar would be nice.*

Irish left his front door and walked past her unit. Curtains were drawn. Good. Her car was parked several doors down. He didn't see anyone loitering. Good again.

He decided to get a couple of hours' sleep. Otherwise he wouldn't be worth anything. It was nine. If anyone meant to strike, they would do it in the early hours of the morning. He would resume his watch then.

Amy looked at the red digital numbers of the clock by the bed. Two A.M. Time to quit. She'd been through one box, which held files dated in the spring of 1945. It seemed an odd collection to her. Why would her grandfather keep such things as duty rosters, sheets of them? Maps? Copies of orders? Written scribbles she couldn't read?

There was nothing that would incite murder.

She skipped through the other boxes. Not much there, either.

She went back to the rosters. Nothing was highlighted, singled out.

Amy was more puzzled than ever.

Her eyes were beginning to blur. She looked at the clock. An hour had passed. She might as well forget any more perusing tonight. Time to get some sleep.

With the dawn, perhaps the fear would leave.

Irish didn't know what startled him, what night sound was unusual.

He had slept several hours, then rose, refreshed, at one A.M. He was like a doctor that way. He could grab pieces of sleep, and that would be enough.

He had gone outside to the little patio. Each was shielded by walls that provided privacy from the adjoining patios. He pulled the chair out a little so he could watch the light in Amy Mallory's room. Sipping a cup of coffee, he relaxed in the cool sea breeze and the gentle lull of the tide washing up on the beach.

Patience again. Another day, and he would head toward Washington, where he hoped he could get his hands on the commission data. And talk to Dustin Eachan. Perhaps Eachan's cousin as well.

Amy Mallory should be through with those papers by then. He wondered how he could approach her. How would she feel about being followed? Watched? Even if the reason was protective, not malevolent. Would she believe that?

He wasn't sure he would, if he had gone through what she had.

Irish didn't know how long he had been sitting on the patio when her light went out. He debated whether he should continue to watch her room, get more sleep, or watch the front. Here was much more pleasant.

He might have dozed off when he suddenly jerked awake. A dog's alarmed bark cut the silence of the night. It was faint, but Irish had damned good ears.

He took running strides toward the sliding glass doors of her room. A light was visible, although the drapes were drawn. He didn't hear anything. He returned and ran through his own room, picking up his automatic as he went.

The door to her room was closed. That meant it would be locked, too. Should he knock? What if the dog had barked at a passing car? Or perhaps the bark came from another dog.

How in the hell could anyone get inside her room?

He hesitated. A sharp bark, then a whine. A cutoff scream.

Then he saw that someone had backed into her car. That's how they had gotten inside. An apology. An explanation.

He could knock. Start a disturbance. *No.* They could kill her and get out the back. He slipped his revolver in his belt and took out his wallet, removing a plastic card. He slid it into the door. As long as the deadbolt wasn't fastened. . . .

It wasn't. He heard a click. The gun was back in his hand. He very quietly opened the door a fraction of an inch. No bark now.

He started in, but then heard a sound—little more than a breath of air—on the other side of the door. Someone was standing against the wall. Waiting for him. Using all his weight, he slammed the door against the wall, and he felt it hit flesh. A gun skittered across the floor as someone grunted with pain.

A man in a ski mask held a gun on Amy. The intruder turned to train it on him, and Amy drove her elbow into his chest. It was just enough to make him drop his aim. He fired just a second before Irish did. Irish heard the soft thud of a silencer and the loud crack of his own weapon. He was aware of a blow to his leg, but not yet pain, as red blossomed across the intruder's chest and he fell to the floor, releasing his hold on Amy.

"Look out," Amy cried, and Irish whirled to see the second man lunge at him with a knife. He twisted out of the way, and the intruder took that moment to get out the open door. Irish started after him, but the pain in his leg stopped him, that and the realization that he didn't know whether the man on the floor was dead and unable to hurt Amy.

As he stood in the door, he heard tires squeal and the roar of a car. He barely got a glimpse of a large black sedan as it sped out of the parking lot.

At least they had one of them. He turned back to Amy. She was kneeling next to her dog, who was lying unnaturally still. Her face was chalk white.

The assailant, head covered by a ski mask, lay still near the bed. Blood spilled over on the carpet. Several people were at the open door, obviously awakened by the shot from his pistol. "Call the police," he said to one of them. "And the office."

He went over to Amy. Her face was pale, but it was obvious that she cared more about the dog than a body in her room. Or her own shock. She wore a long shirt she apparently slept in.

He ran his hands gently over the dog. No open wounds. "What happened?"

"Bo bit one of them and he kicked Bo against the wall. He was . . . trying to protect me."

Irish felt the dog's heart. It was beating. "He's alive."

She looked at him with such fear and yet relief that his own heart nearly stopped. "I need to get him to a vet."

"I doubt the police will let you leave," he said. But he went to the phone and called the office. No one answered. Probably everyone was on the way to Amy's room.

He looked at the dog. Ugly as sin, but gallant. The animal stirred and whined pitifully. "I think he'll be all right," he said, gently scratching the dog's ears. "Brave boy."

Then Irish stooped beside the fallen assailant. No pulse here. He wanted to rip off the ski mask, but he knew the police wouldn't like that. Hell, they wouldn't like anything about this. He placed his own gun on a table.

This was going to play hell with his career. Shooting a civilian while on vacation most likely would be frowned upon.

"Sit down," he told Amy.

Holding the dog gently, she did as he said. Silently. Questions were in her wide gray eyes.

"I followed you," he explained gently. "I was afraid you might still be in danger."

"I was so careful. How . . . ?"

"I put a tracking device on your car. I imagine your . . . visitors did the same. I'll check it out later."

Her gaze studied him. "That's the second time you saved my life. Thank you."

"They might just have wanted your grandfather's papers," he said.

"No. They thought I knew something. They. . . ."

He saw it in her eyes. They had meant to kill her. She'd known it.

Once again, he wanted to pull off the man's mask. Was it the one from the hospital? And why Amy? He had been the one to see the man's face.

Now they were back to the starting line. No more information, except someone very determined was after Amy. He heard the sound of sirens, then a screeching stop. Two uniformed officers moved into the room along with a suit-clad desk clerk who looked at the man on the floor with horror.

Amy stood up, still cradling the dog, who was whimpering.

"Well, damn," one of the officers said as he saw the body on the floor. He immediately radioed for backup.

The other officer, older and obviously in charge, had his revolver out, uncertain as to who to aim it at. Irish pointed to the assailant's gun on the floor, and handed his own automatic to the officer, butt first. The policeman took Irish's automatic and left the other gun on the floor. He'd obviously been trained to leave a crime scene undisturbed.

"Two men invaded this woman's room. I heard her cry and came in. The man on the floor shot at me."

The older man's gaze went around the room, then rested again on the fallen man. He knelt at the dead man's side and checked for a pulse, shook his head, and stood, moving just inches from Irish. "Who in the hell are you?"

Irish already had his billfold out with his credentials showing. "I'm Colonel Lucien Flaherty," he said. "This is Miss Mallory. Amy Mallory. She was attacked in Memphis last week, and came here to relax. I came to provide some protection. I heard the dog bark and came in. Two men were attacking her."

"Two?" the older cop said.

"One left in a dark car. Obviously someone was waiting for him."

"A woman," Amy said. "Middle-aged. Brown hair mixed with gray. She woke me, said she'd accidentally run into my car, and wanted to give me her insurance card. She wanted to do it now because she was leaving. When I opened the door to take it, two men pushed their way in." She shook her head in disgust. "I should have realized. I parked several spaces down."

"They're probably already off the island," the officer said. "Did you see anything of the car?"

"No," Irish said.

The manager or assistant manger or night clerk, or whoever he was, had sat down, eyeing the body with horror. "Nothing like this . . . has ever happened."

The older police officer put a plastic glove on and went back to the body and pulled the mask off. He looked up at Irish and Amy. "Recognize him?"

It wasn't the same man as the one in the hospital. This one had dark hair. The other had light brown. The face was thicker, the lips thinner. "No," Irish said, then turned to Amy. "Do you?"

She looked at the face of the dead man for several moments. Then shook her head.

The officer then looked at the clerk. "Tim, could he be a guest here?"

The white-faced clerk shook his head. "I haven't seen him before."

Bo was trying to move in Amy's arms, but every time he did, he whimpered. Irish went over to them, and put his hand on the dog's body. He was panting hard.

"Look, Officer, we need to get this dog to the vet," Irish said.

The older officer shook his head. "No one leaves here."

"There could be internal injuries," Amy said. "Please."

"She'll be right back," Irish interjected. "I'll stay, of course. She's the victim here, after all."

The officer looked skeptical.

The other officer took a step forward. "I could run her over there. I'll call Stephanie on the way. She can meet us at her office."

The older officer obviously wanted to say no, then relented after looking again at Amy's face. "You take the mutt, Richard," said his partner. "She stays here."

"He's terrified of strangers."

"I'm good with animals, ma'am," the officer said. "I'll treat him real gently."

Obviously hesitant to delay getting him medical help, she reluctantly agreed and handed Bo to him. "His name is Bo. He's five years old and has had all his shots."

Richard nodded, taking the dog, who yelped in dismay.

Amy leaned down. "It's okay, Bo. I'll get you soon."

Her left hand was shaking. Irish took it in his, steadying her.

The officer named Richard left with Bo. Amy looked

white and drawn, her gray eyes huge in her face. Still, she seemed uncommonly collected.

"Now we'll sit down and wait for the detectives," the older officer said. His face changed as he followed Amy's gaze.

Irish looked down to the same spot. Blood was pooling on the floor at his feet.

"You're hurt," Amy said.

"Ah, damn," the policeman said. He used his radio again. "We need an ambulance. Atlantic Motel. Unit 220." He looked disgruntled. "But no one leaves here until the detectives arrive."

Irish shrugged. "It's just a flesh wound."

"How do you know?"

"Otherwise I wouldn't be standing." He tried a cocky grin. He didn't know if he succeeded; the burning was intensifying.

Still, it wasn't much compared to the hole in the man on the floor. He'd heard about elephants on the table. A dead body in the middle of the room had the same impact.

They left the county police department together. He'd spent two hours at the hospital, then joined her at the police department. He'd brushed off her worries about his wound. "Barely a scratch," he'd said dismissively.

The sun was directly overhead. Amy thought it was rather remarkable that the sun rose as usual.

Someone had tried to kill her, and not for the first time, and yet people still walked the streets and drove their cars as if nothing had happened. Once she'd been like that. She wondered whether she would ever be again.

Irish was driving his rental car. Her car had been impounded to check for paint traces. A useless exercise, she thought. The car used by the would-be murderers was probably stolen. And her car would need repairs before she could drive it again.

"We'll get your dog, pick up your things, and find another place," her companion said, breaking the tense silence.

"Another place?"

"An anonymous hotel. Unless you want to return to Memphis."

She was silent. She had no idea what to do now. She thought she would be safe here. She wondered whether she would ever be safe again. She bit her lip. What did someone do when they had nowhere to go?

"I thought we would go to Washington," he said. "The Eachans are there. So are investigators for the commission."

"We?"

"We," he confirmed. "I don't want to leave you alone."

She let that idea rattle around for a moment. It had a certain appeal. But that wasn't Amy Mallory. Spontaneous. Adventurous. Running from killers with a man she barely knew. She'd spent her life trying to be safe.

"Amy?"

"I'm thinking," she said.

"You're very appealing when you think."

She looked at him suspiciously. He had a lazy smile. She liked that smile. She was amazed she could even think about that, and yet she had to think about something other than the events of last night. It was the only way she could keep the terror under control.

Act normal. Maybe things will become normal.

Or would anything ever be normal again?

She thought again about his proposal. "I have to be back for my tenure hearing in two weeks."

"I'll get you there," he promised.

The hearing had once been the most important thing in her life. She had worked so hard for it. She'd taught at a community college for four years before finding the assistant professorship at the college, and she'd worked darn hard all these years to get her doctorate, then achieve this final step.

She couldn't give it up. But what if not giving it up meant giving up her life, instead?

Unwilling to explore that further, she changed the subject. "How does your tracer thing work?"

"It's a global positioning satellite vehicle tracking device."

"What did the police think about that?"

"I didn't tell them," he said wryly. "I thought it better if they thought you knew I was protecting you."

"Will the police find it?"

"Not unless they're looking for it, and I doubt they will be. They just wanted paint." He hesitated, then added, "They might even find a second one."

"Those . . . people?" she said with an anger that sent a chill through the car.

He nodded. "It's the only way they could have found you."

"You didn't know there was a second one in my car?"

"No," he said. "I looked it over several times, but didn't find one. It could have been inside the trunk. Hell, it could have been anywhere."

She read him directions to the veterinarian's office and huddled in the far corner of the front seat, tired and shaken and altogether bewildered. She didn't even protest his following her. She had not done very well on her own after all, and he had saved her life. Twice now.

What if he hadn't followed her? She didn't even want to guess.

"Your leg?" she asked.

"Nothing worth worrying about," he said. "It took a few stitches, nothing more. The bullet barely ripped across the skin."

"I'm sorry," she said.

"Don't be. If you hadn't elbowed that guy, I would be dead instead of him."

She shook her head. "For some reason I'm responsible for all this. Jon. Claude. Now you."

"Don't think that," he said fiercely. "To be honest, I think I bear most of the responsibility."

"You?"

"I made queries after the commission closed its investigation."

He was trying to make her feel better. She looked over at him. Despite everything that happened last night, he looked wide awake. Competent. She flinched at the blood on his shirt and jeans. Neither of them had had a chance to clean up.

He also looked . . . sexy with blond stubble on his cheeks and the sleeves of his shirt rolled up to bare suntanned arms. She, on the other hand, probably looked like something the cat dragged in.

He turned to look at her for a second, and she saw warmth in his eyes. And concern. For a moment, some of the chill left her.

If you hadn't elbowed that guy, I would be dead instead of him.

At least she had done *something. And someone is dead because of it,* another voice interrupted. Not good, despite the fact he was one of the bad guys. Her pacifist mother had indoctrinated her better than she'd thought.

So many conflicting feelings. So many of her values torn asunder.

"Amy?"

"I'm all right," she said, then realized she was hugging herself tightly.

He reached out and touched her gently. "I'm sorry. You're not used to this."

"How do you ever get used to it?"

He chuckled. "I suppose you don't."

She remembered what he had told her about his last posting. "What was the CID doing in Kosovo?"

"Trying to collect weapons and keep them safe," he said. "An exercise in futility."

"Did you get shot?"

"No."

She felt even more miserable.

He grinned. "I did get knifed, if that makes you feel better."

She looked at him. The lines around his eyes seemed deeper. And yet there was humor in his eyes. "Thank you," she said. "I don't know if I told you that before."

He didn't say anything for a moment, concentrating on the road ahead. "You did," he assured her. "I thought you might be angry that I followed you."

"That would be rather stupid, wouldn't it?"

He gave her a quick, approving look. "You're a gutsy lady, Amy Mallory."

"I don't feel gutsy. I feel bewildered. And angry."

"I'll take an angry you any time."

Amy let that sink in. It gave her a warm feeling. No one had ever said she was gutsy before. Smart. Determined. Even nicely aggressive. But no man had ever looked at her with so much admiration.

For killing someone. The bubble burst.

"Is this going to go on forever?" she asked, trying to keep the trembling out of her voice.

"I sure as hell hope not."

"Do you have any idea—"

The beep of a phone stopped her. He looked beside him, where his cell phone sat, then picked it up and looked at the display. "My commanding officer. . . ."

It continued to beep. He made no move to answer.

She waited.

The beeping stopped.

"You're not going to answer it?"

"No," he said curtly, as if to cut off the conversation.

Was he being recalled? The thought of being abandoned by him was excruciating. He was the only island of safety in a sea of terror. Regardless of his motives, he'd risked his life twice for hers. She would take that in a New York minute.

"You're risking your career?"

He didn't reply. Instead, he turned a corner and they drove into the veterinarian's office. . . .

Bojangles was groggy, but he wagged his tail when he saw Amy, and she thought the scrawny appendage the most beautiful thing in the world.

The vet, Dr. Douglas, looked at her sympathetically. "He'll be fine," she said. "His ribs were bruised, and he will be hurting a little." She handed Amy a plastic container full of pills. "This is for pain. Even if he doesn't seem to need it, give it to him. Dogs often don't show their distress."

Amy cupped her hands gently around his head. "Brave boy," she said.

Bo's tail wagged with a little more enthusiasm, and he licked her hand.

She paid the bill with the credit card. After all, it didn't seem to matter now. Everyone seemed to know where she was: good guys and bad guys alike.

Amy gently picked Bo up and took him out. Irish opened the door for her, then the car door, and helped her settle the dog in her lap. Bo whimpered, and she could imagine how he felt. Her own side still ached occasionally from her wound.

She was suddenly aware of tears pooling in her eyes. She'd been so frightened for Bo. The colonel might represent escape, but Bo with all his neediness was the one being that relied on *her.*

She was silent as they drove back to the motel. As they pulled up in the parking lot, she noticed the yellow tape around her unit. "What do we do now?" she asked.

"They want us to stay in the area," he said. "But I don't think the management here is thrilled with the idea."

He opened the door to his own unit, and she went inside. She found a bowl in the kitchenette and filled it with water for Bo, who drank thirstily, then went over and lay down at Irish's feet.

Did Bo know the colonel had saved her life? And probably his? He had ignored the man before. Now he was lying in front of a man who was a stranger to him. He'd never done anything like that before.

Irish leaned down and scratched Bo's ears, then straightened.

"Colonel. . . ." Amy felt awkward. They had been through two shootings together. He had taken her home from the hospital. She'd had more intense moments with this man than anyone, and she still struggled with how to address him.

"Irish," he said.

"I beg your pardon?"

"It's Irish."

Why did he always seem to know what she was thinking? He had asked her to call him that before but she'd resisted. It was too familiar. But Irish *did* fit him, despite the fact that his light brown hair and blue eyes said there was Scandinavian blood as well as dark Irish. Perhaps it was the charm that came so easily.

"My classmates at the Point said I was full of blarney," he added after a moment went by.

"Are you?"

"I used to be," he admitted. "It was always my defense."

It was an oddly personal comment. "Defense?"

He shrugged, then went to the door overlooking the ocean.

She followed. "It's so peaceful. It's hard to believe. . . ." Then, to her humiliation, she started shaking. She reached out to steady herself against the sliding glass door, but her legs were turning to rubber.

His arms went around her. She found herself leaning against him. She heard his heart beat, and that steadied her own. Life. *She was alive. Bo was alive.* She would never take life for granted again.

She was aware of his scent. A lingering smell of after-shave. And blood.

Amy looked at the colonel. No, Irish. His eyes were so blue, so intense. He bent his head, and his lips met hers.

Exploration. But a fevered one. She found herself responding in a way she never had with a man before. Her hands went around his neck, and her body fit into his. The kiss became frantic. An affirmation of life.

She had really thought she would die last night. Then he'd burst in like an avenging angel. But he was no angel. Not with those cobalt blue eyes that were suddenly burning like the hottest part of a flame.

She trembled. She didn't know whether it was because of the aftermath of fear or the new sensations taking over her body. Those were dangerous, too, she knew as the kiss deepened, taking on a wild, fierce quality, given and reciprocated, that made everything else fade into nothingness.

You really know nothing about him. You don't even know whether he is married, though all indications are that he isn't. But the fact is, you don't know what he is or who he really is.

But a blaze had been ignited inside her, and it was growing with every second, with every touch.

Life. She felt so very alive. Every nerve was tingling, every pulse throbbing. Passion ripped through her the way lightning rips through the sky. Sudden. Burning. Dazzling.

His mouth opened, and his tongue met hers in a movement so natural, so instinctive that it seemed destined and oh so right. Hot longing filled her as her body moved even closer to his, nearly melding into it. She felt his arousal, and the need inside her responded to him.

It had been so long since she'd been with a man. So very long. And she'd never once felt like this. Every sense was humming—no, electrified. His lips moved from her mouth, moved downward to her throat, then hesitated as his breath sent new tremors through her body. He nuzzled her as his hands caressed the back of her neck, then his lips went to her ear, nibbling the most sensitive part of the lobe.

Hot longing welled in her as her hands left his neck and explored the sides of his body. Hard. Sexy. Enticing. He trembled slightly as her hands kneaded his skin as he was kneading hers.

When his lips touched hers again, there was an explosion, their bodies locking together in mutual need and hunger. No more exhaustion. No more fear. Only irresistible desire. Heat rampaged through her body, seeking companion heat.

His hand went to her shirt and unbuttoned it, then unhooked her bra. His hand hesitated at the bandage on her side.

"It's all right," she said. "Practically well."

Not really. It still hurt occasionally when she made a sudden move. But she didn't care now, and he was being very careful. His mouth went down, and his lips touched her left nipple, then played with it until she didn't think she could bear the exquisite pain. She felt like a volcano bubbling silently within, ready to break free.

"Amy," he whispered as his lips moved to her other breast, his fingers stroking the curves of her body. Her body arched with all the sensations. The air radiated with hunger, her body becoming a heated mass of desires.

His face rubbed against her skin. It was bristly, and somehow that was erotic. In fact, everything about him was erotic.

She'd never been a fan of eroticism. Now she understood why some were. She knew a sensuality she'd not known existed. Sex previously had been pleasurable. Not essential. Not overwhelming. Not all-consuming.

But there was more than sexuality. Something deeper. She felt a bond she'd never felt before. An attraction that was more than physical.

He moved his mouth back to hers, but he didn't stop there. His hand went to her face, and his fingers caressed her face. She'd never felt anything so gentle, yet so compelling.

She found herself unbuttoning his shirt, her hands running over muscles and planes. Hair. Coarse and springy.

His lips returned to hers. The volcano boiled over.

"Your leg?"

"Something else is far more painful," he said with a smile.

They moved in tandem to the bed, and he separated from her only long enough to guide her onto the bed. He followed, one hand in hers, the other undoing his jeans. Then her own jeans were off. He reached into a pocket, taking out his wallet and a small packet. He turned away for a second, then balanced himself above her.

"Amy?"

She held out her arms, and he lowered himself. He came into her very slowly, very carefully. Very gently.

New waves of heat curled inside her as he probed deeper, then moved in a rhythm that grew more and more frantic, a whirlwind of power and need.

The volcano erupted with magnificent splendor. Thunderous waves of pleasure rolled through her, and she felt as if she were shattering into millions of brilliant pieces as he drove into her one last time. . . .

twelve

Amy woke up to daylight, feeling sleepy and warm and contented.

Then she reached out for Irish. She was alone. And naked.

Panic enveloped her.

Clutching the sheet around her like a mammoth towel, she rose from the bed. No Flaherty in sight. Nor could she find Bo.

Bo! Guilt shoved aside the panic.

She went to the windows on the beach side front of the room and saw the colonel out with Bo. She watched as he slowly matched his footsteps to those of the obviously stiff terrier. The colonel had a slight limp of his own.

He was wearing jeans, and a long-sleeve blue shirt, the sleeves rolled up past the elbow. He looked solid and real and irresistibly attractive. Particularly next to Bo.

She moved into the bathroom and looked at herself. It must be twelve or thirteen hours since two men forced their way into her room. She hadn't had time to wash, or even brush her hair. It was going in all sorts of directions, and her eyes had shadows under them.

She wasn't very appealing.

Amy knew she never should have let last night happen.

It had been fear, relief, gratitude. Certainly nothing more. There couldn't be anything more. She barely knew the man.

She wasn't prepared for this. For its impact on her. She had never believed in this . . . kind of feeling.

Because of her mother, perhaps, she had been wary of relationships. She had not wanted a series of one-night stands, nor even one-month stands. She'd had enough "uncles" come and go to doubt constancy of any kind.

She didn't want that kind of life, but neither did she believe in true love. At least, not where she was concerned. She wasn't the kind of woman who evoked poems and pretty words or attracted the kind of man that she suspected Irish Flaherty was.

Amy had lost her virginity at twenty-two with a fellow student in postgraduate studies. She hadn't moved in with him, although that's what he had wanted. She'd still believed in a ring before cohabitation; he hadn't believed in marriage. And when she was offered a position that he wanted, he became emotionally abusive.

She'd left the relationship. She hadn't hung around for it to evolve into something else. Her mother had done that. Not her.

Instead, she'd settled into her work. She'd been elated when she'd received an offer from Braemoor.

She'd had one more relationship, but it had not lasted. She hadn't looked again because she didn't think many of them really worked. None of those of her friends did. Jon was a perfect example. His wife of twenty years had been talking about seeking a divorce and threatening to take everything they had built together.

That thought brought reality back, to the nightmare her life had become. Until a few hours ago when it was miraculously transformed by a stranger. But that transformation couldn't last. She knew that.

No matter how glorious the last few hours had been, they were over.

She slipped on the clothes she'd worn yesterday. They were all she had. The rest of her clothes were in the unit several doors down, and neither she nor Irish had been allowed inside.

Amy went and stood at the door.

Flaherty turned and saw her. He looked down at the dog, said something, and started back. Bo followed right behind, slowly.

When Irish reached the door, she opened it. He stepped inside and waited until the dog came inside.

Flustered, she leaned down and picked up Bo. He settled happily into her arms and reached up to lick her face.

"He's better," Flaherty said, looking her up and down. She kept trying to think of him as Flaherty. Irish was too . . . personal. Intimate. Even now. Or maybe especially now.

She didn't miss the sudden fire in that gaze as it found the spot where her shirt ended.

It created a corresponding heat in her. "Thank you for taking him out," she said. She feared it was more a mumble.

"He let me know it was necessary," he said wryly.

She sat, and her hand rubbed Bo's ears, his favorite place. She felt guilty that she'd not taken him out earlier. Amy could feel her face turning red at the thought of what had diverted her from giving him the attention he deserved. She sought to change the subject. "Do you think I can get some clothes?"

"Yes," he said. "They have an officer in front and in back, but I see no reason why they won't let you have your clothes."

"My boxes?"

"Did you find anything in them?"

She looked into his eyes, wanting to know how much the answer to that question meant to him. "No. I went through most of them. I don't know why anyone would be interested in them."

"Your friend Jon had them for several weeks. Could he have removed something from them?"

A week ago she would have said that was impossible. She trusted Jon. Now she wondered whether she could trust anyone.

"I don't know," she said simply. "I don't know anything any more."

"Would you object to my going through them? I might see something you didn't."

She deliberated. She was getting nowhere on her own. She nodded. "Can we get them back from the police?"

"I think so. They have no reason to keep any of your possessions."

Amy looked up at him. "When do we leave here?" Not *I*. She needed that "we" at the moment.

"We'll be safe enough here for a couple of days. Police are crawling all over the place. The management said we can be their guests, though I suspect they would be happier if we leave."

She suddenly grinned. "I bet they would."

"On the other hand, I think the local police want us to stay. I don't think any of them has seen a murder before."

"It *was* pointed out to me that I shouldn't leave without letting them know," she replied.

He didn't reply.

"Irish?" It was the first time she'd tried the name on her lips.

He raised an eyebrow in question.

"Are you here because of your grandfather? Or are you part of an official investigation?" It was a question that had been worrying her. She still didn't totally trust him. Or his motives.

"It started because of my grandfather," he said.

"And now?"

"Oh, I still want to know what happened all those years ago, but not at your expense, or the expense of anyone else," he said.

"Then why did you begin probing in the first place?"

"Surely you had questions when the articles appeared?" he countered.

She remembered the moment she'd read the article. She hadn't believed it of her grandfather then, and she didn't now. She, too, had meant to research it.

"I had a lot of them," she said, "but I had my tenure hearing coming up, and I thought . . . later."

"Tell me about your grandfather." His voice was low and reassuring.

She shrugged. "Not much to tell, except he was disciplined and honest and demanding. I can't imagine him doing anything dishonorable. If anything, he expected too much of himself, and of others. Including my mother."

"In what way?"

"He wanted my mother to be like him. His wife—my grandmother—died when my mother was eight. He was gone much of the time, and my mother had one governess after another. She never felt he loved her. Instead, he demanded perfection from her. I think she tried, then discovered she could never meet his expectations, so she stopped trying. She rebelled in every way possible."

She was silent for a moment, then continued slowly. "She took a picture of him when she left, though, and she collected other photos over the years. Part of her never stopped wanting to be loved by him."

"And you? What did you think of him?"

"I hated him, even though my mother said I shouldn't. I knew he'd disapproved of her, and that was why she'd left. I didn't like anyone who disapproved of my mother." She looked at him. "When my mother died, I had to live with him. We went to war with each other. He wanted me to be the lady he'd tried to make my mother into. I resisted him with everything in me. I resented the fact that he was alive and my mother was dead."

"Who won?" he asked.

"Eventually both of us," she said. "I found him crying

one day when he was looking at my mother's photo. He was embarrassed at being seen, but for the first time I realized that he had really loved her. And that he loved me. He just never knew how to show it. Along about then, we declared a truce." She gave him a half smile. "I think that's when I discovered nothing was all black or all white."

"You loved him?"

"Very much, at the end. I always regretted it took me so long to understand how very complex he was. He had come from a family that had nothing. His father died in the coal mines when he was a boy, and his mother migrated to the city, where she cleaned people's houses. He could never understand why my mother didn't appreciate everything she had.

"He was a mustang," she added, "and he was proud of rising from the ranks. But he never forgot the slights he received because he wasn't a West Pointer. He'd had to fight for everything he ever got, and he never knew how to give an inch."

"He never gave an inch with you?"

"It took him a while. He didn't know anything about children. He was gone so much of my mother's childhood, and then he would come home and expect her to be like one of his privates. It wasn't meanness; he just didn't know any other way to do it."

Emotion registered in his eyes. Empathy? Understanding? He always seemed so well contained. At least until last night. But last night was an emotional outlet. Nothing more. And she was talking too much. She'd never talked much about her feelings for her grandfather before. Or her mother. Those memories were too private, too intense.

She could be garrulous about her work, and about superficial things. She'd never been any good at sharing intimate feelings. In fact, she often wondered if anyone really knew who she was. She sometimes wondered if she did herself. The contrast between her mother's carefree lifestyle and her grandfather's structured one had often made her question that.

She wanted to change the subject, and there was nothing like turning the tables.

But then his fingers went up to her face and caressed with exploratory gentleness. She forgot about turning the tables as the heat grew between them again. The sexual awareness they had shared intensified. Knowledge was there between them now. They were no longer two strangers bumbling in a new, enforced relationship. Instead, they had shared a close brush with death, and then let their emotions explode in bed.

Not wise, she told herself. Perhaps not a bond at all, but emotional overflow. Gratitude at being alive and wanting to experience that life to the furthest extent possible. And soon he would go back to his life, and she to hers.

But that was a cop-out, and she knew it. She was afraid. Not only of people trying to kill her, but of wanting something she couldn't have, of experiencing heaven, then losing it. This was something that couldn't last, that—given their own lives—was destined to end.

Still, his very touch was like a live electric wire snapping against her and charging through every nerve ending.

She wrenched away and swallowed hard, looking away from him toward the gray ocean and blue sky and fiery sun. She tried to slow the rapid beating of her heart and calm the need pooling inside her.

Take what is being offered. She wanted to, but that was the reckless side of her, the side she'd inherited from her mother—and was practiced at taming. *Don't get in any deeper. You still don't know what he's after.*

When she turned back to him, his eyes were masked and he'd moved several feet away, as if he knew she wanted—needed—distance.

"I'll see if I can get your clothes and laptop," he said.

"I'll go with you," she said.

He shook his head. "I'll probably have more luck on my own."

"The good old boy cop network?" She couldn't keep a hint of resentment from her voice.

"Something like that," he replied.

She hesitated. She wanted to demand to go with him, to make sure all her belongings were safe, even the accursed boxes. She'd noticed he had said nothing about the boxes to the police. Nor had she. She hadn't wanted them impounded again. Darn, there had to be something in them; otherwise, why was she being pursued?

But she also knew how she looked. Her clothes were wrinkled and, like his, had some blood spots. She hadn't taken a bath since the attack, and she felt nothing like the staid, respected, and respectable college professor she was supposed to be. She must smell like sex as well as blood.

Amy nodded. "I'll take a shower."

"You should be safe. The police are still going over your room, and they're keeping an eye on this one."

"You think someone would try again in the middle of the day?"

"Hell, I don't know what they would try," he said. "I do know they seemed determined for some reason." He paused. "I'll be right back."

There must have been doubt in her eyes, because he approached her again, touching her chin with his right index finger and forcing her gaze to meet his. "We will find out who and what," he said. "And there *will* be an end to it."

She could be dead by then. She still wasn't sure of his motives or his role in all this. She did know he apparently was the only protection she had. It was a galling fact. Even more galling was the fact that she seemed to be putty in his hands. He needed only to look at her. Time in a cold shower would be good.

Very good.

She didn't say anything, but moved away again. She went into the bathroom and slipped off the shirt. Her body was unnaturally hot, and when she looked in the mirror, she saw that her face was flushed. For a moment she looked at herself in the mirror. She had bruise marks on her shoulder where one of the assailants had grabbed her, and the ugly wound from a week ago.

More painful, though, was the want that still lingered in the core of her. She wanted—craved—the feelings she'd had this morning, the wonderful warmth of his body, and the exquisite sensations that followed.

But at what cost?

With a snort of disgust, she entered the shower, first turning on the hot water to cleanse herself, then the cold to cool rampaging feelings. It didn't seem to work. She was just as tingly as before, just as wanting.

And it wasn't only the safety she needed.

Irish traded a few war stories with the officers as one called and asked for permission to allow him to take Dr. Mallory's belongings.

One was particularly interested in the CID. "Nothing ever happens here," he complained. "Until last night," he added quickly after Irish raised an eyebrow. "Mostly just traffic accidents, a few hotel thefts, underage drinking on the beach."

Irish told him how to apply. Many CID agents were civilians, and he seemed like a bright kid, a little intimidated by Irish but not enough to cut him any slack or allow him to do anything without obtaining permission from a superior officer. Irish liked him. He would have told him to use his name, but his name might be more a detriment than a help in the future.

He knew he should call his commanding officer, even though he was on leave. He knew there must have been any number of calls to Doug Fuller. Doug would have to catch him first.

But not if he couldn't get in touch with Irish, and Irish could always justify not keeping in touch with the office by repeating Doug's own words. "Get the hell out of here and don't let me hear from you."

At least he hadn't said, "Don't let me hear *about* you."

It was semantics and it wouldn't wash, and Irish knew it. But at least he didn't have to disobey a direct command. It might not save his career, but neither would ignoring a call on his vacation be a court-martial offense.

He had absolutely no intention of leaving Amy Mallory to fend for herself. He still couldn't avoid the very real possibility that he might well be responsible for starting the chain of events. That made it essential that he take care of it.

She had, though, done a pretty good job of taking care of herself. He hadn't been flattering her when he said she had probably saved his life.

He couldn't forget that, and now her life, her future, was more important than his grandfather's reputation or the mystery surrounding the train. He knew only that their lives were now intimately linked.

Once the detective reluctantly gave his permission, Irish packed her suitcase, grabbed the food for the dog, and left. He would return for the laptop and boxes, he said. He thought about taking them with him, but he had several errands, and her possessions would undoubtedly be safer with law enforcement than in an empty motel room.

The water in the bathroom was still running when he returned. He put the clothes on one of the two double beds.

He looked at the messed bed, and remembered those few glorious moments. He couldn't remember when he'd last felt the emotions he'd experienced then. Amy Mallory had a combination of innocence and passion that was incredibly appealing.

He felt things he hadn't felt in a very long time. Tenderness. He had wanted to give as much as take.

Irish shook his head. He had to be careful. She was vulnerable now. Extraordinarily vulnerable. He shouldn't have given into temptation earlier, but it had been so spontaneous, so completely natural, so irresistible. . . .

And unfair to her. He knew that. He would have to keep his zipper closed. Then, perhaps when they knew each other better, when danger wasn't an aphrodisiac. . . .

But even then she would have to understand the ground rules. He'd decided years ago that his career and marriage would never mesh, and Amy, he sensed, was a forever kind of woman. She'd had enough pain during the past several weeks without him adding to it.

He had made an art out of noninvolvement in the past twenty years. To be good at his job, he'd had to; God knew the devastation and hatred he'd seen in Kosovo had demanded it. But it went deeper. He'd lost one father to war, another to divorce. His mother had been destroyed by the army.

Noninvolvement had centered his life. He had no intention of changing now. With this vow firmly in charge of his libido, he sought to dismiss the image of Amy in bed, her tousled hair framing her face, and the long, dark eyelashes that made those gray eyes mysterious and seductive. Even more daunting was erasing the memory of their lovemaking and turning his thoughts toward something more productive. Like how the bad guys had found her.

He ticked off one possibility after another, then decided to take a look at his rental car. Amy's assailants didn't seem to be after him. They had concentrated all their efforts on her. Still, he was thorough, or at least he tried to be.

He went outside, opened the trunk, and searched it carefully. Then the undercarriage of the sedan. Nothing. Next was the interior. He found the small GPS device tucked between the cushions in the backseat.

They hadn't followed Amy. They had followed him.

To get to her? Or to get to him?

He left the device in his car. For the moment it did no

harm. They knew where both he and Amy Mallory were. There would be a better time to discard it.

He wished he had a gun. His automatic had been taken by the police. He would head into Brunswick and buy a pistol. He shouldn't have any trouble with his credentials. He would certainly pass an instant check. He wanted one for Amy, too.

When he returned, Amy had dressed in clean clothes: a short-sleeve shirt and shorts. For the first time, he noticed how long and shapely her legs were; he'd been too busy earlier studying other parts of her anatomy. Her hair was wet, and short curls framed her face. She was sitting in the large chair looking out. The dog was in her lap.

She didn't look at him but obviously sensed his presence. "Do they know who the . . . dead man is?"

He shook his head. "He had no identification on him. No wallet. No credit card. No driver's license. They'll have to run his fingerprints through the computer."

She shuddered. That said something to her. She watched movies, read suspense novels. "That means he was a professional. . . ."

"Hit man?" he said. "It looks like it."

She was silent for a moment, obviously trying to digest the information. "Then there is more than one?"

He nodded. He noticed how valiantly she was trying to hold herself together. Her lower lip trembled. He wanted to reach out and comfort her, but something in her eyes warned him against it.

After a second, she asked, "And my laptop?"

"We can pick it and the boxes up later. I thought it and the files would be safer there for the time being."

"Can we leave here?"

"*You* can. I just shot a man. I think everyone's agreed it was self-defense, but there are some formalities."

Fear flickered across her face. He remembered how she'd felt early this morning. Soft and passionate and ever so receptive. Because of what she had gone through. In ten days, her house had been burned, she'd been shot, then someone tried to kill her at the hospital, and now this. . . .

She had fallen in his arms because of her need. The fear had to go somewhere, or she would break.

Or would she?

Amy Mallory was a survivor.

He went over and put his arm loosely around her shoulder. "I think your grandfather would be proud of you," he said.

"I don't know what to do next," she said slowly, pain in her eyes. "My tenure hearing is late next week. I have to be back."

He was aware of what a tenure hearing meant. It was success or failure. Those that did not achieve tenure usually lost their positions.

He wanted to promise that she could safely return by then. But he couldn't do that. He didn't believe in false promises. The only thing he could do was find an answer to the puzzle. The attackers apparently believed a key lay in Amy's boxes. But another key could be the grandchildren of the third staff officer, General Eachan. Might they have any ideas as to what happened to the missing gold and paintings?

Amy gently lowered the dog down to the floor, then stood.

"Do you think it would be safe to walk down to the beach?"

"The place is still crawling with the local gendarmes," he said. "I think it's the safest place you—we—can be."

"What about the FBI? Haven't my attackers crossed state lines?"

"We don't know that," he said. "And the local officials have to call them in."

"Can't you?"

He would have to go through Doug. Who would then order him back. There might well be a period of time where she had no protection. Maybe calling in the Bureau would be necessary, but he didn't think they could provide protection for her. There simply wasn't enough proof of a connection to a federal investigation. Someone had twice tried to kill a college professor. That's really all they had.

"Let's go for that walk," he said, holding out his hand. "I think the bad guys are a long way from here now."

He opened the sliding glass door. Bo stood and followed them as they went down the sidewalk toward the beach. Their particular section of the motel seemed curiously still. Irish wondered if most of the guests had left.

The beach, though, was crowded with families. And walkers. Joggers. Once more, he wished he had a gun. But on the other hand, he didn't see anyone wearing enough clothes to hide a weapon.

Amy's fingers tightened around his for a moment, then let go quickly, as if suddenly conscious of—and distrusting—the quiet intimacy. He could feel the tension in her body. Or had she just felt his own? He made himself relax.

The sand was hard, not sugary like so many other beaches. The water was gray rather than blue. Birds skittered over the sand while gulls competed with colorful kites as they soared in a cobalt blue sky. A breeze cooled the warm temperature. It was the kind of day made for vacations.

Not for running from murderers.

Bo stayed right with them. He walked stiffly, but his tail wagged. He stopped to sniff a piece of driftwood, then a dead sea creature. Amy's eyes didn't leave him.

They walked silently for a while. Gulls cried. Waves crashed. It all seemed so normal, Amy thought. It clashed against the fear she felt. She didn't think she would ever believe in normalcy again.

Her fingers burned from Irish's touch. She'd wanted to hold his hand, to clasp something strong and solid. But it was a lie. Oh, not that he wasn't strong and solid. But the emotions she'd allowed to run rampant weren't. He had been convenient. She'd been convenient. And the circumstances had created havoc.

It wasn't real, and she wasn't going to let it be real. She didn't want him to think he had to stay, or that she needed him as much as she did. She didn't want him to believe she felt she had a claim on him because of a few moments of passion.

Not just passion. Not just fear. Not just gratitude. There had been more. Much more. But it had been on her side. Men like Irish Flaherty didn't fall for mousy historians.

She didn't want him to feel obligated.

She tried to turn her attention to the sea. The sea she'd always loved. They could walk miles beneath those oaks, could escape the busy beach for secluded coves, but that would be dangerous. She'd never worried about danger before. She'd never not done something out of physical fear. She hated that feeling.

But the sun eased some of the tension, and the sound of the waves some of the terror. Both, however, made her even more aware of the man next to her, of the masculinity that oozed from his every pore.

They walked farther, and she noticed that he made sure there were other people around. She also noticed that the heads of females turned as they passed.

They sat on an old log and watched the shrimp boats some distance away. She still had trouble putting the two together—that peace and the violence of last night. The rhythms of life—the birds, the skittering small crabs, the children squealing as a wave washed away a sand castle— with the sound of bullets last night and the color red.

The rhythms of life this morning when they'd joined in a whirlwind of want and need. Why did she distrust it so? She shoved the thought aside.

Bo rose painfully and started exploring again. He wandered a little as enticing beach things apparently beckoned to him. Amy watched carefully as he moved a little farther down the beach.

A lone man whistled to him. Bo looked up, apparently undecided as to what to do. The man approached the dog, and suddenly Amy was up, running, calling his name in a shrill voice. Bo turned and started toward her.

The man shrugged and started walking again as she reached Bo and lifted him up. She realized she was shaking.

Flaherty reached her and put his hands on her shoulders. Safe. They were both safe.

For the moment.

Fear for the dog still washed through her like waves. The man was probably just a dog lover.

Probably.

The fast beating of her heart slowed. But fear remained.

Would she ever see a stranger again without wondering if he wanted to kill her?

thirteen

GEORGIA

Amy hated guns. She was a gun control advocate. She was for a waiting period of forever. She had berated her congressman and senators for not supporting such a ban.

And now she stared down at a pistol in her hand, then looked at the target in front of her at the pistol range. Common sense mingled with revulsion. She would no longer be entirely helpless. She despised that feeling, knowing that it justified something she felt was entirely wrong. Too many guns in the country. Too many accidents.

She was angry. Angry at being forced into being a hypocrite. Angry with whoever was responsible for destroying not only her life but her values. Angry with Flaherty for making her see it was necessary.

They had bought two guns at a gun shop in Brunswick. Flaherty had purchased them, because he had both a badge and a carry permit. She applied for her own permit, but it would be several days before it could go through. Still, she could learn how to use the thing. And she would break the law by keeping it near her at all times.

Today was a first for many things. She'd never consciously broken a law before. Not even a speeding law.

The gun felt like a snake in her hand as they entered the firing range. Flaherty had picked it out for her, bypassing the ugly, large pistols for this small, titanium featherweight model. She'd always thought a pistol would be heavy, awkward, but this weighed practically nothing. How could something this light be so deadly?

It was, according to Flaherty. It might not have the range of the heavier pistol he'd purchased for himself, but it had, he said, plenty of stopping power.

His own choice was heavy and lethal-looking. She watched him check it over with an ease and familiarity that sent chills through her. Despite his shooting one of her assailants the night before last, she'd not thought about the fact that his entire life involved weapons and danger. That competence, for which she was grateful the other night, now set him apart. He was someone who lived in an entirely different universe.

It had never been more clear when they stood in the gun shop. Her insides churned while he talked knowledgeably about an assortment of weapons and handled them as if they were a part of him.

The final realization came when she figured out why he was wearing a shirt over his T-shirt. Along with the gun, he'd purchased a belt holster, and she'd watched as he efficiently snapped it on his belt and fitted the gun into it. The shirt covered the weapon.

He'd handed the other to her. "It's a .38 Smith and Wesson," he said. "Five bullets."

He might have been talking about a box of cereal, he said it all so matter-of-factly.

"Try it," he said.

She'd picked it up gingerly.

"There are no bullets in it," he reassured her.

That didn't matter. It was still a gun. But she would be damned if she let him know how queasy it made her feel. Could she ever actually fire it? She wasn't sure.

She was surprised at how well it fitted into her hands . . .

Now he actually wanted her to fire it. He showed her

how to load it, then how to hold it. "Brace yourself. Plant both feet solidly on the ground." He wrapped his fingers around hers, and her back was against his hard body. She felt the heat from both places. His body heat went directly to a place terribly sensitive to it, and his fingers burned hers and sent tingling up through her arm.

She tried to concentrate. His hand was still on hers when she fired, surprised at the *pop* that came from the barrel. The shot the other night had been much louder. This one was higher-pitched, softer.

She'd also expected the gun to jerk, but it didn't.

Even with his help, she missed the target. She had no idea where the bullet went.

He released her hand and stepped back. "Try it on your own."

Amy tried to concentrate, tried to think of the article in her hand as a sporting item, not a deadly weapon. She aimed; squinted at the target, which featured the outline of a man; and fired. She hit the edge of the cardboard. Not the body. Not any of its appendages.

"Again," Flaherty said mercilessly.

She sensed that her bad aim came from her lack of enthusiasm. She didn't want to shoot anyone, not even a cardboard outline.

"What if he was shooting at you?" Flaherty whispered behind her, as if reading her mind.

She tried again. The third bullet.

It missed.

"What if he was shooting at me?"

She missed again.

"What about Bojangles?"

This time she didn't miss.

He chuckled. "Now I know where I rate."

She turned and looked at him solemnly. The slight smile disappeared from his face. He disregarded the other shooters—mainly male—and put his hand to her face.

"It's not a joke to me," she said in a voice that broke despite her best efforts. She turned to go, and he caught her arm.

"I'm sorry," he said. "Please don't go. This is important."

Amy felt her face flush. She felt like a ten-year-old afraid of the dark, not a grown-up someone with such a deeply held antipathy for guns. Her mind flipped back to when she was a girl. . . .

"Hold the gun. Aim it. Damn it, girl, can't you do anything?" Her grandfather's voice. Demanding. Querulous.

She didn't want to. Her mother had hated guns. She'd learned to hate them.

"Do it, girl!"

She pulled the trigger, heard the noise. Then dropped the gun in front of her grandfather.

Four years later, he had taken a gun and killed himself. She'd walked in his study and found him. . . .

The memory was too strong. Her hand lowered with the pistol in it. She almost dropped the pistol.

"Amy?"

She turned and looked at him. The memory flash hadn't happened two nights ago when Flaherty had shot the intruder. Why now?

She closed her eyes and willed herself to lift her arm again.

"Amy?"

His voice was both intrusive and welcome. How could it be both? But then she'd had so many contradictory feelings. Memories revived. Mostly bad. She'd thought she'd banished them into some mental trunk.

"It's all right," she said.

"I don't think it is," he said slowly. "Something happened."

"A lot has happened," she replied, wanting to change the subject.

"Will you try it again?"

"I know how to pull the trigger," she replied.

"But will you? Can you?"

"I don't know," she said honestly.

"Again," he coaxed. "Don't worry about Bo. Concentrate."

But she did worry about Bo. She hadn't wanted to leave the dog in the motel. They had taken him into the gun shop, which had a firing range in the back. The owner had agreed to let Bo stay in his office while Flaherty showed her how to use the weapon.

Anxious to leave now, she aimed once more and shot. This time she hit the edge of a leg. "Satisfied?" she asked Flaherty.

"Once more. Reload. Then we'll go."

Amy swallowed hard, then shot one more time. She simply couldn't aim for the heart. She hit a cardboard leg, then, without looking at Flaherty, she reloaded just as he had shown her.

"Satisfied?" she asked a little bitterly, even as she realized it was unfair. He was trying to help her. He *had* helped her. He'd saved her life. But she still resented being forced into doing something that went against every fiber of her being. While she knew it wasn't his fault, he was the nearest target.

"No," he said mildly, "but it will do. Let's get Bo and something to eat. Then I'll check and see if anyone has identified our John Doe."

She handed him her pistol.

"Put it in your handbag," he instructed.

"I don't have the permit."

He looked at her for a moment. It wasn't condescending. More like patient. He expected her to do the reasonable thing. She really disliked him for doing that: forcing her to make a decision she didn't want to make.

She put it in her handbag. "If I drop it, and it goes off, it will be your fault," she said.

He didn't smile. Apparently he'd learned that nothing

about this was a smiling matter to her. "It won't," he assured her.

They stopped in front of the counter and the clerk, who happened to be a dog lover, opened the office door. Bo wriggled with delight at seeing them. She knew from her own bruises that it must hurt. It was hard, though, for him to contain his exuberance as far as she was concerned. She leaned down and picked him up. "Time for a hamburger," she told him.

He barked as if he knew exactly what she was saying.

"Thank you," she said to the clerk.

He grinned. He was a big guy. He looked as if he walked out of a good ole boy white supremicist movie, but his smile was genuine and she couldn't help but return it. "How did it go, little lady?"

"She was a whiz," Flaherty said.

Amy wanted to hit them both. "Little lady," indeed. And "Whiz" wasn't much better.

"Now don't you forget," the clerk said, "you need that permit. Until you get it, the gun belongs to the colonel."

Amy suddenly knew it had not been for her benefit that he'd kept Bo. It was for *the colonel*, who Amy suspected was the clerk's ideal role model.

A model she'd been raised to distrust.

Irish stopped at a seafood market and bought two pounds of fresh shrimp, then went to a supermarket and disappeared inside while Amy sat inside the car with the dog. The doors of the car were locked, the windows up, the air-conditioning running. The pistol was in her purse.

Still, he hurried. He picked up some potatoes, some corn, butter, milk, and a few other items. After a moment's consideration, he added a six-pack of beer.

Then he hurried out. She was still there. No one appeared to be taking undue interest. Which was good. He wasn't at all sure she would use the weapon. She had disarmed one of her attackers, but she hadn't had to do more.

Her obvious distaste for weapons, he surmised, must have come from her mother. Certainly not from her grandfather.

Still, she had tried. She would know what to do if attacked again.

They didn't say anything on the way back. She held her dog, and he concentrated on checking the traffic around him, though now he knew there was an easier way to track his movements than tailing the car.

He was only too aware of the rigid position of Amy's body. Firing the gun, for some reason, had affected her deeply. She hadn't wanted to do it. He sensed it had taken a great deal of willpower.

It was another facet of a complex person who fascinated him. She'd showed no hesitation in striking one of the attackers, especially after her dog had been kicked. She'd really not shown great sympathy for the dead man. She had shown fear, but he was only too aware that real courage came despite fear.

In twenty minutes they were back at the motel on the island. A yellow crime scene tape still blocked off her room.

He stepped from the car, keys in his hand. Amy didn't wait for him to open her door and scooted out, Bo right beside her.

Irish glanced around, then unlocked the motel door with his left hand, the fingers of his right on the revolver. He walked in carefully, looking first in the bathroom, then past the two double beds to the living area. No one there, but there was a figure sitting outside on one of the patio chairs.

Hell. He knew who it was before the figure rose and turned around, although Irish could have sworn the newcomer couldn't have seen them from his position.

Amy had walked in behind him, carrying the bag of groceries. She stopped abruptly at seeing the man at the patio doors.

Irish sighed. He placed the Glock on a table. "Don't worry," he said. "It's my boss."

Her eyes widened, but she merely nodded as she set the groceries on the table.

Irish went over to the door, and unlocked it. He went out, closing the door behind him.

"Doug," he acknowledged. They had been on a first-name basis since they were classmates at West Point. The fact that now Doug Fuller was a bird colonel, and Irish only a lieutenant colonel hadn't affected that, even when Doug had become his commanding officer after Irish returned from Kosovo.

"Obviously," Doug said, as Irish limped across the patio. "You didn't answer your phone."

"I'm on vacation."

"That's why I'm getting calls nearly every day from every law enforcement agency in the southeast?"

Irish winced. "I'm sorry about that."

"That's it?"

"There's a lady in distress."

"That I believe," Doug Fuller said. "Now let the police handle it. It's not your job." He paused. "I've had some calls from Washington. You have a new assignment. A command position has just come open. In Hawaii," he added with a grin.

It was one of the dream assignments in CID. At one time, he would have grabbed it. Even if it was a desk job. But now . . . it didn't seem so important. There was the ranch . . . and Amy.

"I have more days of leave left."

Doug stared at him as if he'd just turned purple. "It's being canceled."

"I can't leave her now. It might be my fault she's in danger. The police won't give her protection." He turned back and looked in the window. Amy was putting away the groceries. "There've been three attempts on her life."

Doug hesitated. "I'll ask for FBI protection."

"There's no evidence of a federal crime."

"Damn it, Irish. Neither of us are being given a choice.

Orders are orders. Why in the hell do you think I flew to this godforsaken place? You'll face a court-martial if you don't return."

"I can't, Doug."

Irish could see Doug look inside the room. "She must be one hell of a. . . ."

"Lady," Irish finished. "And she is. I would have been killed if she hadn't elbowed a bad guy."

"Gratitude, guilt, or lust?"

Irish grinned. "A little of all three."

Doug didn't smile. "You're risking everything."

"I'd rather risk my career than Amy Mallory's life."

"I'm going to have to meet this paragon."

"It's not only Miss Mallory," Irish said, belatedly trying to be circumspect. "It's my grandfather. His name was put into question in that report."

"No accusations were made."

"They were implied," Irish said, "and I can't help believing that what has happened to Miss Mallory stems from my inquiries. If so, someone is afraid of what further investigation might find."

"You might find that your grandfather was responsible," Doug said.

"Then so be it," Irish said. "If he was, I wouldn't protect him. But I can't believe it. He pounded honor, duty, country into me." He paused. "Give me a few days."

"You know what you're asking," Doug said softly.

"Yes." It was difficult for Irish to answer. They had a lot of history between them, and he didn't like putting Doug in this position. He didn't see another choice.

"All right. I'll say you've left Georgia. I expect you to do that. God knows how they know, but headquarters heard about the killing last night."

"By the way," Irish said, "who called you about my transfer?"

Doug hesitated again, signed. "General Wade."

"Kinda sudden, isn't it?"

"I'm told Colonel Banner was in an accident."

Irish stilled. "An accident?"

Doug nodded. "He wasn't killed, but he's critical."

"Hit and run?" Irish guessed.

Doug looked at him. "How. . . ."

"A professor who had some of Amy Mallory's papers was involved in a hit and run a week ago. He wasn't so lucky."

"Go to the feds. You can't do anything alone."

"I don't trust anyone now," Irish said. "You have to admit my reassignment is pretty surprising. Someone very high-level is making things happen."

From the look on Doug's face, Irish knew he thought the same thing.

Irish held out his hand. "Thanks," he said. "I owe you."

"It's your ass. I didn't see you."

"Come in and meet Amy. . . ."

"I think it's better if I don't."

Irish nodded. "How's Judith?"

"Sad. Our first is off to college in eight weeks."

Irish felt a slight ache in his heart. He'd been to dinner several times at Doug's house. His kids were boys, twelve, fifteen, and seventeen. There had been an affection between the parents and children that had touched him, that had almost made him question his choices. Almost.

And Doug might be risking his career for him.

"I'll be off, then," Doug said. "Try to keep in touch and be back at the base on the twenty-first."

"I'll be there."

"Take care, Irish."

"Yes, sir."

Amy wished she could hear from a distance. She wasn't above snooping, but it would be pretty obvious if she opened the door, and her hearing wasn't good enough to go through glass.

Yet she realized from Flaherty's expression that it had gone the way he wanted it to. *And what was that?*

Would he stay with her?

Bo had gone over to the door, looking like a lovelorn suitor. So much for loyalty.

Amy wondered about starting to boil the shrimp. Would there be two of them? Or three?

Then she saw the man in uniform leave. Flaherty stood where he was for a moment, then opened the door and came inside.

"We have to leave tonight," he said.

"Why?"

"I've just been reassigned," he said with his lips quirking in that appealing way. "They want me immediately."

"Then. . . ."

"I talked my commanding officer into giving me a few more days. But he made it clear we shouldn't stay here."

"A reassignment?" Amy was trying to keep up with what he was saying.

"A command post. There's an opening because of a hit and run."

That did soak in. "Oh, my God," she said.

"Doug is an old friend. He won't tell anyone he saw us. But we have to get out of here."

"The police?"

"I'll see about getting your laptop and boxes. There's really no reason to hold them."

"Supper?"

He hesitated, then shrugged. "We'll leave immediately after."

An icy finger ran down her back. "Why didn't he come inside?"

Flaherty came over to her. "He didn't want to know anything."

"But *can* we leave?"

"The police, you mean?"

She nodded.

"We've been released. Though we've been warned not to leave the area, there are no charges pending. There's really nothing they can do."

But it would hurt his career. "He thought you should return to duty?"

"He understands why I can't," Flaherty said, then turned away.

Did he? Or was Irish risking his job for her? As well as his life?

Irish stifled his apprehension as he went next door. They should leave immediately. But one good meal wouldn't hurt. And he would get everything packed while she got dinner ready.

He went outside and unlocked his rental car. He looked around, then reached in the backseat and took out the GPS device that had been planted there. He walked down the rows of cars until he found one with a West Virginia plate. He looked inside the car. It was locked.

Irish continued until he found an unlocked car. Tennessee plates. Good enough. With luck, the driver would be going west toward Tennessee. Their pursuers might believe they were returning to Memphis. He looked around, then quickly opened the back door and tucked the device underneath the seat.

Then he strode to the yellow-taped room. Minutes later, he had packed Amy's laptop and boxes in the trunk of the car. Then he went in to eat.

Irish enjoyed the shrimp, particularly after the junk food they had had for the past several days. They left the rest of the groceries in the unit. It was dusk when they went out to the car.

Irish saw her look at the ocean just before they left. Her face was strained.

He waited for a moment. Then she seemed to stiffen, leaned down and picked up Bo, and followed him out the door. "Where to?"

No complaints. No tears. No questions. She was indeed a trouper.

"Somewhere we can go over those boxes together," he said.

"What if they find us again?"

"They won't," he said.

"How do you know?"

"They planted the GPS computer in *my* car. I planted it somewhere else."

"How did they know you would come after me?"

"I don't know, Amy. Maybe there was one in yours, too."

"Could there be more of . . . those devices in the car?"

"I don't think so. I've been all over it."

"Where is the device now?"

"A car in the parking lot. It has Tennessee plates. It would make sense that you were returning."

She nodded, but her face looked forlorn. He guessed what she was thinking. When was she going to be able to return?

He wanted to reassure her, but he couldn't. He couldn't lie to her. He still didn't know what was happening, nor why someone was sending professional killers after a college professor. He didn't know, but he sure as hell intended to find out.

fourteen

Irish drove for several hours up to Charleston. They stopped there at a rental car agency and traded in the car for another one. He had no choice but to use his credit card, but at least he knew there wouldn't be any little devices planted in the new rental. He hoped the pursuers, if there were any, were concentrating on the Tennessee car rather than his credit card charges.

They bought food at a convenience mart, then ate it at a rest stop where Amy could walk Bojangles. With the dog resting between them on the front seat, they headed north along I-95. He planned to stop in Myrtle Beach. Plenty of tourists. And plenty of cheap motels, the kind that didn't ask for identification.

Before leaving Jekyll Island, Amy had called her insurance company and arranged for her car to be picked up and repaired when the police finished with it. Since the bad guys obviously knew where she was, all subtlety went by the board.

Everyone also knew the identity she'd been using. That had been a bit of a problem with the police when they discovered she'd registered at the motel under a false name and gave a false license tag number. She had explained somewhat awkwardly that she used a friend's name because of fear.

The police hadn't questioned that, not with the Memphis police backing her story. But Irish had more curiosity about it. Model Citizen Amy Mallory didn't seem the type to have false identities tucked away.

"Did that identification really belong to a friend?" he asked after they'd ridden in silence for an hour.

Amy was still for a moment, and he didn't think she would answer. Then, very softly, she said, "It belonged to my mother. She sometimes traveled with someone wanted by the police. One of them made her this identity. It's been . . . sitting in a box for years."

"You surprise me, Dr. Mallory."

"I learned some unusual things from her and the 'uncles' who came and went."

He bet she did. He knew something about her background, but not the details. He wondered what kind of impact it had had on her. She seemed remarkably well-adjusted to him, but he wondered whether beneath that disciplined exterior there weren't some underlying traumas.

And she wasn't always as cool and disciplined as she liked others to believe. He'd had a brief taste of wildness, a passion that had been unbridled. What else was there under her cool exterior?

She was a contradiction. Prim and proper when he'd first met her, but willing to run away with a forged identity, apparently without any compunction. She disabled an armed gunman and cried over a dog. He saw fear in her eyes, but she had never asked him for help.

She was strong and resilient and resourceful. She was also appealingly vulnerable. Now those qualities were running together in an irresistible package.

He wanted to know more about her mother. A general's daughter turned war protester and flower child. Arrested once for drug possession. Put on probation. Then she'd fled the state and changed her name. Her legal name of

Mallory hadn't surfaced again until she'd died. That much he knew from his own investigation.

"Tell me about your mother," he said. She'd talked about her grandfather but had said little about her mother.

"She was very loving," Amy said, "but not very wise in picking her friends. She often took in ... protesters wanted by the police, or drug dealers who used her sympathies to get her help. She would give her last dime to someone she thought needed it more. In fact, if she saw a one-armed person, she would probably cut off her own arm and give it to them. People recognized that. And used it. But she never changed."

"How did she support you?"

"Usually waitressing. She was also good at crafts. She made dolls and bears, and dresses for both. Happy things. She was the ultimate optimist."

He considered all that. "And your grandfather? How did she feel about him?"

"Sad. But she didn't trust him. She was afraid he would try to take me away from her. One time, she said it might be better for me if he did." Her hands nervously stroked Bo. "I never thought so. I always wanted to be with her." Her voice faded.

Irish was fascinated. There was more to the story. A lot more. "Why didn't she trust him?"

She was silent for a moment. "She had thought she was in love. She was seventeen, and he was twenty-two and a Vietnam war protester. My grandfather had him arrested for statutory rape."

She hadn't told him that before when she'd talked about her grandfather. How many other secrets were there? But he'd learned that silence was the best prompter. He waited.

"The man died in jail. I never knew exactly how or why. I tried to find out. The newspaper account said he was beaten by other inmates. That's when my mother ran away. My grandfather didn't know, but she was pregnant then;

she was afraid he would force her to get an abortion or give up the baby."

"You were the child."

"Yes," she said softly. "My mother could no more kill a child of hers than accept the injustice of what happened to the man she loved. But she didn't have good care when I was born, and she couldn't have other children. I think that's one reason we lived as we did, even when the anti-war movement was over and other people moved on. She always wanted to be around children. When people drifted away from communes, she usually found someone for us to bunk with, or them with us. She needed to be needed, even if sometimes she was more child than adult."

"It takes strength to live that kind of life," he said. "To be true to your own values."

She looked surprised. "I suppose in some ways she was," she said. "In other ways, very naive. She accepted anyone who had any kind of cause, and that often got her in trouble. She just wanted to see good in everyone."

"Except your grandfather?"

"Oh, even him, I think. She didn't tell me everything that had happened between him and my father. She told me part of the story—that my father was unjustly imprisoned and killed, and that she left home to take care of me. My grandfather told me the rest of it; he'd never forgiven himself for what happened."

"But she never contacted him?"

"I think she was afraid he would try to take me and raise me 'properly.'"

"Would he have?"

"I think he would have tried at one time. He hadn't known she was pregnant. I showed up on his doorstep as a distinct surprise." She hesitated. "I hated him for a long time. He had a big house and a lot of money, and I remembered what a hard time my mother and I often had. I thought she would have lived longer if she'd had good medical care.

"It took me a long time to realize that it was the life she chose. And I can never say she was unhappy with it. She marched to a different drummer. She didn't care about money or possessions. Only causes. She attended nearly every demonstration in town. I grew up carrying signs."

"But you didn't keep carrying them?"

"No. I suppose I had too much of my grandfather in me. Although I loved my mother, I always longed for a home and security. I wanted to be good at what I chose to do. But I have a bit of her passion for justice, even if I didn't agree with all her causes."

"And she's why your field is protest movements?"

"Sometimes I knew more than I wanted to know," she said. "But yes, I suppose I was drawn to what had drawn her."

"How old were you when she died?"

"Fifteen. She was ill for several months. Most of her friends had disappeared or died or gone to jail. She made me promise to contact my grandfather."

He allowed her to talk at her own speed. He had put the car on cruise control, and he stretched out his legs, trying to relax his aching body.

But she didn't continue, and he didn't push.

Instead she leaned against the door and looked at him. He didn't take his eyes from the road, but he could feel the intensity of her gaze. He felt himself growing warm, but not because of lust. Instead it was the intimacy that bounced around inside the car.

Words would have shattered it. They were bound together by her earlier comments, ones he suspected she had seldom uttered before. And bound by violence and danger, and a baffling mystery.

And now she trusted him. If not completely, then more than anyone else at the moment. He was damned determined to fulfill that trust.

The question had been where to go. He had only a little money and his credit cards, and he wouldn't be surprised that whoever was after Amy had the resources to trace any credit purchases he—or she—made.

He'd thought about contacting some of his friends, but all of them were either military or law enforcement. He didn't want to get them involved in something that might well hurt their careers. Not unless he had to. He still felt guilty about Doug, and the position he'd put him in.

Irish had never felt comfortable about asking for favors.

After looking at the map, he'd confirmed his thoughts on Myrtle Beach. He'd sensed how much Amy liked the beach and the ocean, and they needed a couple of days both to relax and to go over her grandfather's papers. It was a resort area, filled with tourists, and that was another plus.

The problem, of course, was renting a place without giving identification. It would have to be less than the finest accommodations. But at the moment, any bed would look good to him.

He looked at the clock. Four in the morning. The last road sign said thirty miles. He started looking for the type of motel that expected more John Does than not.

The smell of ocean was back with them. Amy had rolled down her window and leaned her head back. She must be exhausted. Neither of them had had much sleep in the pasty forty-eight hours.

Another twenty miles, and he saw row after row of motels. He picked one—obviously an independent—with a vacancy sign and drove to the office. They would look for something else tomorrow.

Surprisingly, Amy was wide awake. She'd said nothing for the last hour.

"Stay here," he said. He half expected a protest, but none came, only a soft sigh.

Irish paid cash for a double room with two beds. He hesitated before doing it, but two rooms required two names, and perhaps questions. And he wanted to keep an eye on her. He scribbled John Huey on the registration card. It was a byline he remembered from some newspaper and thought it far better than John Doe. He added a fictitious license tag number.

Amy raised an eyebrow after he drove to a room and led her to it.

"We're sharing," he said. "I'm not taking my eyes off you for the next several days."

She didn't protest. She didn't agree. He wondered whether she had reached the limit of her strength. Hell, no one had a better right.

Dark. Hands. Reaching for her. Terror. She tried to hide under the cover like a hermit crab retreating into its shell. Please. Please. Go away. Then she was screaming. . . .

"Amy . . ."

Hands again. Grabbing at her.

Then she felt arms go around her. Not rough or hostile.

"Amy." The voice came again. Gentle. Comforting. The fear stared to fade.

Her eyes flickered open. Her head felt heavy, her throat thick, her mouth dry.

"It's all right, Amy. You're safe." Hands were on her. This time, warm, comforting hands. Even possessive hands. Bo whined plaintively beside the bed.

The memories came flooding back. The men bursting into her room. The gunshot. So loud in the confines of the small room. A shiver of fear remained.

She looked up at him. Pale light was creeping through the drawn curtains behind him. His hair was mussed, and his cheeks had a golden stubble again. He wore jeans but no shirt, and he looked obscenely attractive. The proximity of his body, and the heat radiating from it, comforted her, warming the chill that pushed her under the covers.

He held her for a moment, then she inched away, embarrassed. She'd been embarrassed when they had gotten ready for bed last night. Fortunately they had both been too tired to do much more than fall into their respective beds.

Amy was only too aware they'd slept together the night earlier, but that, she'd told herself, had been reaction to near death. Nothing more.

That's all this is, too.

But despite the warmth of his hand that still held hers, the panic didn't subside, and she knew part of it came from being so close to him.

Her entire world had been turned upside down. All the sanity she worked so hard to construct was gone. And now she was in a motel room with a man she barely knew. It didn't help that he had twice saved her life. He had appeared at the same time as the violence. She had slept with him after only a few conversations.

She didn't know him, or what he wanted. The fact that she had fallen so easily under his protection panicked her even more than the nightmare that had returned after many years. *Don't trust.*

Yet she had. She wanted to. She needed to.

Could there be anything as awkward as waking up with a lover who was a stranger? Even a stranger with whom she'd shared several more than traumatic events? She didn't think so. The silence grew heavy between them, and she knew her eyes were probably something less than friendly.

She saw him straighten. His hand slipped away from her, and he stood.

Bo crawled up on the bed, and she hugged him, a distraction—a needed distraction—from the tall man beside her. She was very aware that she wore only the long T-shirt she usually slept in, that her hair was probably sticking out at every impossible angle.

The last few days had been a blur of pain, fear, and confusion. And now desire accompanied those feelings. It only increased the sense of bewilderment, loss of control, loss of reality, loss of who she was—or thought she was.

Irish combed his hair with his fingers. "You look comfortable. Why don't I take a shower first, then you? We'll get some breakfast and look for somewhere a little better to stay."

Again those conflicting feelings. She didn't want him to leave. He looked so solid and safe . . . and appealing as he was. But the sexual tension that was always between them was rising, too. She didn't need that distraction.

In fact, she needed time alone to think. To assess.

She nodded, and watched as he disappeared into the bathroom.

She'd thought she wanted time alone to think. But that wasn't possible when she heard the water run, and her mind went to the image of Irish Flaherty standing in the shower with steam rising around him.

It made steam rise around her.

She used the remote to click on the television. She wondered whether there would be anything on the news about the death on Jekyll Island. She also wondered whether the world was continuing as always for millions of people while her own had turned lopsided.

It was. A celebrity interview occupied one station, a cooking segment another. She turned to CNN, only to hear market news. The stock market was up.

Good for it.

But the noise was, in an odd way, comforting.

She finally rose and went to her purse, digging out a brush and running it through her hair. She looked in the mirror over a low dresser. Her eyes were bloodshot, her face pale without makeup. Her gray eyes were uncertain, deepened by dark shadows ringing them. Her hair looked lank. Not even the brush helped.

Did all men look better than women when they got out of bed? Or was *she* just plagued?

She went over to the boxes that Irish had brought in. She wondered whether he would discover anything she hadn't. He was a trained investigator, but she was a trained historian, schooled to find the oddity.

And if he did find something? What would he do with it?

Such speculation ran nowhere. The shower had stopped, and she heard the sink faucet turn on. He would probably be shaving now.

Damn it. She'd never been so unable to concentrate on one thing before. Her mind was spinning like a whirling dervish.

Because you don't want to concentrate. You don't want to remember blood exploding on you. You don't want to remember feeling so close to death. You don't want to remember someone holding a gun on you. You don't want to think about Irish Flaherty or what he wants or what will happen when he finds it.

She went to the window, opened the draperies, and looked outside. Rain clouds had darkened the sky and the parking lot despite the fact that it was morning. Rain splashed in the parking lot, and puddles were evidence that it had been falling for some time.

The door to the bathroom opened. Steam drifted into the room, as did a light clean scent.

"See anything?" he asked. His voice, deep and rumbling, rolled across the room.

"Just rain," she said as she turned to face him. His light brown hair was damp, his face was clean-shaven. He wore faded, snug-fitting blue jeans and a T-shirt. She watched as he pulled on a long-sleeve shirt and rolled up the sleeves, leaving the front unbuttoned, then saw him attach his gun holster to the back of his belt. A chill ran through her. He did it as casually as someone might pull on a pair of shoes.

She tried to keep the distaste from her eyes, but when his gaze met hers, his eyes were quizzical and one side of his mouth was turned up in question.

"I'll take Bo out while you use the shower," he offered after a moment's silence, his eyes growing neutral.

"Thank you," she said formally, feeling like a fool but not sure what else to say. Bo, however, broke the awkwardness. He had perked up at the word *out,* and was standing next to the door.

Flaherty, too, seemed unsure of what to say, and that was certainly uncharacteristic.

"You won't need a leash. He trusts you now. He will stay right on your heels."

"He's well trained."

"Not really. He just doesn't want to get lost."

Banalities. They were talking like the strangers they were, not the lovers they had been. Distant. Matter-of-fact. Not as if killers were after them or they had shared death as well as a bed.

But he didn't say anything else. Instead, he opened the door. "Come on, Bo," he said, and the dog followed. She felt a moment's betrayal, even though she was pleased that her dog had accepted him, and he apparently liked Bo. He was, in fact, a natural with him, which meant he was a natural with other animals as well. One could not fake that.

If nothing else, that one thing had added to her trust. She trusted him with her physical safety if little else.

She pulled a pair of slacks and knit shirt from her suitcase, along with her small personal kit with its toothbrush, toothpaste, and minimum makeup. She found a little bottle of shampoo on the counter, which surprised her, then stepped into the shower. She'd always heard that cold showers cooled the heated beast. Hopefully, it might do that now.

She turned the water on and shivered as she was struck by what seemed to be little pieces of ice. Despite the shock, she let it run. After several minutes she turned on hot water and washed her hair.

She would cope. She would use this day to return to normal, as normal as one could be under the circumstances. There was still her tenure hearing. Still responsibilities that called her back to a world she knew and understood and wanted. She let the water run until it started to grow cold, and then she stepped out.

The scent of his aftershave still filled the room. A wet towel had been neatly folded and placed on the sink counter. All his toiletries had been returned to a small leather case.

Stop it, she told herself. Her thoughts were drifting dangerously again.

She looked for a hair dryer, but there was none. She supposed she should be grateful for the shampoo. Using a towel to blot up water, she settled for combing her hair, then adding a touch of lipstick.

Breakfast. Another motel. And always the specter of masked men and guns. She took a deep breath. She would survive this. She would solve the mystery. She would get tenure.

She would remember this as an . . . adventure. Flaherty would remain a . . . partner. She would not become involved with a man she knew so little about. She didn't even know whether he already had a relationship with a woman. Maybe even a wife, though she deeply doubted that. But even the thought of him with another woman hurt. And that was humiliatingly excruciating.

And then there was the fact that she had given herself into his care so easily. She couldn't remember when she hadn't taken care of herself. She'd been the caretaker in her family far more than her mother had been. She'd taken pride in that, and in taking care of herself.

It was time to start taking care of herself again, to stop allowing events to twist her in the wind.

She gathered everything together and went into the other room.

It was still empty. Amy packed everything in her suitcase, then looked out the window.

No Flaherty. No Bo.

Panic started eating at her again.

She grabbed the key and went outside. The car, parked ten spaces down, was still there. Then she saw them. Flaherty was talking to someone. A tall man whose face was turned away from her.

Bo was almost standing on Flaherty's feet.

She waited, willing the stranger to turn around. He didn't, but he gestured toward the road. Directions. She tried to relax. Flaherty was just asking for directions.

Still, as she turned around and went back into the room, an odd disquiet accompanied her.

fifteen

Dustin had asked to be informed about Colonel Flaherty. He hadn't expected to be informed quite so quickly.

"He just killed a man down on the Georgia coast," his informant said. "It was obviously self-defense. A woman was being attacked."

"A Dr. Mallory?" Dustin asked, a sinking feeling in his gut. Things were getting worse and worse.

"Yes."

"Is he being held?"

"No."

Dustin swore under his breath.

"No charges, then?"

"No."

"Where is he now?"

"He disappeared. So did the woman. The police are not happy. They had a few more questions to ask, even though he wasn't a suspect in anything. They considered him one of them—a law officer—and they thought he would stick around."

"The FBI wouldn't make that assumption," Dustin said.

"No. But we haven't been called in. Our interest is totally unofficial, just as you asked."

"I understand he received new orders."

Silence. Then, "You know more than we do. The police down there said Flaherty's group commander says he's on well-deserved leave and doesn't check in with him."

"The police didn't check while Flaherty was in their offices."

"Only to confirm his identity. It wasn't until he disappeared that they started asking more questions."

"And of course he doesn't have a cell phone?" Dustin knew it was a foolish question.

"Out of order. Someone like him wants to disappear, he can disappear, and he's not due back for another week."

"And Flaherty made damn sure he couldn't be found so he couldn't be ordered back."

"Something like that."

Now it was important that Dustin find him, too, or at least know where he was poking around. "Can you look for him? Unofficially?"

"Not without a lot of people knowing about it. Do you want that?"

No, he did not. He'd wanted this whole matter to die of old age and disinterest. Someone else obviously didn't. He remembered Jordan's vague threat. What did he know? And how did he know it?

"Can you check someone else's background?"

"Depends," came the cautious answer.

"Brian Jordan."

"The defense contractor?"

"Yes."

"I don't know."

"Try. And keep me posted on Flaherty." Dustin paused, then added, "Thanks. If you ever need my help. . . ."

"Don't worry. I'll call you."

Dustin put the receiver back in its cradle. Damn, but he wished he knew what had happened. Flaherty was staying with the woman. After what happened in the hospital, he would have been careful. Then how did someone find them?

It had to be someone with resources better than his own.

He felt a chill. Why were they after Amy Mallory? What did the woman know? And why had Flaherty joined forces with her? Did she have information that Dustin had not been able to find?

Three deaths. He would call Sally this afternoon, but not from the office. He was getting spooked if he didn't trust his own telephone. Everything was coming apart.

He tried to turn his attention to the briefing papers, but his mind kept going back to the news he'd just heard. Where was Flaherty going? What did the Mallory woman know? What did Jordan know when he'd thrown out his boast?

His carefully arranged world was falling apart. The strange thing was that for the first time he could remember, it didn't matter as much as it once did. He was too worried about Sally. He stood, walked to the closed door, and opened it. "Judy?"

"Sir?"

"Cancel my meetings tomorrow and the next day. I have a family emergency."

Her face didn't betray anything. He had kept Judy with him for precisely that reason. She seemed to be almost a robot. She was supremely efficient and extraordinarily professional. Never asked questions. She didn't disappoint him now. "Yes, sir."

"I'll phone you tomorrow."

"Is there a number where I can reach you?"

He knew she knew the number. It was her subtle way of asking whether she *should* call. "My cell phone," he said, "but only if there's an emergency."

"I hope everything is all right." It was a statement, not a question.

"I do, too, Judy."

He retreated into his office. He called the deputy secretary of state to tell him that he would be gone for several days and that he was sending up some briefing papers.

No objection, but then, he'd never asked for any time before.

He finished his recommendation, gave it to Judy, then left the building. In a few hours, he would see Sally.

MYRTLE BEACH, SOUTH CAROLINA

Irish felt the chill. He had ever since Amy had awakened in the morning. She was purposely cool. Distant. He didn't try to bridge that distance. That was something she would have to do herself.

He didn't blame her. God, if he had been thrown into the maelstrom of the past few days, then he, too, would question everything and everyone.

Taking Bo with him, he went to the motel office, where he purchased the local paper and picked up a free advertising publication. He also asked directions to Richmond, a precaution in the event anyone inquired.

Another man, dressed in a pair of slacks and sport coat, was in the office. Irish hovered near a coffeepot and poured himself a cup. He was wary of strangers now. And these clothes didn't fit this particular motel on a hot, sunny morning.

But eavesdropping did have its advantages. The man apparently was a salesman for a magazine listing local motels and cottage rentals.

Irish followed him out and caught him at his car. "My . . . wife and I really like this area," he said. "Thought we would stay a bit longer, but we would like something on the beach. Something private."

"There's a realtor who handles rental homes on the beach. Some real nice ones."

"I was hoping you might know of one where we don't have to go through a realtor," Irish said. He winked at the man. "I don't, I mean we don't . . . want anyone to find us."

A leer appeared on the man's face. "You *did* say your wife?"

Irish shrugged off the question. "Look, I'll pay top price if you know of something."

"How long?"

"A week."

"I might know of something." The man's greedy gaze assessed him. "I'll have to do some phoning." He looked down at the dog. "No one much wants dogs."

"As you can tell, he's well-behaved."

"Cost you extra."

Irish nodded. "I'll meet you back here in what . . . an hour?"

The man nodded. "What room?"

"I'll meet you out here."

The salesman thrust his hand out. "I'm Jim Woods."

Irish took it. The hand was damp and the shake was weak, but that was good. He wanted someone who thought Irish had someone else's wife and didn't want any kind of record of it. He would probably be adding a handsome commission of his own, and wouldn't want whoever owned the property to know it. A devil's bargain.

Irish went back into the motel office and poured another cup of coffee for Amy, then returned to the room, a very watchful Bo never moving more than two feet from him.

Holding the two cups of coffee in one hand, he knocked lightly with the other. The door opened quickly.

Amy was dressed. Her hair was damp and curling around her face. A touch of lipstick had brought color into her face. Shadows were still under her eyes, though, and she looked drawn and tense.

She took the coffee, and her gaze met his. "I saw you talking to someone in the parking lot."

"A salesman for several publications, including real estate and motels," he said. "I heard him talking to the manager. I thought he could help us find something for a few days. Without leaving records."

"And can he?"

"He thinks so. He'll be getting back to me. He thinks I'm trying to cover up an illicit relationship. Hiding from a husband."

She looked at him dubiously. "With a dog?"

"That kind of complicates things," he said with a half smile. "Still, he thinks there's extra money in it for him." He hesitated. "I'm getting short on cash. I plan to send for some, but it will take a few days."

"I have enough for what we should need," she said. "And I don't want to be paid back. You don't owe me anything. You've already done more than . . . necessary. Far more."

He shook his head. "I'm as much involved in this now as you. I shot a man."

Her eyes darkened. "And you feel responsible. I know. But you shouldn't. I had planned to look into the commission report myself after the tenure hearing. We don't even know if . . . that's what is behind this." She stood a little straighter, and he could feel the determination radiating from her.

She was trying to let him off the hook. The problem was, he didn't want to be let off the hook. And that thought astonished him. He'd made it a lifetime goal not to get involved with others, particularly those of the female persuasion. He hadn't wanted the noose around his neck, the interference in a lifestyle he'd chosen. Loneliness was not unknown, and sometimes he'd see a sunset in the mountains and wish he could share it. Or he would see a couple, their heads close together and smiles on their lips, and wonder what he had missed. Or see a father and son fishing on a pier. But then he would remember the pain that went with relationships. The recriminations and tears and screaming. The bitterness and often hatred.

And the envy would fade, the emptiness would lessen. If you didn't offer a part of your soul, it couldn't be rejected. Mishandled. Destroyed.

The way his stepfather had been destroyed.

"Flaherty?"

She was calling him that again. Her own mental mechanism for keeping him at arm's length.

She was far wiser than he.

"Sorry," he said. "I was thinking about the next several days." It was a bald-faced lie, but she seemed to accept it.

"Maybe I should just return to Memphis and ask for police help."

"You tried that."

"But now there's been a third attempt. Surely someone. . . ."

"There's probably enough now to bring in the FBI, but there's no guarantee of witness protection," he said.

"My tenure hearing. . . ."

"Under the circumstances, I would think you could get it postponed."

"The committee is scattering after the hearing. And there's my. . . ." She stopped suddenly, and he realized she was going to say "house."

For a moment her face seemed to crumple, but then, like a piece of Play-Doh, it firmed again. He watched her blink back a suspicious moisture in her eyes.

He wanted to reach out and pull her to him, but something in her eyes warned him against doing that. Just as it had earlier.

She turned away. The television was on, and she looked at it, effectively shutting him out. It was obvious she didn't want his sympathy.

"I'm meeting him outside in an hour," he said.

"Can you trust him?"

"I don't think we can trust anyone, but there's no reason he should think anything than what we want him to think."

"How much money do we need?"

"He mentioned fifteen hundred, but I think he was just trying to see how much I was willing to pay."

Amy didn't say anything, but went to her suitcase and

reached inside. She pulled out an envelope and gave it to him. "There's two thousand dollars in there."

"Did you rob a bank?"

"Only my savings. I thought it the better part of wisdom to use it to *have* a future."

He privately vowed to pay her back, whether she wanted it or not. It would, he knew, set back plans for his ranch, but that was of little importance at the moment. Nothing was more important than getting Amy Mallory out of this in one piece. But after looking at the set of her chin and her cool eyes, he knew he would lose any argument now.

Instead, he decided to give her some space. "There's a mini-market up the street. I'll get us something to eat."

"Orange juice," she said hopefully.

"And donuts. Unless I can find something better."

As he left, he saw her pick Bo up. The dog snuggled in her lap. She was looking at the television, but he knew she wasn't seeing anything.

The house was more than two blocks from the beach. It was small, little more than a cottage, but it had two bedrooms and a kitchen.

At least, there would be some privacy, Amy thought. Someplace where she could retreat. She could finish what work she needed to do while Flaherty prowled her grandfather's files.

She hung onto Flaherty's arm, pretending to be his paramour. Not so much pretend, she feared.

She knew the cost was inflated, that their benefactor with the ruddy face and shiny pants saw an opportunity. The house was not prime beach property; it had a "For Rent" sign in front and a shabby look. But at the moment it was a refuge.

Amy watched as Flaherty counted out a number of hundred dollar bills. "You have to be out by next Sunday," the man warned.

Flaherty nodded. They hadn't even signed any paper. She wondered if the real owner would ever know the place had even been rented. She doubted it.

The salesman left. Flaherty looked at the place wryly. The furniture was used rental, but no worse than the motel.

"Sorry," he said.

"Don't be," Amy replied. She felt safe. Temporarily.

Flaherty inspected the kitchen. A usable stove, an old but clean refrigerator. Basic pots and pans. "I saw a store down the street. I'll get a couple of steaks and salad makings." He hesitated, then added, "Keep the pistol near you."

Amy felt her body stiffen.

"Amy?"

"I will," she said reluctantly.

"Good." Then he was out the door, and the cottage seemed an extraordinarily empty place. She watched while he returned to the car. Then she looked around the cottage again. A washer and dryer would be nice, but no such luck. Everything was simply functional, with faded carpets designed to soak up water and sand. She took Bo out into the tiny backyard and he obliged by doing what was required while she stood outside sniffing the ocean air, aching to walk down to the beach.

The boxes were inside, but if she locked the house, she wouldn't be able to get back inside. Flaherty had the only key. At the moment she didn't care if someone stole the damned things. They were soaked in blood. Figuratively, if not literally.

She hesitated, then decided to go down to the beach. She left a note on the wobbly kitchen table. After a moment's hesitation, she picked up the pistol and put it in her purse. Although the pistol was light, she felt as if her purse had taken on the weight of an anvil.

She called Bo and went out the front door, locking it behind them. She crossed the street, walked a block, then found a path crossing the dunes down to the ocean. A hot wind finished drying her hair, and she leaned down and took off her shoes, burying her toes in the sand. She'd done that days earlier at Jekyll Island.

She heard a sudden loud noise, and she froze. Those damned images returned. *Men rushing her. Shots. Blood.* Her heart pounded rapidly. Her mouth felt dry. She tried to tamp the panic, telling herself she wasn't going to let it control her life.

She forced herself to glance around. Another loud sound. Then she recognized the sound. A boom box had been turned on.

Slowly, she tried to relax. She recalled how she'd experienced a jolt of fear when she'd seen Flaherty talking to a stranger. She wondered whether she could ever relax in a crowd or entirely trust anyone again.

She'd trusted Jon. Explicitly. But something had been niggling at her lately. Why had he wanted those papers? Who had known he had them? She'd accepted his explanation of simple curiosity at the time. Yet she had mentioned them years ago, and he'd asked to see them only months ago. Had he known about the commission before its findings had been publicized?

Or did she just question everyone now?

Laughter jolted her from her dark mood. Glancing toward the water, she saw children bobbing up and down on floats in the ocean. Others were building a giant sand castle. No worries except for a particularly aggressive wave that threatened the fragile structure.

The seeming tranquillity clashed with all the recent violence. It was difficult to think that until two weeks ago, her only concern had been the tenure hearing.

Bo inched closer to her. He had been more clinging than usual since the invasion of her hotel room. A small girl ran up to them. "Can I pet your dog?"

No ulterior motive here. "I think he would like that," she said. And he did, as long as she was right there with him. Bo whimpered with pleasure as the child rubbed his ears. The mother called, and the child ran back to her, and a man and another child.

For a moment, she wished she were that woman. Wrapped in the safety and comfort and security of a family unit. She'd wished that before, but she'd never been willing to compromise and her Prince Charming had never appeared on the horizon. Perhaps she'd wanted too much, expected too much.

Or perhaps she was just suspicious of all relationships and unwilling to depend on another person.

She heard the crunch of shoes on sand, saw a shadow darken the sand beside her. A tall, elongated shadow.

She looked up. Flaherty was too damned handsome. Even when she was half-blinded by the sun, the planes of his face were ruggedly attractive. "Thought I might find you here," he said.

He sat down with a fluid ease and offered her a cold soda. Her brand. It was amazing what he'd learned about her in the past few days. He remembered every one of her likes and dislikes. It was . . . disconcerting.

She took it, and it tasted good. Neither of them had had much to eat this morning, and she was beginning to feel the rumblings of hunger deep inside. Unfortunately, there were two kinds of hunger, especially when her gaze met his. She wanted to reach out and touch him. He was reality and substance in her new world of shadows.

But that was too easy. She would never know how much of what she felt was real, and how much was fear and gratitude and even the dependence she didn't want.

She stood. "You wanted to go over my grandfather's papers."

He nodded and unwound his long legs, standing in one easy, graceful motion. Drat him. He did everything easily. She wondered whether he had any self-doubts. She didn't think so.

She reached down and picked up her purse. Two guns

between them now. Her pacifist mother would be turning over in her grave.

Braced by a steak and beer, Irish attacked Amy's boxes. It didn't take him long to see a pattern.

The two of them went through them together for a while, Amy translating some of her grandfather's poor writing. Once he caught on, she moved away, saying that she wanted him to look at them without her input. Maybe he would see something she hadn't.

General David Mallory had evidently kept what he had for a reason, and that reason could be nothing but a book. He didn't keep odds and ends. He'd kept maps with notations on them, orders received from the supreme command and obviously private assessments on how they worked, recommendations for major decorations, casualty list totals, personal observations on division staff and on the enemy command. It was obvious that he often disagreed with Irish's grandfather, feeling that he was too cautious.

The papers were dated from June 6, 1944—the Normandy invasion—and ran through April 30 of the next year. After that, the number of papers declined. There were terrain maps, orders from headquarters and from Irish's grandfather Sam Flaherty. There was, surprisingly, a list of casualties, not just the total number, but individuals. Nothing else. No more comments on staff. No more comments on orders.

A month later, as the American Army approached Berlin, the notes started again, but to a much lesser extent. Now they seemed more reminders to him, not events to be recorded.

A soft breathing distracted him. Amy had fallen asleep on the sofa. Long, dark lashes fringed her eyes, and she looked lovely to him. The tenseness had left her body, and she looked peaceful for the first time.

He felt the damndest urge to touch her. Nothing lustful, just to touch, to make contact, to soothe. He couldn't remember ever feeling that way before. Tender. As if a hole inside him was filling up, shoving aside an emptiness he'd been reluctant to acknowledge.

She had been unbelievably game these past few days. Courage, he knew, came from unsuspected places. And she had shown it that night at Jekyll Island when she'd demonstrated both grit and good sense, throwing off the assailant's aim at just the right time.

It had emerged again when he'd shown her how to shoot. She'd hated every moment of it. Her body language and eyes told him that. Yet she had listened carefully and learned quickly.

The simple fact was, he liked her. He liked the intimacy that had sprung up between them, no matter how hard they had both fought it. He realized it was rooted in the circumstances. Danger was always an aphrodisiac. He'd learned that long ago. But the way he felt now went deeper.

It scared the hell out of him.

He looked at his watch. Two in the morning.

He replaced the papers in the same order they had been in. He wasn't finished yet. But he wanted her input. She had gone over the same material. Had she seen the same pattern as he had or had his military background guided him in a different direction?

Irish stood and stretched. He thought about waking her but merely satisfied himself with finding a blanket in one of the two bedrooms and covering her with it. He didn't remember ever doing that before, either. His hands hesitated as he pulled it over her shoulders, his fingers lightly touching her hair. They lingered there a moment, then he straightened reluctantly. For a moment, he watched the blanket move slightly with her breathing, then checked the doors and windows.

Satisfied the cottage was locked tight, he turned out the lights and went into the bedroom he'd claimed as his. Damn, but it felt impersonal. Empty. Like his life.

You like it this way.

He'd told himself that for years, but now the sentiment didn't have the same fierce pride and defiance it once had.

He hoped for quick sleep, but he knew it would not come. He longed to feel her next to him. He longed to see the warmth in her eyes that had been there the day after the attack. His body, he realized, was tense with need.

Still, he would try. He needed to keep his wits about him. They were one step ahead of a killer. He intended to keep them that way.

sixteen

Dustin felt the familiar ache in his heart as he watched Sally comb her long, honey-colored hair as she readied herself to go out to dinner.

Watching from the door of her bedroom, he caught her glance in the mirror and smiled.

He still felt warm from her greeting an hour earlier. Her eyes had brightened when she'd opened the door.

It seemed natural to open his arms, and she'd stepped into them, enveloping him in a big hug. Her eyes sparkled, her smile was infectious, and it was all for him. He leaned down to kiss her on the cheek, but she moved her face, and his lips touched hers, lingering a moment before moving away.

"I've been going crazy here by myself," she said. "I've already gone through three books."

"Anything good?"

"Romance novels."

She grinned at his expression. "You ought to try them sometime. You might learn something."

"Unfortunately, I'm usually stuck reading briefing papers," he said.

She made her own face at that. "Which is why you aren't any fun."

"Oh, is it?" he challenged with a smile. "I'll have to see about that."

"That sounds interesting."

"I've brought you something," he said. "It's in the car."

She'd raised an eyebrow.

"First get ready for dinner," he said. "We'll go to the best restaurant in town."

She'd disappeared. He went down to the car and pulled out the art supplies he'd purchased at a store in Washington. A sketch pad. Charcoal pens. Water colors. Even acrylics. An easel.

He'd placed them in the corner, then approached her room, where she was combing her hair.

She whirled around, a question in her eyes.

"You look beautiful," he said, and watched a glow spread over her face.

"Thank you."

He went into the living room of the condominium, Sally by his side. She stopped when she saw the drawing materials. "I remembered how much you used to like to draw," he said awkwardly. She had, in fact, loved art, and planned to study it in college until her artist mother abandoned Sally and Sally's father. As far as he knew, she hadn't touched a paintbrush since. Instead, she had flitted from one major to another, spending five years in college and finally graduating with a liberal arts degree that prepared her for exactly nothing. She went over to them, then looked up at him. Her face was tight, strained, as if a plastic mask had been stretched too tight, and he realized she wasn't ready. He had hoped she was. But perhaps she never would be.

He watched her struggle to regain her composure, the carefree attitude she so assiduously cultivated. "Does this mean I can't go home yet?"

Suddenly, he realized that she must have thought he was there to take her home. "I think it's better if you don't," he said. "I told your boss there was a family emergency, and he said you could take unpaid leave as long as you wanted."

She stiffened. "You shouldn't have done that. Not without asking me."

"Sally, someone *else* has died. The woman I told you about, Dr. Mallory, was attacked again in Georgia."

"She was killed?" Horror tinged her question.

"No. Someone heard her scream and came to her rescue. The attacker was killed."

"Then . . . why can't I go home?"

"There was a second assailant. He got away."

"And you still think it might have something to do with . . . Grandfather?"

"I'm becoming more and more convinced that it does."

"My mother?" It was one of the few times he'd heard her mention her mother. She'd divorced Sally's father when Sally was fifteen.

He shrugged. "She's gone back to her maiden name and she'd been estranged from the family for so long that I doubt anyone would even think of her. She certainly wouldn't have anything of your father's or grandfather's."

Uncertainty flitted over her face, and he wondered whether she was finally coming to terms about her mother. "Call her," Sally urged.

"Why don't you?"

"I can't," she said adamantly.

He reached out and touched her shoulder. "All right. But she'll start worrying about you."

Sally didn't reply, but he saw the doubt on her face.

He wished he could wipe that doubt away. Sally had already believed that her mother had left her father for selfish reasons, that she'd never cared about her father, that, in fact, the divorce had led to her father's suicide. He knew it wasn't true, but she had never listened to him. Nor did he tell her that Chloe Matthews called him occasionally to inquire after her daughter, to make sure she was all right.

"I don't think that's right," he said gently. "You never gave her a chance."

"She killed my father," Sally said flatly, "just as if she had pulled the trigger herself."

But Sally still cared, or else she wouldn't have suggested that he call Chloe. Still, he didn't think it wise to pursue that at the moment.

"And you?" she said. "Have you asked Patsy to marry you yet?"

Ah, pain returned with pain. "No," he said.

"How does she feel about you coming up here?"

"I don't know."

"You haven't told her about this?"

"No," he said. "I don't want her involved." But he realized that if he really loved Patsy, he would have told her. Instead, he had been purposefully avoiding her these last few weeks. Excuses about work. About family. Except she knew that his only family was Sally, and he'd seen the questions in her eyes.

She picked up a paintbrush. Dustin saw how she held it. The way a lover held her mate's hand. With reverence. Then she quickly put it down. "I think you promised me dinner."

"So I did," he said.

"When are you going back?"

It was Tuesday. He'd canceled appointments for today and tomorrow. He couldn't stay away longer. "Tomorrow," he said. "There's a party I have to attend."

"In your penguin suit?"

"Afraid so."

"Are you taking Patsy?"

"Yes."

Her eyes clouded slightly. She turned around and laid the brush down, then started for the door. "I'm starving. Let's go."

MYRTLE BEACH, SOUTH CAROLINA

Amy woke to the smell of coffee. She stretched, then realized she was on the sofa as her feet hit something hard. Still feeling sleepy and more than a little stiff, she sat up. Other aromas drifted over to her. She brushed her eyes with her hand and ran fingers through her hair. She was still wearing the same slacks and knit shirt she'd worn all day yesterday, and they were wrinkled and grungy.

She was grungy.

"Breakfast in ten minutes," came a cheerful voice. "I've taken Bo outside."

She wanted to kill him. She did not feel cheerful or chirpy.

Bo nudged her for attention, his tail wagging. She reached out and rubbed his ears, then barely suppressed a groan as she got to her feet. Her mouth tasted foul, she was sure her cheeks had the imprint of a throw pillow, and she'd slept so heavily that she felt drugged. She kicked off the blanket.

Blanket?

There hadn't been a blanket last night. She regarded it suspiciously. Almost like a snake. No one had taken care of her for a long time.

"You slept well." The voice again. Sexy as well, damn it. It just wasn't right at this time of the morning.

She stumbled to her feet and made for the bathroom before he saw her. She took one look at herself. It was a lie that anyone looked good when they first woke up.

Amy did her best to repair the damage. Just brushing her teeth made her feel a great deal better. Then her hair. A splash of water on her face. Finally a touch of lipstick.

Her clothes were in the other room, but she was quickly running out of them. She had not brought many with her. *This is not a date. You are running for your life.*

That thought brought all the nightmares tumbling back.

The last thing she remembered was Flaherty looking through the files. Had he found anything?

She straightened her shirt as well as she could. She would take a shower later.

Breakfast. The smells filtering into the bathroom were intriguing. All of a sudden she was hungry. Flaherty had cooked supper last night, and now breakfast. A man who could cook was a prize indeed.

Except he wasn't her prize.

She stepped out of the bathroom and into the kitchen. He had already set two places at the imitation wood table. Steaming coffee and large glasses of orange juice already graced the table.

When she appeared, he scooped something out of the frying pan onto two plates and presented them with something like a flourish. Omelets. Hers looked and smelled terrific. "Where did you learn to cook?"

"A bachelor usually learns or starves," he said. "But you've seen most of my repertoire now. Steaks and omelets."

She tasted it. It *was* terrific. One of the best she'd ever tasted. There were any number of subtle flavors. Some, like garlic, were readily identifiable. Others were not. She tried to think of that instead of the information he'd just dropped. It didn't work.

She couldn't resist asking the question that had been nagging her. "Have you ever been married?"

"No," he said.

"Why?" It was none of her business, and she always, always hated it when someone asked her that question.

"It's difficult for a woman to be an Army wife," he said. "You have to give up a great deal, including security. You move a lot. There's a lot of loneliness. There's damned little financial reward."

Amy thought she detected a touch of bitterness in the words. The slight smile disappeared from his lips. He took a long swallow of coffee, and she knew he was closing the subject. Had he lost someone?

She changed the subject. "Did you find anything last night?"

He put down the coffee cup. "Did your grandfather ever talk about writing a book?"

She thought back. Her grandfather had a large library, almost all of it pertaining to the military. Mostly nonfiction. Some selected fiction. Toward the end of his life, when his eyesight faded, he would ask her to order books and she would read them to him. But writing a book?

"No, I don't think so. I don't remember him ever mentioning it."

"The notes were interesting."

"Why?"

He hesitated. "The notes didn't seem to have any military value. They were more like personal reminders, observations." He paused, then asked, "There weren't any diaries?"

"I never saw one. And he wasn't the type of man who would keep them."

"What kind of man is that?"

"He was never . . . reflective. He was gruff. Matter of fact. He had decisive opinions he didn't give up easily. I never saw him write anything but a check."

His gaze bore into her. "You read the notes?"

"I skimmed over them. I didn't see anything. . . ." Her voice trailed off. She didn't know what she had been looking for. A smoking gun? Something dramatic? The notes had seemed innocuous to her.

"What's really interesting," he said, "is that papers with notes stopped as of April. There were documents, but no notes. As if he found no reason for them any longer. Or," he added, "someone removed those with private notes."

She should have noticed that. Or maybe she had. Is that why she thought of Jon yesterday?

"You're sure there couldn't have been any more papers?"

"No," she replied. "I'm not sure. But I cataloged everything after his death. The estate had to be . . . liquidated because of taxes. Everything was sold but those boxes of papers and some personal items bequeathed to me. I didn't know why he had saved only those boxes. He'd never mentioned them to me. Since they were in the attic, I just supposed he overlooked them. I went through them to see whether there was anything of value. I was working on my dissertation and didn't have time to really study them, so I stored them along with some furniture and a few other items that had some importance to me."

"What furniture?"

"His desk. It was a giant rolltop desk."

"Was it in your house?"

She stared at him. "No. It's still in storage in Kentucky, along with several other large pieces. I was in an apartment when my grandfather died, and didn't have room for them. Then I just . . . didn't have time to get them."

It was a lie. She *had* had time. She just had never been sure she wanted the desk in her cottage. It was huge, designed for a large study. But that was her excuse. She hadn't been sure she wanted the memories, good and bad, in her new world. Yet she hadn't been able to give it up, either. So she'd shoved it out of her consciousness.

"I think we might look at it."

"Secret compartments?" she scoffed.

"Nothing would surprise me now," he replied so seriously that her halfhearted attempt at humor faded.

"All right."

"First, though, I want to meet with the Eachan grandchildren," he said. "It would be interesting to know whether they have had any of the same . . . experiences we have, or whether they have any documents."

"He was adjutant to your grandfather."

"And he served with yours. I wonder whether he had

the same opinion of my grandfather as David Mallory did."

She recalled some of the notes. It had been obvious that her grandfather had not liked his grandfather, had thought himself the stronger man, but he had never gone beyond Brigadier General and Mallory had his second star.

Amy finished the omelet, gave remnants of her toast to a patiently waiting Bo, and rose to pour them both fresh cups of coffee. "What was your grandfather like?"

Irish played with his cup. "You said your grandfather was gruff and . . . apparently not very good with people. Mine was the opposite. He was warm and amusing, and never met a stranger. After the war, he stayed with the Army for a few years. He ended up teaching at West Point, then bought a ranch in Colorado. I think he knew every person in the county."

"And your father?"

"He died in the early days of Vietnam. I barely knew him."

She was silent for a moment. "Then you grew up without a father, too."

"Not exactly. My mother married my father's best friend, an Army helicopter pilot. He died in a helicopter crash six years later."

She felt her chest tighten. "It must have been terrible for her."

He was silent.

"How did she feel about you joining the Army?"

"She hated it," he said quietly. "She hated the Army. She hated everything about it. I don't think she ever forgave me for going to West Point." He was silent for a moment, then added, "She felt it was a betrayal. I felt it would be a betrayal to my father if I didn't."

"Where is she now?"

"She died three years ago of cancer," he said. "She'd married a dentist, but I don't think she was ever happy." She heard the sadness in his voice. And regret.

She was reminded again of the tragedies that had struck both their families. She wondered about the Eachan family as well.

It was not unnatural that all three grandfathers were dead. They would have been near the century mark in years. But nearly all the members of the second generation were gone, too. And only four of the third generation remained. What were the odds of that?

She cleaned up the dishes while he called Washington on his cell phone. After three calls, he hung up in disgust. "Dustin Eachan's office said he was out of town for two days on family business. I get only the answering machine at their homes."

"Two days?"

He nodded. "We'll stay here today, then drive up to Washington."

She raised an eyebrow.

His mouth twisted in that appealing smile of his. "If you agree," he said.

She'd made her point. She was not arrogant enough not to recognize his expertise in an area totally unfamiliar to her. But neither was she a blind follower.

"I should make sure I have everything ready for my tenure hearing," she said. "Do you think it's safe to call Sherry and assure her I'm all right?"

"Use my cell phone," he said.

"They can't track that?"

"Technically, yes, but it would require very sophisticated equipment."

"But it could be done?"

"Only a general location," he replied. "If they *can* trace it, then we're in real trouble. They will have more resources than I thought."

She considered that, then took his phone. Sherry should be home now that the semester was over. She looked at the clock. Eight A.M. here. It would be seven in Memphis. But

Sherry was always an early riser. She usually ran for an hour before it got too hot. She dialed.

Sherry answered on the second ring.

"Sherry?"

A sigh on the other end, then, "Thank God. I've been worried about you."

"I'm fine."

"I heard about Jekyll Island. Everyone has. Some Georgia cops called, trying to find you. Where are you?"

Amy wanted to tell her. Sherry was her best friend. But now she was paranoid. "I can't tell you."

Silence. "There are questions now. . . ."

Amy's stomach churned. She had worked so hard for her tenure. There weren't that many history positions available. She had one of the best, and only tenure would keep it for her. Jon had been her greatest advocate. *Jon. How could she even think of herself when Jon was dead? No matter what he'd. . . .*

No. She wasn't going to believe it of him. She was so tired of doubting everyone. Of questioning every value she had.

She had to go back. She had to defend what was hers.

"Tell them I'll be back in time for the hearing. Until then, I'm resting with friends. Everything is fine. I'll be able to explain everything." She glanced up, saw Flaherty shake his head. She ignored it.

A pause on the other end of the line. "Are you sure, Amy?"

Amy hesitated. Was she? Safety was important. But so were other things. She'd worked for ten years for tenure. She wasn't ready to sacrifice it. "Yes," she said.

A silence on the phone. "I'll tell them you are still recuperating from the wound inflicted in their building. The doctor says you need plenty of rest," she added in a self-satisfied tone. "I'll also tell them that the attack in Jekyll Island was probably a result of the one in *their* hall. That should alarm them enough to give you a few more days. Keep safe."

Keep safe. They used to be words said in passing. A pleasantry. Now they sounded ominous.

"I will," she said and hung up before she said anything else.

WASHINGTON, D.C.

The voice on the telephone was excited. "We've located them. They used his cell phone."

"Where are they?"

"Myrtle Beach, South Carolina."

"Have you seen them?"

"No. We just know the general area. We're searching the motels now."

"They won't register in a motel. Flaherty's smarter than that."

"Then where . . . ?"

"They're not using credit cards. We know that. So they must have a lot of cash. Try the rent-by-the-hour motels. No one asks for identification there. Then try the real estate companies. See if anyone is renting to someone using cash."

"Should we use the badges?"

"If necessary. I want them. I want them before they cause any more trouble."

"I'll need a few more men."

"Call the office. Get as many as you need."

A pause. "Should we bring them to you?"

"Hell, no. I want them dead. And make it look like an accident."

"With all the other . . . incidents, won't there be suspicions?"

"Mistakes, you mean," he broke in. "But there's nothing to lead them back to us. If accomplished properly, an accident will be accepted by authorities. *If* accomplished properly. Do you understand, Marcus?"

"Yes, sir."

"No more mistakes."

"No, sir."

"And I want no papers left."

"I understand."

"I want you to report back to me as soon as you eliminate the problem."

"Yes, sir."

"Don't take too long, Marcus."

seventeen

Irish wondered whether it would be possible for Amy to return to Memphis even in another week. But he took one look at her determined face and knew it would do no good to argue.

He could only present alternatives. He could not bully her into taking one or the other. He wanted some time. And she needed at least one day away from fear, from running. Either to or from something.

"I'll get you back in time," he offered, "but let's take today and relax. We can't do anything until I can reach Eachan."

She looked at him suspiciously.

"A drive up the coast until we find a relatively deserted beach," he offered. "Bread and cheese and a bottle of wine."

"Bo goes with us?"

"Of course."

She looked tempted. Hungry, in fact, for a few moments of normalcy. And perhaps he could change her mind about returning to Memphis before it was safe.

If she didn't, he would have to revise his own plans. He wanted to reach Washington—and Eachan. But if Amy was determined to return to Memphis, then he would return with her. He would stay with her as long as necessary, even if he had to resign his commission to do so.

She had told Shelly she would return for the hearing, seven—no, six—days away.

But perhaps he could give her at least one carefree day, the kind she'd wanted so much when she'd driven to the coast.

"I would like that," she said finally.

"Good. I'll get everything together."

She disappeared into the bedroom. He would stop at a grocery to get the wine and cheese. He looked at the damned boxes that seemed to be the key to everything, even if he hadn't found anything in them but more questions. He couldn't leave them here. Someone wanted them too badly. He took them out to the car, then examined the house and made certain adjustments. Shades exactly halfway up. A piece of tape at the bottom of the outside of the back door. He would put another on the front door and each of the windows.

Irish was finished by the time she emerged from her bedroom. She was wearing jeans over a black bathing suit. A big, unbuttoned shirt covered her shoulders.

She looked appealing with her great gray eyes, short hair that swirled in curls around her cheeks, and just enough lipstick to put color in her face. A dusting of freckles over her nose gave her a girl-next-door look. Her skin was smooth and sweet-smelling. But most attractive of all was the shining brightness in her eyes.

He opened the door for her and Bo, and as she went down the steps, he quickly stooped and placed the tape at the bottom of the door. Not very scientific, he knew, but it would have to do. The shades were the best indicator. If anyone was prowling inside, the intruder would want them down.

They took Highway 17 up the coast. He stopped at a grocery store and went inside while she waited outside with Bo. He came out with a bag of ice he put in a cooler along with a bottle of wine and some groceries.

An hour later, he found a beach with a parking lot that did not look too crowded. He watched as Amy and Bo jumped out. He hesitated a moment, then took his pistol and holster and locked them in the trunk, along with Amy's purse, which contained her gun. He had watched carefully on the way up, and didn't think anyone had followed them.

He picked up the ice chest and they walked to the beach, moving toward a relatively isolated spot shadowed by a sand dune. She had brought a blanket from the cottage, and she spread it out on the sand. Bo plopped down on the sand and watched the ice chest as if he knew exactly what was in it.

The sun seemed particularly large, the sea splendidly blue, the birds singularly graceful. A sea breeze ruffled through Amy's hair, and the sun blushed her cheeks. He held out his hand and helped her lower herself. He watched as she took off her shoes, then slipped off her jeans. The bathing suit was relatively modest, but it showed her figure to good advantage. Her legs were long and shapely. Too shapely.

He looked away and stripped off his own jeans to reveal a rather cheap bathing suit. He'd bought it yesterday when getting their groceries at a store that had numerous beach items as well as food.

The waves made seductive music, accented by the occasional cry of a swooping gull. But nothing was as intoxicating as the woman beside him. He wished he didn't remember every moment of that night they had made love. He wanted her now with a gut-wrenching need, but even more he wanted her safe. And he didn't know how to make her safe.

He looked at a wheeling gull as it glided above the sea, then dived into the water. Her hand crept into his, and he wondered at how natural it felt. He couldn't remember when he'd just held a woman's hand before. For the first time, he felt a sense of belonging. His fingers tightened around hers and heat built there, moving along his nerve ends and pooling in his groin. Their gazes met, and he knew she felt that same warm energy. Her usually cool eyes were smoky, and her tongue darted out and licked her lips. It was a particularly sensuous movement, and the fact that she seemed completely unaware of it made the gesture even more seductive. He had never met a woman more unaware of her own attractiveness.

If he didn't do something, he would take her then and there, to hell with anyone who might wander by. He stood, although it had been only minutes since they'd sat. "Let's go for a walk."

She regarded him seriously for a moment, then rose. "I think that's a good idea." Bo, who had dug a cool hole in the sand, stood and nudged him, obviously in agreement.

His hand caught hers again, and they walked down to the cool water. He wondered that it didn't sizzle as it met his heated skin. He felt as if he were burning up with need.

This had been a mistake.

And yet as he looked at her and saw the smile on her lips, he knew it wasn't. It was just going to cost him a lot of sleepless nights and jangled nerves, and "what ifs." What if he didn't know that the Army and long-term commitments just didn't go together? Yet she had accomplished what no other woman had: she had wriggled into his soul, and by God she had done it in the matter of a few days.

An intense few days.

That was it. The intensity. And yet there was something else, too, something far stronger than mere lust. It scared the hell out of him, particularly with a woman who seemed to have a death wish. He knew he had to talk her out of returning to Memphis, tenure or not.

They walked for an hour, maybe longer. The sun beat

down on them while cool water crept over their ankles, then retreated. They passed other couples, and yet it seemed as if no one else existed. She stopped where several kids were building a sand castle, and he watched as she released his hand and stooped down, remarking on the excellence of the structure and winning broad grins in reply. He stood by and watched her relate to a six-year-old, and he wondered why she had never married.

He had reasons. Good reasons. He wondered about hers.

When she stood, he took her hand again. And he asked, though he hadn't wanted to. He hadn't wanted to get more involved than he already was. But the question came anyway. "Why haven't you ever married?"

"And you know I haven't?"

He'd been suitably put in his place. They had never talked about it. The only way he could know was by checking into her background. "Not absolutely," he said.

She smiled at that. "I thought you knew everything."

It was a "gotcha" smile. And she hadn't answered his question.

They had passed the children, left them behind, and by silent consent moved within the shadow of a dune where they had some privacy. No one in sight. He leaned down and kissed her. His lips skimmed over her cheek, then settled on her lips. Their nearly naked bodies fused. Her skin was warm, glowing from the sun, and she smelled like sand and sea. Her body arched against his in an incredibly erotic way. He felt himself growing hard under the thin cloth of the cheap bathing suit. She responded, her body snuggling into his. It felt right, natural, real.

All of a sudden, he wondered whether anything had been real before. He had skirted the edges of life, avoiding involvement, avoiding any kind of commitment. The ranch had been the only real home he'd ever had, and he visited it only rarely. Afraid to let it into his heart. Into his soul. Someone might grab that away, too.

He was past forty. He'd had an interesting career. He'd thought he'd kept loneliness at bay. During his life, he'd known only rotten examples of marital relationships. He could still remember his mother yelling at his stepfather. Still remembered the tears. Still remember her accusations. "*All you care about is that damned Army. Well, go sleep with it.*"

Peace had been a rare commodity in the household. He knew it was true of his grandfather, too. How many times had he heard his grandfather say it? "Marriage and the Army don't mix." And the Army was Irish's life.

His body didn't seem to comprehend that concept.

Loneliness and need and yearning welled up inside, and he knew they had been lurking beneath the surface. Could he stop rubbing the lamp and put the genie back in the bottle?

All those thoughts passed like individual frames in a motion picture. He'd edited his own version of his movie, and now he found it highly unsatisfactory.

Irish took his lips from her mouth and moved them lightly across her face, wanting to taste the essence of her, claim it as his own. Heat intensified where their bodies met, and flooded through the rest of his body. He felt the quick, involuntary shudder of her body.

Electricity ran between them, sparking and scorching. Her body softened as his hardened, and they seemed to meld together in complete compatibility. Her arms went up around his neck, and their lips met again. He felt alive again, pulsing with energy. His blood was like currents of liquid fire, searing and sensitizing every nerve, every muscle.

The sound of voices stilled them. Reluctantly, very reluctantly, he stepped back. Her eyes were glazed, her mouth slightly swollen from his kiss. She looked as dazed as he felt. Her hands fell from his neck, and her fingers interlocked with his.

Neither of them moved as a woman and man, and two children walked by. Bo belatedly barked at them.

"Thanks for warning us," Irish said dryly.

"I think . . . we had better go back," Amy said, her voice breathless.

His free hand went to her chin, fondling it with his thumb. "Later," he promised.

"You think we can be good that long?" Amy gave him a trembling smile that was extraordinarily appealing. So was her honestly.

"No," he said.

They started back, Bo sniffing dead sea creatures along the way, and they paused once in a while to wait for him. Their gazes invariably met, the smoky promise of combustion in hers. Only that kept him from feeling like a schoolboy clutching his girlfriend's hand. He hadn't realized how fine a feeling it was. The intimacy. The warmth. The belonging.

The peace of it. The tranquillity of this place. A sky so blue it hurt. A sun so large and bright he felt he could touch it. The song of the sea and the birds. No violence here.

He saw the same wonderment in her eyes. How could two such opposite worlds collide as theirs had?

Amy tried to subdue all the tumultuous feelings raging through her, tried not to throw herself into his arms again. She felt soft and melting all over, and she wanted to feel neither. Or maybe she did, and that terrified her. But she couldn't harness the raging desire that sent tremors through her. Nor the closeness she had never felt with anyone before.

Back. The cottage. A bed. Her fingers tightened around the rough strength of his fingers. She absorbed every touch, memorized the sensations that still lingered inside her, goading and teasing.

They reached the blanket. He looked at her for a moment, asking silently.

"Let's picnic at the cottage," she said.

He grinned at her. It was more than a twist of his lips. It was a full-fledged, honest grin.

She helped him gather up their belongings. The hunger inside her didn't fade. Instead, it seemed stronger with every touch of hands, every meeting of eyes.

In minutes, they were back in the car, driving down the coast. She sat in the corner where she could watch him, watch every nuance. The lover had turned into something else when they'd returned to the car; he'd efficiently checked his gun and replaced the holster on the belt of his jeans. The softness faded from the day. Reality returned, and she didn't want reality.

She wanted to think instead of his kisses, and the warm tenderness.

The two didn't go together. Violence and peace. Passion and danger. Or maybe they did. Maybe that was why her emotions were like a whirlwind, maybe that was why fire still sizzled between them. Every time Flaherty took his eyes from the road and looked at her, she felt scorched.

She tried to focus on Bo. He seemed oblivious to the currents. He was obviously content just to be with them. Settling down between the two of them, he put his head on her lap. But even with him separating them, she felt fire sizzling between Irish and herself.

She knew exactly what was coming, and she wondered whether she was ready for it. It would, she feared, mean much more to her than to him. She'd always been a one-guy kind of girl. Sleeping with someone was a huge commitment to her. She feared it wasn't for him.

Still, she couldn't resist the irresistible, no matter what he was, or who he was, or how long it might last. She wasn't even going to try. She had been caught in something on the beach that she'd never experienced before, and she knew she would not go through life without finishing what had been started. She had no wish to always wonder what could have been.

That's not like you. She heard the whisper, but pushed it aside. Nothing that had happened in the past weeks had been within her realm of reality. Her life had been turned upside down. Black was white, white was black, and she could never be what she had been.

No more caution. No more reservations. No more building walls. She simply wanted him.

And she knew if she did not act now, she might never experience what he offered. Even temporarily. Even though she was determined to return to Memphis and resume her life.

They said little during the ride back. They didn't have to. Intimacy had made him an old friend; words weren't required.

An hour later, they approached the lane with its small cottages. Flaherty drove past it, and she saw him tense. The warmth between them faded as she sensed something was very wrong. She sat up straighter and looked around. "What is it?"

"Maybe nothing," he said.

"But you don't think so."

"I left all the shades exactly halfway up. One is out of place."

She went cold. An hour ago, she was beginning to feel normal and safe again. Even falling in love a little. Maybe a lot. Now fear crawled up her spine again. Her hand dug into Bo's fur.

"What should we do?" she asked after a moment.

"Not you, Amy," he said as he drove around the corner, out of sight of the house, and parked. "Me. I'll go around the back."

"I don't understand. How could they find us?"

"My fault. I shouldn't have let you call your friend. They must have her phone tapped, and through that they can locate us. It takes pretty sophisticated equipment. I didn't think they could have those resources."

"Could they really tap Sherry's phone?" she said, fearing she had put her friend in danger.

He nodded. "It's fairly easy with the right equipment."

"She should know about it. She should know she might be in danger."

"I'll ask someone to visit her. I don't think we should use the phone any longer."

"Why don't we both just drive away now?"

A hard glint came into his eyes. "I want to meet these guys. And a lot of my possessions are still in the house. And yours."

"I want to go with you."

"No way, love."

Any other time, she might have been intrigued by his choice of words. She was not his "love." Not now. Not yet. Did she really want to be?

Because now he had changed. His lips firmed, and his eyes were as icy a blue as she had ever seen. The laughter and banter and warmth were gone. Instead, he was a warrior. It was in the watchfulness of his gaze, the sudden tenseness of the muscles in his cheek. *A warrior.* Everything she'd been taught to hate.

Everything she needed now.

She watched as he left the car, slipping the pistol from his holster into his hand. He came back to the window. "Do you have your pistol?"

She did. It was in her purse, which he'd given her when they'd returned to the car at the beach. She nodded.

"Keep it out and ready," he said. "Stay here."

She wanted to follow him, but as she fingered the weapon, she wasn't sure she could actually use it. She knew she wasn't experienced enough to confront armed assassins. She would most likely put Irish Flaherty in more danger, not less.

At this moment, she knew it took more courage to stay

than to try to be Sue Grafton's Kinsey Milhone. She wanted to follow him with all her heart. But she had seen too many movies in which the heroine did something really stupid and imperiled others. She didn't want to count herself among them.

She put Bo into the backseat, then moved to the driver's side and turned on the engine. And waited. And waited.

Time crept by as if it were a tortoise crawling across a desert. Suddenly, an explosion rocked the car. A ball of fire erupted into the sky.

Bo barked frantically, and she sat transfixed, not sure what to do. Irish expected her to be there.

But what if . . . he was caught inside? Or he was injured?

Clutching her purse with its deadly contents, she rolled all the windows partway down for Bo. She couldn't leave him in a sealed car. She reminded herself of her total lack of police skills. Even survivor skills. But it didn't matter. She heard sirens, then saw someone running. She knew instantly it was not Flaherty. The figure stopped, as if he saw her. The sound of sirens was louder, and he turned again and disappeared between two houses just as a police car passed her, slowed and approached where their rental house was in flames.

Then she saw Flaherty, weaving his way toward her from the back of a house three doors down. His shirt was singed and stained with red. Blood dripped from several cuts on his face.

She started the car and drove to meet him. He eased himself painfully into the passenger's seat. As she started to move out into the road, a fire engine passed them, then another. She turned down a side road and, keeping well within the speed limit, found the main highway.

"How badly are you hurt?" she asked.

"Nothing serious," he said. But he held his left arm awkwardly. "Go left to Highway 17."

"Shouldn't we wait for the police?"

"I don't think so," he said.

"Why?"

He hesitated.

"Now is not the time to keep anything from me," she said. "I already know there's a lot of people out to kill me for some unknown reason. The more I know, the better I can protect myself."

He sighed audibly. "You're right, of course. I think the cottage was rigged to blow when we went inside. I had placed some tape at both doors. Both had been disturbed. I checked the windows. The kitchen window had a slight crack, and I smelled gas. I think the moment I opened the door, a wire would have tripped a spark."

She waited. There was more. Obviously he wouldn't be here if he *had* opened that door.

"Someone must have been watching, and probably had a remote trigger as a backup. When they saw me prowling around instead of going in, they tripped it. I had just moved away from the window, coming to get you the hell out of the way, but part of the blast knocked me down."

"But why not talk to the police?"

"These people have resources like I've never seen before," he said grimly. "They already may have tried to kill someone to get me transferred. If I show up at another police station, I'll sure as hell be hauled back to base. Right now there's nothing to connect us to the explosion."

Nausea settled in her stomach. She was destroying his career. It didn't matter that it was a career she didn't exactly like. It was *his* career. Just as teaching was hers.

She started to turn the car around.

He grabbed the wheel. "No," he said.

"But I can't let you destroy. . . ."

"You don't understand," he said. "They nearly killed someone in Germany in order to get me transferred. What's to stop the from doing the same thing to me? I don't want to be looking under my car every time I get in. We have to find who is behind this."

"Can't the FBI or someone else do it?"

He looked at her. "Someone high in the government is involved, Amy. I have no idea who, yet. Until I do, I'm not going to leave you unprotected."

"I can't let you sacrifice everything for me."

"They've tried to kill me, too. I'm as high on their list as you."

"Because of me," she said.

"No, I don't think so," he said slowly. "I think we've all been targeted for a long time."

"What do you mean?"

"Your grandfather. He committed suicide?"

She nodded slowly.

"Did you think he was suicidal?"

"He was sick."

"But suicidal?"

She shook her head.

"My grandfather had a heart attack, but he'd never had heart trouble."

Silence. She tried to digest what was being said.

"And the Eachan family. General Eachan died in an accident."

Her eyes turned away from the road for a second and toward him. "You think they're connected?"

"I think they could be."

The lump in her throat almost choked her. The implications were too mind-boggling. Unlike her mother, she'd never believed in conspiracies. At least not many of them. And the scale of this was too large for her to comprehend.

"You can't go back to Memphis, Amy. It's not safe. Ask for a delay."

"I'll see if it's possible," she said slowly, not at all hopeful. Any hint of scandal would destroy her chances for tenure. Six days. She had only six days.

"We'll go to Washington," he said, "and talk to Eachan. If necessary, we can fly to Memphis from there."

She looked at his torn shirt, the blood splattered on it, the burn on the back of his hand. He must be in a lot of pain.

She was not going to make it worse. Not now. He was right.

She finally nodded. "We'll go to Washington."

eighteen

SOUTH CAROLINA

Irish hurt. He wished he could think better, but he was
burned and cut and had lost blood. All he knew was his instincts. And they told him to run like hell.

He could still feel the heat from the blast. If he hadn't
stepped back several feet, he would be toast. Again instinct
had saved him. The moment he'd smelled gas. . . .

He'd known instantly they couldn't stay in South Carolina. Too many incidents now. He would be held, and
he sensed she would be released. She would be on her
own.

God, but he hurt. The blast had opened the wound he'd
gotten at Jekyll, and he felt the blood running down his
side. Now neither of them had any clothes other than what
they were wearing. They had only the dog and those
damned boxes.

He said a quiet prayer of thanksgiving that they had
taken Bojangles with them. He didn't know how she
could deal with another loss. Everything had been taken
from her: her home, her friend, perhaps even her livelihood.

He leaned back, closed his eyes and tried to will away
the pain. He didn't want her to know how bad it was.

The worst were the burns. They would have to stop and

get some antibiotic salve and hope that it helped. He didn't want to go to a hospital or clinic. Or even a doctor. They would be looking for him there. They would know he was hurt.

That was, he knew, assuming a lot—that they had access to security or law enforcement agencies. He now feared that they—whoever *they* were—did. He'd underestimated them from the beginning.

Amy didn't say anything as they drove up the coast toward Washington, not when they passed the beach where they had stopped earlier, not when they passed several beach villages.

Finally, she stopped the car and turned off the engine. He opened his eyes and saw they were at a drugstore. She studied him. "I think you should go to a doctor."

"No," he said. "I know about stuff like this. Get some cotton balls, antiseptic cream, gauze and tape, peroxide and aspirin."

She hesitated. "I still think. . . ."

"It's minor, Amy. I—we—don't want to have to explain what happened. The explosion will be all over the state news."

"If you don't feel better tomorrow. . . ."

"We will talk then," he said.

She disagreed. He knew that. But after a moment's hesitation, she left the car.

He tried to think. He had no idea how much money they had left. She had given him several hundred for groceries and gas. He didn't know whether she had left any money in the cottage when he'd had the very bad idea of a brief holiday from running. They had no clothes. He couldn't use the damned cell phone, which was one of the few possessions he still had.

They had to have money. He would have to take a chance and call the ranch. Or would he? There was the woman who ran the general store near the ranch. They had chatted back and forth quite a bit on his visits. Maybe he could call her from a public phone and ask her to contact his ranch foreman. The more he thought about the idea, the more he liked it.

Joe had access to funds in order to run the ranch. It wasn't much, but enough, he hoped, for the next several days.

He closed his eyes again.

He opened them when he heard the car door opening. She tossed a large bag next to him. "I think we should stop somewhere and let me doctor you."

"That sounds like a good idea," he said, forcing his voice to sound lazy.

"I found a couple of T-shirts," she added.

He looked at her. "How much money do you have left?"

"A thousand," she said, adding regretfully, "I left several thousand more in the house."

"I'm sorry."

"It isn't your fault."

He knew, though, that she couldn't have that much money. Not as an untenured professor. She must have taken out everything she had.

Tomorrow he would call Betty Manfield, the owner of the general store, and have money wired to Washington.

Tonight, he needed rest. He was tired. Weak. He knew the signs. Belated shock. Loss of blood. He needed rest. Time for the body to absorb what had been inflicted upon it. His mind worked fuzzily.

She seemed to sense it. "Should I stop?"

He nodded. "Someplace. . . ."

"Cheap and shoddy," she finished the sentence. "I know."

"You'll have to go in. I don't . . . think I would pass inspection, even for cheap and shoddy."

She glanced over at him. "Not exactly what you promised earlier," she said wryly.

"No." It was all he could manage. It certainly wasn't

what he'd promised with his eyes and words and body. They'd needed each other then. Now he needed her.

"How about this?" she asked.

He looked out. Daylight had faded into dusk, then into night. The motel was obviously a "by the hour" type. He suspected most of the license plates would be local. He might switch one of them for his tonight.

He nodded. "Looks good." It didn't look good. It looked terrible. But at the moment any haven would be a blessing.

He watched as she parked out of sight of the office. She was learning. No one to check the license plate, even if they cared. She got out and went inside as Bo gave a half-hearted bark.

In minutes, she was back out with a key attached to a big black piece of plastic. No magnetic room cards here. She got back inside the car and drove around to the corner of the motel.

"We're set," she said. "I asked for something real private." She spoke with a pronounced southern accent.

He reached out and took her hand. "You're one hell of a woman," he said.

"Have I thanked you for getting repeatedly shot, beaten, and wounded on my behalf?"

"On both of our behalfs," he corrected.

She got out of the car, and opened the back door for Bo to jump out. Then she took the bag. He had to struggle to open his door and stand. She went over to him and put his arm around her shoulder, and together they reached the door to the room. She unlocked it, and they stumbled inside. He sat on the bed.

Irish watched as Amy turned on the lights, then the television.

She went into the bathroom and came out with a wet towel. He shrugged off the bloody, torn shirt, then allowed her to help him take off the T-shirt, part of which was stuck to his chest. There were large red marks scattered over his torso and arms. The wound on his side was partially open, and fresh blood mixed with dark dried spots.

She washed around the wound as gently as possible.

"Peroxide now," he said.

She poured the liquid on a cotton ball and gingerly pressed it against the wound. He could tell it probably hurt her more than it hurt him. Her fingers felt cool against his skin, her touch gentle. When she'd finished with the per- oxide, she taped gauze over the wound. She moved to the abrasions and burns, this time using a Benzocaine spray to cut the pain.

They were, he knew, fairly minor, but they still stung like hell. He felt as though a hundred porcupine quills had been stuck in him and set on fire. But at last she was through spreading antibiotic cream. He still hurt, so he took several aspirins, then he watched television with her. The stations were from Richmond. No news of an explo- sion in South Carolina.

They'd had no food. "The picnic," he said.

Her eyes widened, then she smiled slightly. "Not ex- actly the way I imagined it."

Nor the way he had imagined it. A bottle of wine in bed. Cheese. Bread. Strawberries. He'd thought of imaginative ways to eat the strawberries earlier. Lot of good it did him now.

She went out the door, taking her purse with the gun. She was a lot gutsier than he ever imagined. In another minute she returned. She put the cooler on the dresser, then carefully locked the door.

He started to get up, but she stopped him with a look. "Just once let me take care of you."

He decided that was a reasonable request.

She spread out the bread and cheese. There were also a couple of pieces of roasted chicken kept chilled by the ice. The strawberries were a little wilted, but she put those out, too. Then she opened the wine with the corkscrew he'd thoughtfully dropped in the ice chest.

He took a piece of chicken, amazed at how hungry he was until he realized they hadn't eaten since this morning. He hesitated before taking a sip of wine. There was no way anyone knew they were here. There hadn't been time for anyone to follow them. Still, one glass would be his limit.

The bread and cheese were good, more than good. Or else he was more than hungry. But once that ache went away, the others amplified. They shared the bounty with Bo, whose dog food had been blown up with the cottage. Among the three of them, they ate every crumb.

"Go to sleep," she said.

"There's only one bed."

"I know. I plan to share it with you."

"I'm covered with salve."

"I know. I put it on you."

He was too tired to argue. A good night's sleep, and he would be better. Still, he tried again. "We should take turns watching."

"I looked all the way," she said. "There was no one following us, and no chance for someone to plant one of those gizmos."

He raised an eyebrow. "Gizmos?"

"Or whatever they're called," she said.

Her voice was light, and he knew she was trying to reassure him. It seemed strange to be on the receiving end of reassurance. But he liked it.

He slipped off his jeans, which left only the swimming trunks. He would have dearly liked taking those off, too, but he was in no shape to make love, and he had a feeling that come morning he might damn well try. No matter what.

But he held out his hand. She sat next to him, her fingers caressing his in a sure, rhythmic soothing way. He closed his eyes.

• • •

Amy woke up to Bojangles' frantic nudges.

She lay there for a moment, her fingers tangling in his fur.

Then the events of the last twenty-fours flooded over her.

Every moment. The sun, the sea, the kiss. Then the explosion. The blood. The fear as she drove away. The pain she felt in his pain. She felt the warmth of his body beside her. He'd been a quiet sleeper. She touched his forehead. It was cool. And she knew the sleep was good for him. His body was demanding it after all the abuse it had taken.

Still wearing the new T-shirt she had slept in, she slipped out of the bed and pulled on her jeans.

They both needed new clothes, but their money was getting dangerously low. She would have insurance money from the house, but that would probably take weeks, and then there was the problem of getting it.

She knew one thing. Returning to Memphis was now on hold. She was not that foolish. She realized that her decision yesterday had been based partly on fear of Flaherty and the feelings he evoked in her.

How long was this nightmare going to last?

It *was* a nightmare, and yet she was beginning to understand the appeal that danger had for some people. She'd tasted the adrenalin, the heightening of senses, including the terror and then the relief. Everything was more vivid. The senses, the sights, the colors. . . .

How much vivid could she take?

She pulled on her sneakers, found the room key on the chest, then quietly opened the door and slipped out with Bo at her feet. She hadn't asked whether the motel permitted dogs; the privacy of the room, she thought, would allow her to walk him without being seen from the office. If they stayed the day, she would put out the "Do Not Disturb" sign.

Thank God, Bo was not a barker.

A couple with a dog was easier to find than a couple without one.

After scanning the parking lot for anything unusual, Amy walked Bo behind the motel, along the edge of a weed-infested field. As usual, he quickly tended to his needs and was ready to go inside. He was not an adventuresome dog, and preferred the safety of an interior to the dangers of the outside.

Amy took him back to the room. Flaherty was still asleep. She felt his forehead, worrying about him, and thought about waking him. *No.* He'd had precious little sleep this past week.

Instead she wrote him a note, telling him she would be right back. She put the time on the note, so he wouldn't worry. *Eight a.m.*

"You stay here," she whispered to Bo, "take care of him." Then she slipped back out, this time taking the car keys.

She'd seen a fast food restaurant a block away. She drove there and picked up two large cups of coffee, two orange juices, four sausage biscuits, four steak biscuits, some French toast bits, and two orders of potatoes. She also bought a newspaper from a machine.

He was awake when she returned. She heard the water running in the bathroom, and she set the two bags down.

The door to the bathroom was open. He wore only his bathing suit, and she watched the muscles in his back move as he washed. He turned and gave her a wry smile. "No toothbrush. No razor."

"But food," she said as the aroma of coffee filled the room.

He came into the room and slipped on his jeans, then took a cup of coffee with a grateful sigh. "You have no idea how much I hoped you were bringing this."

She watched as he gulped down food. She ate not

quite as quickly, sharing hers with Bo. "What do we do now?"

"Get some clothes, first of all," he said. "And something to shave with. Then I have to make some phone calls. After that I think we had better leave the area."

"I think you need more rest," she said, looking at the burned spots and scrapes on his body. The wound that had opened had bled onto the bandage, turning it a bright red.

"We won't go far," he promised.

"Some doctoring first," she said. "Sit down."

"Yes ma'am." He took one last sip of coffee and placed the cup on the table.

He looked devilishly attractive despite bruises and cuts. The new bristle of his beard gave him a rougher look, and his blue eyes were as vivid and bright as she had ever seen them. His body, despite old scars and new burns and scrapes marring it, was really quite . . . marvelous. Wide shoulders, muscled chest and arms. He was all muscle and power, with the grace of an athlete. She wondered whether he had played baseball or some other sport.

It made her realize once more how little she really knew about him.

And yet she knew everything she needed to know.

She went to the bathroom and tried to find something to use to attend his wounds. Unfortunately the towels—all a pinkish color from tending him last night—lay on the floor. The two plastic glasses had been used for the wine last night.

She took one of the dirty towels, ran it under hot water until she hoped she'd destroyed any germs, then returned to the room. All the salves and bottles and tape were on the table next to the bed.

Her patient looked . . . patient. He raised an eyebrow as he noted the soaked towel in her hand.

"It's all we have," she said apologetically.

"I've had a lot worse wounds and a lot worse nurses," he said.

She sat down next to him and started cleaning the burns and scrapes and abrasions. "Where?"

"South America. Bosnia. Florida."

"Why South America?"

"I was with a drug interdiction team, training a military unit to find and destroy coca fields. There was a little objection to our assistance."

"While you were with the CID?"

"No, I went to CID as a result. The command seemed to think I had a talent for working with my counterparts. I was transferred into the Military Police career field, attended the Police Officer Advanced Course, and did training in terrorism and counteraction, as well as other law enforcement courses. They said I had a knack for working with foreign nationals, so I was sent to Bosnia."

She knew that but wanted more details. "And were you good at working with them?"

He shrugged. "No one was. We were involved in confiscating weapons and making sure they weren't resold to one faction or another. Most serviceman are honorable, but there's always a bad apple here and there."

"Like fifty years ago?"

"It seems that way," he said grimly. "What I don't understand is why anyone cares now. That report would have died a natural death, noted by a few but dismissed as old news by almost everyone. Even if I did make some queries, it shouldn't have started this level of violence."

She gently washed the salve from the burn areas, then swabbed them with peroxide. "Maybe it wasn't you who started this . . . mess in motion."

"What do you mean?"

"Maybe Jon found something he didn't share with me. Maybe *he* asked the questions that started all this. Otherwise why kill *him*?"

"Would he keep something from you?"

"I wouldn't have thought so," she said. "We . . . were friends." Her voice broke slightly. Everything had happened so quickly, she still hadn't entirely absorbed his death, or its implications.

His hand caught hers. "It wasn't your fault," he said softly, as if he knew exactly what she was thinking.

But she was still thinking that. She'd never stopped thinking that. If she had never given those papers to Jon. . . .

Her hands hesitated. What if she had done the same thing to Flaherty? He thought he was the cause of all this, but what if she had led him into danger?

Why had she never taken the time to go through those papers? And why had her grandfather kept them?

Even as doubts about Jon continued to multiply, her hands kept busy, washing one cut or burn after the other, bandaging those wounds that were still bleeding slightly. It must have hurt, but he didn't move through the whole process. Finally she finished.

"Let me help you with the shirt," she said, handing one of the new T-shirts to him.

He winced slightly as he put his arms through the sleeves.

Then he sat still for a moment, as if absorbing the pain.

She sat down in the sole chair in the room. It was as uncomfortable as it looked. "I thought investigators just . . . sort of investigated."

"So did I," he admitted wryly. "I think I'm getting too old for this."

"Have you thought about retiring?"

He didn't say anything. She wondered if he *had* thought about it. But he was already a lieutenant colonel, and now had been offered a command. *If* she hadn't ruined any chance he had. "What would you do if you did leave?"

"I have the ranch in Colorado."

She hadn't expected that. But then she'd noticed his

athletic grace. Maybe it hadn't been baseball, but riding. Or perhaps both.

"Did you ever play baseball?" she asked.

Flaherty looked at her as if she'd lost her mind. After a moment, he nodded. "I played some in high school, then at the Point. Why?"

"You walk like a baseball player. Or a horseman."

"Oh," he said. "And how is that?"

"Kind of a swagger." That wasn't it at all, but she wasn't going to tell him he was graceful.

"Ouch," he said. "No one ever told me that before."

"It's not too bad."

He grinned. "That's a little better. I think."

"Tell me about your ranch."

"Isn't much there now. My grandfather left it to me."

"General Flaherty?"

"Yes."

"Did you know him well?"

"I spent my summers there. My mother didn't like it. She considered him a bad influence. Anything connected to the military was a bad influence. But then she married a dentist, and he and I didn't like each other much. She sent me away to keep peace in the household. But she always hated Grandfather."

"You can't blame her," she said. "Losing two husbands to the military."

The side of his mouth crooked. "That's why I never married. I saw what the Army did to personal relationships."

He stood. His hand reached out for hers, and he pulled her up. She didn't look at him. She didn't want him to see the censure in her eyes. She knew it was there. She would have done anything for her mother. She had, in fact.

His fingers went under her chin and forced it up until her eyes met his.

"You can't let anyone run your life," he said softly, "or

you make everyone unhappy. My father was a hero. I worshiped him as a boy. When he died, I vowed I would make him proud of me."

"Wasn't that letting a dead man run your life?"

"It would have been if I didn't like the military. I'm a gypsy at heart. Always have been. The Army was all I ever wanted."

Gypsy at heart. He was warning her.

"But you mentioned retiring. . . ."

"And I will someday." His voice was also cool.

Someday.

Amy shook her hand loose and turned away. She started putting the peroxide bottle and tubes and bandages in the bag. She put his old bloodied shirt in the trash can.

"No," he said. "I want to take it with us. We'll drop it in a trash bin somewhere."

The words reminded her of how much danger they were in. For a few moments she had almost forgotten. She bundled up the stiffened cloth. Stiffened with his blood.

"Ready to go?" she asked.

"Yes." His voice was still cool. Distant.

"Do you want me to drive?"

"I will," he said. "You keep an eye out for anything unusual."

She didn't protest. They had lost something in these past few moments, and part of her desperately wanted it back. And yet she couldn't change it. What hadn't he said?

Don't judge until you've walked in someone's shoes.

How often she'd heard that. Her mother had said it often, particularly when she had taken up with someone new, or invited a derelict to share their scanty meal, or after they woke and found half of their belongings gone.

But she was judging him, and he knew it.

She opened the door for Bo, then walked around to where the car was parked. The car keys were in her purse and she dug them out, feeling the pistol as she did so. She tossed them over to Flaherty, and he caught them easily. She waited until he unlocked the doors, then opened the door for Bo. When he was settled in the middle of the seat, she got in, Bo between them.

She really didn't have to do that.

There was already a huge barrier between them.

nineteen

Sally's life had always been tumultuous. Her parents' marriage had been volatile. Her father had been a charmer, scooping her up in his arms and telling her she was the prettiest girl in the world.

Her mother made her father's life miserable and finally left him, dragging an unwilling Sally with her.

She had just returned from her senior prom when her mother told her that her father was dead. He'd killed himself. The ultimate selfish act, her mother had said.

Sally had never forgiven her for that statement, nor had she forgiven herself for dancing and enjoying herself when her father was in agony. She had not sensed it the day before when she'd talked to him. Maybe if. . . .

But lives were full of ifs. She'd turned to the only person she felt would understand, her cousin who had always protected her, who had taken her to movies when her parents were having furious fights, who had convinced her that it was not her fault. Had *tried* to convince her. He had also tried to convince her that the fault in the marriage had not been Sally's.

Sally knew she had been wandering. For some reason, she couldn't seem to really grasp anything of importance. She'd loved drawing as a girl, but she blamed her mother's abandonment of her father on her mother's own art and career. Art was the only thing that mattered to her mother, who now owned a little gallery in Sedona, Arizona.

Sally received Christmas checks from her but sent them back. She simply didn't want anything to do with her. Her mother had always been a distant figure, while her father had represented the only warmth she knew. Sally had always believed that if she hadn't been in a hurry that night of the prom, she might—in some way—have prevented her father's death. Her own guilt built on what she believed was her mother's indifference to William Eachan's death.

After Dustin left, she stared at the art supplies for a long time. She was restless. She didn't really understand what was happening, and Dustin had purposely been vague. But she'd trusted him so long that she obeyed.

She was thirty-five. Anyone else would have their life firmly in hand. Instead, she still drifted among the shipwrecks of her family, unable to seize a life raft. Instead, she waited for someone to save her.

It wasn't a very attractive picture. She wondered why Dustin even bothered.

She picked up the sketch pad and a charcoal pen, then curled up on a sofa, folding her legs underneath her. She looked at it for a long time, then her hand began to move across the surface. Slowly at first, then faster. A face began to develop. Strong. Aristocratic. The eyes were partially shadowed, though, the expression enigmatic. It was a face she knew well, but the essence had always escaped her. Dustin masked his feelings, moods, emotions. He was so many people that she never quite knew which one she was with. He could be intolerably sarcastic and mean-spirited, then the next moment do or say something so sweet that it would completely negate his earlier remarks.

Who was the two-faced god in mythology? Janus?

The sketch came to life as she darkened the cheekbones, brushed in the shock of hair that sometimes disobeyed his sense of propriety and fell on his forehead. She hesitated at the mouth. To smile or to frown?

Instead she found herself turning his lips in a quizzical expression, as if even he himself didn't know exactly who or what he was.

By the time she finished, dusk had fallen and she felt hunger gnawing at her. Dustin had left just before dawn. She had heard him showering and had gone out to bid him good-bye. He had stared at her for a long time, then smiled, catching her hand in his.

"You're beautiful, you know," he said, and she'd wondered whether she really heard a wistful note in it. She wanted him to kiss her, to lean down and kiss her as he had long ago in a stable when she had returned to her grandparents' for a visit after her father had died.

Her grandmother had found them. She'd lectured them both at length. They were *cousins.* The very idea was sinful and wrong.

Later Dustin had spent an hour in their grandfather's den, and the next day had left. There had been no good-bye, no note. She hadn't seen him again for two years.

So many years ago. And yet she still remembered that kiss.

Nothing else had matched it. No other embrace had made her feel right.

God knew she had tried hard enough to find its equal.

Oh, he had kissed her since then, but they had been light, feathery, relative-type kisses. Not the intense need that had rocked them.

It had rocked him, too. She knew it.

She stared at the sketch. She had caught some of him, but not all.

Sally finally put it aside. Time to go out and eat. Maybe go to the bar nearby, she thought defiantly. She remembered Dustin's warning. But she'd been here five days now and had seen nothing suspicious.

With that thought in mind, she went into the bedroom to

change clothes and apply some makeup. Just a few hours
away from this room. Otherwise she would go stir-crazy
with all the thoughts of Dusty and the mess she'd made of
her life.

You're just like your father.

Shivers rocked her body for a moment. Her mother had
accused her of that more than once, and as a teenager Sally
had gone out of her way to prove her mother right. Now
she was very careful about how much she drank.

Am I, Daddy? Am I like you?

Why couldn't she take charge of her own life?

Because she had no goal. No aim. She wasn't good at
anything but art, and being pretty. She'd discarded art, and
being pretty meant nothing, especially now that she was
getting older.

You're like your father.

She looked at the paints again.

Maybe she'd try another sketch and have just a sandwich tonight.

She would go somewhere tomorrow.

WASHINGTON, D.C.

Dustin knew he couldn't keep Sally safe much longer. She
was like a caged butterfly.

He stared down at his messages. Among the stack were
three messages from Colonel Flaherty, the last one this
morning, just minutes before he came in.

*Damn it, the colonel wasn't going to let go. Or maybe
at this point, he couldn't.*

He turned on his computer, and logged on to the E-mail.
A message from his contact in the Justice Department. The
police were looking for Flaherty and Amy Mallory for
questioning. They were identified as being at a house in
the Myrtle Beach area that was destroyed in an explosion.
If that were true, why hadn't they remained? Why would
Flaherty risk his career by running?

And how had they been identified? He called his friend at the FBI.

"Should I know why you're interested?" his friend said.

"No," Dustin said flatly.

A silence. "You're not mixed up in anything. . . ."

"No," Dustin said. "He called me a few days ago, something about our grandfathers."

"Don't lie to me, Dustin. I'm going out on a limb for you."

"I'm not. And I'll protect you. Just see if you can find out how Flaherty's name surfaced."

"I'll check on it, but if you're not being straight with me. . . ."

"Then you can do what you have to do," Dustin said. "Thank you."

The phone clicked off, and Dustin wondered whether he'd lost one of the few friends he had.

Flaherty must have checked on him. His name might well surface in some way. He would have to get to Flaherty first.

He called in his secretary. "Judy, next time Colonel Flaherty calls, I want to talk to him. If I'm not here, give him my cell phone number."

She looked at him with surprise. Only a handful of people had that number.

"Yes, sir."

"What did you tell him the last time he called?"

"What I told everyone. You had a family emergency and I didn't know exactly when you would be back."

He would call. Dustin was sure of that. One message two days ago, two yesterday. He returned to his office and called his contact at the Justice Department. "Ed, can you get a trace on a cell phone into my office?"

"I can get a number. As for location, no. Not unless we know exactly when he's going to call. Then. . . ."

"Thanks," Dustin said.

His intercom buzzer interrupted.

"I'll get back to you," he said, hanging up. He turned on the intercom speaker. "Judy?"

"The Deputy Secretary of State. He needs to see you about your recommendation on the sale of those Jordan Industries vehicles."

"When?"

"Now."

Dustin grimaced. He'd finally recommended against the sale. Jordan had obviously gone over his head. He remembered Jordan's veiled threats, but damned if he was going to put those vehicles in the hands of a dictator to use against his neighbors. He would be the one explaining that if the war escalated.

He looked at his watch. "If Flaherty calls, tell him to call back at noon. I'll have lunch here."

"Would you like me to order something?"

"Salad and sandwich." She knew what he liked.

Dustin checked the mirror in his private restroom, straightened his tie, and hoped the rings around his eyes weren't as bad as he feared they were. David Talbot would be sure to ask him about his "family business," if everything was all right. Probably if he planned any more unscheduled trips. And more certainly he would try to persuade him to change his recommendation. Jordan was a very large campaign contributor.

To hell with that. If Jordan won on this one, it wouldn't be the end of his not so subtle blackmail. Dustin was not going to open that door.

NORFOLK, VIRGINIA

Around midday, Flaherty and Amy reached Norfolk. They'd taken secondary roads, feeling they would be safer. They could keep a better eye out for anyone tailing them. He'd also gone over the car once more, checking every inch of it for some kind of tracking device.

They had stopped briefly in a discount department store

in a small city. Amy gave him a list of what she needed, and he'd gone inside. Neither of them felt they could leave Bo, even for a few moments, in a locked car. She rolled down the windows and placed her purse next to her.

Because of long lines, it took him longer than he wanted. He used Amy's cash to pay the bill. Shaving gear. Toiletries. Two pairs of jeans, two T-shirts and a long-sleeve shirt for him; a pair of jeans, a pair of shorts and several tops for her. A dish for Bo along with a bag of dog food. And a cheap suitcase to put everything in.

He also got a six-pack of sodas and several packages of crackers. A the last moment, he grabbed a baseball cap.

He used his ranch credit card at a bank machine to draw out four hundred dollars—the limit from one machine. Hopefully, the bad guys weren't watching that account since it wasn't in his name. Even if they were, he would be long gone by then. He also called Betty, his friend from the general store, waking her because of the time difference. He asked her to drive out to the ranch and tell Joe Mendoza that he'd taken money from the account and might take more. He stressed the urgency of not using the phone. Like many westerners, she asked no questions, figuring he would tell her what he wanted her to know.

He called Eachan, but the official wasn't in yet. When he hung up, he returned to the car. Amy stood outside the car, obviously stretching. She was clutching the purse, and her gaze kept moving. Her eyes lit as she saw him, but then the glow faded as she remembered exactly why they were here.

Still, it was nice that she was lowering her guard a little. The drive this morning had been awkward because of yesterday's conversation. He'd made it clear that he was a loner and a gypsy, and didn't care what anyone thought. Perhaps he'd done so because the mention of his mother raised dangerous emotions and memories.

He didn't want her to think of him as anything but what

he was. He was no paladin, no saint, no selfless hero. Hell, he'd been caught in this situation as much as she.

He hadn't been that competent, either. He should have anticipated the attempts on them. He'd always been the hunter, never the prey, and he didn't like it at all. Neither did he like the feeling of impotence it gave him.

Most of all, he feared that growing feelings for her were dulling his instincts, and that would be fatal for both of them. He had to keep his head. Falling into bed with her almost guaranteed that he wouldn't.

He stole a glance at her as they reached the city limits of Norfolk. He had decided to stop here for several reasons. One was its military population. Another was the large number of motels and trailer parks serving that particular population. Equally important, Washington was only about three hours away.

"Hungry?" he said.

"Yes."

"Anything special?"

"A salad," she said hopefully.

"I'll see what we can do."

They went past a number of motels, hotels, and hamburger places. He pulled in at a self-proclaimed delicatessen. "A sandwich, too?"

"A hot pastrami, if they have it," she said.

He nodded. "Then we'll find some place to stay for a day or two."

"Any ideas?"

"A few." Except his last one didn't work all that well. How had someone found them? He would try to be a little more creative this time. And he still had to call Eachan again. He might have a missing puzzle piece.

He disappeared inside the deli, stopping first to pick up several newspapers. They were late for lunch and early for supper, so business was light. Within five minutes, he left the deli with two bulging sacks of food.

They didn't eat there. Instead, he drove around until he

found a park. They all needed to get out of the car. Bo was particularly eager, especially after Irish filled the dog's new dish with water from the park restroom.

"What now?" she asked as she fed Bo part of a sandwich.

"This is a Navy city. Sailors live here six months, then ship out. There are lots of visitors and a lot of turnover in trailer parks."

"How long do you plan to stay here?"

"Until we can arrange a meeting with Eachan. See if he knows anything about my sudden transfer."

She didn't say anything, but her gaze stayed on him, her big gray eyes solemn and just a little distant. They were far more cautious than they had been yesterday on the beach. He felt as if he'd lost something very valuable.

It was for the best.

They finished in silence. He looked at the paper. Nothing about either him or Amy. He skipped over to the want ads. He was aware that Amy had stood and walked away, obviously taking Bo for a stroll.

He found trailer parks, then rentals. He circled three. Then he turned to the used cars section, and he circled several offerings. When he finished, he stood, waiting for Amy to return.

They had to get a place to stay. He was still weak, still hurting. They needed a temporary headquarters, and he knew the language of the military. He would bet his last dollar that the trailer parks were either owned or managed by retired sailors.

He considered his appearance. He needed to do something about that. When Amy returned, he headed for the car and his newly acquired goods, including his shaving gear, and returned to her side.

"Do you mind staying out here for a few moments? I should get cleaned up."

"I'll be fine."

"You have the pistol with you?"

"Yes."

"If you see or hear anything suspicious, come after me."

She nodded and sat down.

He didn't want to leave her again, even for a few moments. But he had left her earlier when he'd gone shopping, and that would have been a better opportunity for an attack than this. Too many people here.

The public restroom was empty. He shaved at the sink. Then he changed clothes. Jeans. The long-sleeve shirt with the sleeves rolled up. His face still looked as if he'd been in one hell of a fight, but there was nothing he could do about that. He might even make it work to his advantage.

It was the damned telephone call to Eachan that bothered him. He no longer felt he could use his cell phone. Nor did he want to use a public phone anyplace close to where they were staying. Once settled, he would drive to Portsmouth and call from there. Fifty miles away. He didn't like it, but he no longer underestimated the other side's resources.

Amy tried to relax as she waited for Flaherty. She'd hated the tension that had accompanied them today, but she didn't know how to break it.

She tried not to think of him inside the restroom. His face had been darkened by stubble this morning, and the assorted bruises and cuts made him look as much the ruffian as she'd ever seen. They went with his cool, detached words this morning about his mother, about his dedication to a life that allowed little intimacy.

It contrasted so completely with the gentleness and warmth he radiated on the beach yesterday. Before the world crashed in on them again.

She swallowed hard as he exited the restroom. He was completely changed. He was clean-shaven, and he wore a cap that in some way changed everything about him. His jaw seemed more slack, his eyes not quite as wary. Only that intriguing crook of his lips seemed the same.

She had seen actors change their appearance not through makeup or clothes, but the way they carried themselves, the facial expressions that distinguished a businessman from a street person. She'd never known anyone who could do it.

"You look different," she said.

"That's the idea," he replied with a quirk of his lips.

She stared at him, wondering if she knew him at all. "Have you worked undercover before?"

"A few times."

Something else she hadn't known but should have guessed. She'd known, of course, that he was with CID, and she knew a little about that agency. After meeting him, she had found its site on the web. The most interesting things were its independence from the regular chain of command, and that most of its agents were warrant officers or civilians. But he obviously had been groomed for command within the service.

He was, all in all, an enigma.

She followed him to the car. "I should change, too."

"You're perfect as you are," he said.

Knowing exactly how she looked, she wasn't sure what he meant by that.

They got into the car. "Where now?"

"Gas and a city map," he said. "Then we're going to find a suitably disreputable truck and rent a trailer."

"Why a truck?"

"We can't drive up to a trailer park in an upscale rental car and claim we've been mugged."

"We've been mugged?"

"Better than what really happened. Also explains why we don't have identification."

"Then how do we have money to pay for anything?"

"A friend wired us some."

She looked toward him and lifted an eyebrow. "You're a very good liar."

"Sometimes it's a necessary skill in my line of work." He hesitated, then added, "You're Lori Hunt. I'm Al Hunt. Retired Chief Petty Officer."

"Lori," she said, tasting the sound of it. "I always wanted to be a Lori."

His lips turned up. "Why is that?"

"Lori sounds exotic."

"I think you *are* exotic."

"I'm a plain, ordinary history teacher."

"Is that what you think?"

Amy didn't answer. They were turning onto a main road. As had been her habit in the past week, she scanned the streets behind them. But she knew she used that as an excuse. Her description was *exactly* what she'd thought. Her life had certainly taken on a certain . . . complacency. She'd given up notions of a white knight, of a great romance.

She had great reservations as to whether Irish Flaherty could ever be that. He certainly had made it clear that he wanted no permanent bonds, but maybe that was a necessary quality for knight errants.

She just wished it didn't hurt so much. As much as she wanted to save her physical self, she also wanted to protect her heart.

Flaherty made a turn and she saw several used car lots. He drove into one. "This shouldn't take long," he said.

She really wanted to go with him. She was becoming fascinated with the Machiavellian way his mind worked.

But she couldn't because of Bo. And, she suspected, she might well ruin Flaherty's plan. She waited.

"I want cheap transportation for my son," Irish told the salesman. "He's turning seventeen next week. But," he warned, "reliable."

The salesman gave him a huge grin. "Got just what you

want. We specialize in old but well-maintained vehicles. Now what sum are we thinking about?"

Irish noted the *we*. "I was thinking about something around five hundred."

The grin faded a little. "Now that might be asking a little much. Hey, what happened to your face?"

"Mugged," Irish said. "Last night." He shoved the bill of his cap a little farther down on his forehead as if in serious thought. "Why don't you just tell me what you have?"

"Can't get anything manufactured in the nineties for that."

"Didn't think so."

"Well we might have an '88. But can't let you have it for less than eight hundred. Be losing money if I did."

"I'll look at it."

He was led to the back of the lot, past a number of brightly washed cars with prices scribbled on their windows. There were a few sad-sack vehicles at the very back.

The salesman led him to one. "Trade-ins," he said. "Haven't had time to pretty 'em up. But we wouldn't have taken them if they didn't run right."

There were three vehicles. All of them probably headed toward the junk heap or the salvage dealer. One was an old station wagon. Two were sedans from the mid-eighties. No pickup.

"My kid wanted a pickup."

"Sorry. This is all we got."

Irish eyed the station wagon. But no kid would want that. He moved to the second sedan. An ugly purple. But a kid might like it. If it ran.

"How much is the purple number?"

"A thousand."

Irish raised an eyebrow. "Does it run?"

The salesman looked indignant. "I'll bring the keys."

A moment later, Irish turned the key in the ignition. It turned, but sounded rough as hell.

"Piece of junk," he told the salesman. "But my kid is good with cars. Tell you what, I'll give you that five hundred I mentioned."

"Nine hundred," the salesman said.

"Can't get that much by selling to salvage, and you know that's all it's good for."

"*You* want it," the salesman retorted.

"Want is an exaggeration. I'll take it off your hands for, say, six hundred. Not a penny more."

The salesman looked pained. "My boss will have my hide."

"Your boss will be ecstatic. You won't have this eyesore sitting in your lot."

"You a Navy man?"

Irish grinned widely. "How did you know?"

"Do a lot of business with 'em. Was in the Navy myself."

"My kid's planning to enlist when he finishes high school."

The salesman's face cleared. "I think we can arrange something."

"I hoped you could," Irish said.

Minutes later, with car registration papers proclaiming Al Hunt as the proud new owner of a purple eyesore, Irish returned to the car. "We passed an apartment complex down the road. I'll meet you there. We'll leave the rental car there."

Amy eyed the purple car dubiously. "Do we have to?"

"I'm afraid so. It's just for a couple of days."

She sighed, then moved over to the driver's side and started the car. He followed her to the apartment complex, and they transferred all they owned. Bo. The boxes of her grandfather's papers. The suitcase with their meager belongings. Her laptop computer. The cooler.

He drove the recently purchased car out of the complex. It was like riding in a tank. The air-conditioning didn't work. Her window came down halfway, then stuck. "You have a real eye for cars," she observed.

"I think so," he replied with equanimity.

He handed her a map. "Can you find Fourth and Cedar? It's southeast."

She found the spot on the map and guided him easily. He found himself smiling at the precise, concise way she did it. She did so much just like that. She concentrated, and never let anything get in her way.

He would miss her. He would miss her very much when this was over.

More, in fact, than he ever wanted to admit.

He shoved the thought aside as a string of trailer parks appeared. He found the one he was searching for, and drove in, parking in front of a building with an "Office" sign outside.

The trailers and their small sites looked neat and well-kept. He wasn't sure whether that would be an advantage or a disadvantage. Well, he had several other prospects.

He got out of the car and went around to Amy's side. He opened the door. "Ready, Lori Hunt?"

Her gaze met his and never wavered. He was beginning to understand that she liked challenges. She might not know it, or recognize it, but she was a competitor, a warrior in her own right, on her own terms.

She left the windows open and Bo in the car. He understood now that Bo was never going to go anywhere on his own. He was still amazed that the shy, affectionate dog had attacked someone in that Jekyll Island motel.

They opened the door and went inside. A man in his fifties—a paunch showing in what obviously had once been a fit body—sat at a desk. He looked up, scanning their faces. His gaze lingered on Irish's battered one, then at the newspaper ad in his hand.

"Can I help you?"

"You had an ad for a furnished trailer?"

The man nodded noncommittally.

"I'm Al Hunt. This is my wife, Lori. Our son's a squid on a sub that's due in next week. We're planning to stay a couple of months and visit with him."

At the words, the man's face relaxed. "We have a lot of sailors here."

"I thought we'd be more comfortable here. You see, I'm retired Navy myself. Finished my twenty a few months ago, and my wife and I drove here from California. Problem is, we were mugged last night, attacked in a state park. Lost all our identification. A friend wired me some money, but. . . ."

"Retired Navy, you say. Me, too. Retired fifteen years ago. Chief Petty Officer." He stuck out his hand. "Sam Beard. Don't worry about anything. I'll see you get what you need. Your kid's following the old man, huh? My kids couldn't get far enough from the Navy. One's a banker," he added with disgust.

"Yeah, I'm lucky," Irish said. "It's hard on the wife, though."

Sam Beard looked at her enviously. "Forgive me for saying so, ma'am, but you hardly look old enough to have a grown child."

Irish put his arm back around her. "We were married real young. Worked out good, though, didn't it, honey?"

"Yes, darling," she cooed.

"Nice to see a couple together after all those years. Mine left me. Gone too much, she said." He looked at Irish's face. "Those muggers did that?"

"Yeah. Didn't see one hiding in the shadows. They started roughing up my wife, and I took exception. They might have done something worse if they didn't hear someone coming." He hesitated. "I thought someone might be following. . . ."

"You don't need to worry about anything here," Sam said. "I'll be keeping an eye out for you. Lots of wives stay here alone when their husbands ship out. We look after our own."

"It's not myself I worry about," Irish said. "It's the missus."

The manager nodded. "The trailer is four hundred a month. Includes utilities. Usually ask for a deposit, but seeing as to what happened, I'll waive it."

Irish hesitated. "She has a small dog. Found it on the highway."

Sam shrugged. "As long as it doesn't bite. We have children here."

"He's afraid of his shadow."

"You pay for any damages."

"There won't be any. Never saw a better-behaved animal. That's why I let my wife keep it."

Sam nodded.

"I owe you, Chief." Irish took out his billfold and counted out two hundred carefully, as if each bill was dear. "I'll give you the rest at the end of the week. Those damn muggers . . ."

The manager nodded. "You don't want to see it before you pay?"

"It looks great from the outside. I can tell you take real pride in the place. It'll be fine, won't it, sweetie?"

"Just dandy, lollipop," she gushed.

He had to swallow a chuckle. Certainly no one had called him lollipop before. But Sam Beard looked amused. And approving.

They would be safe here.

He just wasn't sure how long.

twenty

It was an interesting crowd. A real mix. Young swinging singles. Several older couples who were obviously tourists. Some locals. They were easily identified by both their clothes and their comradeship with the bartender.

Sally had selected the bar carefully. A munchies bar. A place where people went on their way home from work or a place tourists went to get free hors d'oeuvres and often stayed longer than they intended. It even had ferns. She'd thought ferns had gone out ten years ago.

Most of all, it seemed reputable with plenty of reputable people. Safe. She needed people.

Dusty didn't understand that. He was so self-contained that he didn't need anyone. But she'd spent six days alone. She'd started painting again, working feverishly during the last two days. A sketch of Dusty, then an acrylic. She'd even attempted a seascape from the vantage point of her balcony. It might not be technically good, but she knew the colors were right. Vivid. The spurt had, at first, exhilarated her. Then depressed her. She would never be more than mediocre.

The loneliness deepened. So did the desperation. She feared she would lose her job, and she didn't want to lose another job. She knew her life resembled a locomotive headed downgrade without any brakes. She was in her mid-thirties and had a hundred friends, but none—except Dustin—with whom she could really be herself. For everyone else, she was a facade. A sparkling facade that had nothing behind it.

A bar was perfect for that. You could be with people—have human contact—without needing to make a commitment of any kind. You could walk away. She was very good at walking away.

She sat at the bar. The bartender was a good-looking young man with a tan and sun-bleached hair. Although he was probably ten years her junior, he was demonstrably attentive to her. A woman sat to the right of her. She was with another woman. Several minutes after Sally sat down, a couple of guys took the stools to her left.

As usual, she was careful. Ordering a glass of wine and listening to conversation. The man next to her was arguing about baseball scores. She just enjoyed the conversation around her, the noise.

The man on her left turned to her. "Here on vacation?"

He had a pleasant face. Hazel eyes and a nice smile. Unlike most of the other customers, he was dressed in a suit. That probably meant a salesman of some type.

"Yes."

"Where are you from?"

Sally remembered Dustin's warnings. He hadn't told her not to go anyplace, but he had asked her to be careful. She could do that.

She shrugged. "A lot of places." That, at least, was the truth.

"Where are you staying?"

"With a friend. She'll be here a little later."

He looked a little disappointed. "Can I buy you a drink?"

She had a policy about that. "Thank you, but no. I'm not ready." She smiled to soften the refusal. "What do you do?"

"I'm a lawyer."

That was interesting. "What kind of law?"

"Criminal."

She wrinkled her nose. "Murderers."

"Innocent people," he said with a chuckle.

"All of them?"

"Of course. Now tell me what you do."

Something made her hesitate. She could not tell him she worked for the State Department. She was using another name. She hesitated, then said the first thing that came to her mind. "I'm an artist."

"I'm impressed."

"Don't be. I'm not very good."

"How does a not very good artist support herself?"

"She has a gallery." Somewhere in her mind, she was conscious that she was using her mother. She wondered what a psychiatrist would say about that.

He eyed her speculatively.

She took a sip of wine. And while she did, her eyes wandered to his ring finger. Habit more than anything. Nothing on the ring finger. Of course, that didn't mean anything.

"Do you live here?" she asked.

"About three miles down the coast road."

"Any good restaurants?"

"Any number of them. Can I take you to one tonight?"

She remembered her excuse. "Sorry. I'm meeting a friend for dinner."

"Then tomorrow night?"

"I have plans, but thank you."

"How do you like our city?" He wasn't going to press, and she was grateful. She was also aware that the bartender, as busy as he was, was keeping an eye on her. She felt better. She took another sip, then another. She was aware that her companion gestured to her glass, and this time she didn't complain. He was obviously not going to be a problem.

And he was interesting. Attractive in a cool, assured way. A lot like Dustin.

Despite his easy bar talk, he was reserved. There was something dangerous in his eyes that appealed to her more than it should.

"I need to powder my nose," she said.

"I'll hold your seat."

She left and went into the restroom. She splashed water on her face, then looked at herself. *Why was she even here?* She didn't like one-night stands, and here she was mouthing all those bar clichés and even considering . . . hell, she didn't like what she was considering. She shouldn't have come. She'd just been so damned lonely.

Lonely enough to make a really bad mistake.

She ran a brush through her hair, then left, starting to wind her way back to the bar.

"Miss?" She turned around. The bartender was there.

"Yes?"

"The gentleman—the man—next to you put something in your drink."

Her heart seemed to stop. "What?"

"A pill of some kind. He didn't think I'd see it, but there was something . . . about him. He's never been in here before, and yet he seemed to want you to think he had. I could have just spilled your drink, but I thought you should know. . . ."

Her heart started again. In fact, it pounded. She started to dig in her purse for money to pay her bill.

"Never mind that, Miss. I'll keep him busy if you want to leave."

"The . . . police."

"I could lose my job over this," he said. "It would be better if you just leave."

She gave him a twenty-dollar bill. "Thanks again."

She waited until he went back to the bar and leaned over, talking to the stranger. She slipped out the door.

An attempt at date rape? Or something else? And it

would have worked if not for the bartender. She hadn't taken Dusty seriously about the threat.

What to do now? If it wasn't just a chance encounter, she must have been followed. They knew where she lived.

Panic seized her.

She had difficulty unlocking the car door. Her gaze was moving back and forth, to the bar's door and around the parking lot. Finally she opened it and got inside.

She wouldn't go back. Washington was six hours away. She would go straight to Dusty. He would know what to do.

NORFOLK

The trailer was old, but remarkably well-kept. It had two bedrooms, a kitchen, and a living area. The bath was surprisingly spacious.

Amy had certainly lived in a lot worse when growing up. For a young just-married couple, it was even kind of cute. One previous resident had decorated the kitchen area with dancing teapot wallpaper; another—or perhaps the same one—had painted a window on the back wall of the bedroom, which had none.

They took their belongings inside, inventoried the kitchen appliances, then he went to a nearby store. He returned with a large bag of groceries, a pizza, and sodas for two.

"Lollipop," he said in disgust as he took a slice of pizza.

She smiled sweetly. "I think the chief liked it."

"He liked *you*."

"You really are a very good liar."

"It wasn't much of a stretch. I've been around army towns all my life. Navy towns, too, when we had joint investigations." He paused. "But I'll need your computer to research ship deployments. I have the feeling Sam Beard might well want to share experiences."

"You can always say you were in the SEALs," she offered with just a hint of sarcasm. Or was it really a query?

She was beginning to wonder what he'd really done in South America.

"I think that might be pushing my luck."

She held his gaze. "Do you really think we can get lost in here?"

"It's by far our best bet at the time. There's no record."

"But if you call this Eachan?"

"I'll call in the morning from Newport News, and tell him that we're traveling up that way. I can't use the cell phone anymore."

"You think he's a part of what's happening?"

"I don't know. But I'm not taking any more chances."

"I think riding in that purple car is a chance."

"You're right about that. But we're just using it to and from the apartment complex."

"Isn't someone going to question strange cars?"

"It's too damn big. It could be anyone visiting one of several hundred units. It's safe enough."

Part of her admired his ingenuity and guile, but another deplored his ease with lying, particularly to good people. Bo whined, as if sensing her discomfort, and offered a paw. Instead, Amy patted her lap and he crawled up, one tentative paw after another.

Flaherty studied her. She felt the intensity behind his gaze. Warmth moved up her spine. She didn't want it there. She feared every tingly sensation that spread throughout her. Neither of them was dead tired. Neither had immediate fear. Neither had anything pressing to do. It was just the two of them.

The two of them.

He would go away when this was over. He would return to a life filled with excitement and danger. And she still didn't know exactly who he was. He'd been a good old boy just a few moments ago. It seemed to come as naturally to him as being a hard-eyed soldier who killed automatically, who handled a gun as easily as most people handled a pen.

He could be warm and tender, and yet her heart had chilled when he'd spoken so dispassionately about his family.

But as the air around them grew even more explosive, she knew she could no more resist what was happening than a moth could resist a flame. *It was too bright, too promising, too full of splendor.*

Bo whined as if he sensed the growing whirlwind.

"It's okay, Bo," she said, even as she heard the tremor in her voice. He didn't believe it either. He whined again.

"Down," Flaherty said.

Bo regarded him for a moment, then jumped down with obvious reluctance. He folded one front paw over the other and put his head on them, looking up with a disgruntled expression. But his tail wagged.

She leaned down and scratched his ears, and he looked less offended.

Flaherty moved over to her and held out his hand. She took it.

Fire roared between them. Flash point. She'd heard the expression but never really understood it until now. Her heart beat more rapidly. Blood pulsed in all the places it shouldn't. A trembling excitement reverberated inside, like the first rumblings of an earthquake. They stood still, caught for a moment of endless time in which she knew she was making a momentous decision, that her life would never be the same. If she surrendered to him now, she would be surrendering her heart.

A conscious decision. Not like the night on Jekyll Island when fear and relief and gratitude and bewilderment combined to throw them together.

Then his hand touched her cheek in a gesture so gentle her last reservation faded. She felt his breath against her hair as his fingers traced the curves of her face. They did so lovingly, as if she were beautiful. And she knew then that she *was* beautiful in his eyes. She found herself leaning her cheek against his hand in a gesture that said more than words could.

His face bent down, his lips met hers, and their bodies came together, his arms around her neck, hers around his. The heat that seared her also branded him. She could feel it in the tension of his body, and the hardening of it against hers.

Her own body changed, too. Her breasts grew taut and tender, the center of her body expectant and wanting.

She shivered, and his hands left her neck and ran up and down her body, stroking reassuringly as his lips gentled, then moved to her earlobe, nibbling it. Every touch, every brush of his lips was a caress, fine and arousing and intoxicating. His breath sent waves of pleasure through her.

She turned her head so her lips met his again, and the heat became an explosion. The gentleness was lost in hunger. Their lips turned frantic. Her mouth opened, and his tongue entered. Exploring. Seducing. Awakening every erotic nerve in her. Her body was composing a song, and she was swaying to the rhythm of it.

The hunger in her grew, a craving, a longing even stronger than before. Its call was irresistible.

His lips left hers, and he looked at her, his blue eyes as brilliant as a rare blue diamond and his mouth swollen by its contact with hers. "Amy?"

She swallowed hard. "Yes," she said. "Oh, yes."

His gaze lingered a moment. Hot. Wanting. But warning. Then his lips twisted into that appealing smile. He took her hand in his and led her to the larger bedroom. Still standing, he unbuttoned her blouse with such erotic grace that she was trembling. Then he unzippered her jeans and inched them down along with her panties.

She had never thought she had a beautiful body. She was too tall. Not thin enough. She'd always thought herself awkward. Yet his hands moved along it as if every curve were a thing of beauty. And she felt beautiful and glowing. And expectant. So expectant.

His hands ran through her hair and tightened around her shoulders. She closed her eyes to the gentle assault on her every sense, every emotion. She felt his arousal, and her own body responded in an explosion of expectation.

"Don't move," he said. He reached in his pocket and took out a package, putting it on the table next to the bed. Then he slipped off his clothes. She saw the bruises and cuts that were barely scabbing over. "Should. . . ."

"Of course we should," he said gruffly. "Or I'll be in a lot more pain."

She had to smile at that. She was beginning to understand exactly how he felt.

Their bodies met, fitting against each other as if they had been designed for that one reason. Raw, physical hunger seized her. She heard him groan, and she didn't know whether it was from restraint or the physical agony of their bodies stretching and bending toward one another.

He broke away and took out the contents of the package, then came back to her. Moving in concert—wordlessly, because they no longer needed words—they reached the bed. He guided her down and sat next to her, his fingers loving her with his touch. Then he was above her, balanced on his elbows while the lower part of his body teased and tantalized her.

Tantalize. She'd never really understood that word before, either. It wasn't just want or need. It was more . . . a crazed craving that had to be sated.

His lips returned to hers. Their tongues met, playing a sensuous game that heightened every sense. Even her toes tingled with a wonderful, electric tension. His mouth left hers and moved down to her left breast. He nibbled, then licked, and her body shuddered with reaction. She felt the change in his body, and her own responded. It was as if it was reaching out in some desperate quest. A greedy fire needing fuel.

The throbbing yearning deepened as he prolonged the agony, made her body arch up to meet his. His slow, deliberate entry only intensified the sensations, each movement creating billows of sensation.

He moved in and out slowly, preparing and exciting her until she thought she would go mad with wanting. "Irish," she whispered as she felt his restraint, his obvious effort to leash himself, to move slowly, ever so slowly.

Too slowly.

A cry of pure agony burst from her. But still he restrained himself, raining kisses on her eyes, her cheeks, the corner of her mouth until the throbbing inside became unbearable. Then the tempo of his movement quickened, and their bodies danced together in a sensuous waltz of two bodies in instinctive harmony.

One last thrust ignited rapturous bursts of pleasure, turning into a fireball of sensations. . . .

WASHINGTON, D.C.

"You fool!" The speaker could barely contain his anger. "Can't any of you do anything right?"

"I'll find her again," came the voice.

"You don't have to look. She'll be running straight to Eachan, and he'll protect her. I needed her as leverage, damn it. You're supposed to be so damn good, and you let a stupid bitch outmaneuver you."

"I almost had her. I don't know what happened."

"You said you could handle her alone."

Silence.

"She'll be on the road to Washington. Get to Eachan's before she does. Stop her before she goes inside."

"Yes, sir."

"Your employment depends on a successful conclusion of this matter."

The phone went dead.

twenty-one

It was pouring rain.

Sally could barely see in front of her. She hated the rain. She particularly hated driving in it.

She remembered driving all the way from Arizona to Maryland when her father died. Her mother had a show opening, and refused to go east to the funeral. She didn't want Sally to go, either. *Nothing you can do, honey. You can mourn him here.* But it wasn't the opening of the show, Sally knew that. Her mother hated everything to do with the Eachan family.

Sally had taken the car keys from her mother's purse during the night and started driving. She'd taken money from her mother's purse, too. Not that there was that much.

She'd known she wouldn't be in time for the funeral, but she kept driving. She could barely see the road through tears. It had been the loneliest time of her life.

Sally was pulled over in Louisiana. Her mother had called the cops on her. She'd spent the hours of her father's funeral in a jail cell.

She never forgave her mother. She ran away again and again. She even threatened to sue her mother after she heard of someone underaged doing exactly that. Her mother finally gave up, and Sally went to live with her grandparents, the Eachans. And after the death of their first-born, they had finally welcomed her.

She remembered every moment of that drive. It had been raining. She'd always equated the death with rain. It was the one thing she'd never told Dusty. . . .

The rain came harder. She reached the interstate, hesitated, then continued, hands clenched around the steering wheel. She drove another twenty miles, saw a rest stop, and turned off. Instead of taking the branch marked for cars, she followed the truck signs. Finding a number of the tractor trailers parked, she drove into a place between two of them. She had great faith in truckers.

She turned off the ignition and sat there. She had left so suddenly, she hadn't really thought much ahead. Now she did. She had three credit cards and a hundred dollars cash. There would be phones inside. She could call Dusty. She had his cell phone number. She could call from the pay phone here.

How did someone find her?

The only way was through Dusty. He wouldn't let anything slip. She knew that. He was the most cautious man she knew. That meant someone was tracing phone calls.

Would she bring danger to him? And if she called, could someone start tracking her movements? Would someone be waiting for her?

What would have happened if she'd taken that drink?

She shuddered. Why had she gone there?

The rain pounded against her windshield. On the roof of the car. A lonely sound.

Maybe she would rest a few moments. Try to think. She checked her doors. Both were locked. If anyone even tried to approach she would lean on her horn and wake up every trucker in the parking area.

The thought made her feel better. She tried to think of safe things. Dustin. That reminded her of the sketch of him in the apartment. She wished she had it now.

She wished she had *him* now.

NORFOLK

The world was a different place in the morning.

Amy knew it when she woke in Irish's arms. It might not last—these hours—but she knew she would never regret last night. She couldn't imagine now going through life without the experience of last night.

She had never known what lovemaking could be like. It certainly had never been like this with Alan. It had been comfortable with him. Not fire and storm.

Did fire and storm last?

She moved, and his hand reached out. "You're not leaving, are you?" Flaherty's voice was low and lazy and sexy.

She looked at the window. Dark outside. She wondered for a fleeting second what time it was, then discovered she didn't care, not when his arms pulled her closer to him. She felt his lips on the back of her neck, and she squirmed with the shudders that started deep inside.

"Shouldn't we . . . ?"

"Most definitely," he said.

She realized they weren't exactly talking about the same thing, but he was nibbling her ear, and his body was growing hard, and hers was growing taut; they, at least, were in harmony. Such wonderful harmony.

She turned to face him and began nibbling his ear as he had done hers. It tasted a little salty and really wonderful. He groaned, and she cherished the idea that she could make him do that.

He pulled the sheets off and moved against her. His hard, hot arousal made her ravenous.

He paused a moment, took a precaution that she had not considered. Then he was inside her again. She had thought nothing could match the intensity of last night.

She was wrong.

• • •

When Amy woke again, light was streaming through the window, and she smelled coffee brewing. She also realized that there was another difference between Flaherty and herself. His body clock and hers were not in sync. She was a bear in the morning, unwilling to roll out of bed. He was Mr. Marvin Sunshine. She really, really hated that.

Yet a small glow of satisfaction shoved away her usual morning moodiness. He was still here. Making coffee and, from the aroma coming from the other end of the trailer, something else. How extraordinarily . . . domestic.

Don't. She told herself that for the thousandth time. *Don't even think of anything beyond the next few days.* He had never mentioned words like "love." Their normal worlds were so far apart that they could never come together. He was a wanderer. She was a homebody. He was a warrior. She was a pacifist.

Does a pacifist ever carry a pistol in her purse?

How far had she traveled from her roots in these past few days?

And could she ever settle down to her usual routine once this was over? Could she ever go to bed again without thinking about the warmth of his arms? Could she ever wander about without looking for people in the shadows? Could she ever crawl back into her world of history and books? Once you felt the rush of adrenaline, could you ever forget it? Or did ordinary life turn gray, colorless?

She would have to ask Flaherty.

She reluctantly climbed out of bed, pulled on her T-shirt, and went into the bathroom. She washed her face, brushed her teeth, and looked at herself critically. Something had changed last night. Her eyes seemed brighter, her color more vivid. Her lips were slightly swollen. She felt she had never looked better. In fact, she seemed to glow, even first thing in the morning.

Did men glow, too?

She ran a comb through her hair and went into the small kitchen.

"Good morning," she said.

"It's an extraordinarily good morning," he replied with a grin.

"That good?"

"Not for you?" he asked with feigned disappointment. Or *was* it feigned?

"I'm not usually fond of mornings. Particularly since waking up to someone trying to kill me. But today is a decided improvement."

He put his fingers on her cheek and brushed back a curl from her face in a gesture so intimate and possessive it made her hurt inside. She wanted to run her fingers through his hair.

Instead, she stepped back. "I smell something."

His hand dropped, and he gave her a wry grin. "I told you I can cook two things. Steak and omelets. This is the omelet again."

"I'll cook tonight," she said.

He nodded as he divided the omelet and put her share on a plate.

"Will we be here tonight?"

"I think so. I'll make some calls in Newport News today."

"What if he's avoiding you?"

"I plan to take care of that little matter," he replied grimly. "I'll let him know that my next stop is the newspapers."

"What if he doesn't care?"

"I've learned a great deal about Dustin Eachan. He'll care, all right. He has grander ambitions than being an assistant to a deputy. I would bet my last dollar that he's the one who maneuvered my new posting."

"Didn't you say someone was injured? Would someone in the State Department . . . do something like that?" The moment she said the words she knew how naive she must sound, and how could she possibly be naive after everything that had happened? She knew a lot about human nature, but still . . . what had been happening was so outside her range of experience.

"I don't know," he said slowly. "I don't know the man. I only know his reputation."

"What if he doesn't know anything? Or won't tell us anything?"

"Then we try something else," he said. "Someone thinks you have some information that endangers them. That idea must have come from somewhere."

She hesitated, then finally gave voice to the thought that had weighed heavily in her mind. "What if Jon found something? And took it?"

His eyes told her that he had already considered that possibility. "You knew him," he said. "I didn't. Would he have taken some papers and used them in some way?"

"He was my friend," Amy said. "But everything seemed to start with those papers."

"I thought it might have started because I made queries," Flaherty said.

"But they didn't come after you, not until you interfered," she said slowly.

"I'm not so sure of that. Maybe they just didn't know where I was. I was on leave."

"They seem to know everything and how to get to anyone," she observed, taking the last bite of the omelet. "It's just a matter of time."

"Such little faith," he said. "But back to your friend. Do you think he was capable of making a few calls of his own without telling you?"

"What do you mean?"

"Was he capable of blackmail if he found something in those boxes?"

She hesitated. She didn't want to think what she was thinking. But now was no time to hold back. Flaherty's life was in danger, too. "Two weeks ago I would have said no way. But the more I think about it, I wonder. He was having marital problems. He might have needed money. If he found something he thought he could use. . . ."

She left the sentence hanging.

He nodded. "If he did take something, where would it be?"

She shrugged. "His office. Home. I don't know."

He played with his coffee cup. "If I don't get Eachan today, maybe we should pay a visit to the widow."

"If he had taken some papers and the bad guys want them, why haven't they searched his home?" She found herself using his words for the assailant. They fitted as well as anything.

"Maybe they have," he said.

"Could his wife be in danger?"

"He died in an auto accident. I doubt if anyone would want another accident this soon."

A chill crept through her.

"I'm sorry," he said. "Your friend may not have done anything."

"I hope not," she said softly. She couldn't even imagine going to Jon's house and asking his widow if she could go through his things.

There was a question in his eyes.

"No," she said. "There was never anything between us, but from what I understand, his wife thought there might be. That was one of the problems. She thought he was cheating with everyone because he couldn't stand being home. We had lunch sometimes. Coffee. He was my mentor. He supported my tenure, but that was all there ever was."

He nodded, and she wished she knew what he was thinking at that moment. He didn't say anything, but helped himself to another cup of coffee and poured one for her.

She was amazed, however, at how at ease they were together most of the time. She had never felt this way before, not even with Alan, the man with whom she had a two-year relationship. There was no juggling for control, for position. No sense of competition. He listened to her, gave her opinions credit. She hadn't known that two people could have this kind of ease. A lump lodged in her throat. For the first time she wasn't sure she wanted to catch the bad guys. Once that was done, he would leave. She remembered what she'd thought about earlier and meant to ask him.

"Can you ever go back?" she said.

He gave her a quizzical look. "What do you mean?"

"I never understood the appeal of danger," she said. "I never understood why some people choose dangerous jobs, like policemen or fireman or Special Forces, or driving race cars or jumping out of planes." She didn't know if she was making herself clear or not, but he had put down the coffee cup and was studying her intently.

"Now," she continued, "I know what is meant by adrenaline. I . . . understand its appeal. It must be a little like a drug."

"It can be," he said. "It is for some."

"Are you one of those some?"

He hesitated. "I personally think it's overrated. I don't like getting shot."

She didn't either. She remembered only too clearly the pain that followed her first brush with danger. And yet . . . life had never been so vivid. "Once . . . you experience it, can you ever go back?" That was the big question. But then she wondered whether it was the danger, or Irish Flaherty.

He looked at her thoughtfully. "I suppose it depends on who you are. I always thought it made peace more precious."

"Then why do you continue doing what you do?"

"I usually don't get shot at. And I like solving puzzles. Most of the investigations I conduct involve paper trails. Dishonest contractors and procurement fraud. Unsafe equipment. That kind of thing."

"But not in Bosnia?"

He shrugged. "That mostly involved preventing weapon theft."

"And in South America. Wasn't that dangerous?"

"That's why I transferred to CID," he said with a self-deprecating shrug.

She didn't quite believe that. He'd not shown the slightest fear or hesitation since she'd met him. Instead, he'd plunged in at every opportunity. *To protect her.*

Why?

But she had no opportunity to ask more questions. He stood up and took the dishes to the sink. "Time for me to leave."

"Should I go with you?" She wanted to.

He shook his head. "You have Bo, and I know you want to do some work. Why don't you do that, and if you have time, check on Navy deployments about ten years back?"

She had almost forgotten about the tenure hearing after the last couple of days. It was less than a week away now. She would have to return by then. It would not hurt to review everything. But her life in Memphis seemed a hundred years and thousands of miles away.

He was right. She did have work to do. She did have her own life.

"Keep the pistol handy. Don't open the door to anyone but the chief. I should be back by midafternoon."

If you're not. . . .

He wrote something down. "If I'm not back, call this number. It's my commander. He's also a friend. He'll help you." He leaned down and kissed her slowly and thoroughly. "But I *will* be back."

WASHINGTON, D.C.

Dustin left his Georgetown home and drove to a gas station that had a pay phone. He dialed Sally's number. The phone rang and rang and rang.

No answer.

Damn. She didn't have a cell phone. She hated the things. He should have insisted. He looked at his watch. Seven in the morning. She should be there.

He had been awake all night, reviewing the meeting he'd had earlier in the day with his superior. He had, more or less, been ordered to change his recommendation. He hadn't agreed. He hadn't disagreed. But he knew it was damned wrong, and could well come back to bite them all in the ass. The sale of those vehicles would mean one more dictator could more easily slaughter his people. He just wasn't sure how far he would go to deny it.

Jordan, damn it. He suspected he would have another call from the man today.

That was one call he planned to avoid.

He did hope Flaherty would call.

And where in the devil was Sally?

He felt like a juggler who had lost control. Balls were bouncing all over the damned place.

Fifteen minutes later he strode into his office. His secretary wasn't there. Sally was.

She looked terrible. She wore no makeup, and her clothes were wrinkled. She was in his arms before he could say anything. He held her for a moment, then pulled back. "Why are you here?"

"I didn't think I should go to your house. I was afraid to go to mine."

"Why?"

She rubbed her eyes. "I went out last night. To a bar. It was a respectable one," she added after looking at his face. "I met a guy. He looked okay, and we talked a little while. He asked me out, and I said no. There was something . . . in his eyes that warned me. When I went to the powder room, the bartender came after me and said the man sitting next to me slipped something into my drink. I couldn't think of anything but getting away."

"You drove here last night in the rain?"

She nodded.

"Why didn't you call me?"

"You told me not to. I assume you had a reason," she said indignantly. "I was also afraid to come to your house. But I didn't think they would check every door in the State Department. I had my credentials with me, and I waited until seven. I knew you came in early."

He studied her face. He saw the fear in her eyes. Yet she'd kept her head. Everyone had always underestimated Sally, had always expected little from her. He'd been guilty of the same thing. "It could just have been someone who wanted to score. . . ."

"I don't think so. He seemed friendly enough, but there was something about his eyes . . . and the bartender said he'd never seen the man there before, although the guy told me he was local."

"You did exactly right in coming here," Dustin said.

"I'm not exactly dressed properly."

He took her hand and went to his door, unlocked it, and drew her inside.

"I'll send my secretary to get you some clothes," he said.

"Won't she resent that?"

"I don't think so. I don't ask things like that often. She'll know it's important."

She digested that for a moment, then changed the subject. "Why would they come after me?"

"I wish to hell I knew. Can you draw a picture of this guy?"

She nodded.

He took several pieces of paper from the computer printer and handed it to her, along with several pens from his desk. "Sorry I can't do better."

"I'm sorry, Dusty. I didn't know what else to do, where else to go."

"Not to worry, Squirt. I'm glad you did. We just have to figure out what to do with you now."

"If I hadn't gone to the bar . . . ?"

"If they found you at the bar, they knew where you were staying. They would have gotten to you in another way. Perhaps a more violent one."

"But how could they have found me?"

"I don't know." And he didn't. There were several possibilities. Cecil Ford knew where she was. Some kind of device could have been placed in his car. He didn't think anyone could trace calls going into or out of his office. Since some very publicized security leaks in State Department offices, security was very good. No one would have been able to tap phones.

He didn't know whom to call now. He'd exhausted most of his resources, people he thought he could trust. Unfortunately, he could count them on one hand. Half a hand. But Sally's drawing first. He wanted that while the man's face was still fresh in her mind. Maybe the FBI would have something on him.

Dustin went over the schedule Judy had left for him. A staff meeting at ten. That would be held in the conference room. A luncheon with a congressman at noon. He had to make that. Two more meetings this afternoon. A dinner tonight at the French Embassy.

A knock on his door. Sally stiffened.

"Judy. My secretary," he said. "I recognize her knock."

She visibly relaxed. She had talked to Judy several times.

He opened the door and went outside, closing the door behind him.

"Good morning, sir."

"Good morning."

"I'll make the coffee."

"Sounds good."

She hesitated as he continued to stand there. "Is there anything I can do for you, Mr. Eachan?"

"My cousin is here," he said.

"Here?" She looked confused.

"In my office. She had a scare last night. Someone attacked her."

"Is there anything I can do?"

"Yes, there is. She's going to stay here today. There's really nowhere else to go. Whoever attacked her has her address and house keys. I don't want anyone other than myself—or you—going into my office. I know it's not your job, but I would appreciate it if you could watch out for her."

"Of course I will."

"Thank you," he said formally.

He waited for other questions but, as he expected, none came.

He went back inside his office. Two hours before his staff meeting. Judy had already prepared the agenda, but he had to review the items.

He knew, though, that it was time to make some decisions. Until now, he'd hoped that the whole treasure train matter would fade away. It was quite obvious now that it would not.

If he went to the FBI, it could blow wide open. Sally's life was worth far more than his career. But first he wanted to hear what Flaherty had to say. Then he would have to make some hard decisions.

Sally looked up from her drawing. He gave her what he hoped was a comforting smile, and she went back to work.

What in the hell was he going to do with her?

NEWPORT NEWS

Irish found a phone booth near Newport News. He looked at his watch. Eleven. He dialed the State Department number and asked for Dustin Eachan.

A woman's voice answered.

He had heard it before. He was sure he would get another "he's unavailable."

"Mr. Eachan," he said.

"May I tell him who's calling?"

"Colonel Flaherty."

There was a brief pause. "He wants to speak to you, but he's in a meeting now. He asked if there was a number where he can reach you."

Progress, of a sort. Except he was not about to tell anyone where he was or was going to be.

"I'm moving around," he said. "Tell me when he will be there, and I'll call."

She hesitated, then said, "Noon. But he has a luncheon at one, so call right on the hour."

"I'll do that," he said, and hung up. He stood at the telephone for a moment. He hadn't been on the line long enough for a trace. He'd made sure of that. Now he had an hour to waste.

After a moment's hesitation, he called the ranch. He knew Joe wouldn't be in his house at this time of day, but he left a message that he was all right and would call him later. Then he made a third call to Doug Fuller, his commanding officer. He had to know what was going on.

He was put through immediately. "Get back here," Doug said without any preliminary greeting.

"If it's about that promotion. . . ."

"Hell, there won't be any promotion. You're wanted for questioning in North Carolina. Something about arson. Both you and the woman. And there are some questions left in Georgia. Dammit, where in the hell are you? I can't protect you any longer. Hell, we're the ones who are supposed to be solving crimes, not committing them."

"We weren't involved in arson," Irish said. "That was meant to kill both of us."

"Why?"

"Damned if I know," Irish said.

"You're not any closer than before?"

"No. Except whoever is behind it has resources we could only dream about." He hesitated. "Can you find out where my new assignment came from?"

"You don't think. . . ."

"I think they have killed a lot more people than we know about. And over a longer period of time. It's possible they killed three generals, including my grandfather. Now that takes some kind of organization."

"That's ridiculous. You told me yourself your grandfather died of a heart attack."

"That's what I thought, until I discovered the other two generals who served with him when the Nazi train was captured, died somewhat mysteriously. My grandfather never had heart trouble."

"That doesn't mean. . . ."

"It looked like a heart attack, and because of that there was no autopsy. You and I both know that there are drugs that can cause attacks."

"Then come back, and we can order a new autopsy."

"I can't leave Amy Mallory."

"You don't have a choice, Irish. Any number of officials want to talk to you. I've been putting them off, saying that you had no obligation during leave to check in with me. But they are getting impatient."

"Doug, I can't leave Amy Mallory now. There've been three attempts on her life."

"Let the police or FBI protect her. You can't do it alone."

"You haven't been listening, Doug. If they have enough power to ensure a promotion or change of assignment, they have enough power to have sources in the FBI."

"You're not Superman, Irish."

"I need a few more days."

"You don't have them. I can't protect you any longer. There's a record of this call. You have been officially ordered to return to base."

"I can't."

"You can be court-martialed for disobeying a direct order. I can almost guarantee you will be. Are you willing to give up everything you've worked for?"

Irish closed his eyes for a moment. But then he'd made his decision days ago. It had stopped being about his grandfather. It had started that way, but now it was all about Amy. It was about giving her safety and security and her life back.

Would he leave if he thought she would be safe?

He wasn't sure. He was fascinated by Amy Mallory. He was even more attracted by the bond between them, the instinctive knowledge they had about one another, the sense of belonging he'd never had with anyone else. He'd been intrigued by their conversation this morning, by her admission that she was more than a little attracted by danger. It wasn't the fact that she had been. He'd mused about that before. It was the fact that she admitted it, picked at it, weighed it.

She was like that about everything. He'd watched her as they had driven up the coast. Everything interested her.

The simple fact was he didn't want to leave her. He didn't want to risk anyone else looking after her.

The thought was unsettling at best.

"I'll take my chances, Doug. I have to go now." He hung up before Doug could say anything else.

He'd just burned his last bridge.

WASHINGTON, D.C.

"I thought I'd hired the best. A graduate from a correspondence school detective course could do better." The voice on the phone was angry.

"We know she's with Eachan now," his employee said.

"Ah," the caller said. "And how do you propose getting to her? We needed compromising photos. We have no chance of getting them now."

Silence.

"Keystone cops. You were supposed to be the best of the best, but you've let two women get the best of you."

"We hadn't anticipated Flaherty."

"I pay you enough to anticipate everything."

"I have a tracking device on Eachan's car."

"You had one on Flaherty's, and it didn't do a damn bit of good."

"I'm putting two more men on Dustin Eachan."

"Watch his house but don't bug it. He's just recently had the department sweep it, and he'll do it again. No sense putting him on notice."

"We're putting the rest of our resources on finding Flaherty and the woman."

"Have you narrowed it down?"

"The last credit card was in North Carolina. He's obviously heading north."

"But why?" the call's originator asked. "To see Eachan? That would be very unfortunate. We can control Eachan by himself. If they join forces. . . ." A pause. "Flaherty's smart. He can't use credit cards; we would have that information immediately. That means no upscale hotels. We already know they've used some hourly hotels. But we've been checking those." A pause, then, "He's military. He'll know how to get lost in military communities. Check them up the coast from North Carolina. Motels. Trailer parks. Rooming houses. I don't care what it costs."

twenty-two

Amy tried to concentrate. Hour after hour passed. She reviewed everything for the tenure hearing and found little to add. She knew her answers to probable questions, could back her research, present pending grants and future research projects. Included in her material was a prospective publisher for her proposed book. She needed only to give them the first three chapters.

She knew it was a sound package. Student assessments of her courses had been excellent. She thought she had the support of most of the faculty, although Jon had been her strongest advocate. Would his absence change the dynamics?

The tenure hearing, though, seemed a million miles away at the moment. It just didn't seem that important any longer. And that simple fact scared her. This . . . adventure was not going to last forever.

Amy sighed, fighting herself, tamping down all those wayward, traitorous, foreign thoughts.

She went back into the boxes. She decided to take every name she found and research it on the net. The final list included those recommended for decorations, staff members dating back from Normandy, everyone mentioned in his notes.

She started going through the last box again, making a list of those names. When she was finished, it was noon. Her back muscles were tired from leaning over the laptop. She stood, stretched.

Bo nudged her leg with his nose. She decided to take him for a walk. When she got back, she would start tracking down the various individuals on her list.

The day was hot, humid, smothering. The sky looked as if a storm was in the offing. Dark, thick clouds hovered. She felt the electricity ready to explode.

Her gaze moved around the parking lot, from trailer to trailer, to the roads that branched like veins in a hand. Toddlers played in a playground, and she walked Bo over to them and watched. Mothers who looked more like high schoolers than married women watched them and chatted together. She felt an ache deep inside. She'd often thought about children. She thought she would probably make a good mother. But she'd wanted them only with someone she truly loved.

Until now.

She'd substituted career for family, and she'd never regretted it. Not really. But now, as she watched children playing, running to their mothers, a yearning hit with unexpected intensity. What would Irish's child look like? Dark hair? Inscrutable eyes? That odd little twist of his lips?

She finally forced her gaze away from the children. They'd stirred ridiculous thoughts. Impossible thoughts. She and Flaherty had sex because they'd been caught in a storm of danger. And need. Even dependence. It was nothing more than that.

She looked around. Bo growled, and she stiffened. Then she saw it was only another dog.

Amy forced herself to walk away from the playground. She went to the office, where she'd seen a newspaper vending machine. Putting in a quarter, she took out a newspaper and returned to the bench. She wasn't ready to go back inside.

She read the front page. More trouble in the Middle East. A battle in Congress. A robbery. A trial. She looked inside. Nothing about an explosion farther south. She read it, as she always read newspapers, scouring every article and filing the contents in the cabinet of her mind.

Bo sniffed the areas immediately around her, then came over to her and put his paws on her lap. "You miss him, too, huh? Well, buddy, we have to get used to it."

She gave one last look toward the children, then returned to the trailer and started her search. There were any number of people search sites, and she started with the name at the top of her list. She soon found that most, quite naturally, were dead. Some had died during the war. Some shortly afterward. She eliminated one after another. She was finally left with nine names.

She didn't get any further. She didn't have the skill to gain access to the sites she needed. She did find something interesting, though. She stopped and just stared at the notations next to two men.

Amy rose and looked outside. It was nearly five. Panic started building up inside her. She wasn't used to it, and she didn't like it. Had something happened to Flaherty? *Irish.* She was beginning to think of him that way now. It was more personal.

A lot more personal.

Then she saw him driving up in the purple car, and her heart did a little jump. She went back to the computer, turning to the Internet, then focused on North Carolina newspapers. It was then she saw the article.

The door opened. Flaherty filled the trailer with his presence. She hadn't realized how empty it was until then.

She looked toward him. She didn't want to say how much she had missed him. She only hoped she didn't convey the message in other ways.

"I reached Eachan. He wants to meet with us."

She waited for him to continue.

One of his eyebrows arched. "No questions?"

"Why should I? You'll tell me when you're ready."

"Patience?"

"No. I just think it's quicker this way."

He gave her that lopsided grin. "You think differently from any woman I've ever met."

"Is that good?"

"Different," he insisted. She was aware that he didn't want to destroy the mood by returning to the issue. The life and death issue.

"Tell me," she finally said.

His smile disappeared. "It'll be dangerous. I want to send you someplace else."

"No," she said. "I'm a part of this as much, if not more, than you are." She hesitated for a moment, then added, "And I feel . . . safer with you."

"I'm not sure we've done the right thing. I've been thinking that perhaps you should contact the local and state authorities."

"Why?"

"I talked to my commanding officer. The local police in Myrtle Beach want us for questioning because of the explosion. Apparently they received an anonymous call that we were the ones in the house just prior to the explosion. Our friends are trying to smoke us out."

"And your commanding officer?"

Flaherty shrugged. The gesture said a lot, however.

She swallowed hard. He could well lose his career, even his freedom. Disobeying a direct order could have significant penalties. "You should go."

"I'm not ready to surface. Not until I hear what Eachan has to say. But you can."

"Do you really think we can trust this Eachan?"

"He has some questions of his own, it seems," he said. "Apparently his cousin has been having some unsettling encounters."

"Sally Eachan?"

He nodded.

"They like picking on women, don't they?" she observed indignantly.

"Easier targets than an Assistant Deputy Secretary of State."

"And a CID officer."

"I think the bad guys knew Eachan just wanted to bury the entire matter."

"And you?"

"They probably thought they could buy me off with a new assignment, get me out of the country."

"So the promotion didn't just happen?"

He didn't answer.

"Where are we going to meet?"

"Here," he said.

She looked at him curiously.

"It's as good as any place."

"When?"

"Tomorrow night. I want to meet with them when the park is full of sailors."

"I don't want anyone else to get hurt."

"They won't. I'll meet them in Newport News and drive them here. I'll make sure no one follows."

"Them?"

"His cousin is coming." He paused. "I can try to find some place for you to stay . . . just for the evening. Maybe even with the chief."

She shook her head. "The violence seemed to have started with me." She knew her face must have shown uncertainty, or he wouldn't have pressed her to leave. It wasn't what he thought. She wasn't reluctant to meet with them. But she knew she and Irish would have to leave here then. She just wasn't sure she wanted to do that.

The trailer had become a temporary refuge.

And the place where she'd fallen in love.

"I'm not going to leave," she declared. Then she

changed the subject. "I made a list of everyone my grandfather specifically mentioned in the papers. Of thirty-one, twenty-two are dead. I found addresses for three of the others; I couldn't find anything on six of them." She decided to leave her biggest find to the end, to lead him there.

He sat down in a chair. "How many of the thirty-one survived the war?"

"Fifteen were reported as killed in action in the war."

"That's a high number," he said. "What about the others?"

She gave him the list. She had listed the dates of their deaths next to name and rank. All were either high-ranking officers, sergeant majors, or staff sergeants. He leaned forward in his chair, studying the list. His eyes were that piercing blue she saw when he was focusing on something.

She watched his eyes pass over the names, then linger over the three names and addresses she'd found as well as the six names that remained elusive. She knew the second when he continued on and noted the dates of death of those who had died. Flaherty's grandfather and her grandfather both died in 1980. Nothing unusual about that. They were both elderly. What was unusual was that they died within a month of one another. Flaherty of a heart attack; her grandfather, a suicide.

"Coincidence?" she asked.

He shook his head. "I didn't look at the dates. I should have."

"We haven't exactly had time."

"Or we found something better to do with it," he countered.

The low, sexy tone sent tingles up and down her spine. How well she remembered the "something better."

She tried to return to the subject at hand. It was safer. "It seems that some of my thirty-one were murdered," she said.

"I wonder whether they were involved in the warehousing of the treasure. I have to see the investigators' notes and interviews."

"I would think that should be easy, particularly for you."

"It should be," he said. "I requested them but they are still being 'reviewed for security reasons.'"

"What security reasons?" she asked incredulously.

"That's what I asked. That's why we're headed to Washington. I want to know who has restricted access and try to get it. In the meantime, we'll try to find out more about these deaths."

"How?"

"We can't use my cell phone," he said. "They can probably track that. Your computer should be safe enough. I'll check with the jurisdictional police departments where the murders may have occurred and see whether there were any arrests or convictions. Then we'll have to find the death certificates and police reports."

"How can I help?"

"You've already done it, love, and very well. You may have found the only clue, which is a lot better than I did. But only one of us can use the computer, and I can get into sites you can't."

His gaze met hers. They knew time was running out for both of them. He had already jeopardized his career. Her tenure hearing was less than a week from now.

Just as she knew he couldn't disobey orders and keep his career, neither could she ignore her tenure hearing. Postponements were rare. And what was her excuse? A growing number of dead bodies and destruction?

It wasn't exactly what a private, conservative college wanted to hear.

Time. Neither of them had it.

And yet she could barely think about leaving him. They had been in a cocoon these last few days. A cocoon built from danger, but still a world of its own and far from ordinary life.

He leaned over and touched her face with his fingers. "It *will* be over," he said.

She wondered what her face had just revealed. Obviously not what she had really been thinking. It wasn't solving the puzzle, it was losing him. Losing this partnership, intimacy, whatever it was. She swallowed hard and nodded.

He sat at the computer.

She moved her chair next to his. There was nothing else she could do now except watch.

After five hours, Irish stretched. This was a job that should take half a dozen skilled people days. The simple fact was, they didn't have several days.

He had hunted down only two of the nonmilitary deaths. Both murders. Both unsolved. One was a captain who had been stabbed to death eight months after the war ended. A street robbery, according to the report. No suspects.

The other was a staff sergeant who had received a dishonorable discharge after being charged with pilfering items from a government warehouse. He'd been found hanging from a light fixture. Initially it had looked like a suicide, but according to a police report one of the investigating detectives insisted it was murder. It was never solved. Irish found the name of the detective. He would be in his seventies now.

She sat by his side for most of the time, then together they prepared a supper of salad and hamburgers. The air between them was intimate, full of energy and intensity and power. Even watching her eat incited desire in Irish.

That desire was dangerous. He knew it was dangerous. In both the short and the long term. He needed to keep his mind free and clear, and yet. . . .

The longer he stayed with her, the more he liked her, the more he wanted to be with her.

Irish tried to keep his mind on the list, but his gaze kept wandering to her face, to her gray eyes that always said so much, to her breasts straining against the T-shirt. He re-membered exactly how they felt, how they had hardened under his fingers. . . .

They had hours of work to do tonight.

But then. . . .

Her eyes seemed to darken, the usual clear gray turning to heated, smoky depths.

Hours of work.

And then. . . .

Twenty-four hours later, Irish picked up Sally and Dustin Eachan. He liked Sally immediately. He disliked Dustin just as quickly. He didn't like to think it was the cock of the walk syndrome. As a military man, he knew that attitude well.

Perhaps it was the disquiet he felt in leaving Amy alone. Every decision he made had consequences, and he would have to live with them. Would she be safer at the trailer park or with him? After weighing all the factors, he opted for the trailer park. He asked the chief to look after her.

If Dustin Eachan was indeed a part of whatever con-spiracy was in the offing, the greatest danger would be in those first few minutes of their meeting. If his senses picked up anything, anything at all, he would not return to the trailer park. He was even having second thoughts about bringing these two to the park at all, but he'd discovered Amy had much to offer. Her researcher's mind was the equal of his investigative one. Amy knew her grandfather; she was the only one who could answer questions about him.

If Eachan really was as concerned as he had sounded on the phone, then the four of them needed to meet and ex-change the various threads of information that each had.

They met as planned. Irish had told Eachan to be at a restaurant at noon, and he had called him there, watching from the parking lot of a nearby hotel he'd staked out ear-lier. It did not appear that they were followed.

He knew that one of them—Eachan or his cousin—could easily be carrying a tracer just like the one that had been placed in his car.

Once he had picked up the cousins, he had gone through her purse and patted Dustin down, which did not improve the State Department official's mood. All the way back to Norfolk, Irish had watched for someone who might be following them. He'd then changed over to the purple car in the apartment parking lot.

He had, quite simply, taken every possible precaution. He'd used the rental car to pick them up. Once the meeting was over, he planned to drive Dustin back to his car, and then he and Amy would leave the trailer park. There would be one more stop for them: the warehouse in Kentucky where Amy kept her grandfather's desk. It was probably a wild goose chase, but at this point Irish was willing to try anything.

Eachan had been silent most of the way, as if he, too, was wary. Sally Eachan, on the other hand, tried to find out everything there was to know about him. Irish quickly decided it was not guile on her part, but the never-met-a-stranger quality that she had. She tried to draw him out while revealing very little about herself.

Dustin had grimaced when they transferred to the old purple car. Irish shrugged. "You can stay here," he said.

Dustin ignored the jibe and opened the car door for Sally, then squeezed in beside her. Irish noticed that there was more than a little protectiveness in the gesture, and he didn't miss the quick, familiar glances between the two.

He was acquainted with those kinds of glances. He'd exchanged a few of them with Amy in the past few days. Filing away the observation, he asked Dustin questions about his position at the State Department. He didn't want to ask anything else until all of them were together. He had come to value Amy's instincts.

He was already well aware of Eachan's position and responsibilities. He specialized in western African nations, and was considered one of the rising stars of the State Department. He was one of the people who recommended humanitarian and military aid to some of the poorest countries in the world. He would move to another desk soon.

Irish looked at him and saw an ambitious bureaucrat with more than a little arrogance, but perhaps that was because of everything he'd learned and heard about the man. He had the classic good looks of a young Brahmin and wore casually elegant clothes. He was everything Irish disliked.

"Where in the hell are we going?" Dustin asked him.

"You'll find out."

"I have to be back in Washington tonight."

"You will be," Irish said. He glanced at Sally Eachan, and some of his belligerence faded. She was an extraordinarily pretty woman, but she looked strained and tired.

"Your cousin said you were attacked," Irish said.

"Someone tried to slip something into my drink," she corrected him. "I wasn't exactly attacked."

"A stranger to you?"

She nodded.

"What did he look like?"

"Forties. Dark hair. Solid build. Brown eyes."

It could have been one of the men in the Jekyll Island attack. But that description would fit thousands of people.

"How did you get away?"

"A bartender saw him do it and warned me. I was able to leave without him seeing me." She paused, then said, "Dusty said another woman had been attacked."

Dusty. He kept the surprise from his face and looked at Eachan, who met his gaze, the slightest chagrin in his eyes.

Irish wondered whether he would have to change his opinion.

"You'll meet her. Now, in fact," he added as he turned in the trailer park and drove to their temporary home.

The lights were on. He left the car and waited until his two passengers did the same, then knocked on the door.

To his surprise, the chief opened it, a beer in his hand. He saw Amy rise from a chair and approach them.

"Mighty fine woman you have here," the chief said as Irish stepped inside. "Knows a hell of a lot about baseball."

Irish chuckled. He should have known. Amy seemed to know a lot about everything. "Thank you for looking after her."

"My pleasure," the chief said gallantly, and Irish had the impression he didn't say that often. "I see you have company, so I'll leave. You just let me know if you need any little thing." The message was clear. He knew something was up, and he was going to be on watch.

He passed the Eachans with the barest nod as he went out the door, though he had thoroughly investigated them with his eyes. He had judged Dustin Eachan much as Irish originally had. Irish had seen the flash of almost contemptuous disregard with which many enlisted men eyed authority.

Once he left, the four of them regarded each other cautiously. Suspicion and wariness and uncertainty radiated between them.

It was Amy who made the first move. She stuck out her hand to Sally.

"Let's see if we can find out what in the blazes is going on."

twenty-three

Amy felt the tension in the room. Not knowing what else to do, she did what she'd done most of her life. She'd thrust out her hand and butted in.

"I'm Amy," she said.

The woman who'd entered was attractive. Very attractive. Perfect blond hair and blue eyes that were darker than Irish's but every bit as startling. She smiled, and it was a natural, spontaneous smile.

"Sally," the woman said.

Amy's gaze went to the man. He was not quite as tall as Irish. And they—Irish and the newcomer—seemed as different as day and night. The latter, blond with green eyes, looked uncomfortable in the trailer. He was slender, leaner than Irish, and wore an expensive shirt and creased slacks.

Irish wore jeans and an inexpensive sport shirt, and lounged quite comfortably against the wall of the trailer. He was at home anyplace. She had noticed that before. Possibly because he had moved so much, he made anyplace he was at, home.

"Mr. Eachan?" she said after a momentary silence.

The stranger smiled then. It was a cool expression, yet there was an odd charm about it. She suspected one could succeed in diplomacy without having some of the latter.

"Now that the pleasantries are over, can we begin?" Irish didn't like Eachan, and he didn't care that he showed it.

Amy held out her hand toward the chairs in the living room. "I have coffee. . . ."

"I'd like some." Sally said. "I'll help you."

The kitchen wasn't far enough from the living area that they could not hear.

"Were you responsible for my transfer?" Irish's voice was low but angry.

"You should be grateful." Eachan's voice was smooth, confident.

"You can take your damn promotion and stuff it up your ass."

Amy looked at Sally. "It seems to be going well."

Sally grinned at her. "Dusty can be rather obnoxious."

"Dusty?" It suddenly made the man human.

"He hates the name. I'm the only one allowed to use it."

Amy noted the fond way she said it. It was said in the same way that Amy thought of Irish. She poured the coffee. "Cream or sugar?"

"I like it black. He likes cream."

Amy poured it. Both she and Irish liked it black.

They took two cups each to the table. The two men were glaring at each other.

"What else did you do, Eachan?" Irish said. "Did you hire someone to burn down Amy's house?"

"No, but I imagine your interference probably had something to do with it. If you hadn't started dredging up the past. . . ."

"Why, what do you have to hide?" Amy had heard the edge in his voice before. This time it was like the sharp edge of a knife.

"Look, I don't know what you thought to gain by dredging up a fifty-year-old episode, but it was your grandfather who was the commanding officer, and therefore responsible. I don't appreciate your spreading the dirt to my family."

"There was dirt?"

The words were low. Probing. Dangerous.

Eachan wasn't cowed. "I don't know what you want, but I'll be damned if I'm going to let you put my cousin in danger and ruin our family's name."

"If your grandfather didn't do anything, there wouldn't be anything to ruin."

"At least I don't leave a trail of dead bodies behind me. The authorities are looking for you, you know. Both of you."

Sally set the coffee down and put her hand on Eachan's arm.

Amy was more direct. "This isn't getting us anywhere. I'm the one everyone seems to want to kill."

They all looked at her. Irish had the grace to turn a little red. Dustin Eachan looked taken aback. Sally gave her an approving glance, then said, "And I'm the one they burglarized and tried to kidnap or worse. If you two want to see who has the biggest. . . ." She stopped, then winked at Amy.

Irish chuckled. "You're right, Miss Eachan. And Amy." He looked at Eachan. "Truce?"

Eachan grimaced. "What do you want to know?"

"What has been your part in all this?"

A silence. Long and painful.

"Dusty?" The prompt came from Sally.

He sat up. "I did try to get you transferred. I thought you were stirring up things best undisturbed."

"What else?" Irish asked coldly.

Another silence.

"We're not going to give you anything unless you give us something," Irish said coldly. "In fact, we might just be visiting some newspaper offices soon."

A muscle throbbed in Eachan's throat. "I've had nothing to do with the violence. I have asked certain agencies to find you. They weren't," he added wryly, "very successful."

"Why?"

"I wanted you out of the country," Eachan said. "I thought that when you left, all the queries would end."

"Someone was seriously hurt to get me that position," Irish accused.

Eachan looked genuinely surprised. "I honestly don't know anything about that."

"And Miss Mallory?"

"I didn't have anything to do with that."

"Who does? Who would have a reason?"

"God's truth, I don't know," Eachan said.

"It's certainly someone with a lot of power and a long reach," Irish said. "You have both."

"I also have a career that's important to me."

"Is that why you're here?"

"No. To be honest, I would rather have you picked up by the FBI and shipped back to your command."

"To be court-martialed?"

"Hell, no. That's the last thing I wanted. All would have been forgiven. I do have some influence there. It will still be forgiven."

"If I return now? Is that it? You're still trying to silence me?"

"Three days ago, yes. But now Sally's in danger."

"To hell with Amy Mallory, is that it?"

Amy saw Irish's features darken, his jaw clench. He was ready to tear the man opposite him to pieces. *So much for the truce.*

Irish continued, "Her house was burned, she was attacked twice, and was nearly blown up. And you sat there and did nothing." Irish's voice was as frozen as an Alaskan ice floe.

"He's here now," Amy said. "We don't have much time."

"Understand, Eachan, that we'll be leaving here immediately after you."

The message was clear enough. There was precious little trust between them.

"I came," Eachan said, "because I think Sally has also
become a target."

"But not you? I wonder why?"

They were bristling like two junkyard dogs. Amy
moved her chair closer to Irish's and reached out to put her
hand on his leg. She turned to Sally. "What happened?"

"I thought someone had gone through my apartment, so
Dusty took me to the coast. While I was there, I went to a
bar for dinner, and someone tried to drug my drink." She
gave them a weak smile. "It might have just been someone
who thought he could . . . score."

"But you don't think so?" This time it was Amy.

"I might just have been spooked," she said. "Dusty told
me to be careful, but there was something about the man's
eyes. They had a . . . soullessness."

"She was spooked enough that she didn't go back to her
room and drove all night through pouring rain," Eachan
broke in.

But it was the word *soullessness* that hit Amy like a
sledgehammer. It expressed exactly her impression of the
man who'd broken into her room at Jekyll Island. Her face
turned to Irish's, and he raised an eyebrow.

Eachan looked at his cousin.

She looked back and nodded.

Eachan took a piece of paper from his pocket and un-
folded it. "Sally drew a sketch of him."

"You didn't tell me that," Irish said.

"I didn't know you," she said.

"You don't know me now," he reminded her.

She smiled for the first time, and it was breathtaking.
"Yes, I do," she replied.

Dustin Eachan frowned, but handed the paper to Amy.

Amy looked at the drawing. It was good, very good,

and she readily recognized the face. It resembled the police sketch based on Irish's description of the intruder who tried to assault her in the hospital.

Irish took it then. He nodded. "That's the man who tried to kill Amy at the hospital." He looked toward Eachan. "Do you know who he is?"

Eachan shook his head. "I sent a copy to an acquaintance in the FBI to see whether they could find anything on him. There hasn't been time for them to run it through the computers. Particularly quietly."

"You didn't report it to the police?" Irish's question was sharp, accusing.

"Did you report that explosion in South Carolina?" Eachan retorted.

It was Sally who broke the tension that was building again. "I had no proof. Not that anyone was in my apartment, or that the man in the bar had planned anything ominous. The bartender made it clear he didn't want any part of an investigation. I . . . owed him that."

Irish looked at her for a long moment. It was a searching look, and for a moment Amy felt the tug of jealousy. Sally Eachan was everything she wasn't: Slender, blond, perfect features, naturally elegant.

Even worse, Amy liked her.

But then Irish turned to her and winked, taking her hand in his. As before, it was as if he knew what she was thinking. And that, at the moment, was very humiliating.

She rose and got the coffeepot, filling up the cups again. Dustin Eachan had barely touched his. "We have some beer and a bottle of wine," she offered.

Eachan shook his head. "I have to drive back tonight." He seemed to relax a little. "It wouldn't help anything if I were arrested for DUI."

Irish nodded. "Now we know this has to be connected to the commission report. At least one of the men showed up twice, once attacking Amy, the other obviously attempting to get to Sally." He picked up the picture again.

"Let's call him John Doe for lack of anything better. John could also have been the man who shot Amy at the college." He turned to Amy. "Could it have been the burglar at the college?"

"I don't know," Amy said. "He wore a ski mask. But he could have been, from your description as to height. Anything else . . . it just happened so fast. . . ."

Irish stood. "It's obvious that one of our band of assassins has left us for Sally. Probably because I saw his face. At least, they don't seem to have unlimited reserves."

His gaze returned to Dustin Eachan. "Do you have any idea who might be involved? Or why?"

"I hoped you did."

Irish raised an eyebrow. "Or is this a scouting expedition to learn how much I know?"

"Damn little, or you wouldn't have been desperate to meet with me."

Irish's lips clenched again. "If you'd had the courtesy. . . ."

"I don't owe you anything, Flaherty."

"If you care about your cousin, you'll help us end this."

Amy watched as Eachan's gaze went to Sally and lingered there for a moment. He cared about her. A lot. It was, she knew, the only reason he was here.

"All right," Eachan said. "I found out about the commission two years ago. I kept track of what they were doing. It seemed as if they were going to whitewash the whole matter until there was such an outcry about Switzerland's role in the looting. Then everyone stood up and took an interest. We had to clean our own house. They hired some effective investigators. Two died, the third left. I was able to look in the files. Documents that should have been there were gone."

"What documents?"

"A list of items that were supposed to have been restored to their owners. Paintings, other valuables that could be positively identified. The file did contain an inventory of what was liberated from the train. There was also a list of items taken to New York and sold at auction. The disparity between the two was enormous, including two trunks of gold dust. The difference was explained as items claimed by the rightful owners, but that list is missing. No one explained the lost gold."

"What else was missing?"

"The list of people who had direct access to the warehouse."

"But there should be duty rosters at the very least. Who supervised the warehousing, who went in and out?"

"There should be, but there aren't. And after losing several investigators and running into stone walls, the commission issued a report full of conclusions. It was done quietly, and not many newspapers even picked it up. I checked to see whether there was any evidence connecting my grandfather to any theft. That's when I discovered some of the original documents were missing. The commission apparently wasn't overly worried about it. After all, it was half a century later, and records have a way of getting lost. I thought the whole matter would just fade away. Until I heard that you had asked for records under the Freedom of Information Act."

Irish was listening intently. His expression never changed. She understood why he was very good at his job. But he looked at her, and she knew what he was thinking. That's why he hadn't been able to get reports, why he'd been put off by security excuses. The information Irish wanted was missing, and no one wanted to admit it.

Irish turned back to Dustin Eachan. "The investigators. What happened to them?"

"One was killed by a car in Germany. The other had a sailing accident."

"Convenient, wasn't it?"

"I thought so," Eachan said, "but the local police didn't seem to have questions."

"And you didn't want to bring any attention to it."

"No," Eachan replied, "I didn't. It happened fifty years ago, for God's sake. No one who has a claim is alive today. It should have been dead and buried a long time ago."

"There's snakes in that burial pit," Irish said. "They're very alive. Someone was willing to go to any lengths to keep them that way."

"You mean these past few months."

"I mean for fifty years. I think someone killed all three of our grandfathers."

Eachan's eyes narrowed. "My grandfather died in a plane crash."

"A small private plane."

"How did you know?"

"I'm an investigator. But Amy put it together. My grandfather had a heart attack, but he'd never had heart problems. Amy's grandfather supposedly was a suicide. They died within a month of each other. Your grandfather died six years later, right after your own parents."

Dustin and Sally were staring at him as if he were mad. "You're saying someone's been killing people all these years?" Eachan said. "That someone would be damned old."

"And damned powerful," Irish said. "I think one of the three generals must have found out something and talked to the other two. And there's been more premature deaths of people who served in my grandfather's command."

Sally gave a little cry. Eachan continued to stare at Irish as if he'd just escaped from a mental institution. "But my grandfather survived the other two; that means. . . ."

"It could mean anything," Irish said. "It could be that he was rendered harmless in some way."

Eachan slumped in his chair. It was obvious that he was trying to comprehend everything.

Amy knew exactly what he was feeling. Even now, after she'd had a chance to understand the enormity of what had suddenly eclipsed her life, she was still bewildered by it. How could so many deaths go unnoticed?

Of course, she knew. They were in different parts of the country. They were mostly seen as accidents. There was no way anyone could have picked up on it.

It certainly said something about the power and influence of the person behind it.

It had to be someone who had access to the treasures during the period they were warehoused in Europe.

And apparently that someone believed *she* had information about it.

She was suddenly aware that everyone was looking at her.

It was Eachan who broke the silence. "Did your grandfather have any records?"

She looked at Irish.

"Some. We've placed them in a storage locker," he lied. "And. . . ."

"And we have some names of people who served with Amy's grandfather," Irish said. "We've been checking them out. Where they are today."

Eachan's brows furrowed in concentration. "Wouldn't they be in their eighties or more?"

"Most of them are dead, and have been for a long time. More accidents," Irish said wryly. "There was either a curse on that train or we have one hell of a serial killer tottering around."

"Or a successor," Eachan said.

Irish nodded.

Amy decided to enter the conversation. "We thought if we could get together, maybe our recollections might give us a clue. My grandfather never talked much about the war, though I once asked him why he didn't write a book. It was just before he . . . died."

"What did he say?" Sally asked.

"That no one wanted to read an old man's recollections. He said something else, though, something that never really rang a bell until last night. He said he'd tried to be honest all his life, and he didn't want to start lying now. He said it rather sadly. I thought he just meant that autobiographers had a tendency to shade events on their side. Now I wonder whether he meant something else."

"Eachan?" Irish asked the question.

"My grandfather talked about the military all the time. I think it was the best time of his life," Eachan said. "But he made his fortune years after he left."

"He became a consultant?" Amy had done her own research. "To defense contractors?"

"There's nothing wrong with that," Eachan said defensively.

"Of course not," she said soothingly. "It's just that he's the only one of the three to go into the private sector."

Sally started to say something, then looked at Eachan and hesitated. Amy's first impression of someone who was pretty and not much else had faded during the conversation. Sally had said little, but what she had said had been quiet and insightful. Her description of her attacker, and her subsequent actions, along with the drawing had changed Amy's mind completely. "Sally?" she asked.

Sally looked at her cousin. They exchanged looks, but Amy didn't know them well enough to decipher it. A warning from Dustin Eachan. Defiance from Sally.

"I'm going to tell them, Dusty," Sally said.

Eachan shrugged. "It doesn't really mean anything."

"It could," Sally said. "And too many people have died." Still, she bit her lip for a moment before continuing. "My grandfather gave my father a painting. It's one that's on the original list. Part of that list is missing, but the painting was on what remained of it."

"Is there anything else?" Irish asked after a moment's silence.

"Not that I know of," Sally said.

"Eachan?"

Dustin shook his head. "The only thing I recognized was Sally's painting."

"That makes sense," Amy said. "The newspaper story

said some of the items were used temporarily in headquarters offices. Silver, linen, china. Even paintings. The houses that were confiscated for their use were mostly empty. It seemed easier to use some of these items, especially since things like china and silver probably couldn't be traced and returned to the rightful owners." She turned to Sally. "Is it valuable?"

"It's not a masterpiece," Dustin said. "But it's a well-known Spanish artist. It's probably worth fifty thousand today."

"Did the commission know about it?"

"Not where it is today, no," Dustin said. "It was one of the few things Sally's father left her. There is no known owner today. I . . . checked."

Amy saw Irish raise an eyebrow. "I assume you think that makes it right?"

Sally rushed to her cousin's defense. "He didn't know until recently. All we knew was that it belonged to my grandfather, and he'd given it to my father, who gave it to me. It didn't look like anything special. But it was important to me because . . . my father left it to me. Dustin knew that."

"It doesn't matter," Amy said. "What does matter is who feels that this is so important he has to kill for it. I suppose there's a statute of limitation for theft."

"But not for murder," Irish said pointedly.

"Now it's your turn," Eachan said, turning his gaze to Irish. "What part did your grandfather play in the theft and its cover-up? He *was* the ranking officer." His voice was deliberately sarcastic. "Didn't he ever say anything?"

"He avoided the subject," Irish said. "I don't know if he left any papers. I was out of the country when he died, and I was gone most of the succeeding years. I do know that when I started looking a month ago, I found a lot of papers, but none involving the last six months of the war."

"Which leaves us with no more information than he had," Eachan said.

"Not exactly," Amy countered.

"What do you mean?"

"The list I've compiled from my grandfather's memoirs." She looked at Irish. "I think they should see it."

Irish shrugged.

Amy took it out of a folder and handed it to Eachan. His gaze moved down the names with almost frightening speed. She knew he was reading—and cataloging—everything. She suspected that his elegant good looks cloaked a brilliant mind.

She also saw that his eyes suddenly curtained at one point. She knew he recognized a name. So did Irish. She could tell by the way his body tensed.

"What name?" Irish asked.

Again Eachan hesitated.

"Tell them," Sally said.

Dustin Eachan's face had paled in those few seconds. "I didn't see that name anywhere else," he said. "It's not on any of the documents I've seen."

"Which name?" Irish asked again.

"Sergeant Major Hawkins Jordan." He hesitated a moment. "I remember him visiting my grandfather twenty years ago. Just before my grandfather died. He was working with my grandfather on a military project. He's founder of Jordan Industries. His son, Brian, is now CEO."

Amy's blood ran faster. Hawkins Jordan. He was one of the few survivors of the command staff.

"He must be eighty or more now."

"And he still plays golf four times a week," Eachan said. "Mostly with senators and congressmen, and he can beat most of them."

"A big rise for an enlisted man," Irish said. "He had to have influence . . . and seed money."

"The gold," Amy said.

"And blackmail," Sally said after a short silence.

Dustin hadn't entered the speculation, but his face was still pale, his lips had thinned. "The bastard," he whispered. "My grandfather died a week after Jordan visited him."

Irish spread the palms of his hands on the table. "We have no proof. Only speculation. And if we're right, is it Hawkins Jordan or his son who's responsible for what's happening now?"

"The son was in my office a few days ago. He wanted me to sign off on the sale of armored personnel carriers to an African country," Dustin said, and for the first time Amy saw a passionate anger in his eyes. It was followed by sudden comprehension, even hatred. Then they all disappeared, and blandness settled over his face.

"Did you?" Irish asked.

"No," he said simply. "But it might go through anyway."

The comment said far more than the actual words did. Eachan was saying that this Jordan had more influence than he himself did and that, in fact, Eachan had qualms about the man. It revealed a glimpse of integrity that she knew Irish didn't think Eachan had.

"What do you know about him? Or the company?" Irish asked.

"Which one?"

"Both," Irish said impatiently.

"As I said, the old man has enormous influence, mainly because of campaign contributions. The son is something else. Smooth. Charming. Ruthless."

He stopped, as if suddenly realizing what he had said. Amy saw another look pass between Eachan and Sally. She asked the question: "Do you think he might have been involved with the attempt to drug your cousin?"

"To use against me?" Dustin asked. "Possibly. And it might have nothing to do with that damned German train. He wants that sale. He might have thought that if he photographed my cousin in a compromising situation, it would change my mind."

"I wonder if it would be that benevolent," Irish said. "Murder isn't much of a step further than blackmail."

"There's no proof that the Jordans are involved," Dustin pointed out. "We're just speculating here. And the African sale has nothing to do with a robbery that happened fifty years ago."

Irish shook his head. "If a conglomerate the size of Jordan Industries was found to be established on a foundation of stolen gold, I don't think it would last long. There would be a hundred suits filed, not to mention bad publicity."

"We don't know they have the gold," Amy said. "Maybe someone is still looking for it. Maybe it was never found. Maybe someone thinks I might have a clue to it."

They all stared at her.

"I don't think my grandfather had any of it," she said. "He lived well, but not that well. From what Irish has said about his family, I don't think his grandfather had anything to do with the theft, either." She turned toward Dustin and Sally. "Could your grandfather have taken any part of it?"

Dustin hesitated long enough to make Amy wonder. Then, "Jordan emerged from the forties as the wealthiest of all," he said. "I think he's as likely a suspect as any. If, in fact, the gold wasn't just lost in the last days of the war. It may not be connected to anyone with the command. It could have been lost anywhere along the way. From Salzburg to New York."

"The trunks of gold disappeared in Salzburg," Irish said.

"They were stored there for months," Dustin said. "I don't suppose it was inventoried every week, so we have no idea—nor did the commission—as to when it actually disappeared."

"And the other items?"

Eachan didn't say anything.

The tension between the two men still ran high. Amy decided to try to cut it. "This Brian Jordan. Would he have the power to do everything that has been happening to us? My house destroyed, accidents, murders?"

Eachan nodded. "Probably. He has one hell of a security department. But that's normal in his business. He produces and sells very advanced weaponry, including some classified equipment."

"Would they have access to government investigative agencies? Like the CID or FBI?"

She glanced at Irish. He was leaning lazily against a wall, but she suspected he was way ahead of her. In another second, he confirmed that. "Most large corporations recruit from federal agencies. I've had offers myself."

"So they might still have contacts in those agencies?"

Irish nodded. "It's one of the reasons these people are valuable. The companies are buying contacts as well as experience and training."

Eachan didn't add anything. Instead, he appeared relieved that the conversation had veered away from him.

"So if Sally's drawing is sent around to agencies, someone might recognize the picture?" Amy addressed that question to Eachan.

"Possibly," he said.

Amy was thinking out loud now. She was sure Irish must have run through this himself, but he seemed content that she was doing the asking. Eachan didn't become quite as defensive with her. "Then wouldn't whoever sent this man after us find him rather an embarrassment?"

Irish smiled approvingly. Eachan looked startled, as if the thought hadn't occurred to him. Sally looked surprised, too.

"They don't seem overly concerned about killing people. So why should they concern themselves about embarrassment?" Sally asked.

"Except for the attempt on Amy's life in the hospital, everything could be an accident or a random crime. A house fire, a gas explosion, a hit and run, a simple burglary. They're becoming more and more desperate."

"They must know now that we can identify at least one of them," Amy said.

Irish turned to Dustin Eachan. "It might be productive to start looking for fresh unidentified bodies," Irish said.

"Or they could send him overseas," Dustin said. "Get him out of the country. Jordan Industries has interests throughout the world."

Sally, who had been quiet until then, interceded. "But he doesn't know I can draw. I don't think anyone does."

Eachan turned to her. "Did you leave any of those sketching materials in your room?"

Sally's face tensed. "Yes."

"Then we have to assume they know. Whoever," he said pointedly, "they might be."

"I don't think we can wait around until the man is identified," Irish said. "I can't be gone that long, and I'm not leaving Amy alone."

"What do you propose?" Eachan raised an eyebrow. "Brian Jordan is one of the most politically connected men in the country. We have no proof."

Amy studied his face and thought something else was at stake, too. Of them all, only Dustin Eachan had escaped threat of bodily harm. Because he was too visible a target? Or was he alive because he could still be used for some purpose?

"Are you willing to wait and risk your cousin's life? I sure as hell am not going to risk Dr. Mallory for your goddamn career. Or mine."

"I'm waiting for a suggestion," Eachan said.

Irish returned to the chair, put his foot on it and looked at Eachan thoughtfully. "We have to make them come out of the shadows."

"How in the hell are we going to do that?"

"A trap," Irish said.

twenty-four

Irish drove Eachan and his cousin to the parking lot where he'd left the rental car, then handed the keys over to Eachan.

Eachan looked at the purple car dubiously. "Are you sure it will get us back to my car?"

"No," Irish said cheerfully. Then he took pity on Sally. "It will get you there."

She laughed. It was a pleasant sound, the first time he'd heard it tonight. "I never thought otherwise, Colonel."

Eachan hesitated a moment, then took a key ring from his pocket and detached a key, handing it to Irish. "I'll call you at my Maryland house in two days. Will that give you time?"

"I hope so. We're running out of it."

"Take care of my house."

"Are you sure you want to risk it?"

"We don't have time to rent one."

Irish made no attempt to leave. "What about your cousin? She can stay with us."

Eachan shook his head. "You seem to be the main target right now. I'll find a place." He hesitated, then held out his hand. "Good luck."

Irish nodded, then watched them drive out. He wasn't

sure he could trust Dustin Eachan. But he had damned little choice. He went to his rental car. Another thirty minutes, and he and Amy would be on their way again.

He planned to stop at the chief's trailer and tell him they
had received a check, enough to rent a car and pay him,
and planned a weekend trip to Washington. They might
even stay a few days longer, since their son wasn't expected until late next week.

Irish used a flashlight to inspect the car thoroughly for
any device that might have been planted. Then he got in
and drove back to the trailer. Amy had packed most of
what they had. They left some food in the refrigerator, saw
the chief then drove out.

Amy was quiet, and when he glanced at her, she smiled.
But it was a wan, tired smile. He couldn't even begin to
imagine what a toll this must be taking on her. Moving
from place to place, always aware that killers might be just
behind them.

"What do you think?" she asked.

He shrugged. "We don't seem to have many choices."

"I liked Sally Eachan."

"What about the Assistant to the Deputy Secretary of
State?"

"*She* likes him."

"What about you?"

"I don't know," she said. "He doesn't give much away."

"No, he doesn't. But I think I trust that more than I
would have his ready assent."

"Can you get what you need?"

He reached over and took her hand. "I'll be calling in
every marker I have."

"Do you trust Dustin Eachan?"

"Up to a point," Irish replied.

"What point?"

"Let's just say not entirely," he clarified.

She leaned back, and he hoped she was relaxing. They
would drive through the night to the Kentucky facility

where she'd stored her grandfather's desk. They would check it for any clues, then leave her boxes of papers there.

He found himself constantly looking in the rearview mirror, taking exits off the interstate, then catching up with it again a few miles ahead. He only hoped that he hadn't missed any kind of transmitter. He would soon find out.

Irish stopped several times for coffee. One time, Amy woke before curling back into a ball and going back to sleep, Bo next to her. The other time he took Bo for a short pit stop. He found a public phone booth, and made four collect calls. No way to trace those, unless his opponents had taps on every person he'd ever met. It was five in the morning, and none of the calls were immediately appreciated, but he'd wanted to catch the recipients at home. He told each what he needed, then thanked them.

They had a breakfast of fast food. Thank God for it now, though he usually abhorred the stuff.

"Why don't I drive for a while?" Amy asked as they looked at the map. A hundred miles to go.

"Good idea," he said.

"Any luck?"

He looked startled.

"When you called."

"I thought you were asleep."

"Not entirely. Did you get what you need?"

"Yes," he said. "They'll meet us in two days in Maryland."

"All of them?"

"One's unavailable. The other three will be there."

She reached over and touched his arm. "They know it's dangerous?"

"Oh, yes. They also know there could be legal problems."

"They must be very good friends," she said a little wistfully.

Friends. Maybe. Strangely enough, they had not seen each other much in fifteen years. There were a few phone calls. One drunken reunion five years ago. Promises to keep track of each other. And they did, by long distance. One had asked him a favor three years ago. They all owed each other. But friends? Friends kept in contact with each other.

Their bond was too painful.

In fact, he'd really hated calling them. He'd always disliked asking favors. But now he had no choice. And these guys were the best.

PIKESVILLE, KENTUCKY

Amy drove into the old storage facility and confronted a locked gate. She sat in the parked car for a moment, then stretched. She was stiff. So was, she noticed, Irish. Both their bodies had taken something of a beating in the past few days. And it had been a long drive to eastern Kentucky, where she had once lived with her grandfather. As they had driven through Pikesville, she remembered the main street, the church cemetery where her grandfather was buried, the rolling hills that he loved. It had been twenty years since her grandfather died, five years since the last time she was here. She'd inventoried her grandfather's items then, weighed the possibility of taking them home, and driven past the grand old home he'd owned. It had been sixty years old when he'd died, and had always needed something fixed. But there was a wrap-around porch, and she could still see him in her mind's eye, sitting on the porch, his gaze wandering out toward the hills and the mines where his father had once worked.

He escaped that fate, but he'd never escaped the lure of the hills.

Suicide. It had been hard to bear then, even though she knew he had been ill. Now her heart hurt even more. She wondered whether he knew what was coming.

She'd been in her second year of college. Just eighteen. She'd finished high school a year early. . . .

The storage facility was old, not like the new, gleaming acres of storage facilities sprouting up everywhere in an increasingly mobile society. There was no office outside the gate, only a number to call in case of an emergency. Unfortunately her key was long gone. She paid the rent once a year and usually forgot about the space until the next bill came. And she hadn't given it a moment's thought when she'd fled Memphis days ago.

She spread her hands helplessly as she looked at the phone number.

"It's probably a wild goose chase," she said.

"It won't be my first," he replied with a wry smile. "And we have the time. My friends won't be in Maryland for another day."

"Could they possibly know about this?" *They* was the only term she had for those who had turned her life into a roller coaster. Irish called them "the bad guys." That wasn't descriptive enough for her.

"You didn't leave a bill around your house, or a key?" he asked.

"No."

"Then it should be safe enough." He looked at the sign. "Let's find a telephone."

Twenty minutes later, an old man unlocked the gate and led them inside the office. "Miss Mallory, isn't it?"

Amy tried not to show surprise that someone remembered her. She was ready with her identification. She was sorry to say she didn't recognize the man.

He looked down at Bo, who was huddled next to her.

"Fine fellow," he observed.

He'd instantly endeared himself to her. Not many people were that discriminating.

"Hugh Avery," the man said. "I remember when you rented this place, then when you came back. I kinda check to see if you renew every year. Didn't want to see your grandfather's stuff go to auction. Used to have breakfast with your grandfather. He sure was proud of you. Said you were the smartest young lady he ever saw."

Her grandfather had never said that to her. She felt a blush of pleasure along with a stab of regret. They had grown closer after a few initial years of pure hostility. But never as much as she now wished.

There would have been so much he could tell her.

And he was the last of her family.

"Thank you," she said. "It's good to know that."

He beamed at her as he unlocked the gate. "Have your key?"

She shook her head.

"Well, you don't need identification." He turned and looked at Irish. "This your husband?"

"Just a good friend," she said. "Has anyone asked about me?"

"Nope," he said, his glance still running over Irish speculatively. "Should they? I don't let anyone in unless they have the proper authorization."

"Of course not," she soothed him.

He led the way inside, and went into the small office, returning with a key. "Here you go, Miss Mallory. You just keep it. I'll get another one made. It will open the gate, too. You just stay as long as you want, and lock it when you leave."

"Thank you," Amy said. "You've been very kind."

He looked pleased, then left, apparently sensing that they wanted to be left alone.

Irish switched on the lights. The small area was crammed. The desk sat against the wall. A huge chair was next to it. There were several crates of books. Some, she remembered, were novels. She picked one of them up. *The Silver Chalice.* A historical. He had argued history with her, had been responsible for her love of it.

She saw him in her mind's eye. He'd had a full head of gray hair cut very short, like a newly minted Marine. His blue eyes never lost their intelligence, and they were

shaded by heavy dark eyebrows. He needed reading
glasses, which he hated and always lost. As long as she
knew him, he was whipcord thin.

Probably because he worked so hard in his garden. He
loved gardening and had a green thumb with both vegetables and flowers. It had always seemed strange to her that
he was gentle with vegetables but so hard on people. He
barked at them. She'd hated it in the beginning, but the
housekeeper had taken her aside and said it was just his
way. He'd simply been in the military too long. Everyone,
to him, was a subordinate of some kind. Amy had understood why her mother had hated it. She had not been good
at confrontation, and her father had never respected anyone who didn't stand up to him.

But Amy had learned to stand up to him. And he had
taken interest in her, then pleasure. They had learned to
like one another.

The desk had been a part of him. He always sat at it and
leaned back in the chair. He often held a glass of fine
whiskey and smoked a cigar. She could almost smell it
now.

Bo whined next to her, as if he felt her disquiet. Then
she felt a hand on her shoulder. "Amy?"

"It's all right," she said. "Just some memories."

"Good ones?"

"Mostly."

She moved the chair and sat down. Irish went over to
the door and looked out. *Standing sentinel,* she thought.
She wondered if he was wearing his gun in its holster.

Her hand ran over the oak. The desk was old, dating
back approximately a hundred years. She'd known it
would bring a fine price, but she'd never been able to sell
it, nor keep it close. One of these days, she'd have to balance those two. It was a crime to keep it here.

She opened each of the drawers. They were all empty.
Well, it had been a long shot at best.

She ran her fingers along the inside of the left drawer. It

didn't appear as deep as it looked. Secret compartment? That only happened in books. And yet . . .

But if there was something, she couldn't find it. She knocked. No hollow sound. She started to move away, then hesitated. "Irish?"

He walked over to her.

"I think there might be something here. The top left-hand drawer, but I can't find anything."

He touched the edge of the drawer. As she had done, he felt the bottom, investigated the sides. Then he slipped the drawer out of the desk and turned it upside down. He saw an indentation and pressed it. A spring lifted a false bottom of the drawer. Underneath it was one sheet of paper.

He handed it to her. Across the top was the letterhead of Jordan Industries. Then a long number. Under that were dates and sums. Fifty thousand dollars during five years. Ten thousand dollars a year, ending the year he died.

She looked toward Irish.

"It looks like it might be a numbered account," he said.

"Who was paying whom?" she said as a heavy lump lodged in her throat.

He shook his head. "I don't know."

"When he died, there was little left," she said. "That's why I sold the house. He was deeply in debt. I paid that off and had just enough to finish my undergraduate degree."

"Then I suspect he was paying Jordan rather than the other way around. But why? If your grandfather . . . had stolen anything, he would have more money than you thought he had. He should have had a damn good retirement."

"Not necessarily," she said. "A general's pay wasn't that high."

"Could your grandfather have blackmailed *him*?"

Her first instinct was to say no. But the figure was odd. Ten thousand was a great deal of money twenty years ago. But blackmail? Either receiving or taking it? It just didn't fit her picture of her grandfather.

All it did is point another finger at Jordan Industries.

She took the sheet, folded it carefully, and put it in her purse. "Do you think this might be what someone was looking for? Or trying to destroy?"

"Fifty thousand dollars nearly two decades ago? I doubt it."

"But we have a number."

"We don't even know if it exists now," he reminded her.

"Still, it could be more bait for the trap," she said.

He scowled. "I don't think I like your enthusiasm."

"Do you think there's anything else here?" she asked.

He explored the desk as she had. "I think that's it." He looked around at the boxes and crates. "We might as well go through those."

By midafternoon they were hungry and covered with dust. There had been nothing but books. She took out some to take with them and vowed to finally do something about the rest.

When she found a new house. That reminded her she had no home. She would need this stuff. Perhaps, she thought, divine intervention had kept her from taking her grandfather's belongings home. At least now she had a desk and chair.

"Amy?"

"I was just thinking about my house. I'll have to get a new one when I get back. There's insurance, and . . . damn, the hearing. It's Friday." She'd been able to block those things from her mind for a little while. Now she felt overwhelmed, batted around by fickle winds, out of control.

She hated to feel out of control. She'd had so much control over her life just three weeks ago.

He leaned down and kissed her lightly, his hand going to her neck and massaging it gently. "I can't even imagine what it's like for you," he said.

She looked up at him, and her arms went around his neck. She needed his warmth.

His mouth met hers, and the kiss wasn't gentle. It was hungry and demanding. The warmth turned blistering.

It was partly her need, partly his urge to comfort, but it so quickly turned into something else. Today had been a journey back into her past, a reminder of losses. She felt them stronger today than she had since the day of the general's funeral, the terrible emptiness and loneliness she had then. To be completely alone in the world had been terrifying at first. She had never really gotten over that hollow feeling, and yet something in her had feared relationships. Because she'd wanted too much? And feared disappointment? She'd seen that disappointment too often in her mother.

But now she grabbed for a piece of another person. It was in the way their lips met and searched and finally plundered in an almost desperate quest. The way their bodies arched toward each other as if they belonged together, as if it was destined to be. She felt passion and power and strength in his deliberate, gentle touches and in the rigidity of his body. She felt safe and. . . .

This isn't forever, she warned herself as the kiss intensified.

The ground rumbled. The air sparked with electricity. Her every sense spiraled out of control.

His lips left hers and he went over to close the door, then locked it. When he returned, his arms went around her, bringing her body as close into his as could. "Ah, Amy. You have one hell of an effect on me."

Instead of answering, she lifted her hand, her fingers tracing the angles and planes of his face, stopping to touch the crook of his lips that was so attractive to her. She memorized it by touch and by feel. Seized by an emotion so strong she nearly cried out with its impact, she stepped back. Her gaze met his, and she trembled with the knowledge that this man evoked feelings the size of an earthquake that hit eight on the Richter Scale.

His hand captured hers, and its warmth drifted down to her insides, causing small tremors and explosions.

Irish leaned down. His lips were smooth and hard and gentle. And what they sought, they found.

Amy had never made love anyplace but a bed.

She discovered she had really, really missed something.

WASHINGTON, D.C.

Dustin wasn't going to take any chances with Sally now. He still cared about his career. After all, he had worked toward one goal most of his life. But now her safety was of paramount concern.

He drove from Virginia directly to Ronald Reagan Airport.

"Where are we going?"

"You're going to Sedona," he said.

"No," she said.

"I talked to your mother when we stopped to eat," he said. "And I got you a flight out today."

"Then I put her in danger."

"She knows everything. At least, she knows what I know," he said. "She has friends. She believes you will be safe there."

"My name will be on an airline manifest," she countered.

"Someone is meeting me with an identification for Mary Jones. It's not uncommon for couriers."

She winced at that. "Couldn't you have been more imaginative?"

"Then you *will* go?"

"No."

He saw a rest stop and pulled in. He cut the motor and turned to her. "Please, Sally. For me." He used the one dirty trick he had. "This is the first time I've ever asked you to do something. Just for a week. No more." He handed her a cell phone. "I know you don't like cell phones, but keep it with you. For me."

She was silent for a moment. Then another.

When she looked up, her eyes were full of pain. "Don't do this to me, Dusty."

"I can't do what needs to be done if I'm worrying about you," he said flatly. "It will make it far more dangerous for all of us."

"And you think I'm useless," she said, hating the trembling of her lips.

"No. I think you have been extraordinarily strong. It's me. I can't concentrate if I feel you're in danger, and I can't keep you with me every moment."

"Is this going to hurt you?"

"My career, you mean?"

"Yes."

He shrugged. "It probably would, one way or another now. It's gone too far not to become public. People have died. My career isn't worth more lives, and if it's hurt by this, then so be it."

He felt her hand move onto his leg. She scooted over and laid her head on his shoulder. For the first time in his life, he really felt proud.

And free.

twenty-five

MARYLAND

Amy stretched in the bed, watching through the bathroom door as Irish shaved. There was something extraordinarily sexy about that act, or maybe it was the warm shudders she still felt from the morning's lovemaking. Bo, who had jumped up on the bed as soon as Irish left her side, snuggled next to her.

It was just after dawn. About six. Her body reacted again even as she remembered each of the night's explorations in exquisite detail. Her newly awakened sensuality had responded in any number of imaginative ways since the afternoon in the storage room.

This morning had been especially wonderful. She'd awakened to the sight of Irish leaning on an elbow, watching her. Instinctively she'd reached out to him and touched his rough cheek.

A minute later, he came into her hard and demanding, and she'd found herself moving with him, against him, in a primitive rhythmic dance that exploded in a fireball of glory. Great satisfying sensations cascaded through her, and she had a wonderful feeling of well-being.

She told herself it was a false security. Tomorrow should end everything once and for all, and it would be dangerous.

But for now. . . .

For now she gloried in the intimacy of the morning.

Irish came into the room, a towel around his waist. He was incredibly beautiful to her. That was the only word she could use. Even the scars, including the still angry recent ones, emphasized the sculpted strength of his body.

He leaned over and kissed her, slowly. If she hadn't known the schedule for the morning, she would have pulled him down again.

She should be satiated. She wondered whether she ever could be.

Did anyone ever get tired of such an adventure?

Or did danger heighten the pleasure?

And what about the knowledge that it could not last, that their time together was running out?

"Your turn for the shower," he said in the voice that had become just a little more husky after their lovemaking.

Reluctantly she left the comfort of the bed. It was another of the pay-by-the-hour motels where credit cards weren't a necessity. They had checked into it last night after driving several hours from Pikesville. They would be in a different one tonight, one near Maryland's eastern shore, then tomorrow they would go to the cottage owned by Dustin Eachan.

She had been as surprised as Irish when Eachan offered its use along with the home next door. His neighbors were in Europe, and he had the keys to both houses. They'd needed a place they could stay and control for several days. They'd needed a place where they could be found.

Amy took a shower and washed her hair. She wanted to blow it dry, but she didn't have a dryer. Nor the time. The call had to be made at seven. She applied just a touch of lipstick and regarded herself quizzically. She looked different. Happier. More contented. How strange when she was running for her life.

She dressed in a T-shirt and a pair of jeans, then went out to the room.

"Ready?" he said.

She nodded.

Irish picked up the phone, took out a credit card, and punched in some numbers.

"Eachan," he said after someone answered the phone, "this is Lucien Mallory."

She couldn't hear the other end of the conversation, but she knew its content. They had written the script the night before last. They were betting on Dustin's home being monitored.

"I have something I have to talk to you about," he said. "Evidence involving your grandfather, something about his connection with Jordan Industries. We found it in General Mallory's desk." Just enough truth to make it believable. She couldn't hear Eachan's reply, but Irish said, "When can I meet you?"

Another pause on Irish's part. Then, "Tomorrow night?"

Silence again as he listened. "All right. I'll call you tomorrow for a location."

He hung up without any more words.

"That should concern the bad guys." She'd started adopting his own words.

"Particularly now that they know we're in touch with Eachan."

"Isn't he in danger now?"

He shook his head. "He's too important. Besides, they will probably want to know what we have. If anything happens to Eachan, they know we'll go to the authorities, and this time they'll listen to us. They will want the three of us together."

"So we have a day and a half."

"My guys should be there today," he said.

"When do we call Brian Jordan?" she asked.

"In the morning. From Eachan's Chesapeake Bay house. *After* I know that all the equipment is in place."

"What if you can't reach him?"

"Oh, I think he'll make himself accessible." He took her hand. "I don't want you there."

"You can't leave me out now."

"I can," he replied grimly. "I'll find you someplace else to stay."

Amy knew from his tone she would have no success arguing with him now. But she had been with him every step of the way, and she didn't intend to wait alone in a motel or some other nondescript place to hear whether or not he was alive.

She clamped her lips together and turned away.

"Amy?"

"We had better leave," she said.

"This is not open for discussion." His voice was controlled.

She felt a sudden chill as the recent heat began to seep from the room. He was all business now, and she saw a hardness in his face. It was as if it had turned to ice. She supposed she was seeing what others had seen, perhaps even the essence of the man. No hint of gentleness now. Only a steely determination that brooked no opposition.

Bo huddled next to her, and she knew he felt it, too. But then he was extraordinarily sensitive to moods. She leaned down and rubbed his ears, reassuring him that all was well.

Irish took advantage of it. "And Bojangles," he said. "What would you do with him? We certainly don't want him barking or wandering about."

She didn't say anything. She didn't consent.

She didn't dissent.

He looked at her suspiciously.

"I think it's time to go," she said.

SEDONA, ARIZONA

Sally was surprised to see her mother waiting for her in the Phoenix airport. Sally had not called her. Dusty must have.

He must have thought that if someone wasn't there, she might turn around and take a flight back.

She could have cheerfully murdered him, she thought, then reconsidered. It was amazing that a comment easily uttered in past days now took on a sinister overtone. Still, she resented the interference. She hadn't planned to get on the next plane back, although the prospect was enticing. She'd planned to drive up to Sedona. She'd even rented a car. She'd wanted time to prepare herself. In truth, she'd put off thinking about her mother on the flight from Washington.

She'd found herself thinking about Dusty instead. She'd wondered what would have happened if they weren't cousins. He probably wouldn't have given her a second look. Patsy was the kind of woman he'd always gravitated toward. Sophisticated, well put together, well educated. Classy.

Certainly not a woman who chose to work in a bar, or who escorted dignitaries because her cousin had wrangled the job. She knew good manners, of course. She knew the walk and the talk, which was why she could do her job at the State Department. But she'd also mocked all those graces, and had often thought so many people had all the right credentials and wrong values.

And yet she had run to the Eachans, who embodied that particular dichotomy, when her father died. Away from her mother.

She hadn't seen her mother in years. Chloe Matthews— she had taken back her maiden name after her divorce— looked older, and her hair, once dark and sleek, was touched with gray and worn in a long braid. Her colorful dress was cinched by a silver belt, and her jewelry consisted of long, dangling earrings and a silver necklace with a large chunk of turquoise. Except for the anxious expression on her face, she looked tanned and healthy.

Sally recalled her mother as she had been in Maryland. Before she'd taken Sally and left the Eachans for a museum post in Phoenix. Her hair had been coiffed and she'd worn fashionable clothes, but there had been tenseness in her face, even in her movements. Even when they moved to Phoenix, there had been something like fear. Sally recognized now what she couldn't recognize then. Perhaps because of her own current fear. She'd never known before what it was like to be terrified.

Had her mother been terrified of her father? The thought curdled her blood. Had she been wrong all her life? She had blamed her mother for leaving her father, for taking her away, for the night her father had taken a gun, put it in his mouth, and pulled the trigger.

Now an insidious little voice inside wondered about her father's choice. Whether there wasn't selfishness behind it. Had he ever wondered how she would feel? Had he cared?

She could feel her mother's nervousness now. She had a forced smile as Sally approached her. "Dustin called," she said.

"I wanted to surprise you," Sally said.

Her mother's right hand was curved into a tight ball, and Sally sensed it was to keep from reaching out to her. She had been rebuffed before.

Spontaneously, Sally reached out her own hand and her mother grabbed it, holding onto it like a lifeline.

"Did Dustin tell you why I came?"

Chloe shook her head, but her eyes were wary. Twenty years had passed since Sally had run away from home. In those years, Sally had rebuffed every attempt to reconcile.

Sally saw the love and concern in her mother's eyes, and she shrank from what she had done during those years. She'd always thought she blamed her mother for her father's death, but in a second of blinding clarity, she knew she'd felt his death had been *her* fault. She had not loved her father enough. If only she had been there . . . had known what he was thinking hours before, when she had talked to him. She had been punishing herself all these years.

Her mother waited patiently. Her face was creased, aged by the sun as much as by years, and yet Sally sensed that the lines around her eyes came from humor rather than worry. There was an ease about her, despite immediate apprehension about confronting a daughter she'd not seen in many years.

"It's a long story," Sally said, letting go of her mother's hand, which had lingered in her own. "I'll tell you on the way."

Chloe looked at her purse. "Luggage?"

She shook her head. "I'll have to buy a few things."

Her mother raised an eyebrow but said nothing, just led the way in quick steps to a cavernous covered parking lot. Chloe unlocked the doors of a Jeep, and they got in.

She remembered Phoenix. She had hated the city when they first arrived. She'd loved the green, green hills of Maryland, the large house the Eachans had owned, and the stable of horses. They had lived with her grandparents as her father had tried his hand at several businesses. She had been popular in high school, and in love with Dustin even then. She'd felt torn away from everything she knew and loved. She hadn't, she knew, made anything easy for her mother. She had complained endlessly. Phoenix was gray, dry, lifeless.

And now the woman beside her was someone she really didn't know, and that had been her fault.

They exchanged small talk as they maneuvered through Phoenix to the interstate leading to Sedona. Yes, the flight was nice. The weather was hot. Dustin was fine.

They had been on the road for half an hour before her mother turned to her. "You said there was a long story."

Sally hesitated. But she knew it had to be told. Her mother could be in danger. She doubted if anyone knew about her, but she couldn't be sure.

"Did you see Grandfather's name in a news story about a month ago?"

"No," her mother said. "I don't see anything but the local paper."

"He was named in a special commission report on missing items from a Nazi treasure train in Europe at the war's end. He was one of three high-ranking officers when the train was captured."

Her mother was silent, listening. Sally knew how much she'd disliked the general. She'd blamed him for everything wrong with Sally's father.

"When the report was made public," Sally said, "things started to happen."

"Things?"

"Accidents."

"To whom?"

"To the granddaughter of one of the other officers named. Her house burned, then someone tried to kill her. I think someone tried to search my apartment, and. . . ."

"And . . . ," Chloe prompted in a controlled voice.

"I think someone tried to drug my drink. I'm not sure what they were after. . . ."

"And Dustin . . . ?"

Sally hesitated. She couldn't tell her mother what Dustin planned. It was too dangerous. "Nothing has happened to him."

"Why did you come here?"

"Dustin. . . ."

Sally saw disappointment flash over her mother's face at her answer. "I'm afraid you might be in danger, too," she continued.

"It might be difficult for someone to find me," her mother said. "I cut all ties from the family."

"I really doubt whether they know about you. I used a different name to book the flight. But if they looked hard enough, they might locate you. I just wanted you to be . . . aware. Dustin . . . and I think you should go somewhere."

"I can't leave my gallery."

"Who is looking after it now?"

"A friend, but it's not fair. . . ."

"It's not fair if anything happens to you, either," Sally said. "This other woman, along with the grandson of a third man, have been attacked several times now. They were almost caught in a house explosion. These people . . . are very determined."

"Why would they bother with me? I haven't had anything to do with the Eachans for twenty years."

"They seem to think one of us might have some . . . information. I don't know if it concerns someone who might be hurt by revelations or whether they think one of us has some of the items that were missing."

"I don't have anything," Chloe said.

"I do," Sally said quietly.

Chloe turned toward her for a fraction of a second.

"That painting Daddy gave me when I was sixteen. The wild sea. It . . . had been on the train."

The car nearly went off the road. It hit the shoulder, and gravel sprayed against the Jeep. Chloe straightened the wheel and went back on the road. Then she said hesitantly, "It wasn't your father's to give to you."

"What do you mean?"

"It had been stored in the attic. Your father found it. He . . . took it without your grandfather's knowledge. That was the last straw for your grandfather. He disinherited your father. He allowed you to keep it, though. He hadn't the heart to take it from you. You loved it so."

They were both silent the rest of the way.

WASHINGTON, D.C.

Dustin resisted the urge to call. There could be no link to Chloe. He didn't think anyone knew about her. She had cut all her ties to the Eachans two decades ago, had even dropped the name.

Dustin liked her. He'd always liked her. He hadn't always agreed with her, though. She shouldn't have kept her husband's violence a secret from her daughter. But she'd realized that she was a reserved, internal person who could never express affection as her husband had done. Except her husband had used affection like a weapon.

Dustin would have told Sally about her father years earlier, had he not promised Chloe. Chloe had been willing to give up her daughter to preserve her faith in her father. He had not thought that necessary, that Sally was a lot stronger than Chloe thought she was. He often wondered whether Chloe wasn't hiding something else.

He also realized he should call Patsy. She had called several times, and he'd not returned her calls. But he didn't know what to tell her. He knew she'd expected a proposal for the past month.

He'd been prepared to make it, too. But that was weeks ago. Now something had happened. He found he wasn't willing to settle for a marriage that would be little more than a pleasant convenience. How long, in fact, could that kind of marriage really last?

The damnable fact was that he couldn't get Sally out of his mind. When he tried to think about Patsy, he saw Sally instead, her long hair swinging as she walked, her green eyes sparkling. She was a natural rebel, in contrast to his conformity.

And Patsy might not want anything to do with him after this weekend. If everything exploded as he thought it could, then his career was over. Oh, he had skills. He would probably remain with the State Department. But he would go no higher and would be damnably lucky not to be demoted.

As he thought of Sally, he realized that a lot worse things could happen.

He looked at his watch. Eight in the evening. He wasn't the last person in the building, but his office had pretty well cleared out. He wondered how things were going at his Chesapeake Bay home.

He wanted to call, but he couldn't. He couldn't have

anything to do with this other than loaning his Maryland cottage to an old friend of the family. He hoped he wouldn't regret mentioning the vacant house next door to his.

He wondered how Sally was doing with her mother. Getting them together was something he'd tried to accomplish for the last decade at least.

He hoped she was doing better than he was.

What in the hell was happening at his house?

twenty-six

Irish and Amy headed back to Washington and Chesapeake Bay. It seemed they had spent a lifetime beside each other in a car. The small space wrapped a deceptive web of intimacy around them.

They had stopped at a pistol range on their way. Irish wanted her to take another lesson, make sure she remembered everything.

She did. Though she handled the gun awkwardly, she held it safely, loaded it safely, and hit at least part of the target that was fifteen feet away. If she had to aim a greater distance, they would both be in deep trouble.

She placed the gun back in her purse, and he put his in the holster at the back of his belt, again wearing a sports shirt over it. They'd also stopped at an outlet store and bought a few shirts, and some dog food.

Irish knew that she intended to go with him, no matter what he said. But he had his own plan. He had no intention of letting her anywhere close to Eachan's house. He had asked one of his friends to stay with her, to make sure she was safe. It was the best he could do for her. And Bojangles. Hell, he'd fallen for the damn mutt, too.

Dropping her off was going to be the hardest thing he'd ever done. And the most necessary.

They were setting a trap for a man or an organization with nearly unlimited assets. The only advantage on their side was that the bad guys needed to make things look like an accident. They could not spray bullets all over the place. He suspected they would send a team of three or four.

He and his friends could take care of that. Unless, of course, a woman and a dog stood in the middle of gunfire.

There was also the question of Dustin Eachan. They hadn't shared the information they found in the desk. Irish still didn't trust Eachan completely. His rise in the State Department had been a little too fast. He had friends. But he'd also seen the man's concern for his cousin. His feelings obviously went a lot deeper than cousinly affection. Irish just wasn't sure how far that went. Or, indeed, whether it was any of his business.

For a moment, he wondered whether he knew that because of his own feelings. Amy Mallory—practical, pragmatic—had insinuated herself so deeply into his life that he wasn't sure he could ever let her go. He'd never felt . . . committed before. He'd certainly never felt that he couldn't live without a woman.

He felt that way now. He couldn't imagine returning to his solitary life. And that scared the hell out of him. Her profession and his just didn't go together. She was about to get her fondest dream: tenure at a very good college. And he . . . well, he was used to traveling with only a toothbrush and a spare shirt in his duffel.

There *was* the ranch. He'd been thinking about that steadily now. But that wouldn't solve her problem. There were no colleges and universities within commuting distance to his ranch. And if he retired now, he would have barely enough money to live on, much less make the ranch a self-sustaining proposition. Nor would she be happy as an officer's wife. He shuddered every time he thought of her at a military wives' club, explaining that her entire life had been antimilitary.

She would wither. He couldn't do it to her.

Nor could he move to Memphis and give up both his career and the ranch. That would eventually destroy *him*.

That was, if he still had a career after this. He had not directly disobeyed an order, but his conduct had certainly been questionable. At least to the military. He'd probably ended any chance at promotion, and he knew that meant he could well be forced out eventually. You either went up or went out.

Regardless, their lives—his and Amy's—did not mesh. So he treasured every moment he was with her, the feeling of companionship as well as unbridled lust. No one had ever ignited every sense as she had. No one had brought out the tenderness he hadn't realized survived twenty years of his occupation. No one had ever given him a sense of home and belonging before.

But it would come to an end this week. It had to. Today was Tuesday, tomorrow was Wednesday. He had to have her back in Memphis by Friday, or she might lose everything she'd worked for.

Still, it was going to be hard leaving her. She would feel abandoned. Hurt. Angry. She might never forgive him.

Nothing else to do.

She didn't have a car. And she had the dog. She wouldn't be able to come after him.

But he knew that while he was plotting to leave her somewhere safe, she was plotting just as hard to find a way to stay with him. In the intense days they had been together, it was the first time their needs and emotions and desires veered in different directions. He didn't like the distance it placed between them, the fences they both were building so that one wouldn't know the other's thoughts.

When they stopped for lunch—again fast food take-out—they ate in silence. There was little to say. The almost mystical bond of knowing what the other was thinking had faded. Bo watched them both carefully, and Irish realized the dog felt the tension. But he didn't know how to cut it, how to bring back the camaraderie, the connection. He felt, in fact, that he was betraying her even while trying to protect her.

She didn't want protection that way. She'd made that clear. She wanted to be a part of whatever was planned. After Jekyll Island, she felt prepared to cope with anything, but she still didn't understand the impact of violence. Of causing another's death, or risking your own. Then it had been thrust upon her, and had happened so fast, she hadn't had time to think. This would be planned. Carefully plotted.

He knew he could—and probably should—bring in the police, but he feared Hawke could smell it out and then cover his tracks, only to strike later. He couldn't take that risk, not without more evidence.

So they continued their journey. Five more hours and they would reach Chestertown. One of his former team would meet them there. Sam Reynolds would stay with her at a motel. Mike and Tag would go with him to the house.

"You said you had a ranch," she said suddenly, surprising him. He'd thought she would argue about staying behind. New tack.

"Hmmmmmm," he muttered noncommittally.

"Where is it?"

"The Cimarron Valley in the Black Mountains."

She smiled at that. "I like the name."

"My grandfather called it Flaherty's Folly. Somewhat less poetic. It's in central Colorado, nestled in the mountains."

"Do I detect longing?"

"Probably," he said, glad that the conversation had moved from the next day.

"Is it a cattle ranch?"

"That's an exaggeration," he replied wryly. "That's why he called it Flaherty's Folly. We have a few cows. A foreman. And two thousand acres, some of it public land we lease. The taxes and maintenance take most of my pay. But it's damned good land for cows. And horses. When I leave the service, I'll probably try to raise horses or turn it into a dude ranch. That's the only way something like Flaherty's Folly can survive."

"Will you miss the excitement of your job?"

"Most of it isn't excitement. Most of it is just plain tedious."

"I've never been to that part of Colorado," she said.

He wanted to show it to her. He wanted to share the grand mountains with her, the rich green valleys. He really wanted to be with her when she watched a sun glide behind a mountain, spreading a blanket of gold and orange and coral across the sky.

Irish could almost see the delight in her eyes, the sense of wonder and awe that always grabbed him.

She was silent, and he looked toward her. Her eyelashes were closing over her eyes. "Get some sleep," he said softly.

A soft sigh escaped her lips, and she put her hand on a sleeping Bo. A drowsy smile crossed her lips. "Okay," she said.

Something warm settled inside him. Not lust, but a deep sense of belonging. He took one hand from the wheel and briefly touched her cheek, then returned it to the wheel. In seconds her head drooped slightly.

Five hours later, he made a turn off the interstate onto another road. In a few moments, they would be in Chestertown, Maryland, about an hour from Eachan's Chesapeake Bay home.

The sun was going down, and the air was humid. Dense and hot. It was smothering, and he smelled a coming storm. He didn't know whether that would be a hindrance or a help. But then, with the weather on this coast, it might well be gone tomorrow.

CHESTERTOWN, MARYLAND

Irish drove up to the motel Sam had suggested. He was from the area and knew it well. In fact, he was a fisherman now, a far cry from the Special Forces member he once had been.

The others had gone into security work.

Irish found himself anxious to see them again. It had been years.

His gaze scoured the parking lot. Then he saw Sam perched on a chair beside a small swimming pool. He immediately rose.

"Hey, man." Sam wore swimming trunks and looked as fit as always. His face and arms were bronze. His military crewcut, though, had been replaced by long hair tied back by a piece of rawhide. But his smile was as blinding as ever, revealing white, even teeth.

Irish raised an eyebrow, and his eyes lingered on Sam's hair.

Sam grinned. "Middle-age rebellion."

"I seem to remember you were always a rebel."

"I tried being respectable for a while. Didn't work."

"Can you still shoot?"

"That's something that never goes away," he said, sobering instantly. "Like riding a bicycle."

"Not exactly," Amy said.

Sam turned all his attention on Amy. "Your lady?"

Irish liked the way that sounded. "Yes," he said. "Remember it." Then he turned to Amy. "Amy, this is an old friend, Sam. Sam, Amy."

Amy held out her hand, and Sam held it a fraction of a second too long. "I'm glad to meet you, Sam."

Sam looked at Irish. "A winner, my friend."

Irish watched as his old friend eyed Amy with appreciation. Sam was four inches shorter than Irish, and had to look up slightly to meet Amy's eyes, but that didn't seem to faze him. For a moment, Irish regretted contacting Sam. Sam always had been a ladies' man.

"How's your wife, Sam?" he asked.

Sam's green eyes twinkled. "Long gone. Thought fishing was as bad as the military. Never at home, she said."

"Hell, and I thought you were the safe one."

"I am, old buddy."

Irish raised a warning eyebrow.

Sam's grin immediately faded, and he nodded. He took a key out of his pocket and handed it to Irish. "Room one-twelve. I'm room one-fourteen. I checked you both in. Mr. and Mrs. David Saunders."

"No problem with the dog?"

"I slipped the clerk an extra twenty." Sam glanced down at Bo, who was slinking between Amy and Irish, and panting heavily. Panic attack. Well, he'd been dragged over hell and back.

Irish leaned down and picked Bo up. "This is a friend," he said.

Sam held out his hand and let the dog smell him. Bo hesitated, then his tail started wagging slowly.

"He's a little timid," Amy offered.

"Not a good watchdog, huh?"

She looked at Irish and smiled. "He can be. When absolutely necessary. He just doesn't like conflict."

"Well, that's perfectly okay. I like that kind better." With those words, Sam won Amy's heart.

Sam turned back to Irish. "The other guys are at the house. It should be ready by this evening."

"All the sensors? The phone tapped? Rooms wired?"

Sam nodded. "Everything you requested, including the weapons."

"I'll go over there. Directions?"

Sam held a piece of paper out to him. "I wrote them down for you. Pretty fancy digs."

"I want you to stay here with Amy."

Amy stiffened next to him. "At least let me stay until you make the call. Then I'll leave."

Irish shook his head. "I don't want you anywhere around there."

"There's two houses," she reminded him. "Dustin Eachan's and the neighbor's."

"Yeah, and our friends—if they're any good—will probably check out the neighboring properties."

"But not until you call them. I'll be gone by then."

"What about Bo?" Irish asked.

"I can take him with me."

Seeing the plea in her eyes, Irish surrendered. It would be safe. At least for several hours. Then . . . she wouldn't feel as left out. Sam could make sure she didn't return. Reluctantly, he nodded.

Sam had looked from him to Amy and back again, obviously trying to ferret out the dynamics of their relationship. Then he shrugged. "Whatever. I'll change. I thought this was the most unobtrusive way of watching for you."

"Unobtrusive?" Amy said with a grin. With his tan and build, he would attract any number of stares from admiring women.

He grinned back, then walked toward the motel.

Amy watched him with more interest than Irish would have liked. He put Bo down and took her hand. "Let's unpack," he said. "Then we drive to the house."

SEDONA, ARIZONA

Sally tried to dissipate the awkwardness. Her mother was no more the cuddly mother she'd always wanted than she had been during Sally's childhood. Instead, she was hesitant and reserved. Watchful and wary.

Sally understood that. As she had grown older, she'd regretted not having a relationship with her mother, but she hadn't known how to change it. Particularly since part of her heart died that hour she'd heard about her father's death.

Dustin had tried to tell her that her father was not all she had believed, that there were reasons her mother left. He had been abusive when he drank, and he drank often. But Sally had never seen that part of him. Never. She had been his princess. He'd bought her her first pony and taught her to ride. He'd hadn't always been there, but when he was, it was magic time. Her mother, on the other hand, had been silent and withdrawn. She remembered screaming at her mother, "You never loved Daddy. You took him away from me."

But now, sitting in the office behind the gallery her mother owned, she felt an odd affinity for the woman whom she'd effectively cut from her life. She looked at the paintings and realized they shared more than blood. They both had a love of art and painting. Why hadn't she realized that before? Was it because her mother hadn't taken her in her arms and hugged her as other mothers did? She looked at her mother and realized for the first time that it might not have been lack of love, but her mother's own reserved emotions.

In the first hours after arriving at Sedona, they had stopped at a specialty clothing store and bought some clothes for her, then went to her mother's house, where they had tea. Sally once more had tried to get her to leave Sedona.

Her mother had flatly refused. "This is my home. No one is going to scare me away."

Sally had been frustrated, but grudgingly impressed. She'd looked around the house, which was filled with western paintings, and saw her mother's signature on them. "You still paint?"

"For pleasure," her mother said. "I'm not good enough to do it commercially."

But she was. Sally knew that from looking at the paintings, and instantly she knew they had something else in common. If they couldn't be the best, they opted not to compete. She studied each painting. If there was a problem, it was control. They were technically wonderful, but there was no sense of freedom in them.

"You see it, don't you?" her mother said.

"They're very good."

"Not good enough."

After tea, they went into the gallery. It featured western paintings, both originals and prints. There were also sculptures, including one Remington. Sally fondled the sculpture with wondering hands.

She was aware that her mother was watching her, and she turned, offering a tentative smile. "You have beautiful things."

"You used to draw, too," Chloe said. "Do you still?"

"Not for a long time. But Dusty brought me some supplies, and I played with it a little."

"I'm glad. You were good. You had talent I didn't have."

Stunned at the admission, Sally turned to her. "I always thought you were wonderful."

Her mother shook her head. "I can draw what I see. I can't go beyond that." She hesitated. "That's what your grandfather told me, and he was right."

Sally was beginning to see an uncomfortable picture. She knew her grandfather was a connoisseur of fine art. She also knew how hard he was on people, particularly people who disappointed him. What had he done to her mother?

"I'm glad Dustin got you started again." Her mother nervously played with a pen. "I remember you used to call him Dusty. No one else could get away with that."

"He's been a friend." She realized she was biting her lip, something she used to do as a child.

But something in her voice must have alerted her mother. She sat up, and her eyes narrowed. "Nothing more?"

"He's my cousin," Sally said simply.

"Cousins have . . . married before."

"Not in our family. Grandfather pounded it into us that it was a sin."

"Do you love him?"

"Of course I do. He's my cousin."

"And if he wasn't?"

"And if pigs fly," Sally answered.

"Maybe pigs can fly under certain conditions."

Sally stared at her mother. "What are you trying to say?"

"Dustin isn't your cousin."

WASHINGTON, D.C.

"You don't know where they are?" The voice was laced with ridicule.

"They left no tracks," came the defensive voice over the telephone line. He was calling from a cellular phone to what he knew was a safe line. It bounced off any number of satellites.

"Strange," said the caller. "*I* know where they are. That should have been your job, not mine."

Silence. "Where is he?"

"Flaherty called Eachan. There's a connection between all three now. Exactly what should not have happened if you'd done your job."

"If you tell me where. . . ."

"Then you would probably mess it up again. Destroying that house was sloppy. There were questions."

"There shouldn't have been."

"Two strangers without names? You didn't think there would be questions?"

A little desperation came into the voice. "Tell me where they are. I'll take care of it. My men. . . ."

"Are as sloppy as you. How many chances have you had now? Three? Four? You said you were the best."

"I am. My men are."

"I think they could be headed toward Eachan's second home on the Chesapeake. I'm not positive, but we intercepted a phone call between the two. Since Flaherty maintained silence until now, it's possible he knows we're listening. However, he might also believe that Eachan is untouchable because of his position. His house would be swept frequently for bugs."

Silence on the other end.

"Find out what it is," said the caller. "A trap? Or has our Colonel Flaherty made a mistake?"

"How do I do that?"

"Do I really have to tell you your job? I thought I hired the best security people in the business. I would hate to discover I made a mistake. I want Flaherty and the woman dead, and I want it to look like an accident. Once they're gone, I can handle Eachan. He's a very ambitious man, and he has another weakness. So find his cousin as well."

He slammed down the telephone.

CHESAPEAKE BAY, MARYLAND

Eachan's house was everything Amy had dreamed about. Traditional and roomy and comfortable. A second-story balcony overlooked the bay. A sailboat was anchored just off a dock and boathouse. The house itself was more comfortable than imposing, and that surprised Amy. After meeting Dustin Eachan, she'd expected *Architectural Digest.*

Amy had driven with Irish to the house. Sam had followed. He was, she knew, to take her back to the motel. Irish would make the all-important call, then wait with his friends to see what developed.

But now she and Irish and Bo explored the house. She wanted to know everything about the house, about the preparations.

The home to its left was more elaborate, the landscaping more formal. She wondered whether that was the vacationing neighbors' house.

Amy recalled the fire that ruined her own house. She shuddered to think the same thing might happen here. But Irish felt he had taken precautions against that happening. Brian Jordan, if he was the person behind all this, couldn't afford another explosion.

Once inside, Bo followed her into the living room. Two men inhabited a cozy living room filled with overstuffed furniture and books.

They rose as she entered. Unlike Sam with his long hair, these two had short, neatly trimmed hair. They were clean shaven, and their bodies were obviously in extremely good shape. They had enough age that character was carved in their faces. They looked lethal.

Irish introduced the two just as Sam walked in. Mike and Taggart. Mike was a big blond in jeans and work shirt. Taggart wore expensive slacks and a dark blue sport coat over a blue shirt.

They both grinned. "Long time, Irish," Taggart said.

"Thought you've given up all this for the ranch," Mike said. "It was all you talked about."

"I didn't choose this," Irish said. "It chose me."

Mike looked at Amy. Raised an eyebrow. Then shrugged. "We've rigged the house. There are two separate telephone lines. We bugged both of them, as well as every room. Doors have sensors. Also installed sensors along the hall. You'll know if anyone's coming."

"I appreciate it. Send me your bill."

"You're crazy, Irish. I've been waiting a long time to pay back a debt." Mike, the big blond, looked at Amy. "He saved my life a long time ago. Whatever he wants, he gets."

"You couldn't pay my price," Taggart, the dark-haired one, added with a grin.

"Things that good, Tag?"

"Executive protection is a big business."

Amy turned her attention to Mike. "What do you do?"

"Worked with New York P.D. for ten years, then went into business for myself."

"He's a private dick," Tag said. "Tried to get him to go in with me, but he would rather work for shyster attorneys."

It was obvious to Amy that this was a frequent argument. The two men argued like old friends while they regarded Irish with some awe. She stepped back and looked at the four of them. Irish had always struck her as a loner, and the others made it clear they hadn't seen him in years. And yet they came from God knew where when he called.

Still, he seemed separate from them. When she had first met him, her initial impression was that he kept people at arm's length. In the past week, some of that feeling had faded. They had become close in so many ways. And yet, she realized, it was still there. Irish Flaherty was a man who never totally lowered the barriers.

She also knew, from looking at these men, that she didn't belong here. They all lived on the edge of danger. It was as much a part of their being as academia was a part of hers. She looked away from them and toward the Chesapeake, which sparkled through the window. Distant sailboats danced on its surface, and the sun sent ribbons of gold rippling over the water.

If there had ever been a portrait of peace and tranquillity, the bay was it. If there had ever been a portrait of violence, the four men in the room represented it. The juxtaposition sent waves of anguish through her. While the past weeks had made her feel more alive than she'd ever felt in her life, she knew deep within her that she needed something else. Tranquillity? Safety? Normalcy? She had built her life around those goals.

"Amy?"

She turned around at the sound of Irish's voice. Deep. Reassuring. *Loving?*

She closed her eyes against the pain she suddenly felt,

then quickly opened them, hoping the others didn't see that moment of weakness.

"I'm here," she said. "I was just looking at the bay."

"Would you like to see the rest of the house?" the one called Tag said.

She nodded.

Tag led the way, pointing out the location of the phones, the sensors, the tiny cameras hidden in heating vents. She was familiar enough with the concept. She knew that such technologies were readily available to the public now through catalogs and even through stores that specialized in ways to spy upon your neighbor. As a civil libertarian, she had been appalled. She had certainly never thought she would be involved in their use.

Still, despite the little spying devices located throughout, she fell in love with the house. Her opinion of Dustin Eachan, who'd seemed a little arrogant and pompous, ratcheted up a notch. There was a large kitchen with shining pans hanging from hooks around an island. Two large bedrooms downstairs. One large bedroom and balcony upstairs. It looked pristine. If nothing else, Dustin Eachan was a very neat person—or he had a very competent housekeeper.

Then they went down to the living area that looked out over the Chesapeake.

Irish looked at his watch. "Four-thirty. It's time for the call. Hawke Jordan will be at home, and Brian Jordan should be at the office."

Amy had listened as they discussed the best way to approach the Jordans. It was obvious that the older Jordan was the catalyst for what had happened. How much did his son know? That was the question.

Hawke Jordan was eighty years old now, but Dustin Eachan had said he still went into the office each morning, though now he left about 1 P.M. He apparently had been loath to entirely surrender the company to his son, although Brian Jordan was chief executive officer.

Irish picked up a cellular phone that had a tap inside.

Amy put her hand on his. "Won't he wonder whether it's a trap if he can trace the number?"

"Tag's an electronic genius. This signal will be bouncing off several satellites. He'll be able to find us eventually, but it's going to be very, very difficult. I don't think he'll figure out that we really want him to know where we are. Or that it's plan b." Irish dialed the home number Tag had obtained from hacking into the Jordan Industries computer.

Amy moved next to him, close enough to hear. Bo curled himself around her feet in his possessive mode.

A woman answered the phone. "Jordan residence."

"I would like to speak with Hawke Jordan."

"That's impossible. Mr. Jordan suffered a stroke several days ago. He cannot be disturbed."

"He's home? Not in a hospital?"

"There's a nurse with him."

Amy saw the look on Irish's face. Disappointment. Did Dustin Eachan know about this? She felt the same disappointment.

Irish tried one last time. "Tell him an old friend wants to talk to him. Tell him that Flaherty is on the phone."

"I don't think. . . ."

"Just tell him."

A pause, the sound of a telephone being laid down on a desk.

Several moments later, the woman's voice came on again. "He's sleeping. I won't wake him. If you leave your number and location, I'll give him your message."

Location?

"Is his son there?"

Hesitation. Then, reluctantly, "Yes."

"Then I want to talk to *him.*"

"He is with his father. He cannot talk now. As I said, if you will leave a message. . . ."

"Tell him I know about the gold. If he doesn't talk to me now, I go to the police."

An audible gasp. "I'll . . . tell him."

Irish winked at Amy and formed an O with two fingers for the others.

In a moment, she heard a deep voice rumble through the receiver. "Brian Jordan. What do you want?"

"I want you to call off your dogs."

Amy inched closer so she could hear better. Her head and Irish's were nearly together.

"I have no idea what you mean. My father is a very ill man, and I don't want him disturbed."

"You have more than disturbed my friend Dr. Mallory, and me," Irish said in a voice that could form ice cubes. "And now I want something for our trouble, plus a guarantee that nothing else will happen to her."

"You should write fiction, Mr . . . Flaherty, is it? Or perhaps visit a psychiatrist. And now I am going to hang up."

"I have a number that might interest you," Irish said. He recited the number that was found in General Mallory's desk. Amy knew neither of them were sure whether it had any validity or any meaning to Jordan, but it was the best chance they had.

A silence again.

"I also have a written account from General David Mallory about what happened fifty years ago. I wonder whether the federal government is aware that Jordan Industries was financed with stolen gold."

"About that psychiatrist, Mr. Flaherty, I advise you to visit him soon."

"That's very good, Mr. Jordan. But you might ask your father before you turn down my offer. He might have a reservation or two. . . ."

"Look, if you want a job with the company . . ." Brian Jordan was obviously being very, very careful as to what he was saying.

"I want a lot more than a job," Irish said. "Perhaps we can make a small trade."

"Again, Mr. Flaherty I've no idea what you're talking about."

"All right, *Brian*." He emphasized the last word. "Then I'll take what I have to the FBI tomorrow."

Pause again. "Your grandfather was a friend of my father's," he said. "I *would* like to meet you. What about my office?"

Irish laughed into the phone. "I don't think so."

"Somewhere convenient to both of us, then?"

"You're in Baltimore?"

"Yes."

"Annapolis, then. City Dock. There's always a lot of people there."

"And Miss Mallory?" Jordan said.

"I don't think so."

"I do. Or else I'll wait until we can all get together."

Irish started to say no. She shook her head. "I'll consider it," Irish said.

"Noon?" Jordan said.

"Noon it is," Irish confirmed.

"Where do I find you?"

"I think you will recognize me," Irish replied dryly. "*I* know what *you* look like. I think I can find you."

"I'll try to be there."

"No, my friend," Irish said. "You be there, or my next stop is the FBI. And, oh, Brian. . . ." Again the disrespectful familiarity.

"Yes?"

"I have insurance. A lot of it."

Another pause, then a firm "Good day, Colonel Flaherty." The phone went dead.

Irish switched off the phone.

"I'm going with you," Amy said.

"No," Irish said flatly.

"Yes, I am. Otherwise he won't show."

"He probably won't show anyway. He'll have his lack-eys there."

"We don't know he's involved with all this. It might be his father. Maybe he doesn't have anything to do with it."

"Then he wouldn't have agreed to meet."

"Won't he believe it's a trap?"

"I'm sure he will. But he'll have someone there any-way, and hopefully we can either take them or identify them. They have to know what we have, and he'll want to size us up. Hell, Jordan thinks he's smarter than us. People like him usually do. Arrogance is a weakness. And from what Eachan said, our Brian Jordan is very, very arrogant."

"Then what?"

"If he decides we don't have anything, then I think we'll continue to be in danger. We know about him. Either he or his father or someone working for them doesn't want any loose ends."

"And if he decides we do?"

"He'll try to find some way to get it. Payoff, maybe. But he knows, and I know, that wouldn't end the possibility of exposure. He'll come after us."

"So it's a matter of sooner of later?"

He looked at her levelly. "Yes. Our best chance is to make him so angry he gets careless."

"Then I have to go. Tag will be there. And Mike. Sam. I'll be okay."

Irish's lips twisted into a wry smile. "Tag. Mike. Sam. What about me?"

"That goes without saying."

"Does it?"

"And I have my pistol."

"Could you actually shoot someone?"

She hesitated. She didn't want to lie. She simply didn't know. Had she changed that much in these past weeks? Could she actually take a life?

"I don't know," she admitted.

He leaned over and kissed her. "You are the most honest woman I've ever met."

"Then I can go?"

"Absolutely not. Bo needs you. And Sam's going to look after you both."

Maybe. But not if she could do anything about it. But she didn't say that. She would convince him.

Tonight.

twenty-seven

Sally looked out the window as the plane flew over the desert.

It helped calm her. Her heart had stopped beating so rapidly every time she brought back her mother's words.

They had not come with tears. Instead there had been a quiet dignity as she'd recited a story that had never been told before.

Her mother had been an art student when she met Sally's father. He'd been overwhelming for a girl who lived with her single mother and attended college on a scholarship. He and his family—the house and the wealth and the pedigree—had been like a fairy tale.

She'd fallen in love and eloped with him. His family made it clear they were unhappy with the match. But the marriage had been made public, and his family had said he'd made his bed, so he had to sleep in it. It was a long time before she realized she was his rebellion.

They took her in hand. Taught her how to dress, how to use a multitude of silver utensils, how to sip wine graciously. She lived in a grand house with her grandparents-in-law. Robert's parents were overseas.

But they didn't like her, didn't approve of her family or what she was. She'd continued with her art studies, even earning a master's degree, but her own art always drew criticism. She was told she wasn't good enough to be a successful artist and that her degree couldn't get her a job. She'd begged her husband to move from the house, but Briarwood was his identity. He never earned enough to buy anything similar, and his dependence on his family made him more and more bitter. It was a vicious cycle. The more he drank, the less he succeeded, and the less he succeeded, the more he drank.

His parents threatened to disown him. The only thing that would save him, he told her, was a son. Then they would love him as much as they loved his brother, the very proper Duncan Eachan.

They'd been married three years and no sign of a pregnancy. She was tested at an out-of-state fertility clinic and the doctor told her there was no reason she should be barren. Then he'd been tested. He was sterile, probably as a result of teenage measles. He begged her to use sperm from a donor. She thought a child might repair their marriage, and she'd never been able to deny him, not when he was at his most charming. She agreed.

Unfortunately for her husband, the child was a girl, not the boy he wanted. Still, there was a grandchild, and Robert doted on her. His obvious affection for her gave both his wife and his parents hope that he was ready to settle down.

And for a while he did. He got a job with an insurance company. His family had a lot of friends with a lot of insurance needs.

Only Chloe saw the restlessness. He blamed her for having a girl instead of a boy, although when others were around, he acted the perfect father. Only she knew that he was using Sally to keep his place in the family. If she ever left him, he said, he would make sure that he got custody. He had the money and family and connections to make the threat very real to her. It didn't matter that she wasn't his; his name was on the birth certificate.

Chloe knew she should leave. She discovered years later that she'd been emotionally abused to the point that she felt totally inadequate and unable to make decisions on her own. She could never raise a child alone, and Robert swore that she would never get a penny from the family. She believed him.

Robert was seldom around, but when he was, he was alternately neglectful to Sally and charming.

Chloe had watched her daughter worship hopefully at his feet, always grateful for whatever crumbs he threw her way.

Chloe realized she'd never been able to get close to Sally. Chloe had precious little love as a child, and she simply didn't know how to give it. Robert had taken to calling her the ice princess. But she tried. She really tried. It nearly killed her to see Robert's easy manner with Sally when their own relationship was strained.

Then one night the emotional abuse became something else. Chloe realized that was only the beginning. She called every friend she had, and one knew of a curator's job at a small museum in Arizona. It didn't pay much, but it spelled freedom to her.

For the first time, she fought back. She threatened Robert with a blood test to prove that he wasn't the father. She had the documentation Robert thought she'd destroyed. He agreed to let her go. Let them both go.

She'd never told Sally. Sally adored him too much. Chloe never wanted her to know she was a tool in Robert's arsenal. Instead, she had taken Sally's abuse for eighteen months, until she ran away when her father died. Then Chloe had a choice: should she destroy a young girl's version of her father now that he was dead? Would Sally even believe her?

It was different now. Dustin had never married. Sally had never married. There had always been something about the two of them. And Chloe saw the light in Sally's eyes when she spoke of him.

This was a gift she could give her.

At least she hoped it was a gift. The exchange of an illusion for reality. . . .

A voice came on the intercom. They were reaching cruising altitude. Sally looked down at the hands clasped in her lap. Twenty years ago, she wouldn't have understood, much less believed. Maybe not even ten years ago. She had never felt loved by her mother, and now she knew her mother had loved her in a way that was so totally selfless that it humbled her.

She wondered how much Dustin had known. He had tried to tell her over the years that her father had not been the god she'd thought him. But he had always couched his criticism carefully. He had been afraid, she realized now, that she would cut him off as she had cut off her mother.

And now she had to tell Dusty.

And she was going to get rid of the damn painting she'd kept all these years in her father's memory. It belonged to someone else. She would make sure the rightful owner received it. If no member of the family was left, she would make sure it went to one of the Holocaust survivor associations.

She should have done it weeks ago when Dusty told her it might have been stolen property.

Dusty.

Would he care that they were not blood kin? Would it make any difference to him?

She could only pray.

For that, and for Flaherty and Amy Mallory. For herself. She shouldn't go back. She knew she shouldn't.

But no one would know. She'd used the Mary Smith name. She'd disappeared completely.

She'd be safe enough. And now she had to tell Dustin what her mother had told her. She had to. *She had to know how Dustin felt.*

ANNAPOLIS

In the end, Irish had no choice.

At least, he thought not as he drove Amy through the historical city of Annapolis.

The only way to keep Amy safe would be to tie her up, or lock her in the room, but he would wager almost anything that she would find a way to escape, even with Sam watching her. She'd already made a friend of him, finding out everything—nearly everything—there was to know about shrimping, and even a great deal about his past life in special services.

She had explained her reasons for going very logically last night. Nothing would happen at City Dock. It was too public. Second, Jordan was on a fishing expedition. He wanted to know what they had. Then he would have them followed. If anything, she would be safer with Irish than by herself.

She certainly couldn't make herself *more* of a target than she already was. And she had a right to know her enemy. To see for herself what she was up against.

She explained all this while in his arms. Before and after they had made love. And love was exactly what they'd made. Frenetically at first, then slower and more erotically. Even thinking about it, he felt waves of desire sweep him again.

But she'd made sense. That was the problem. She always made sense. She was never emotional or irrational. Instead, she laid out her case carefully. And she was right. He had learned to value her judgment, and Jordan might well not appear unless they were together. But he'd made her promise, in return, that after this she would stay well away from Dustin's home and do what Sam said.

This time she'd agreed. And he trusted that. Not once had she lied to him. She was always painfully honest.

But he'd instructed Sam, who had gone ahead with Mike and Tag, not to let her out of sight once they reached

City Dock. He was confident that Sam would do just that. He'd never seen his friend respond so readily to anyone as he had to Amy. Perhaps because Amy listened to him intently, as if every word was gold. Or perhaps he just recognized authenticity.

But after today, they would have to separate. He would wait at Dustin's house for their enemies. He and his old team.

Bo was not with them today. Sam had a sister thirty miles away who loved dogs and agreed to look after him for a few days. Surprisingly, Bo had taken to her immediately. He'd wanted to leave with Amy, but he'd also obviously enjoyed the companionship of the woman's two friendly dogs.

Irish had seen how much Amy had hated to leave Bo, but she'd hated even more to leave him in a house that was no longer safe, nor could she have left him in the car while they went to City Dock. And if there was trouble, a dog would only compromise an escape.

It had been one of the conditions Irish had made for her to accompany him to Annapolis. In truth, he thought she would probably stay under those conditions, but she made it very clear that she thought Bojangles would be in more danger the longer this continued. A bad guy wouldn't recognize—or care—that Bo would be of little threat to him. Or maybe not. Bo had been uncharacteristically brave in the motel room. Or maybe it wasn't uncharacteristic at all. Maybe there had just never been anything important enough before to evoke such a guard dog mentality.

In the meantime, Irish enjoyed her rapt expression as they drove through Annapolis, and he gave her a running commentary. He knew the area well. When he was posted in Washington for a while, he often drove to Annapolis. It had a pull for him, and he realized it had a pull for her, too.

Someday, perhaps he could bring her back. . . .

He drove down to City Dock. He had to drive around several times before finding what appeared to be a rare parking place. He looked at his watch. Eleven-thirty. Half an hour to go.

Sam was following them. Mike and Tag should already be there.

Irish checked his watch. It was a tiny microphone that Tag had provided. Amy had earrings, one of which contained a second microphone. Both could be easily detected with a pocket sentry.

What he hoped couldn't be detected was the parabolic microphone that Mike held.

It probably wouldn't work, but it was worth a chance.

Irish stepped out, went around the car, and opened the door for Amy. She usually bounced out before he had the chance. But they had already discussed this. She would not leave the car until Sam was out of his, and nearby. It had been Irish's condition.

When he finally saw Sam find a parking place not far from his own, he opened the door. He held out his hand to Amy, who looked surprised for a moment, then took his hand and squeezed it. No words. Just warm communication.

Pleasure flushed through him, even as his gaze left her face and roamed over the open area. To the left were the docks. To the right were restaurants and gift shops.

Her eyes bright with interest, Amy pulled him toward a bookstore.

He resisted for a moment as he searched the area. He saw Tag, dressed in a flowery shirt and looking every bit the tourist, talking to a woman.

He didn't see Mike immediately. Sam was locking his car, obviously waiting to see what direction to take. His hair was loose today, and he wore a tight T-shirt that outlined his heavily muscled chest and arms. He sported an easy grin and resembled an aging hippy unless you looked too closely into his eyes.

Irish felt a sudden tension, as if unfriendly eyes were on them. It made sense that the opposition would have their people here, too. He felt Amy's fingers tighten in his and followed the line of her gaze. Two men stood together. They were dressed casually, but their stance was watchful.

Amy had found them faster than he had. He leaned down like a fond new husband and brushed her cheek. "Very good," he whispered in her ear.

She tried to smile, but it was a little stiff.

"Let's go to the bookstore," she said. "We still have a few moments."

"Whatever you say, love," he said. Looking like a tourist suited him, even though he knew he and Amy had most certainly been marked. Pictures were not hard to find. Or take. There were probably any number of theirs in hostile hands.

Whatever you say, love.

Amy liked the sound of that. It was meant to relax her, she thought, as was that brief kiss.

She had enjoyed the drive to Annapolis and Irish's commentary. She'd never been to Annapolis before, though she'd always been fascinated with it as one of the cradles of American democracy. Under any other circumstances, she would have fallen completely in love with it. The old brick buildings and narrow streets and the old State House exuded history.

Midshipmen in uniform strode down streets lined with eighteenth-century buildings. She wanted to get out and wander with them. Perhaps someday. . . .

And then they'd reached the City Dock. Signs advertising cruises ruined the view of sailboats. Tourists were boarding a river boat. . . .

She saw Tag, dressed in shorts and an obnoxiously colorful shirt with flowers. He had a video camera in hand. A woman was with him, and Amy wondered whether he'd just picked her up. He was taking pictures of her, asking her to stand against several backdrops. He was very good at looking the tourist. His hawklike face appeared to have softened into blandness as he aimed his camera at anything and everything. Then she saw Sam as he left his car. She should feel nothing but fear, but instead she felt excitement and a sense of belonging. She felt safe with these men. She'd looked around and seen two individuals who looked out of place. She didn't know why. She wondered whether she would have noticed that weeks ago, or whether her every sense had been sharpened.

Then she felt the warmth of his approval as his lips caressed her cheek. For a moment, she wanted to forget why she was there. She wanted to be exactly what they were pretending to be, a honeymooning couple—although a bit on in years—madly in love. Almost in denial she looked toward the bookstore. Like a hunting dog flushing birds, she could sniff out a bookstore in minutes.

She wondered for a moment whether she wasn't just denying what was actually happening. And yet it was as good a thing to do as standing in the middle of a square, waiting for a killer.

It did take her mind from the immediate meeting for a few moments. She browsed in the history books as Irish tried to look doting while scanning the exterior. In reality, it was the very best place to be. From one angle, they could see without being seen.

She looked at her watch. Ten minutes. She picked up a book, realizing how foolish it was. And yet it represented sanity to her. She paid for it with a credit card. It didn't matter now. Everyone knew where she was.

Irish gave her a smile. She knew he didn't expect anything to happen here, or he never would have allowed her to come, despite her threats to get there anyway. This was a thrust, an intelligence op, as she'd heard Tag say, not a battle. Even she understood that.

They left the store. She didn't see Sam but knew he must be nearby. She did see Mike. He was meandering down the street with headset on and a tape player around his neck. She had seen them in the store. The tape was probably "Historic Annapolis Walk with Walter Cronkite." If there was a tape in the player at all.

Irish, her hand again tucked in his, walked purposefully toward a restaurant. He was wearing his uniform: jeans, T-shirt with a long-sleeve, loose shirt draped over it, and the gun in the small of his back. She clutched her purse with her small revolver in it.

The area was full of people. Mothers, fathers, kids. Midshipmen. Young professionals.

A shiver ran down her back. She felt like a quail with a hundred shotguns aimed right at her. She resisted turning her head back and forth like a submarine periscope. She had completely put her trust in Irish and his friends. Her hands clutched her purse.

One of the men who had looked out of place approached them. He was dressed in expensive slacks and a sport coat over a golf shirt. That's what captured her attention. A sport coat in this heat and humidity. Like Irish, he was concealing a weapon. Her mouth went dry.

"Colonel Flaherty?" he said in a neutral voice.

"Yes."

"Our friend couldn't make it. He asked me to talk to you. I understand you have a business proposition, and he is always interested in new opportunities."

Amy realized instantly that the microphones were for naught. Well, Irish had said as much. He'd also believed Jordan wouldn't appear.

"Sorry, my proposition is for his ears only." He turned and tugged at her hand. "Come on, love. We wasted our time."

"I have an offer."

"From Brian Jordan?"

The man raised an eyebrow and seemed to look over her shoulder. She wondered how many others were with him.

"You can tell him we're not interested," Irish said.

"My principal needs an indication of what you have to offer," the man tried again.

"Quite a bit," Irish said. "Some real masterpieces."

Then he looked down at Amy. "We will take our offer elsewhere."

"How can we get in touch with you?"

"You can't, friend. You just blew it." Irish took his hand from Amy's and put his left arm around her. "Let's go."

The man maneuvered in front of him. "I'll take you to him."

"I don't think so."

The man's hand moved quickly. Amy felt a hard object jab into her side.

"I do," the man said. "My car is the blue one."

Fear crept up her spine and settled firmly into her stomach. She tried to remember her self-protection class. Nothing came to her. She looked into eyes so cold she shivered. There was no excitement now. No adrenaline. Just plain terror.

Then she saw a change in his eyes. The pressure in her side relaxed.

"A stand-off," Irish said in a lazy voice. "There are more of us."

Sam was behind the man. Tag was to his side, a hand in the pocket of his shorts.

Aware now that there was more opposition than he expected and that the scene was probably being taped, the speaker shrugged. He backed off slightly. Amy didn't know what had been in her side. Whatever it was, it felt like a gun, but it never left his sport coat.

Suddenly the man in front of Amy fell against her, shoving her to the ground. She reached out to grab something and found Irish's hand but her knees hit the cement and she couldn't stop an exclamation. As she righted herself, she saw the man disappear into the crowd, two others with him.

The blue car was already moving, and the three men

piled into it. Tag and Sam started to go after it. "No use," Irish said.

Tag was staring at the license plate. Memorizing it, Amy assumed.

"I thought she might have been hurt," Sam said apologetically. "I should have grabbed him."

"Then we probably would have had the gunfight at the O.K. Corral," Irish said. "People might have gotten hurt. Maybe this wasn't the best place."

"A public place was best," Tag said. "Otherwise they could have brought an army."

"But now they know we have help."

Tag smiled, and Amy, whose body was still trembling from the aftermath of fear, didn't think it was a particularly benign one. She knew she never wanted Tag as an enemy. "But, old buddy, they have no idea how many or who we are. He's off-balance now."

"We still don't have anything to take to the police, though. Nothing on tape. Or even assault," Irish said wryly. "No one actually saw a gun."

"We knew it was a long shot," Mike said. "But Tag should have their photos. Between your sources and mine, we can probably identify them. They're going to be running out of soldiers before long."

"I have a lot of photos and video," Tag confirmed. "I'm going to make several copies of this tape and send them off. We might even have some photos of the assault, although it was done very carefully. He could say he just tripped."

Irish turned back to Amy. "Are you all right, love?"

Amy nodded. "Some people are so rude."

Irish grinned. "Let's go home, love."

They walked to their car, Sam staying with them. "Follow us," Irish told him. "Make sure we are not being trailed. Then you take Amy to the motel."

Despite her promise, Amy wasn't so sure she was willing to leave him. Still, she tried to hold her tongue. They had skills she didn't, and she still felt tremors of fear as well as that odd exhilaration.

Irish helped her into the car.

Sam hesitated. "He was very close to you," he said. "Check your purse."

Amy knew exactly what he meant. She was becoming expert in the spy business. Swallowing her embarrassment, she dumped the contents of her purse on the car seat. Everything tumbled out: old receipts, several lipsticks, compact, billfold, pens, keys, dog biscuits, loose coins, the gun.

Irish raised an eyebrow.

"I'm a pack rat," she admitted as she sorted through everything. She stopped when she saw an expensive-looking pen. She was a fan of fifty-cent pens.

She handed it to Irish, and he looked at it, weighed it with his fingers. "Bingo. Sam hasn't lost his instincts."

He started the car. "I'll take care of it," he told Sam.

Sam stepped back and saluted. "See you later, Irish."

Irish pulled out of the parking place.

"When will they come?" she asked.

"Soon."

WASHINGTON, D.C.

Sally opened the safe deposit box. In the silence of the bank's private room, she stared at the painting that had meant so much to her. It was dark, violent. A ship tossed in a vicious storm. The strokes were bold, the colors exquisite in their shading.

At one time, she'd thought the ship gallant. Now she saw it as foundering, doomed. How could she ever have loved it?

It was deceptive. Like her father. Like everything in her life.

Stolen art. She'd had time to get used to the idea now. It had been a month since Dustin told her about the possibility. Her first thought had been to keep it safe. She hadn't wanted to give it up. For some reason, she connected it with her father, with all she knew of him. If she were to believe her mother, her father was weak, an alcoholic. Not a monster. Just weak. Her mother had loved him once. Sally had loved him all her life. And now she had to deal with the knowledge that he was never her blood father, that she would never know her blood father.

Strangely enough, it didn't matter. She'd grown up in the past few days. She would always love the man she called Father, though now she could view him through realistic eyes. She had little curiosity about the man who was paid to provide the sperm that contributed to what she was today.

The most important thing was Dustin. And giving the painting back to whoever should have it.

She hoped that her motives were altruistic and not just the reaction to learning that much of her life had been a lie. In any event, she just wanted to get rid of it, and Dustin could help her find the best way of doing it.

Sally's finger traced the oils, then she turned the painting over, wondering whether there were any markings there. The paper in the back was wrinkling, and looked stained. It was, she noted, cheap paper. Why would someone put such cheap backing on a valuable painting?

A piece was peeling back. Very gingerly, she eased it back as far as she could without tearing it. She saw a sheet of paper under the backing. More recklessly now, she pulled it farther, not caring if it tore. Between the painting and the cheap backing were three sheets of paper. She eased them out and stared at the bold black handwriting. She turned to the back page. It was signed by her grandfather. Her heart beating rapidly, she leaned against a wall and read them. Sally put the sheets of paper in her purse, then used the cell phone Dustin had given her to call him.

He was in a meeting with the Secretary, the assistant said, and shouldn't be disturbed. Was it an emergency? Sally hesitated. She'd interrupted Dustin's work repeatedly. No, she finally said. She would meet Dustin at his Georgetown home. She had a key.

She needed time to think. Neither of them thought that Dustin would be attacked directly. His home had good security and she had a key. State Department phones were swept on a regular basis, and he'd told her his personal phones at work and home had been swept. No one knew where she was, and there would be no reason for anyone to look for her at Dustin's home. Not after she'd disappeared so thoroughly. She'd even used the Mary Smith name on her return. Once she got to Dustin's, she could E-mail Amy Mallory and Irish Flaherty. They needed to know, and all four had agreed on using E-mail for communication.

Satisfied that she was doing the best thing, she rewrapped the painting, replaced it in the box. She left the bank and found a cab outside. She gave the driver Dustin's address.

twenty-eight

His hand shook slightly as he tried to dial the number. Things were getting out of control. It should have been easy enough to take out a teacher and an over-the-hill Army officer. Attempt after attempt had failed.

Now it had become crucial. They might well have information that could destroy the family. Could destroy *him.*

A voice answered. Defensive. "They got away."

"How this time?" he asked with deceptive patience. He didn't feel patient at all.

"They had help. And there were too many witnesses."

"You fool. Why didn't you realize they had help?"

"Until now. . . . "

"Another excuse. Now they know your face. How many others?"

"I don't know."

"We have to guess they saw all of you. That makes at least five men they can identify now. We can't use them again. Not until Flaherty and Mallory are dead."

"I can move them to another country."

"Do it. And I want Flaherty's background checked for past associations."

"That will take time."

"What about Eachan's Washington house? Has anyone been there?"

"Just Eachan. And some business associates. Should we take *him* out?"

"Not yet. That's a last resort. There would be a hell of a stink at his death. The other—Flaherty—he has any number of enemies. He's put enough people in Leavenworth to keep cops looking for months. Still, keep an eye on Eachan's house. I want to know who's coming and going."

"Yes, sir."

"And get rid of that damned interfering Flaherty."

A silence at the other end of the line. "Do we know where he is now?"

"We pinpointed the location of the call. It's the area of Chesapeake where Eachan has a second home. Someone is checking out the house now."

"And if they're there?"

"I want them eliminated. But no more gas leaks or fires."

Silence. "What about a burglary gone wrong?"

"Just make sure nothing comes back to me."

"I'll hire some freelancers. They won't know who's paying them."

"This is Wednesday night. Time is critical now. I don't want them talking to anyone else. There will be a hundred-thousand-dollar bonus."

"And Eachan?"

"We'll take about Eachan later. If he's put his oar in this water, then we'll have to find a way to take him out, too. We'll just have to be a bit more creative."

The receiver crashed down.

MARYLAND

Irish stopped at a busy-looking restaurant and dropped the pen/transmitter in the back of a pickup. He waited until the truck drove off, then he and Amy and Sam, who had been following, went inside for lunch.

"I want you to go with Sam to the motel," he said as they finished a lackluster meal.

"I would rather stay with you."

"You promised," he reminded her.

She frowned, and reluctance was evident in the set of her chin. But he knew deep down she would agree because she had promised. In addition to being so damned honest, she had more integrity in her little finger than most people had in their entire body. He was determined to minimize the risk to her as much as possible. The opposition knew now that they had help, and possibly had incriminating information. They would have to move swiftly.

"Please," he said. "I'll get back to you as soon as possible. And you, my love, need to see whether your tenure hearing has been postponed. If not, Sam will drive you back to Memphis and stay with you. No one knows him."

"If you think someone's coming to the house, I want to be there."

"No." His rejection was absolute, and he saw that she recognized that.

She didn't say anything, but merely toyed with the rest of her food.

When they left the restaurant, she reluctantly turned toward Sam's car. Irish's hand caught hers, and he pulled her to him. He leaned down, and his lips touched hers. His fingers caught in her curls. "I'll miss you," he whispered. "But this shouldn't take long. It's our best chance at catching them actually doing something."

She looked at him, and her heart was in her eyes. His own thudded. Was he right? Would she be safer with Sam?

No one knew about Sam. No one knew his car.

She had to be safe. *He loved her.* It was the first time he'd admitted it to himself. He didn't know what in the hell he would do about it. Could do about it. Their lives still didn't mesh. Couldn't mesh. Still. . . .

His lips moved back to hers, and the kiss deepened. Desperation was in it. Love. Fear for her. Her fear for him. For a moment, he felt he was drowning in their combined need. His body coiled like a tight spring as he struggled for restraint. The fire that was always between them crackled and flamed.

It took every ounce of his control to step away.

"We'll talk when this is over," he said.

Tears glistened in her eyes. That hurt more than anything.

"I don't want to lose you now," she whispered.

"You won't," he said. His hand took hers. He lifted it to his lips in a gesture that was new to him. It was a salute.

Then he turned away and didn't look back until he heard the purr of Sam's car fade away.

Amy asked Sam, her new bodyguard, to get her a soft drink. Really, she didn't need it but she did need a few moments of privacy, and she didn't know how to tell him that without hurting his feelings.

Once the door was closed, she opened her laptop computer and checked her E-mail. A message from Sherry. She'd convinced the tenure committee that Amy had a family emergency, and the hearing had been postponed until Monday. It could not be postponed any longer because the department head planned to leave for Europe for the summer.

Amy sat still for a moment, then realized she'd been holding her breath as she read the message. "Yes!" she said. Then quickly wrote to Sherry, *"Great job. Will be there. I owe you a dinner, no, a week of dinners. A year of dinners."*

She continued to read her E-mail. Some spam messages. One from a graduate who wanted to tell her he'd won a professorship he wanted. Her heart lightened at that.

Then an E-mail address she didn't immediately recognize. Its heading, though, was "Urgent."

She opened it. "Found information you wanted. I'll be at Dustin's house in Georgetown. Need to see you as soon as possible." It was simply signed, "Sally."

Amy typed her own message. "Coming." Then, "Address?"

If she couldn't help Irish, perhaps she could retrieve the information they needed.

All she had to do was convince Sam.

But she knew she couldn't. He wouldn't leave without Irish's okay, and Irish, she suspected, would not be amenable.

Dustin's house would be safe. He obviously thought so, if Sally Eachan was there. There would be protection. He was the one of the four who had not been touched. She would be careful. And Irish was making sure the bad guys would be after him. He was waiting for them.

If Sally Eachan had really found something, they could get the attention of federal authorities.

But how to get rid of Sam?

He entered then, a six-pack of soft drinks in hand and a container of ice. She turned on the television, trying to get CNN, but there were only a few local stations. Sam sprawled on a chair next to her.

They would have to go for supper before long. She'd never committed car theft before, but she was seriously considering it now.

Someone had been in Dustin's bay house. Whoever it was had been very careful, but the slight aroma of aftershave hovered in the room.

Irish and Tag looked at each other.

Tag didn't say anything but went immediately to the cameras. The film in two was in place, but a quick look showed it had been exposed. Apparently the intruder hoped no one would check that. Two others, one in a chandelier, the other in a cavity hollowed out in a thick frame of a painting, appeared untouched. Both had film that should have been exposed when the sensors detected movement.

"They're good," Tag said. "Not good enough. He—they—evidently didn't have any film for replacements."

"Let's see the film before we conclude that," Irish said wryly.

Mike checked the windows. All but one were locked. The one that was unlocked was shielded by bushes.

They exchanged glances before continuing. Mike checked the house for strange smells, objects that shouldn't be there, such as bombs or accelerant. He also used Sentry, a detection device, to spot any new listening devices.

They ate some sandwiches Mike had bought earlier. Tag took a stroll around the neighborhood. No strange cars, but that didn't mean much. When it grew dark, they went to the vacant house next door, leaving several lights on upstairs and a makeshift silhouette form in the window of Eachan's home.

In the neighbor's darkened house, the three took positions that could not be seen from the road.

They waited.

WASHINGTON, D.C.

Dustin received Sally's message as he cooled his heels in the Executive Offices. War had broken out in one of the African countries he oversaw, and its president had been captured. There was no way he could leave now. It wasn't only his job he worried about. It was the situation. The African leader could well be killed if diplomacy didn't free him. Renewed civil war would create another orgy of mass murder.

He didn't want to call his home. After Flaherty's call, he'd had a professional check his phones. The expert had found—and removed—a listening device, but still . . .

Yet now he had no choice. Sally had given him none. She didn't answer the cell phone he'd insisted she keep.

He called his home. When his message center came on, he said, "Sally, if you're there, answer."

He hung on for several seconds and then heard her voice.

"Why in the hell are you here? You're supposed to be at. . . ." He stopped suddenly, knowing how much she hadn't wanted her mother involved.

"Something happened that I have to talk to you about," she said. "Several somethings, in fact."

Dustin considered asking her to leave there immediately. But where would she go? What if she were followed? "You've locked everything and put on the security system?"

"Yes."

"I'll ask a friend to get someone over there," he said. "But don't let anyone in the house. If someone shows up at the door with credentials, make them identify themselves by asking them for a word we agree on."

"You think that someone with credentials might be. . . ."

"Credentials can be faked, and you wouldn't know the difference. Think of something."

"Remember when I was sixteen, and you asked me what I wanted for my birthday."

Dustin paused. He remembered only too well. "I don't think that will work. What about the color you hate most."

He heard her laugh. It was relaxed. What did she want to tell him?

"All right," she agreed. "But I like mine better."

He grinned at that. He did, too. What she'd wanted was a kiss. A kiss that had turned into something more altogether. "Go, now, and make sure the house is secure."

He hung up and called his friend at the FBI. "I've had a threat. Can you send someone over to my house? My cousin is staying there. I want to make sure she's safe."

"You know a request needs to go through channels."

"This is an emergency. If anything happens to my cousin, I'll have your job."

"Dammit, Dustin. You have no idea how to make friends. Does this have anything to do with the photos you sent me?"

"It could."

"Would you like to explain that?"

"Yes. Probably. But not now. I'm waiting to meet with the President."

"I'm impressed."

"Don't be. I'm one of many."

A sigh. "I'll send someone out there tonight."

"Now."

Another sigh. "All right."

"Tell him—or her—to identify themselves to my cousin. A word."

"Something exotic, I suppose."

"Purple."

"Purple?"

"Just get someone over there. I'm being called."

He turned off his phone as he saw someone gesturing for him. He straightened his tie, made an effort not to smooth his hair, and followed the escort. For the first time, he felt no thrill at the prospect of being in the presence of the President. He just wanted to be home with Sally. He wanted to make sure she was safe. But Damon would see to that.

Home with Sally.

He erased the idea from his mind and, instead cataloged the options he had to offer the President.

MARYLAND

Amy suggested to Sam that they go somewhere for dinner. She'd planned to leave her purse in the car when she went inside the restaurant, then ask for his keys to retrieve it. She would then take the car.

She'd thought about it, but when they arrived at the restaurant, she couldn't do it.

It wasn't lack of will, it was too much conscience. She'd never used subterfuge. She wasn't going to do it now.

Instead, once they were in the car, she asked Sam if he could contact Irish.

"Not unless there's an emergency."

"There's an emergency."

Sam looked at her for a long moment. "Yes ma'am," he said.

Although she was worried about Sally and the others, she felt a warm glow inside. This man, this dangerous man who had a heart of gold, respected her. Maybe even more, if she was right about the gleam in his eyes. For someone who'd never really enjoyed male attention, she was bemused by the situation. Had she changed that much in the past few weeks that she could attract a man like Irish? And Sam?

How could she go back to an ordinary life?

Sam was dialing a number. He handed the phone to her.

"Irish?" The sound of his name came very easily now.

"Amy? Anything wrong?"

She delayed a moment. "Anything happening there?"

"No. But someone's been in the house. We're waiting."

"Can they wait alone?"

"Why?" His voice sharpened.

"Sally E-mailed me. She's at Dustin's. I think she may be alone. She says she has something we need. I think Sam and I should go."

Hesitation on the other side. A muttered conversation she couldn't hear.

"I'll go with you," Irish said. "Sam can take my place here."

Amy was suddenly very grateful to her conscience. Her throat was too tight to reply.

"Amy?"

"I'm here. Where should we meet you?"

He hesitated, and she could almost see him with that frowning twist of his lips as he considered the problem. "I'll be at the motel in forty minutes. It'll take about two hours to get to Washington."

"I'll call Sally."

"No. There might be a tap on the phone."

"Surely Dustin would have had it swept."

"How recently?" It was a rhetorical question.

She had no answer.

"I'll be there soon," he said. The phone went dead.

WASHINGTON, D.C.

Sally tucked her legs underneath her. Dustin's phone was next to her on the sofa. She had all the lights on in the den, the curtains drawn against the blackness outside. Dustin had called to make sure someone from the FBI had arrived, and they had. Several hours earlier. She had invited him in, but he'd preferred to wait outside in the car.

The alarm system was on. Hopefully, Amy Mallory would be here soon. Then Dustin. Hopefully, the nightmare would be over. But for the moment, she felt safe.

She mulled over what she wanted to tell Dustin. How would he accept the information secreted in the painting? She knew how much the family name meant to him. Should she show it to him before confiding in Amy?

She checked the clock once more. Near eleven. Where was Amy? Dustin, she knew, could be gone all night.

She stood, went to the front window, and looked out. She loved Dustin's house and the picturesque street it fronted. The FBI car was in front. In the light from the porch, she could see the figure in the front seat. Perhaps he would like some coffee. And making coffee would give her something useful to do.

She padded out to the kitchen.

MARYLAND

Sam and Mike heard the cars approaching at the same time.

It was as if the last twenty years had never happened. Each knew exactly what the other would do without words.

They wanted the opposition to get inside Dustin's house. Once there, they would become burglars. Irish wanted a hold over the prowlers. He also wanted them alive. He wanted names.

Tag was already outside, watching from across the street. His job was to take anyone waiting or standing watch for the intruders.

Mike watched from the window as a car drove up. He waited a few moments, then pressed a button that turned off the upstairs lights of the Eachan home. All the lights were off now.

They expected the intruders to wait as long as an hour or so.

Wearing night vision glasses, Mike watched from the darkened front window. Sam went to the back, where he had a view of the back of Eachan's house. They did not want to be surprised.

Minutes ticked off. Then an hour. Mike didn't move. Then he saw a figure snake through the shrubbery, then another, both headed toward the window that had been unlocked.

They were not as professional as he'd expected. Perhaps good help really was hard to find these days.

A true professional would have been suspicious, even of a window he knew should be unlocked. These guys weren't. He watched as one went around the side of the house, probably in an attempt to turn off the alarm system. Tag had rigged it so it wouldn't be that difficult. That should have made them suspicious, too.

It didn't. He watched as one man entered the house,

then the second. When it was apparent no one else was following, he left the room and met Tag. "There's one watching in the back," Tag said.

"Hopefully Sam has taken care of the driver," Mike said. "Take the back. I'll take the window. Sam will take the front door."

Tag nodded. He was the most successful of the three of them, but they had reverted into an unit where each knew where his—and the others'—talents lay.

Another moment, and Mike saw Sam moving toward the front. Tag signaled Sam with two fingers, then went to the back. Mike waited at the window. When two minutes went by, Mike lifted himself and quietly entered through the window the intruders left open.

He heard cursing above. The intruders had seen the dummy forms in the bed, maybe even the dummy in the chair in the other room. He stood just inside a door that led to the stairs. They would be down soon. Sam pressed himself against the wall next to the stairs. Tag appeared from the kitchen.

The intruders *were* amateurs, at least in Mike's opinion. Anyone with an ounce of sense would have left someone downstairs as lookout.

The cursing was louder. So were the footfalls coming down the steps. The room was dark, but he had his night vision glasses. The intruders did not.

As the third reached the bottom of the steps, Mike stepped out, jabbing his Glock into the man's side. Sam suddenly appeared at the back of the last man down the steps. Tag took the middle one.

"What the hell?"

"Call the police, Mike," Tag said. "We've caught ourselves some burglars."

Keeping his weapon on "his" intruder, Mike turned on the lights. The men were all dressed in black and wore ski masks. Tag used his gun to poke the mask off his target, then pushed it back down. "No wonder you wear a mask."

Seeing an opening, the man swung at him. It was exactly what Tag wanted, Mike knew. As the man swung, Tag landed a blow in his midriff, then another on the back of his neck as the intruder bent over. Tag stepped back as the man spiraled and fell to the floor.

"Who are you?" one of the downed man's companions asked.

"We are guests of the high Department of State official whose house you have just invaded with illegal weapons. It's not only burglary but assault on a federal officer. And now, gentlemen, you can each take off your masks. We are going to have a conversation."

Mike admired him. The federal officer bluff was a huge one. The intruder's face paled. He probably had a lengthy record.

Still, it was obvious he knew where the conversation was leading. "What do ya want?" he said morosely.

twenty-nine

Sally made the coffee, found an insulated mug, and filled it. She realized then that she didn't know what the agent liked in it.

She wondered whether Dusty ever got used to having bodyguards around him. She knew he often had security when he traveled overseas. The thought made her wonder again when he would be back. She wanted him. She needed him.

She took the coffee out to the car. That certainly should be safe enough with a real-life FBI agent outside. The window of the car was down, and she looked into the dark interior. The agent was slumped in his seat. She knew enough about first aid to check his pulse. Thank God, there was one. Then she saw the blood running from his head.

Panic seized her, and she froze in place. Her gaze darted around the street. All the houses were dark. She forced herself to move toward the nearest one, her throat too constricted with terror to scream. She had taken only a step or two when a figure stepped out from behind one of the large trees that lined the street. He put his arm around her neck, and his other hand went over her mouth. She felt him hesitate a moment, then move again, as if he'd made a decision. He dragged her back into the house and slammed the door shut with his foot. Another intruder appeared from another room. He must have slipped inside when she approached the car.

She could barely breathe. What a fool she'd been not to be more careful. She hadn't thought anyone would actually attack Dustin's home. And then she'd felt safe with the agent outside. Dear God, the agent. He needed help!

She slumped against her assailant for a moment as if she were fainting. He had to let go of her neck, and she spun around and kicked him in his crotch. Then she started for the door, screaming as she went.

A rough hand grabbed her and turned her around. She saw a fist coming at her and tried to squirm away. Pain slammed through her. She struggled to keep on her feet, then the second blow came. Everything went black.

"We have the Eachan woman."

"Where are you?"

"In Eachan's home."

"What about Flaherty?"

"I haven't heard anything yet."

Hesitation. "Get the hell out of there. Now."

"Should we take her?"

Hesitation. "You've been listening?"

"We managed a new tap on the telephone this morning. She said she had 'something' to tell him."

"Hell, that could mean anything." A loud curse. "Find out if she knows anything. Then give her an overdose and leave her there. Make it look sexual."

"That should be easy. She's a sexy number."

"Get what you need and get out of there." He paused. "Do you have something with you . . . to give her a nice long sleep?"

"Heroin?"

"That should neutralize Dustin Eachan. How is he going to explain a woman dead of a drug overdose in his house?"

"I thought you wanted him in office."

"He's not as malleable as I thought. And now he's trouble. Do it as soon as you find out what she has."

"Yes, sir."

The phone slammed down.

Amy straightened. They were passing Rock Creek Park. They should reach Georgetown soon. For a moment, she allowed her mind to wonder about Dustin. Two homes in very expensive places. She wondered where he'd gotten the money.

She wondered if Irish had the same question. She moved closer to him, placing her hand on his knee. She felt the heat of his skin under the denim of his jeans. He glanced at her and gave her the crooked grin she loved. It was probably meant to be reassuring. She didn't need reassurance when she was with him.

It was only when . . . he wasn't with her. Then she realized the emptiness of not having him in her orbit. She'd never really felt empty or lonely before. She'd always thought she had a wonderfully rich life. Now she couldn't imagine living without him.

Irish's cell phone rang. He'd been forced to turn it back on. He had to know what was happening in Maryland.

"Yes?" he said.

She couldn't hear the other end of the telephone, but she saw the frown on his face and the almost invisible slump of his shoulders.

"What did you do with them?" His voice tightened.

Then, "Well, it was worth a try. Thanks, Mike."

Irish put down the phone. "Everything went exactly as planned," he said.

"No one hurt?"

"Nope."

"Then what's wrong?"

"The . . . burglars were out-of-town talent. They received a telephone call. A voice they didn't recognize offered ten thousand dollars if they burglarized a certain house and disposed of the people in it. They weren't among the best Mike has seen."

"How did they get paid?"

"They picked up the money in a locker at the train station in Baltimore."

"Are they lying?"

"I don't think so. Tag has a way of convincing people to talk."

"Tag?" she said incredulously.

"Tag," he confirmed.

"What did he do with them?"

"Called the police. They said they were Dustin's friends, staying at his house. Came home, noticed a window open and the alarm turned off."

"But we don't know any more than we did?"

"Not immediately. There might be some string leading back to their employers, and now that Dustin is publicly involved, I think we can find substantial interest from the feds. Your Sally Eachan might also have something interesting for us."

She stared at him. "You planned that," she accused.

"What?" he asked innocently.

"That something would happen in Dustin Eachan's home so he *would* become more involved."

Irish shrugged. "He knew what we were after."

"Did he realize he would be in the headlines? He thought he would be involved only in your meeting someone from the opposition and planting the seed that you knew more than you did."

"He had to consider the possibilities," Irish said.

"But they *did* attack his vacation home," she said. "They might go after his home here now."

"They used freelancers posing as burglars. I don't think they would try anything at his Washington residence."

A ripple of apprehension ran through her. Although there had been an apparent effort to take or embarrass

Sally earlier, no one had directly attacked Dustin. Until now.

And Sally was at Dustin's house.

As if he sensed her change in mood, he speeded up. Within minutes they were in front of Dustin's house. A light was on upstairs.

Cars were parked tightly across the street. Irish parked across Dustin's driveway, behind a car with official government plates.

"Stay here," he said.

She watched as he went over to the car. In a minute, he was back. "Someone is lying in the front seat." He handed her the cell phone. "Call the police. Tell them there's an officer down. That will get them here fast."

After she made the call, he told her to call Dustin's home number.

It rang three times, then a machine answered. She shook her head. "No one answers."

The light upstairs went off.

"Someone's there," he said. "I'll go to the back in case they leave that way. If anyone leaves from the front. . . ."

"I'll press the horn," she said.

"Then get the hell out of the way."

They heard a distant siren. Without another word, Irish sped around the back.

A minute passed. Or was it an hour? Then a muted noise, like a soft pop. A shout. The sound of sirens grew louder. *Something was wrong.* Amy took the pistol from her purse.

He'd told her to wait. She hated stupid heroines in books. But what if Irish had been hurt? And Sally?

A shot rang out, then another. She couldn't wait. But could she even use the gun?

She left the car and moved around to the back. One man was on the ground. Another was shooting. She saw Irish go backward and knew he was hit. The sirens were almost on them now. The assailant's attention was on Irish, who'd dropped his gun. He aimed at Irish.

Amy lifted her pistol. Her hand shook, and she used the other to steady it. She pulled the trigger.

The man grunted and swung around, his gun still in his hand.

Then they were surrounded by blue uniforms. "Get down, get down, get down." The order echoed through the neighborhood.

Amy obeyed. The man with the gun didn't. He turned toward the police, still holding the pistol.

A shot. Then another. A third. He went down.

An officer came over to her. He looked at the pistol she'd dropped. "Ma'am?"

She turned to Irish, who was kneeling. "He's been hurt. Can I go to him?"

"What happened here?"

She ignored the question and darted toward Irish. It would take more than one officer to keep her away. Or two. Or three.

She knelt next to him. "Irish?"

In the light of the officers' flashlights, he looked pale. Blood was dripping from his right wrist.

Anguish filled her. He'd been wounded repeatedly on her behalf. She tore off a piece of her shirt and wrapped it around his wrist. "You never duck, do you?"

His good hand clasped hers as he looked at the officer. "There should be a woman inside."

Three of the uniforms went inside. In a moment, one yelled. "We found her. She's unconscious."

Another siren. Medics pushed her out of the way. Another ran inside.

Amy clung to Irish's hand as he refused a stretcher but agreed to go to the hospital. "Sally first," he told the medics.

They followed as the stretcher was carried from the

house to the ambulance. Amy saw a too pale face. Emotion hit her then. Rage. Grief.

She said a prayer that Sally would live, that the sparkling smile would continue to charm.

And then there was the knowledge she—Amy Mallory—had shot someone. After seeing Sally, she knew she would do it again.

Dustin was called out of the meeting. A Secret Service agent, along with a uniformed police officer and plainclothes detective, met him.

He tried to mask his apprehension.

"Sir, there's been an assault on your home," the detective said after displaying his credentials. "Shots fired. A woman—I believe she might be your cousin—is in the hospital."

"Where?"

"Washington Memorial."

"Can you take me there?"

The detective nodded. "We also got word from Maryland that intruders were captured in your house there. Had you loaned or rented it to someone?"

Dustin nodded. "Yes, friends of mine."

"That solves one problem. Quite a coincidence, wouldn't you say?"

"Look, I'll answer any questions you have, but first I want to see my cousin."

"An overdose of heroin," the doctor said. "But we found her in time."

"She doesn't use drugs," Dustin said as he sat next to her bed. She was still unconscious, but his fingers intertwined in hers.

"We checked her arms. There were no needle tracks."

Someone entered the room. "I'm Susan Etheridge, hospital spokesman, Mr. Eachan. Members of the press are in the lobby. They want to talk to you."

Dustin looked at Sally's pale, battered face, the dark lashes sheltering her eyes, her limp hand. "No," he said simply.

The door opened and closed again.

"How long will she be unconscious?"

"I can't tell you that," the doctor said.

Grief—and guilt—coursed through Dustin. He should have been with her. He couldn't even imagine the horror she'd experienced. Had she been conscious when the narcotic had been injected? Had she known what was going to happen?

He leaned over. He ran his hand through her hair and touched her cheek. He loved her. He'd always loved her. He hadn't wanted to admit it because he thought it had been so damned wrong. But now he knew he would risk anything to keep her safe, to keep her happy, to keep her with him.

He willed a movement. The flicker of her eyes. He wanted her to know he was next to her. He didn't give a damn about his job, about some small country thousands of miles away. He didn't care about the family name. Hell, at this moment, he wished it was Smith.

Irish refused to stay the night at the hospital, although the doctor urged it. He was silent, though, after he saw some of the other scars on Irish's body. "You live dangerously, don't you?"

"I try to keep you in business," Irish quipped as the doctor bandaged his wound.

Amy glared at him.

The doctor looked from one to another as he finished. "It's going to hurt like blazes. The bullet nicked the bone. I'll write a prescription."

"I'll make sure he takes it," Amy said.

The doctor nodded. "There's a slew of detectives outside. Want a few moments alone?"

Irish gave her the crooked smile that always affected her heart in erratic ways. "Thanks."

After the doctor left, Irish touched her face in the gentle way he had. "Thank you," he said. "I think you saved my life."

"I barely hit him."

"Hit is the operative word," Irish said. "Enough to distract him. You're a pretty gutsy lady. Especially for someone who hates guns."

She felt her face growing red with pleasure.

He bent his head and kissed her. Hard.

Gratitude?

Her lips parted, and she tasted him. She closed her eyes and uttered a prayer of thanks that he was here. Next to her. Alive.

Then she felt something wet on her cheek. Tears. She felt his lips wiping them away. She bit her lower lip. She didn't want to cry. She wanted to be brave and unemotional. Just like him. Not some teary-eyed woman.

"Ah, love," he said, and his voice was ragged.

Not unemotional. Her heart sang. She clung to him like an emotional woman. He hugged her tight like an emotional man.

Their lips met again, and they kissed like two people glad to be alive and in love.

"One of them is still alive," said a detective. "He knows the other is dead, and he can be charged with murder as a consequence of a criminal act, as well as three counts of attempted murder, assault on a federal officer, burglary, and assorted other felonies."

The detective, an FBI agent, and a member of the CID, along with two uniformed officers, sat in a conference room in the hospital. Amy and Irish refused to leave for the police precinct until they saw Sally Eachan. They had agreed to tell all they knew in what was called a "preliminary" interview.

"Why didn't you contact the police?" the detective said.

"We did. In Memphis. They couldn't help us. They said they didn't have the resources to protect Dr. Mallory."

"So you decided to take matters in your own hands?"

"Not at all. We had an appointment with Miss Eachan tonight. We didn't know. . . ."

"I've talked to your office, Colonel. They've been try-ing to find you. Seems you leave chaos wherever you go."

"Not him," Amy said. "Me. He's just been trying to pro-tect me."

"And Mr. Eachan? What's his part?"

"He has no part. I sought him out after learning that his grandfather and mine served together. . . ."

Amy watched Irish as he told the story. The FBI agent took notes, then stopped the conversation and made a phone call. In thirty minutes, two other agents appeared, and Irish started again, quickly running through everything they knew or suspected.

"So you were involved in the burglary of Mr. Eachan's Maryland home?"

"Only in that we were staying there. Some buddies of mine were helping protect Dr. Mallory. They apparently walked in on the burglary in progress."

Amy knew he was protecting his friends, possibly sac-rificing his own career by not being entirely truthful. She had always insisted on the whole truth, black and white, and now she was seeing varying shades of gray. She de-cided to try to change the subject. "What about the man who was wounded?"

"We'll talk to him. He's in the hospital prison ward. I think, with everything we have, he might be willing to talk to us."

"He should be guarded," Irish said. "Now."

One of the agents nodded. "I'll see to it."

Irish looked at his watch. "It's four in the morning. I'm tired. I know Dr. Mallory is. We want to see Miss Eachan. Can the rest of this wait until tomorrow?"

Amy chimed in. "The doctors even wanted to keep Colonel Flaherty here. He needs rest. He's lost a lot of blood. And we're the victims here."

The detective who apparently had jurisdiction looked at the others. The leading FBI agent nodded.

"Noon tomorrow," the detective said. "I want your word you both will be at my office."

"Make it two," Irish said.

"Two, then," said the detective as he rose from his seat.

Amy and Irish went down the hall to Reception, asked about Sally's whereabouts, then took the elevator to Critical Care.

They found Dustin pacing outside. "The doctor's inside," he said.

"How is she?"

"She's still on a respirator, but the doctor thinks she'll make it. Thank God they left a syringe next to her so the doctor knew what he was dealing with. A few more minutes. . . ."

"I'm so sorry," Amy said.

"Don't be. If it weren't for you, she probably would have died. They meant her to die," he said with rage he didn't try to hide.

"Is she conscious yet?"

He nodded. "Just barely. Not enough to answer any questions."

"We don't know what she found, then?"

"No, and at the moment I don't care," Dustin said. "I just want. . . ."

His voice broke, and he turned away.

Irish was silent a moment, then said, "We're going to a hotel and try to get some sleep. The police want to talk to us at two. Perhaps we should talk first. . . ."

Dustin frowned. "Just tell them what happened. I intend to resign. Sally doesn't have anyone. . . ."

"Don't do anything too hasty," Irish said. He held out his hand.

Dustin took it. "I'll call you on your cell phone if anything happens. No one can approach the house. It's taped
off as a crime scene. I also asked that it be guarded."

"Our friends should be in shock now."

"I just hope it's over."

"She'll be all right," Irish said. "She and Amy have a lot
in common. They're both resilient. And a lot tougher than
they look."

"She is, isn't she?" Dustin said wryly. "I always thought
she was fragile . . . like a butterfly. She said I was like a
drone bee."

"I don't think she thought that at all," Amy said, reaching for his hand and squeezing it. "Her eyes always said
something else altogether."

Dustin pulled out a credit card. "Use this when you
check into a hotel. It's a State Department credit card.
After today, I doubt they're in any position to go after you,
but you might as well be safe."

"And you?"

"A necessary expense," Dustin said. "Use the name of
John Smythe."

"Smythe?"

"Our couriers use it sometimes. It's a little better than
Smith."

Irish thrust out his hand. "You'll be all right?"

Dustin took his. Their gazes met, and Irish saw something there he hadn't seen before. Uncertainty. Warmth.
"Yes," Dustin said. "You can find me here if you need anything."

Irish still hesitated, then said awkwardly, "Tell Sally
we'll be by tomorrow."

Dustin nodded, then turned back to the door of the
room.

Irish lay awake and looked at Amy. His wrist hurt like hell,
and he couldn't sleep, but he didn't want any pills.

It wasn't over yet. They had won a number of battles, but he wasn't sure they had won the war.

He liked looking at her. She slept quietly. Her head lay against his arm, and her face was turned toward his. It wore a tranquil expression.

They'd not made love this morning. *She* obviously feared hurting his wrist. *He* knew she was emotionally and physically exhausted. They just needed to be together, to savor the presence of the other without any demands, to revel in the warmth of each other's bodies, to relish just being alive. They hadn't needed words.

They hadn't, he realized, needed them for a long time. She was as much a part of him now as any of his appendages. He couldn't imagine breathing air that she didn't breathe, or living a day without seeing her, or sleeping without her at his side.

He put his arm on hers. He really didn't want to sleep. He hadn't worked out a way for them to be together.

He could give up the military. He had little doubt that after the past few weeks, he'd effectively destroyed any chance of promotion. He had more than twenty years in, and he could retire—but to what? His ranch in Colorado was fairly isolated. It would be impossible for her to find a comparable teaching position.

Unlike Tag or Mike, he didn't want to spend the rest of his life protecting fat cats or investigating wayward spouses. He wanted the clean air and blue skies and snow-covered mountains of Colorado.

He wanted *her.*

How much could either of them give up for the other without eventually destroying each other?

thirty

Sally woke in stages. Her throat hurt. Her cheek ached. Her world was heavy, foggy. She flitted in and out of consciousness, trying to open her eyes but finding it too much of an effort. She was conscious of a hand holding hers, though. It felt good. Safe.

Then fear came. Through the fog she saw the large man coming toward her while another held her. Her face stung. Her chest ached. She remembered the pain of the blows. The angry face as she refused to answer questions. She kept saying there was nothing to find. She knew he wouldn't let her live. She'd seen his face. And their grandfather's message was the only thing that could pinpoint her murderer, that could save Dustin and the others.

Rage had twisted her tormentor's face like some fun house mirror.

"The police are going to find you in your cousin's bed," he said as he raised a needle and plunged it in her arm. "Beaten. Dead of an overdose. He'll have a hell of a time explaining it." He smiled. "You'll feel very good for a few moments," he said, "but it will be a very few minutes."

Dusty. That was the worst of it. Sinking out of consciousness, knowing that Dusty's life would be destroyed.

"No," she screamed hoarsely.

The hand tightened on her hand. "Sally, it's Dustin."

She tried her eyes again. Part of her didn't want to leave the cocoon she was in. But now nightmares were intruding. "Dusty?" She barely recognized her own voice. It was hoarse. But it was audible. She was alive!

Her eyes finally opened. He was leaning over her. "I didn't tell them," she said.

"Tell them what?"

"Didn't tell him 'bout . . . Grandfather's letter."

"To hell with any goddamn letter." His hand practically squashed hers. He leaned over and kissed her gently.

Some of the heaviness lifted, but she still felt . . . drugged. "How . . . ?"

"Colonel Flaherty and Amy got there, apparently just after they injected you. One of the men who attacked you is dead. The other was shot. He's in the hospital here. The police want to talk to you as soon as they can. There's one just outside the door. . . ."

Sally felt the fear again. It bubbled up inside, and she thought it might burst inside her like a huge boil. Her fingers clasped his. "Don't go away."

"I won't," he said in a tone she'd never heard before. It . . . quavered. Even trembled. She felt an enormous tenderness that he was so affected. "I really *am* all right."

As if to show him, she tried to move, and then felt as if a sledgehammer slammed across her. She couldn't stifle a cry. Her face hurt, and she lifted her fingers to touch it. One cheek was swollen and a bandage covered an area near her cheek.

"God, Sally. . . ." He started for the door.

"No," she said. She didn't want him to go.

He returned, but he used her buzzer. In seconds, a nurse was beside her. "She's awake. That's wonderful."

"She's in pain," Dusty said hoarsely.

The nurse frowned. "She shouldn't have anything."

Sally nodded. She didn't want anything. Not until she told Dusty what she had to tell him.

But she couldn't. The nurse was there, and what Sally wanted to say had to be said in private. She waited impatiently as the woman took her blood pressure, then her temperature, before hurrying out of the small cubicle with its one wall of glass. *Intensive care.* With sudden horror, she realized how very close she must have come to dying.

She clutched Dusty's hand and felt it wrap comfortingly around hers. No more time. She was not going to waste any more time. "I have something to . . . tell you."

"So you said," he said. "It seems a million years ago. I lived through every one of those years waiting for you to wake."

"The letter. I started to tell you. It was behind that painting my father gave me. Not . . . really a letter, I guess, but an account. It tells something of what happened all those years ago. Hawke Jordan was responsible for much of the . . . theft."

"Much . . . ?"

"All three of our grandfathers used some items in their personal quarters. The painting, and a few other items, showed up in Grandfather's personal effects that were shipped home. . . ." She stopped. "It's complicated. The letter is in a book in your study."

His brows furrowed. "Why did you put it there?"

"I don't know. I just thought it would be safe until I was able to show it to someone." She hesitated. "I didn't tell . . . the bastard that hit me."

"Ah, Sally. Don't you know nothing is as important as you are?"

She tried to smile, but it hurt too much. "I knew he planned to . . . kill me anyway."

He cursed. "I wish I killed him myself." His voice was

so unlike his usual cool, dispassionate one. It sounded . . . ragged. And fierce.

She hesitated, then continued, "I told Amy Mallory that I'd found something, then had second thoughts until I talked to you. It could hurt our . . . your . . . name."

She could care less about the family name. But she knew he did.

"Do you really think I would risk people's lives because of that name?" he said wryly, even a bit sadly. "Hell, it's obviously not worth preserving. I should have seen that years ago when my sister died. I just . . . bought into the whole damn thing because there was nothing else. At least I didn't think so then. I thought you were lost to me, and I made my career my life. Only problem was, it wasn't really my career. It was my father's and grandfather's career for me, and I went along with it." He paused, then continued, "There's been too damn many cover-ups over these past years."

"There's something else," she said carefully. Even fearfully. What if he didn't care that she wasn't really his cousin?

He frowned.

"My mother. . . ."

"Your mother?" he prompted.

"You're not my cousin."

He looked at her as if she'd lost her mind.

"Not a *blood* cousin," she added, watching every movement of his face.

His fingers tightened around hers. "Then . . . what . . . ?"

"I came from a sperm bank or whatever it was back then."

His mouth dropped open so wide she chuckled. She wished it didn't hurt so much, but he looked so . . . incredulous.

"My . . . father apparently was sterile. He wanted a child." She didn't say that he wanted a child to maintain his place in the family. She had not allowed herself to totally believe that. She couldn't. She still had difficulty thinking of him as a brutal man, too. But now she had flickers of memories of times he'd brushed her aside. Memories she had locked away somewhere in her mind. "He . . . took Mother to a fertility doctor."

She saw the news register on his face. "She doesn't know who the donor was, but it wasn't my . . . William Eachan."

His fingers tightened around hers.

"Dusty?"

"It's taking me a moment to adjust to the idea."

"I'll always love you," she said.

"Like a cousin?"

She hesitated. "Like any way you want."

He leaned over and kissed her. He kissed her the way he had kissed her many years ago. With longing and wanting. And passion that he'd always controlled before. She felt every nuance of emotions he'd never allowed to show before. She resented it when he drew away.

"Come back," she said.

"You are sore and hurting and weak, and you've just gone through a terrible experience."

"I'll go through an even worse one if you don't kiss me again."

He did.

Amy and Irish stopped by the hospital before going to the main police station. Dusty was holding Sally's hand. She was in a regular room, and though she looked pale and battered, she was smiling.

"You look much better than the last time we saw you," Irish said.

"Dusty tells me you saved my life."

"I wish we'd arrived a few minutes earlier."

"I'm just grateful," she said. Amy saw her fingers tighten around Dustin's. She'd never seen him look so relaxed. Despite wrinkled clothes and unshaven cheeks, he had a glow in his eyes she hadn't seen before. It was almost as blinding as the one in Sally's.

"Dusty just asked me to marry him," Sally said. "We found out we're not blood cousins."

"It wouldn't have made a difference anyway," Dustin said. "To hell with convention." He looked particularly pleased with himself for saying so.

An ache mixed with pleasure. Amy wanted to sport that same contented expression. But though Irish had been warm and loving today, he'd not mentioned the future. *Not today.* She'd clung to his earlier words that they would "talk later."

There wasn't much "later" left. She had to leave tomorrow to make her Monday tenure hearing. He was due back to his base. He could no longer claim that he was on leave and "unreachable." He'd received direct orders yesterday to be back at his post Monday.

They had one day before returning to their respective lives.

She looked at him standing there. He was freshly shaven with a razor supplied by the hotel. He wore a white shirt with the sleeves rolled up, showing tanned arms except for the patch of white that covered his latest wound. He looked at home everywhere, while she was comfortable only in the classroom. *Had* been comfortable only in the classroom.

He had changed that for her. In the past weeks she'd been completely accepted for what she was. Accepted and liked. And respected. Not just for her scholarship. For *her*.

He'd given her a lifetime gift. He'd given a confidence in herself she'd never had before.

She wanted more.

Dustin stood. He took some keys out of his pocket and wrote a note. "Sally put a document in a book in my study. Graham Greene's *This Gun for Hire.* Sally's sense of humor," he added wryly. "This note should get you in the house to pick up some personal belongings. I understand it's still under police guard."

"We'll stop over there before going to the police station. Anything you want us not to say?"

"Sally's already told them everything. No need to hold back anything."

"Is it going to affect your career?"

"I think yours is in more trouble than mine. It doesn't matter to me, anyway. I want more time now that I'm going to marry. I think I want to try to enjoy life for a while. I'm resigning tomorrow, and then will look for a job in a think tank. I've been approached by several previously, and they could give less of a damn about my pedigree."

"I don't think the State Department will, either."

Dustin shrugged. "I don't want the hours. I don't want the politics. I was being pressured by superiors to let Brian Jordan sell very lethal weapons to people who have no business having them." He smiled slowly, and Amy thought how attractive it was. Not like the man who several days earlier had struck her as so plastic. "I understand that the man Amy wounded, Marcus Kelley, is singing a song. Turns out he's deputy director of security for Jordan Industries. It was the father who directed things, but the son had to be involved. Both will face a number of charges, including conspiracy to commit murder, and murder."

Dustin hesitated, then continued. "I know Irish felt he might have started this. But according to Kelley, he didn't. A professor found some documents in Amy's possessions, recognized the name, dug a little deeper, then tried a little blackmail. The documents were never found. The professor must have hidden them somewhere. Hawke Jordan believed Amy must have known about them."

Irish put his arm around Amy's shoulder, holding her tight. He'd known how she felt about Jon Foster, and now he was conveying his sympathy. Some of the terrible sense of betrayal faded.

She found herself leaning into him. Natural. *So natural. But for how much longer?*

It was Irish who broke the awkwardly painful silence. "You're not leaving, then?" he asked Dustin.

"Not until she does," Dustin said. "I'm not leaving her alone again."

Irish's hand pressed a little harder on her shoulder. The same protective stance. She liked that. She also liked being a partner. Just as he had saved her life several times, she'd been able to return the favor.

"I think we had better go," Irish said.

Amy was reluctant. There was so much warmth in what was usually a cold, sterile room. She took his hand and walked to the door.

General Eachan's document was in an envelope tucked, as Dustin had told them, in the Graham Greene book. There was a row of Greene books, each a first edition.

Amy took it but didn't read it. It belonged to Sally and Dustin. They would return to the hospital once their police interview was over.

She tucked it in her purse, then they went off to confront the minions of the law.

The questions got personal. What was their relationship to Sally and Dustin Eachan? They'd answered the questions before, but they did so again. Why had they fled the explosion in South Carolina? Surely an experienced investigator like Colonel Flaherty knew it was the scene of a crime. He could be charged with obstruction of justice.

The questions went on for hours. Then they got to Brian Jordan. Did they know him? Did they know why he might be involved with murder?

Amy thought of the document in her purse. Not yet. They could say they found it later. It was Dustin's call.

She realized that weeks ago she would have been appalled at the very idea of withholding information.

They finally left at six and returned to the hospital.

Dustin was still in Sally's room. A policeman was still outside her door. For protection now. She'd answered most of their questions and had identified the wounded man as the one who injected her.

Amy handed Dustin the document she'd retrieved.

He read it so quickly that she wondered how he could comprehend it. But then he must read thousands of documents.

Without a word he handed it to Irish. She waited until Irish had finished and handed it to her.

It was dated July 4, 1986, and written in a neat cursive hand. On purpose, she discovered. He hadn't wanted any doubt about who wrote it. It was, he said, an insurance policy for the family.

To whom it may concern:

"Forty-one years ago in Austria, I was involved in the capture of a train carrying items looted by the Nazis. The contents were cataloged and kept in a warehouse. Attempts were made to discover legitimate claimants. Few items were claimed and, after the surrender of the German Army, the remaining items were shipped to New York for auction. The proceeds were to go to survivors of the Holocaust.

I didn't learn until much later that two trunks of gold never reached New York, along with a number of other items. It was another year, when I returned home, that I learned personal property sent to my home by aides included items from the train, items used in headquarters and my own personal quarters while we were in Austria. It was standard procedure during that time to confiscate household furnishings for official use.

I was up for promotion for my first star. Any hint of scandal or impropriety would have destroyed my career.

I said nothing, and that was the greatest mistake I ever made.

Ten years later, I ran into Hawkins Jordan, who had been sergeant major at the time. He had improved his situation considerably and had joined an arms manufacturer. He seemed to think I owed him special consideration in his bid for an army contract. I refused to give it.

He then said I had stolen Nazi property, and he could prove it. He had an inventory of items shipped from my quarters back home. They included a valuable painting, silver, and crystal. If I didn't make sure he received the contract, he would give the information to the newspapers. I took the coward's way out a second time, and then I was his.

I had a detective check on his background. He left the Army in 1946. Until then he was always in debt. Suddenly he was very wealthy. He bought himself into a small arms concern, took it over when the owner died three years later, and apparently put a great deal of capital into it. No one knew where it came from.

When I learned of the discrepancy—the deep discrepancy—between the items we liberated and those that actually appeared in New York, I went back and checked to see who had access to the warehouse. Hawkins Jordan was among them. Then I found the inventory. It had been altered.

I called Generals Flaherty and Mallory and told them of my suspicions. They both told me they, too, had found stolen items in their belongings. Apparently, Hawkins had tried to set each of us up. His men were responsible for packing our belongings. He included items we'd put to temporary use in our headquarters building. He'd done it deliberately.

Mallory had paid blackmail for years, afraid that his career would be ruined. Flaherty had reported the items he found when he'd returned, and thus put himself outside

Jordan's reach. But because the thefts occurred under his command, he was quietly forced into retirement.

We decided to meet. Before we could, both of them died. One of a heart attack, the other a suicide.

I looked into their deaths. There was no indication of foul play. I made another poor decision. It's strange how a human being can justify almost anything. I could ask for investigations and destroy my family's name and my son's career. There were both the stolen Nazi items and some questionable contracts I made with Jordan Industries. Or I could checkmate him. He would leave me alone; I would leave him alone. I told him I had insurance, letters that would be mailed if there was any suspicion of an unnatural death. Any accident, and they would be sent.

He then made another threat. If I said anything, my son would die. I knew from the deaths of David Mallory and Sam Flaherty, Jordan was all too capable of it.

But now I'm a sick old man, and I know I made a pact with the devil. I justified my actions by believing—trying to believe—that I more than balanced it by my service to the country.

I don't know what will happen to me now. I might well die in a way that cannot be traced to Hawkins Jordan. So I am leaving this to try to explain a man's arrogant foolishness.

Enclosed is the original inventory of goods signed by Sergeant Major Hawkins Jordan. Because I countersigned it, I kept a copy. I don't know if he knew that. I understand that the original inventory has disappeared, as have the duty rosters for the warehouse. There is also a signed affidavit from a man who removed some of the items with Jordan. He died shortly after making it.

There were a lot of deaths around Jordan.

I will go to the grave regretting that I did not step forward. With each mistake I made, I dug my hole deeper. I never had the courage to step up and face the truth or the *consequences of that first mistake and the ones that followed. We were a proud Maryland family, and I couldn't bear to see our name dragged through the courts. I always told Dustin to uphold its honor. I never told him how I disgraced it.*

It was signed *Edward Eachan*. The name was not followed by his rank, the customary way for retired officers to sign papers.

The other two documents were with it.

"Is it enough?" Amy asked.

Dustin nodded. "Together with the testimony of the man who tried to kill Sally? I think so. My source at the FBI has also identified some of the photos you sent me. They have previous Army service, some with Special Forces. All are employed by Jordan Industries."

"Have they arrested him yet?" Amy asked.

"Teams have been sent to talk to both Hawkins Jordan and Brian Jordan," Dustin said. "Now we have a motive."

Amy remembered that when Irish had called the Jordan home, a maid had said the older Jordan had had a stroke. "Is Hawkins Jordan well enough to interview?"

Dustin frowned. "I know him. He's a tough old bird. I wouldn't be surprised if he wasn't faking it to protect himself."

"What are you going to do with this?" Irish asked about the document written by Dustin's grandfather.

"Give it to the police. Tell them I found it in a book you brought me."

"Your family. . . ."

"My only family is in a hospital bed," Dustin said. "I want those bastards in prison."

He reached in his pocket and came up with a card. He went over to the phone and dialed a number. "Detective Baker, please. This is Dustin Eachan. You might want to call Special Agent Damon Gordon with the FBI. Tell him to meet me at Washington Memorial. Room 4420."

Irish gave him a slight smile. "You don't need us, do you?"

"No."

"Amy has a tenure hearing day after tomorrow. I'll face court-martial if I'm not back at the same time. She should be safe now."

"When are you leaving?"

"I'll be flying to Fort Lewis, Washington, tomorrow."

"Good luck."

"Thanks." Irish took out the credit card Dustin had given him. "I think I can use my own now."

Dustin took it and stood awkwardly. "I suppose we'll see you at some trials."

Irish nodded.

Dustin's eyes were curious as he turned to Amy. "Are you returning to Memphis?"

She nodded. "I have a dog to pick up first."

He smiled, and she thought it was a very nice smile indeed. "I remember. He didn't like me much."

"He doesn't like anyone much."

"Until next time then," he said.

The hotel was a very, very nice hotel. Irish had hardly noticed last night. He *had* noticed it this morning when he'd called the desk and asked for shaving gear, and it appeared almost immediately.

It was more expensive than ones he usually chose. But tonight was the last one he and Amy would spend together. They would be flying back tomorrow, she to Memphis and he to the state of Washington. He'd called Sam, and Sam said he would drive Bo back to Memphis. Amy had been reluctant to take Bo on the plane. She didn't trust airlines to take care of pets.

Too many horror stories.

And she already had enough of those. Amy would live with the nightmares for a long time. Maybe forever. She might well have occasional flashbacks. He wanted to be with her if it happened.

He wanted to be with her all the time.

He'd never planned to marry while in the military. He suspected his military career was over, no matter what. He had disobeyed direct orders. He had obstructed an investigation in the South Carolina case. He had possibly obstructed justice in a major case.

Strangely enough, it didn't matter now. The ranch in Colorado looked mighty good to him. It would look particularly good with Amy beside him.

How could he ask it of her?

A renegade part of him hoped she wouldn't make tenure. Then he wiped the notion from his head. It was so unfair to her. It would hurt her deeply, both personally and professionally. He cared about her too much to wish that on her.

Care, hell. He loved her.

"Let's have dinner in the room," he suggested.

"I'd like that," she said. He saw uncertainty in her eyes, though.

By now he knew her tastes. "Steaks?"

"Sounds good."

He quickly ordered, adding a bottle of wine.

"I don't think I ever want fast food again," she said, sitting primly on the bed.

"There's lots of beef on a ranch," he said, not quite sure what had prompted the remark.

"To eat?" She raised an eyebrow. "I don't think I could partake of a cow I know."

"You don't get to know them personally," he said. "But we can buy from a store if you prefer."

If you prefer.

A proposition? A proposal? Even he didn't know.

But there was a glow in her eyes, and that was promising.

"When I was a girl, I always wanted to ride a horse."

"You've never ridden?"

"Nope. But I read all the books. *Smokey. The Black Stallion. Misty of Chincoteague.*"

Though her tone was light, he could see the question in her eyes. Was he saying what he might be saying?

Hell, he didn't know. He'd never proposed before. Never even considered the possibility. He was forty-four, and he had no idea how to be a husband.

"Will you marry me?" he blurted out, feeling like the biggest fool in the universe.

"Yes," she said.

He was so stunned he couldn't move. Couldn't say anything. He hadn't meant to ask the question, not until they could solve some problems. He'd never thought she would accept without any of those solutions.

"But. . . ."

She smiled at him, a gentle, wondering expression that made his heart bounce in his chest. "Going back on your offer?" she said.

"No. It's just your tenure. You've worked for it so long, and. . . ."

"I love history, Irish. I can teach anywhere. And I still want to write my book, even if it's on an Army base. I can do that anywhere, too. In fact, I can give it the time I've wanted to give it."

"I'm resigning my commission, even if they don't toss me out," he said. He stretched. "I'm too old to risk any more holes in my body."

"I like that fear."

"Money will be tight," he warned. "Ranching isn't what it used to be. We just barely manage, and that's with my service pay."

"Maybe I'll make a million dollars on my book."

Now he raised *his* eyebrow. "On overaged hippies?"

"A typical military question," she said, but there was only teasing in her eyes.

"I love you, Dr. Mallory."

"I love you, Colonel Flaherty."

"Your mother would be horrified."

"Your grandfather would be appalled."

"Not as much as you think. He was a very tolerant kind of guy."

She was leaning against him now. His heart beat harder. Other parts of his anatomy responded.

"What about the tenure hearing?"

"I'll go. They have tried hard to accommodate me, and I owe them that. But I'll tell them I can't take the position."

"Are you sure?"

"Absolutely?" she asked. "I would be lying if I didn't admit to a twinge or two. But I would have many, many more if I didn't grab and cherish and nurture whatever there is between us." She grinned. "I'm getting accustomed to adventures."

There was a leer in her eyes. He liked that leer. He liked everything about her at the moment, particularly her lips. "Room service," he warned.

"Let's leave a note telling him to leave it outside."

"Someone might steal it," he said as he nibbled on her lips.

"That's entirely all right," she said as her hand played with the back of his neck.

Their lips met and promised. Not just this hour or this night.

His arms went around her, and he knew that it was right. He would give her the freedom she needed to make her life valuable. If the ranch wasn't it, then together they would find their own unique future. She was ready to give up everything for him. He would do the same.

Her lips left his, and she leaned back in his arms and gazed up at him. Her eyes were open and bright and happy. She was incredibly beautiful.

He heard a kind of music he'd never heard before, one with lyrics he'd never believed until now. Friend. Companion. Lover. A home. A real home. Everything he'd wanted as a boy and feared as an adult.

No more. And, as always, he felt the same wonder in her.

She went into his arms again.

Forever.

epilogue

Dustin and Sally attended the wedding in Colorado. It was at a small church in a small town with a few friends.

It was everything Amy ever wanted.

Irish had received his retirement a week earlier. He'd wanted to wait until then, to get over the uncertainty of his position. He still could have been charged with obstructing justice.

He wasn't, thanks to his commanding officer.

Amy had driven across the country two weeks ago with Bo. Irish had wanted her to see the ranch, to be sure she could live there. She'd already applied at the local high school, thirty miles away. Luckily a history teacher had just left to get married, and the spot was open. Her lack of educational courses was a handicap, and she was obviously overqualified, but she was accepted on a provisional basis until she completed those pesky education requirements. What really appealed to her was filling young minds with the love of history that she had. In college, she'd taught those who had already found that love. She wanted to get others early, to teach them that history could be more exciting and intriguing than any movie or piece of fiction. She had a piece of that history as a personal example.

So much for thinking she could finish her book anytime soon.

She loved the ranch. The house was one-story, sprawling. It had wood floors with colorful rugs and plain but comfortable furniture. A large picture window looked toward the mountains and the limitless sky that was so blue it hurt.

For a week, she'd ached terribly from her first horseback ride, but now the aches had faded. While she still wasn't sure of herself on even the gentlest of horses, Irish said she was a fast learner. He was a lovely liar.

And Bo was in canine heaven. All sorts of marvelous smells and people he liked. He even shyly allowed the ranch foreman to pet him, and made instant friends with the man's sheepdog.

He was at the wedding today, a ridiculous bow around his neck. Irish had put it there in an unusual moment of whimsy. She was seeing more and more of that in him.

She loved him more each day. He was obviously delighted that she wanted to live at the ranch, and had filled the house with flowers when she'd arrived. She never would have expected that from the matter-of-fact, practical, no-nonsense investigator she'd met.

The most surprising thing was his invitation to Dustin and Sally to attend their wedding. He had not told her, only said he had a surprise for her yesterday, and drove her three hours to the Denver airport.

The Eachans had married six weeks earlier. She glowed, and Dustin didn't seem able to keep his eyes off her.

"Thanks for coming," Amy said, pleased beyond words that she would have someone for her at her wedding. Somehow Irish had sensed that. Sherry had been unable to come because her mother was ill.

And she and Irish and the Eachans had gone through a lot together. It had created a uniquely intense bond between them. They would go through even more when a series of trials took place.

Dustin had resigned from the State Department and was

now with a Washington nonprofit group. He'd suffered weeks of newspaper scrutiny with an openness and dignity that had impressed Amy. It seemed that once unleashed from a family legacy, he'd emerged a stronger, more independent, and more thoughtful person. Or maybe, she thought, some of it had to do with Sally.

Hawkins Jordan had died of a heart attack the day he was to be arrested; there was some suspicion that he might well have used a drug that stopped his heart. Brian Jordan had been charged with multiple offenses, including conspiracy to murder and murder for hire. His deputy chief of security would go on trial for murder. Several others of their security personnel were charged with arson, attempted murder, and other crimes. The story had been all over the papers for weeks.

After all the publicity and interviews, Colorado had been a very good place to go.

Amy often woke up with nightmares, and it had been particularly bad when she'd been alone. But now she had Irish's arms, and his warmth and his love.

She knew he would always be there for her.

Just as he was now. . . .

She wore a simple blue dress, and there was no hiding from the groom, not even for a few hours before the wedding. Instead, he had joined her and presented her with a bouquet of forget-me-nots, another fanciful touch that now no longer surprised her.

She and Irish went inside the chapel. The minister was already waiting. A friend of Joe Mendoza's, Irish's foreman, sang the song she had selected, "When I Fall in Love."

His hand tightened around hers, and their gazes met and pledged even before the vows were said.

Whatever would come, they would face it together.

He gave her a slow, lazy grin before turning back to the minister. And she knew nothing had ever been so right.